L IS FOR LARCENY

The Horsemen Series

Zoe Dunn & C.M. Bowen

Ebook ISBN: 9798883224422
Print ISBN: 979-8-9924435-1-6

Cover image created by:
https://getcovers.com/

Shattered Sirens and the colophon are registered to Shattered Sirens.

Published by:
Shattered Sirens, LLC
https:// www.shatteredsirens.com/

Dedication:

We know why you're here.
It's gonna hurt like a motherfucker.

CHAPTER ONE

Leighton

"Get him on the table," Harrison barked as he stormed toward the cabinets lining his dining room wall, gathering medical supplies.

We hadn't wasted any time after Rich collapsed; Craig and Joey loaded him into the back of Craig's Mercedes while Az helped Victoria into the front passenger seat. Az had taken the driver's seat while the other two worked to maintain pressure on Rich's wounds, tearing out of what remained of the garage with me close behind on my motorcycle. By some miracle, Rich was still breathing when we hauled him into Harrison and Mags' apartment above the Spotted Cobra.

Victoria stumbled forward, reaching out for Rich's prone form just as Craig and Joey laid him out on the dining table. Tears tracked down her cheeks, and her body shook with silent sobs, but her eyes never moved from the slight rise and fall of his chest.

"What the hell have you boys been into?" Harrison scowled, producing a pair of safety sheers to cut away Rich's tux jacket and button-down shirt. "On second thought, don't tell me. I don't want mixed up in whatever caused this."

My hands curled into fists at my side as I watched him work. We'd been in plenty of tight spots before, but it wasn't looking good for Rich. I'd done enough damage to our enemies to recognize a man on the precipice of death. Victoria's wail broke through my thoughts, and my eyes flitted in her direction just in time to see her knees give out. Az made it to her before I could react, wrapping her in his arms as he went to the floor beside her.

Without a word, I grabbed some gauze and tape from

the open cabinets behind Harrison that were filled with medical supplies. I quickly bandaged the bullet wound in my shoulder before I turned and slipped out of the apartment into the night.

The emotions in the place were stifling, something I was wholly unequipped to deal with and still maintain some sense of self-control. But there was *something* I could do. We needed information before word got out that Rinaldo was dead. Pulling my phone from my pocket, I shot off a quick text before heading to my bike, intent on seeing what would be found in Marino's home.

Forty minutes later, I was deep in Jackal territory. Stashing my bike behind a dumpster, I pulled a hoodie from my saddlebags and put it on over my bloodied tux. Pulling up the hood, I crept through the shadows toward my destination. I stopped at the edge of the manicured lawn that Marino's old Victorian was nestled on. My gaze remained locked on the darkened house as a mousy brunette approached in my peripheral vision.

"You crack it?"

"What do you think I am? An amateur?" She scoffed. "I'm no Craig, but I know my way around tech, Leighton. Speaking of, why did you call me for this instead of have him do it?"

"You know better than to ask questions, Sarah. Just tell me what I'm looking at inside Marino's and then get out of here."

"Whatever you say," She shrugged, sliding a backpack off her shoulders and retrieving a tablet. Her fingers tapped rapidly against the screen before she turned it to face me. "As far as I can see, the place is empty. No security around the property. No alarms silent, or otherwise, either. It's like everybody just up and left the place unprotected, which is strange for your lot."

"Good, now show me the fastest route to the main office and my quick exit. Without the additional commentary."

Sarah cut her eyes at me but wisely launched into the information I needed. "Take the stairs straight from the front door; as soon as you're upstairs, hook a right here." she continued, her finger lining a path on the screen. That's the main office, as far as I can tell. If that's not the one, then take this hallway, here, all the way to the last room on the left. There's only two ways out of this place, though, Leighton, and they're both on the first floor. You might have to jump from a window or something if you get in trouble."

"Worried about me, Sarah?" I chuckled.

"You? Never. I just don't wanna explain to the rest of the Urchins why I got caught up in Jackal territory packing your ass to safety."

"I doubt they'd be surprised considering the trouble we all got into before I found my family." I shrugged, reaching into my pocket and pulling a handful of bills. "Here, for your services, and extra for the risk of being caught with a Horseman this deep in Jackal territory."

"Nah," Sarah shook her head, shoving my hand away. "I did this for old times sake. Just because you moved on to bigger and better things, Urchins stick together. We'll always have your back, Leighton."

"Sentiment is gonna get you killed one day, Sarah. I hope you don't expect me to come to your funeral when it does."

She threw her head back and laughed before stuffing her tablet into the large zipper pocket of her backpack. She didn't bother responding as her laughter died, shooting me one last broad grin before disappearing into the shadows

.

I strolled across the silent lawn toward the house's front door once I was sure she had been gone long enough not to be suspected if something went wrong. On a whim, I turned the knob and couldn't help laughing when the door creaked open.

"Thanks for making it easier, arrogant prick." I chuckled to myself before slipping inside.

Following Sarah's directions, I made my way to the first office on the second floor. Even in the dark, I could make out the sparse furnishings and bookshelves that lined the walls. My gut told me there wouldn't be much to find, but I pulled my phone out of my hoodie pocket and switched on the flashlight anyway.

I tore through the office as quickly as possible, ripping open drawers in the small desk and pulling books from the shelves. It became clear as I worked that the office had been set up for Victoria. I'd found her donor list from the youth center tucked away in a ledger on the bookshelf and various stacks of blank paper with the Bristol Foundation header. Part of me appreciated how thorough Rinaldo had been in ensuring Victoria would have everything she needed to continue her work had he managed to take her. The rest of me raged at the thought of anyone other than the five of us laying a finger on her.

Satisfied that there was nothing to be found in the first office, I slipped down the hall to the second one Sarah had pointed out on her tablet. I knew I'd struck gold when I stepped into the oversized space. Unlike the barren desk in the first, this desk was laden with papers and books, a laptop as the centerpiece of the organized chaos.

Not wasting any time, I rifled through the desk drawers, grabbed anything that looked important to Jackal business, and laid it all on top of the laptop. Marino's office was more utilitarian than the one he'd created for ma petit démone, making it easy to grab anything that might be useful to us. Taking one last look around, I grabbed the stack of papers, ledgers, and Rinaldo's laptop and stuffed them against my chest beneath my hoodie before deciding to check out the rest of the house.

I methodically searched the remaining sixteen rooms and closets in the old Victorian, taking care to check every so often for any Jackals roaming around the grounds. It was nearing four in the morning when I finally slipped from the house, confident that I'd gathered anything that could give us an answer, an edge, and had it safely tucked against my chest beneath my hoodie.

It wasn't until I'd nearly reached my hidden motorcycle that I ran into trouble. Lenny Moretti leaned against the dumpster while another person rolled my bike into the open. My upper lip curled in disgust as I pressed myself against the nearest building and slipped off my hoodie. Folding it so everything I'd stolen from Marino's wouldn't shake loose, I tied the arms tightly to secure it and set it carefully on the ground.

"Shit, boss. This looks like a Horseman's bike." The man pushing my motorcycle hissed.

"Pretty sure those fuckers are pushing up daisies about now," Moretti snorted. "Rinaldo sent a strike team to take them out and grab that bitch that he's had us running around like headless chickens over. Someone probably just brought it back as a trophy."

"And stashed it here?"

Peeking around the corner, I saw Lenny shrug. "Probably didn't want Rinaldo getting wind of it, you know how he is about that shit. Gotta claim territory and property by the book and all that. Besides, no way a Horseman would be this deep in our territory without the alarm being raised, even if they pulled off a miracle and survived what the boss had scheduled for 'em."

The second man muttered something under his breath before turning so his back was fully toward me. Seeing my opening, I crept toward Lenny, snagging the gun he had tucked in the back of his pants just as my other arm wrapped around his neck.

"Boo." I cackled, aiming the pistol at the other man and pulling the trigger.

Lenny's grubby hands shot up to claw at my arm as his comrade collapsed to the ground. I was no Joey when it came to marksmanship, but I suspected even Victoria could have dropped a body at such close range. Lenny continued to struggle against my hold as I squeezed my arm tighter, crushing his windpipe. As much as I wanted to draw out his death and make him suffer forever, making us doubt *la petit démone*, I knew I needed to get out of Jackal territory before the rapidly lightening sky gave way to the sun.

"Consider this a fucking gift," I gritted out as I placed the gun against his temple and fired.

Doubling back, I grabbed my folded hoodie, making sure to put another bullet through each Jackal's head before I made it to my bike, and stuffed my prize in my saddlebag. I didn't bother giving either body a second glance as my motorcycle roared to life, and I took off, heading back to the Spotted Cobra.

Harrison scowled at me when he cracked open the door to his apartment over the bar. Stepping back, he pulled it open to allow me to step inside. My eyes bounced from his blood-soaked shirt to my friends seated around his living room. All three faces wore grim expressions, their eyes rimmed with dark circles, and their shoulders slumped forward. Glancing toward the kitchen, I realized Rich wasn't on the table where I'd last seen him.

"Where?" I asked.

Joey's eyes snapped up from the floor, his features twisting in rage. "Where the fuck did you go?" He demanded, stomping toward me. "You just fucking vanished with Rich on his fucking deathbed. I know you don't feel shit like us, but even you have to know how fucked that is."

"There was nothing I could do here." I shrugged. "So, I went somewhere there was. I raided Marino's house." I held up my still-bundled hoodie.

"Do you have a death wish?" Joey bellowed, moving close enough to jab my chest with his finger. "You should have been here. You never should have gone into Jackal territory, not with Rich bleeding out, and not alone."

"That's enough," Mags' voice cut through the room. My eyes flicked over Joey's shoulder to find her stepping into the living room from a connected door. "Your friend is in there barely hanging on and your girl is a wreck, refusing to leave his side. She doesn't need y'all at each other's throats right now. Whatever this is," She continued, motioning vaguely toward us. "Stow it. None of you get to be angry, not when you're the reason she's in this now. So, settle the fuck down and take care of her."

"Mags is right." Harrison interjected. "Your boy isn't out of the woods yet. I did the best I could, but his gut wound is worrisome. I couldn't find the bullet without risking more problems. If he makes it through the night, he'll need the vet bright and early. You can stay until he's stable, but you all know my rules. Whatever this infighting shit is, it's not gonna happen here. Outside of patching you gangsters up, your fighting doesn't come into my territory. If it does, well, you know the rules. We'll leave it at that since I know emotions are running high right now."

Mags looked at her father and gave him a quick nod before turning her attention to us. "Get cleaned up, take care of your girl, and get whatever shut eye you can." She ordered before moving to head down the hallway next to the kitchen.

"You need to get checked out and patched up, Leighton." Az spoke. "Mags already took care of the rest of us while Harrison worked on Rich."

"I'm fine, I was just grazed. Already stopped bleeding hours ago."

Harrison snorted, shaking his head. "Come on into the kitchen, let's get it cleaned up anyway. I won't have one of you chucklefucks dying from an infection on my watch."

Grinning, I stepped around Joey and followed Harrison into the kitchen, dropping my bundled hoodie on the coffee table as I left the room. I stripped off my tux jacket and button-down so he could access the wound on my side. Harrison pinched his lips together and snagged the first aid kit and a bottle of antiseptic from the counter. Without any preamble, he sprayed the antiseptic solution on my side, causing me to hiss at the sudden stinging sensation as he worked to clean me up.

"Doesn't need stitches," He grunted, wiping away the last of the antiseptic and taping gauze over the area. "Keep it clean, and you'll heal up fine; probably have a scar, though."

"Just another for my collection." I chuckled.

Harrison shook his head and stood. "I need to hit the rack and get some sleep. Me and Mags will take turns checking in on your friend tonight, but gonna need all the shut-eye I can get to fix him up completely if he makes it overnight."

I muttered my thanks and pulled my button-up back on before following him out of the kitchen. Az, Craig, and Joey were silently sitting in the living room when we reentered. It wasn't until Harrison broke off to head up the hallway that anyone spoke.

"What did you find?" Craig asked once Harrison was out of sight.

"Documents, ledgers, and a laptop." I grinned, strolling to the coffee table to snag my hoodie and hold it up.

"What you did was stupid and reckless, Leighton."Az spoke from the couch as Craig moved to take the bundle from me, "But I can't say I'm mad about the information you came back with. Especially not when we have to go to ground for a while."

"The call already go out?" I asked, moving to sit in the recliner at the other end of the room.

"While Harrison worked on Rich." Az confirmed. "Once Rich is stable, we need to get out of Sacona while we recover and regroup. The rest of our men have been told to pull all the product into the heart of our territory and to stay off the streets until we give word."

"What about our pest problem?" I asked, my lip curling in disgust.

"Phil's going to work through the suspect list and report back to us." Joey said. "Right now, he's the only one we can trust."

"Good," I nodded. "I have a place we can hole up in the meantime. I'll make the arrangements in the morning."

"No more slipping off alone again, Leighton." Az warned. "I mean it. If Marino's attack on us tonight wasn't enough to declare war, his death sure as hell was. We can't risk any of us getting caught out while we're weakened. We have to be smart about this. When the time is right, we'll make our move, as a *team*, and wipe the fucking Jackals off the map. But until then, you need to keep your shit together and not go off on your own again."

"Aye, aye, captain." I smirked with a mock salute. "Now, if you're done scolding me, I'm gonna go check on our girl."

CHAPTER TWO

Victoria

Watching Harrison work on Rich had been brutal. I couldn't tear my eyes away even as Az tried to coax me out of the room. Seeing Rich stripped bare as his life hung in the balance was unsettling. It took everything in me not to rush forward and cover him. If I did, it would only hinder the work that needed to be done to save him.

It wasn't until his wounds were bandaged, the one in his abdomen packed and strapped tightly, that I allowed myself any sense of relief. Rich was still breathing. For now.

Harrison had instructed Az, Craig, and Joey to carry his unconscious body carefully into a spare bedroom just off the living area of the apartment. I kept out of the way as they positioned him in the bed, covering him to the waist with the comforter. Harrison's movements were precise and efficient in a way I'd only seen in films. The moment Rich was situated, he'd run an IV, murmuring about the need for fluids and pain medication to keep Rich comfortable. I didn't ask where a man who owned a bar had come by the supplies he used. I was just grateful he had them.

When Harrison left the room, the guys remained, closing in around me as I watched Rich. One had moved a chair to the bedside, though I couldn't say who. It was Joey who guided me to sit, ensuring that Rich was still within reach of the chair. I can't say how long I sat there, the three of them surrounding me as I watched the rise and fall of Rich's chest with an intensity that should have scared me. Eventually, though, they left me to my vigil, needing to take care of whatever business needed to be settled in the wake of the night's events.

"You're not allowed to die, bossy pants." I spoke finally, reaching my hand to grasp Rich's. "I'm not done fighting with you while you try to tell me what to do."

He didn't stir, his only movement from his shallow breathing. Tears continued to track down my face as I took in his deathly pallor. My fingers tightened around his limp hand, desperate for any reaction.

"Please don't leave me like this," My voice cracked. "You have to fight. I... I need you to wake up. You're not allowed to die on me, Rich. You fucking hear me? We were just starting to get somewhere. I-I thought maybe..." I let my voice trail off as sobs ripped through me again.

For hours, I sat there, holding his hand and alternating between sobbing, begging, and demanding that he live. My body grew stiff from being in the same position for so long, but I couldn't move. Not until I knew he'd survive. The guys would come in and check on me from time to time, and I saw how their expressions grew more tortured each time. They finally stopped when Mags appeared.

"Hey, honey. How ya holding up?" She asked, setting another chair next to mine.

I tore my gaze from Rich to look at Mags for the first time since we'd arrived. "Just peachy." I deadpanned. "All dressed up and ready for a night out." Hysterical giggles bubbled up in my throat as soon as the words left my mouth.

Mags watched me, her brows drawn down in concern as my hysteria grew. The whole night had been a shitshow. I was still wearing the gown I'd put on for the hospital charity event. The once gorgeous dress was now torn and covered in blood.

"I don't know what I'm going to do if he dies." I whispered when I finally got control of myself again.

"Rich is strong. He just has to hang on a few more hours and Pops will get him to the vet to finish fixing him up." Mags replied, grabbing my hand and giving it a reassuring squeeze.

"I don't understand why we can't just take him to the hospital. He needs a hospital."

"Honey, the hospital has to report gunshot wounds. That means police. I know you're new to this world, but the police are bad for business. There's a vet in midtown that's on these guys' payroll. He has the same equipment and can patch your man up. He's just gotta hang on a few more hours."

"Rich isn't... He's not my man." I said slowly, not really sure what else there was to comment on. Mags raised a brow and smiled at me gently, her expression tinged with amusement.

"Yeah, sure sweetie... That's why he took several bullets to keep you safe." Arguing erupting in the other room caused her to pause, looking at the door with a frown. She gave my hand another squeeze as she stood. "And why you're in here crying your heart out over what it could have meant for him to do that."

I stared at her momentarily, before turning my gaze back to Rich's unconscious form. I heard the door click close, signaling her departure, and turned her words over in my head. I could hear her scolding the rest of the guys through the door but was too focused on the man in front of me to understand what she was saying. Whatever it was worked, their voices grew quieter before Leighton slipped into the room.

"Hey beautiful. We should get you a change of clothes, and somewhere to get some rest. I can take over your vigil and wake you if anything changes." He spoke softly.

"Get out, Leighton. I don't want you near me. Anyone else, but not you." I spat, not taking my eyes off Rich.

"Please, *Petit Démone*-"

"Get out. Get the fuck out!" I shrieked.

I heard him sigh before the door clicked open and shut, leaving me alone with Rich once more. The early morning hours settled into a rotation of the others coming to check on us. Harrison or Mags would come in from time to time to check

11

on his IV, but we were largely left alone in between.

I think I dozed at some point in the chair; dawn filtering in through a small window in the room pulled me from a sleep I didn't know I'd slipped into. Sitting up slowly, I groaned against the stiffness in my back and stretched.

"Good. You're awake." Mags spoke, startling me. "I've got a change of clothes for you in the bathroom. You should get cleaned up and dressed so we can get Rich to the vet."

Nodding, I stood from the chair and let her lead me through the apartment to the bathroom. After stuffing my destroyed gown into the small trash can, I quickly showered and dressed in the sweatpants and oversized t-shirt Mags had left for me. Nothing could be done for the dark circles under my eyes or the sense of dread that had settled under my skin.

"Sweetheart?" Joey called, rapping on the bathroom door. "We're ready to move, but me and the others talked it over. We think you should stay here while we get Rich patched up the rest of the way."

Jerking the door open, I scowled at him. "Absolutely not."

Joey rubbed the back of his neck with an apprehensive look. "It'll be safer for you here. None of us want to see anything happen to you, and we're not exactly in a good position to keep you safe out in the open like that."

"Listen here, *Joseph Innocenti*, if you think for one fucking second, you're leaving me behind, you've got another thing coming. No way in hell will I sit here not knowing what's going on while y'all are out there. Not over my dead body."

"Let her come," Az called from somewhere behind Joey. "We don't have time to waste arguing with her, and she's proved during the attack that she can handle herself just fine."

"Thank you." I said as Joey shot an angry glare over his shoulder.

I could feel the anger and worry radiating from him as I pushed past him out of the bathroom and strolled toward where Az stood at the end of the hall.

"Quit fucking around. We need to get moving if you

want your boy to live." Harrison spoke, appearing at the end of the hall. "The other two already got him loaded into the van. Let's go."

Fifteen or so minutes later, Harrison pulled his cargo van into the empty parking lot of Sacona Animal Center. I practically jumped from the vehicle as the guys helped Harrison unload Rich's unconscious body through the back doors and pack him into the vet's office. A man in his mid-forties met us at the entrance and ushered us into the back.

"Alright, everyone out so I can get these x-rays." The man said, shooing us out of the exam room after the guys had laid Rich on the table.

"Come on, Bunny." Craig spoke, wrapping his arm around my shoulders to lead me back to the waiting area.

Craig helped me into the hard plastic seat before he settled in beside me. My eyes immediately sought out the ticking clock hung on the wall behind the receptionist's desk. The minutes dragged into hours as we waited. Each of the guys took turns sitting beside me, whispering words of comfort that I didn't hear. I was so consumed by worry that I didn't bother pulling away from Leighton when he replaced one of the others.

The door that led to the exam rooms finally opened, and the vet strolled out with a smile. "He's waking up now if you'd like to see him."

I shot to my feet and ran toward the door, barely noticing Az take the man aside. Footsteps echoed through the hall behind me as I made my way to the room we'd left Rich in. I tore through the clinic so fast I'd have missed the room if it hadn't been for the door propped open. A sob threatened to break free when I laid eyes on Rich, still sprawled on his back across the exam table. He grimaced as he turned his head toward me.

"Hey Baby Girl... You look like shit." He croaked out.

My knees almost gave out at the sound of his voice after

being so scared I'd never hear it again. I felt an arm around my waist and took a moment to steady myself.

"You aren't looking like a bouquet of roses yourself, big bro." Joey quipped over my shoulder, moving us closer to the table.

Rich chuckled, then let out a pained groan. "Fuck you, Joey. Next time, you take the bullets."

"I vote no one takes anymore bullets," I said after I found my voice again.

"We should get moving," Az interjected as he entered the room. "Harrison said he wants to keep an eye on Rich for the next few days. That will give us time to find a place to lay low, but we gotta get Rich loaded up and head back to the Cobra before anyone gets wind we were here."

I made my way back to the van and made sure I was out of the way while they loaded Rich in the back. He wasn't entirely out of the woods yet, but he was awake, and he was alive. The somber tension that had hung over our heads was finally a little lighter, and it felt like the hand around my throat threatening to strangle me had finally started to let go.

CHAPTER THREE

Leighton

I let the phone ring twice before disconnecting the call and doing it again. It was our signal when I couldn't call from my own phone. Call three times, allowing it to ring twice each time, and I'd be answered on the first ring of the fourth call no matter where I called from.

"What kind of mess have you gotten yourself into this time, Leighton?" Her tone was clipped.

"The usual. You know me, Lacey." I laughed. "I need somewhere to lay low for a while, I was hoping you could get the cabin ready for me."

"Just you, or are the other four coming with?"

"Six of us, actually."

"For Christ's sake LeLe, who have you mixed up in this mafia business of yours?"

"She'd have been mixed up in it without us. We're just trying to keep her safe." I retorted. "And don't call me LeLe, you know I hate it."

"What can I say, little brother? I wanted a sister and got you instead." Lacey's laughter tinkled through the receiver.

"Can you have the cabin ready, or not?"

"I'll have it ready. Try not to get yourself killed before you get there." Lacey replied.

"Good. I'll call you with our eta when we're on the way."

She didn't bother saying goodbye before she hung up the phone. Shaking my head, I pulled the sim from the burner and dropped it on the ground, crushing it beneath my heel before tossing the phone in a trash bin nearby as I made my way back toward the Cobra. We'd been staying in Harrison's apartment above the bar for the last five days, waiting for him to say Rich was well enough for us to leave.

Tensions were running high with all of us in such a small space, and *la petit démone*'s refusal to be around me only made it worse. Unable to deal with everything, I'd spent the last few days gathering supplies and making arrangements. The call to my sister was one of the last things I needed to do. Getting us a vehicle that couldn't be tracked was last on my list, but that would have to wait until we were ready to leave. Couldn't risk whatever car I stole being reported before we were on our way out of town.

Looping the handles of the plastic bag that held all the burners I'd bought over my arm, I headed back toward the Spotted Cobra. Making sure nobody was watching, I slipped around the back of the building and took the stair access to Harrison and Mags' apartment.

"Innocenti, if I catch you up without the cane we gave you again, I'm gonna make sure you can't get up next time." Harrison scolded, holding out an oaken cane toward Rich, who had his arms crossed over his chest.

"I'm not using that, Doc. I'm fine, just stretching my legs." Rich retorted stubbornly.

"Bro, you need to do what they say. You've only been able to move around for a few days." Joey jumped in, Craig nodding in agreement just behind him.

"We really don't have time to be arguing about me using the damn thing! I'm fine!" Rich argued.

"Which is exactly why you should just do it." Az offered, coming into the room.

"Rich, please, use the cane. You need to be careful so you don't reinjure yourself... We almost lost you not long ago," Victoria said gently. Her brown eyes were big and pleading. "It won't be long before you don't need it."

Rich grumbled something under his breath before snatching the cane from Harrison. "Fine, fuck! Can we just get on with it now?"

I chuckled at his quick change of heart after Victoria asked him to use it. Big softie.

"I've got good news, boys." I interjected. "We've got a place to lay low. Just waiting on the word from Doc that we can get outta dodge."

Harrison scowled at Rich before turning to address me. "As long as he agrees to use the cane, you boys are free to leave. Not much I can do for him now. He needs to rest, take the pain meds, and heal." He said before shifting to address Victoria. "You make sure he keeps the wounds clean and doesn't over-exert himself since he'll listen to ya, girl."

"Well boys," I grinned, rubbing my hands together. "Looks like we just need a car, and we can bust outta this joint."

Two hours and another phone call to my sister later, the six of us were stuffed into an old, beat-up, gray minivan I'd stolen. Rich had given me an incredulous look when I pulled up to the Spotted Cobra in it, but we needed something big enough and unlikely to get noticed. Az had wanted to drive and only conceded to having me behind the wheel when I reminded him that I'd not disclosed to any of them where we were headed.

It was a full day's drive through the mountains east of Sacona to my family cabin. We'd made good time, but only because none of us wanted to stop in a public area to stretch our legs or take a piss. *La petit démone* had scrunched her nose at the empty Coke bottle I'd passed back when she complained of needing to pee, forcing us to pull over to the shoulder of the empty mountain highway so she could relieve herself. The enraged look she gave me when I told her it was the roadside or the bottle was enough to let me know I had dug an even deeper hole for myself.

"Thank fucking God," Craig muttered as my family cabin came into view.

Lacey's Maserati Quattroporte was parked off to the side of the gravel drive, a massive white box truck blocking most of the view of the cabin. I frowned as I watched two men moving furniture from the back of it and carrying it inside. Easing the dilapidated van into park on the other side of the box truck, I cut the ignition and climbed out, not bothering to wait for the others as I stomped toward my sister.

"What the fuck, Lacey?"

"Oh, LeLe," She sighed. "These men are on *my* payroll. They know how to keep their mouths shut. You had to know I'd need movers to get this place ready for you. You can't have expected me to do it myself."

"The whole point of me calling you to get this place ready was so that nobody, not even our parents, would realize I was here." I hissed.

Lacey rolled her eyes and crossed her arms over her chest. "Father has no interest in this place. And as I said, these are *my* men. They are loyal to me and me alone." Her gaze traveled over my shoulder, and she continued speaking as if it were an afterthought. "I've secured everything you need. One of my men will restock your food stores in a week's time. If there's anything in particular you need, just tell them and they'll have it on the next run."

"Lacey, good to see you." Az spoke behind me. "I didn't realize this is where Leighton meant when he said he had a place for us."

"Az." She nodded curtly before a saccharine smile spread across her face. "Richard, how lovely to see you again, darling. You're looking a little worse for wear."

I turned to see Rich slowly making his way to the cabin porch, gritting his teeth as he relied on the cane Harrison had insisted he use. Craig and Joey were on either side of him, a very worried-looking Victoria trailing a few steps behind.

"I've been better." Rich replied.

"Do let me know if you need a little extra care to nurse you back to health. Our last encounter was rather enjoyable."

Lacey winked.

Rich stiffened slightly as he moved, and I caught the sneer of jealous outrage that momentarily painted Victoria's face.

"Back the fuck off, Lacey." I bit out.

"What, worried your little toy there will get jealous?" She whispered back low enough that only I could hear, never dropping her smile.

"I doubt it, Lacey," Rich said slowly. "I'm in good hands."

I kept my gaze pinned on Victoria as she moved closer to the porch. Her body seemed to relax, and an easy smile painted her face with Rich's words.

"Wait," She spoke, recognition flashing across her features. "You're not Lacey Laurent? Of *the* Laurent's?"

"I am, and you are?" Lacey replied, raising a brow. I knew damned good and well my sister knew who she was.

"Victoria Bristol. We've met a few times at charity functions."

"Ah, yes. I remember now. Lovely to see you again." Lacey's fake smile never wavered.

Victoria turned to me and slapped me on the chest. "You didn't tell me you were one of *the* Laurents. I can't believe you didn't tell me, you ass."

"I haven't exactly been in high society for a while and my family doesn't claim me, so why should I claim them?" I shrugged.

"Don't be modest, Leighton. According to our parents you're doing such lovely work on your mission trip. Last I heard, you'd even proposed to a local." Lacey laughed. "Mother and Father are just *so* excited for their trip to visit."

I couldn't help the derisive snort that left me. "Is that what they're telling people these days?"

"I thought he was working with Greenpeace. That was what your mother said at the last charity event we were both at." Victoria piped in.

"Oh, darling, that was ages ago." Lacey said before

shifting her pitch higher to mimic our mother. "He did such wonderful work with Greenpeace, but then he got the calling, you know. When one is called to act by God, one must answer."

"You sound just like her." Victoria laughed, causing Lacey to give her a genuine smile. "I'm sure my father was all," she dropped her voice as low as it could go, "I can only imagine how proud you are of his good work, even if his loss at the business is felt."

"Spot on, darling. Hugo always loved to rub it in my father's face that his only remaining heir was a woman. As if you weren't his only child." Lacey said, rolling her eyes before returning her amused grin to me. "And Lele, you'll be pleased to know, the girl you're engaged to now is just the *prettiest* girl in the village." She clasped her hands together in mock glee before reaching into her purse and retrieving a photograph.

"They did not!" Victoria squealed in delight as Lacey handed her a photograph of what appeared to be me, minus the tattoos, and a woman that looked suspiciously similar to Bitch Barbie. "Is she supposed to look so much like Tiffany Humphreys?" Victoria continued to laugh, noticing the same similarity I had.

"If you ask my mother, they look nothing alike. But if you ask the guy they paid to make these, that is absolutely Humphreys, just a bit darker in skin tone and hair." Lacey cackled.

"If you two are just gonna continue with this weird bro-ship you've built on mocking me, I'm gonna head inside." I huffed.

"Oh, Lele, don't be like that!" Victoria called after me as I stomped across the porch toward the door. I couldn't help the smile that lit my face. "You can't leave until you've given me an invitation to the wedding!"

Shaking my head to hide my amusement, I continued into the cabin. Lacey and Victoria's laughter echoed behind me.

I stood in the den for a moment, taking in the cabin

we spent our summers in as children before I started poking around the rooms to see what Lacey had set up for us. Her movers had set up most of what was needed in the common rooms and were pulling furniture into the bedrooms as I looked around.

I saw Lacey heading for me with a slightly frustrated look before she looped her arm in mine and pulled me back toward the door. Victoria had turned her attention back to Rich and was fussing over Joey and Craig, situating him on the pull-out.

"Lele, let me show you where I've had the motion-sensitive lights installed so you can show Craig when you have a moment," she said by way of excuse. I doubted anyone else could hear the edge to her voice that I did. When we were a little away from the door, she let go of my arm and whirled to face me directly.

I sighed and crossed my arms, having seen this look enough to know that a lecture was coming. "What Lacey?"

"Really? The *Bristol* girl?! The daughter of the most powerful prosecutor in the area. *That's* who you've dragged into your underground shenanigans?" She clipped, poking me in the chest with some force.

"Lacey–"

"Leighton. If I've told you once, I've told you a thousand times, when you play, play smart. This is not smart. It's decidedly one of the worst people you could have pulled into your shit."

"Are you done?" I drawled.

"Are you about to tell me that there's a really good reason that you've got a direct line to prison following you five around?" She sneered.

"She was in the shit whether or not we were involved, like I said on the phone. Someone's after her in a rough way, and we were hired to protect her. Shit just... went sideways."

"You expect me to believe that Hugo Bristol hired five mafia men to protect his precious darling? Get real, Leighton.

21

You may be able to convince others of whatever you want them to believe, but we are the same, you and I. You can't lie to me."

"And what, exactly, do you think I'd gain from lying to you?"

"That's what I've yet to figure out. But this has the whole Angelica situation written all over it. You're not telling me *something* and I will find out what it is. I'm not going to help you cover up another obsession gone wrong when this goes sideways on you lot. I have more to lose this time."

I rolled my eyes and sighed heavily. "Lace, the only thing I didn't bring up before is that everyone in that house is in love with her."

We both stiffened as soon as the 'L' word was out of my mouth. My hand moved to my chest, and I rubbed it with my knuckles to ease the strange sensations I'd felt there lately. I wondered briefly if that's what they were. Love. But it couldn't be. I wasn't capable of it.

"Your brand of *love* is deadly, Leighton." Lacey said, her words dripping with venom. "Because it doesn't exist for you. There is only obsession and obsessing over the Bristol girl will lead to no good."

"Is that why you decided to marry Harry, Henry, Hank, or whatever his boring ass name is?" I scoffed. "Because you didn't want to risk *obsessing?*"

"We're not discussing me. We are discussing you and the fact that your obsessions tend to die, leaving me to clean up your mess. Don't let playing house with this girl make you forget what you are, Leighton."

Before Lacey could continue her lecture, the slight squeak of the front door alerted us to someone coming outside. I turned to see Victoria standing by the door.

"Everything okay out here, guys?" she asked casually.

"Of course, darling. Are you all set?" Lacey said, her entire being switching back into a friendly and social air in the blink of an eye.

"Oh yes, and we can't thank you enough. Are you going

to be able to stay for dinner? Craig can whip up just about anything, and it's the least we could do."

"That sounds lovely! It's been too long since I was able to catch up with my brother, and I'm sure you could do with a break from being surrounded by these Neanderthals." Lacey remarked with a laugh, moving back toward the door with a discreet warning look toward me before the topic was officially closed.

"Are you coming, *Lele*?" Victoria asked smugly, enjoying the nickname she'd been gifted from my sister.

"Yeah… just a minute," I said absently, causing Victoria to frown slightly. She said nothing; just nodded and moved inside with Lacey.

I leaned against the wall and stared into the distance without focusing on anything particular. I rubbed my knuckles against the strange feeling in my chest again. Whatever it was, it definitely wasn't *that*. Lacey was right. Our whole family was all monsters just playing at being people.

CHAPTER FOUR

Victoria

The shift I'd noticed in Lacey between the time I stepped outside and when I spoke was unsettling. Even with her back to me, it had been noticeable. With the things I'd been through in the last few months, it put me on edge. When Leighton said he needed a minute and didn't use the pet name he'd given me the first day we met, that only heightened the worry coiling in my gut. Plastering a smile on my face, I worked to convince myself I was just being paranoid after everything that had happened.

"How did you meet my brother?" Lacey asked as she followed into the den. "If you're here with the five of them, then you know what they're about. I'm struggling to wrap my head around how you got mixed up in their line of work."

"Honestly, I have no idea." I sighed, my shoulders slumping forward. "I'm sure you heard about the gala fire last year and Az being arrested for my attempted kidnapping."

"I did. You know how it is in high society. News spreads quickly." Lacey confirmed.

"After Az was released and the charges dropped for lack of evidence, I don't really know. My father told me he hired the guys to be my bodyguards and that was that."

Lacey arched a brow at me. "And you went along with it? I'd been under the impression that you weren't reliant on your father's money."

"I'm not." I scowled at her. "But he threatened to stop donating to the Sacona youth center, and that would have been a devastating loss for them."

"How... altruistic." The minute amusement in her tone and the slight upturn to one side of her lips were all I needed to get the distinct feeling that she was laughing at me internally. "The more interesting question here is evident, I think. Was sleeping with them part of your plan, or was it more of a 'it just happened' situation?"

My mouth dropped open for a second, and I considered my answer momentarily. "I'm not like Tiff in that way. It just kind of... happened."

"Things are known to just *happen* when it comes to Leighton. I'd thought you'd have been smart enough to avoid them from what little I know of you." Lacey replied.

I bristled slightly at her insinuation. "What happened with Leighton... I was just a pawn in whatever fucked up game he was playing with Az's head about me."

Lacey gripped my arm tight enough to bruise, turning me to face her. Her mask of civility was gone, replaced with a cold, calculating glare, her hazel eyes void of emotion.

"You seem like a nice girl, but I'll only warn you once. I have no desire to clean up my brother's messes again, and I assure you, if you continue to play his games you will be the mess, he leaves for me to deal with. You can't play with people like us and make it out unscathed." Her icy tone caused a shiver to run up my spine.

"There you are," Craig's voice called from behind Lacey. I watched in horror as her cold demeanor shifted to something more lighthearted and playful like a switch had been flipped. "Leighton said you're staying for dinner, Lacey. Thought I'd see if you had any requests."

Lacey dropped her hand from my arm and turned to face Craig with a smile. "Oh, darling, I've been dying to have your Italian Roulade since you last cooked for me. It's impossible to find it anywhere as good as yours. I will never understand why you won't accept my offer to leave the criminal world behind and become a head chef in one of our restaurants."

"That's very sweet of you, Lace. But you know these guys are my family." Craig chuckled before turning his attention to me. "Rich is finally set up on the pull out if you want to go check on him, Bunny." He said, pointing to the nook at the far end of the den.

Grateful for the out, I nodded and went to the nook, where Rich sat on the edge of a pull-out bed. He was scowling at Joey and Az as they attempted to situate him.

"I'm not a fucking invalid." Rich growled. "I can do it myself."

"And bust open your stitches?" Az scoffed. "Stop being such a stubborn asshole and let us help you."

"Yeah, bro. Don't be an *Az-hole*." Joey snickered, causing Az to glower at him.

"Be a good Daddy and listen to them, don't be so stubborn." I interjected, pleased to see the way it caused Rich to freeze for just a moment.

Joey and Az exchanged glances before they started trying and failing to cover the laughter threatening to escape. Rich recovered more quickly this time and glared at them.

"I can get myself into position, but these shits keep trying to move me into place. If they keep pushing and pulling on me like I'm a sack of potatoes, then *they'll* be the ones to pop my stitches." Rich grumbled, slowly shifting on the pull-out until he was more comfortable.

I turned away to cover my snickering. When I regained my composure, I turned back to the guys and shooed Az and Joey out of my way. I handed him a small pillow and stood close while he slowly moved himself into position on the pillows that would support him as he propped up.

"They're just worried about you. Don't be too hard on them for trying to help."

The sound of the front door creaking open interrupted Rich's grumbling, and I glanced over to see Leighton stroll in, his face drawn into a scowl. When our eyes met, his dour expression was replaced with his usual manic smile.

"You managed to wrangle Rich into submission I see."
He cackled, making his way toward us.

"I used my powers of persuasion," I said, grinning.

"The hell she did." Rich grunted at the same time,
causing Leighton to start laughing.

"You're so whipped, bro," He wheezed as he wiped the
tears his laughter had caused from his face.

"Only one of us has been following her around like a
lost puppy. And it hasn't been me." Rich clipped the traces of a
sneer on his face.

Leighton winked at me before turning his attention
back to Rich. "I wouldn't say I'm lost, but ain't no shame in my
puppy game."

"Hey, L," Az called as he reentered the den. "Lacey said to
ask you where the fold away tables are. Dinner's almost done
and it's probably better we bring dinner to Rich instead of the
other way around."

"Yeah, this way." Leighton said, motioning for Az to
follow him into another room.

In a matter of minutes, they'd returned with three
square folding tables and began sitting them up so that they
connected, with one positioned directly in front of Rich. Joey
followed close behind with folding chairs, placing them at
intervals around the tables that would allow everyone to sit
and eat comfortably. They finished just as Craig strolled into
the den with a steaming pot, Lacey close behind him with a
pan of garlic bread.

"LeLe, be a dear and grab the dishes." She smiled
brightly.

Leighton scowled but complied. I could hear cabinets
opening and closing in the kitchen before he reemerged,
carrying a stack of plates, glasses, and silverware. After a few
moments of shuffling, everyone was positioned around the
tables so we could all eat together. The pot of spaghetti and
pan of garlic bread was passed around the table, and I dug in
as soon as I'd filled my plate to hide my amusement at the fact

Craig had ignored Lacey's requested meal.

"So, Rich, how have you been, aside from," Lacey spoke, waving her fork toward him to indicate his current condition. "This?"

"I get why some people see 'may you live in interesting times' as a curse." Rich responded.

"I'd love to get together while you're here." Lacey smiled, her tone dripping with innuendo.

"How's Kenneth?" Leighton interjected harshly.

Lacey raised one perfectly manicured brow in his direction. "Dull, as ever. That man wouldn't know interesting if it slapped him in the face."

"You married him." Leighton shrugged.

"We all make our sacrifices. Marrying such a dullard was mine. The connection to Apex Accounting has proven quite lucrative." She shot back.

"I didn't realize that you married as a business move," I spoke up, instantly regretting it under Lacey's withering stare.

"How is Benson, darling? The last I heard, the two of you were yet to set a wedding date."

Dishes on two of the folding tables clattered as the guys shifted in their seats, anger painting their faces. Joey's fist clenched around his fork, the glint in his eye making me wonder how hard he was fighting against sticking it through Lacey's eyeball.

Lacey smiled, casting her gaze around the table. "I see I've hit a sore spot. Did they not know you were engaged?"

"Perhaps the news hasn't reached you yet, but we split up over a year ago. I was under the impression that you were relatively well connected, so I had assumed you knew." I said, unable to stop the sarcasm that dripped from my words.

"Harrison and McMillan are fucking." Leighton blurted out, causing everyone to turn and look at him.

"What?" I asked, confused at his interruption as Craig choked on his food.

He leaned back in his chair and grinned, shooting

everyone a conspiratorial look. "Yeah, I guess they keep their relationship on the down low, but with how many times Harrison has patched me up, I noticed. Ol' Lorna seems to like having her world rocked by the neighborhood medic."

"How is that any of our business?" Az groaned, slapping Craig on the back to help clear his throat.

"For as much good as both of them have done for the community, I'd say they're entitled to their privacy however they choose to relieve stress," Rich said, exasperated.

"Come on, you guys can't tell me that's not some hot goss. What with how buttoned up McMillan is?" Leighton laughed.

Joey, looking horrified, added, "That woman is like my second mother! I'd really rather not think about that. Can we not?"

"I'm going to have a therapist send you the bill for the treatment I need to get that out of my head, L." Craig finally said after he'd managed to get his food down.

Leighton poked out his bottom lip and crossed his arms over his chest as he pouted. "I thought that would be the revelation of the century. You're all a bunch of uptight pricks."

"I believe that would be my cue to leave." Lacey drawled, dabbing the corner of her lips with a paper napkin before pushing away from the table. "Someone will be here early next week with fresh provisions. If you need anything in the meantime, LeLe, you know how to reach me."

We watched in silence as Lacey strolled toward the cabin door. She paused just inside and looked over her shoulder, pinning her gaze on Rich.

"If *you* feel up to a little fun while you're here, you have my number." She winked before disappearing outside.

A stab of jealousy tore through me, but I quickly forced it down. It wasn't like Rich, and I had any connection beyond him acting as my jailor. There were definitely sparks, and I enjoyed pushing his buttons, but that was as far as it went.

"She's not going to hand us over to the enemy the first

time it's convenient for her, is she?" I asked after the sound of Lacey's car leaving faded. I nearly cringed at the harshness bleeding into my tone.

"Lacey is a world class bitch, but if there's one thing she's good at, it's keeping secrets." Leighton replied.

CHAPTER FIVE

Victoria

"So, how are we supposed to kill time while we're stuck here?" I asked Craig as I stood beside him, drying the dishes from dinner.

Craig paused from washing the plate in his hand and shot me a sidelong glance. "I... can think of a few ways."

"Craig!" I laughed and flicked him with the towel.

"I may not be as blunt as the rest of them, but I'm still a man." He smirked. "And we have plenty of time for me to answer the question you asked in my room back at the manor."

My brows dipped in confusion. So much had happened that I didn't know what he was talking about. "What question?"

"The rope, Bunny." His tone had dropped low, and there was heat in his eyes when he turned to look at me. I couldn't help the blush that crept into my cheeks.

"I found a movie collection you guys! Az is picking one now and Leighton said there should be some popcorn in the cabinets."

"That sounds great!" I beamed, rushing to grab the last dish from Craig while Joey rifled through the cabinets until he found the snacks.

Once the dishes were dry, Craig shooed me out of the kitchen while he finished cleaning up. I made my way to the open area of the den where the couch, a loveseat, and the entertainment center were. Leighton had claimed a spot on the loveseat, so I moved to sit beside Az on the sofa. He reached his arm around me and tucked me into his side.

"What movie did you pick?" I asked, curling my feet under me and leaning into him.

"You'll see," he smiled. "Just waiting on the other two to get their asses in here so we can watch it."

"What about Rich?"

"He knocked out while you and Craig were cleaning up." Leighton sighed, watching me and Az with a sad gaze.

"Good. That's good. He needs his rest." I nodded.

"Who needs their rest?" Craig asked, strolling to the couch with Joey behind him, both carrying bowls of popcorn.

Noticing the open seat beside me, Joey elbowed Craig out of the way and raced to plop down in the empty spot on the couch. Craig made a frustrated noise before settling in on the loveseat with Leighton.

"Everyone ready?" Az asked, his face grave as he lifted the remote and brought up the menu.

The moment the menu screen popped up, I choked out a laugh, covering my mouth in an attempt to stifle it.

"Is there a problem with my movie selection, Love?"

"No, no problem." I shook my head. "I just didn't think you'd be the type of guy into 'Up'." I snickered.

"It's a good movie." He protested. "The only people who don't love this movie are heartless bastards."

"In my wildest dreams, I'd never have pegged you for such a softy." I grinned, playfully poking him in the side.

"Come on, guys, back me up here." He groaned.

"He's right, 'Up' is in my top five all time faves." Leighton said, causing me to shoot him an incredulous look.

"They're not wrong. It's definitely more than it looks." Joey said before shoveling a handful of popcorn into his mouth.

"Really? Well, I suppose I'll have to take your word for it. I don't generally watch kid movies." I said with a shrug.

In response, four shocked gazes turned to look at me as Az hit 'play' on the menu.

"Good thing we're about to rectify that travesty,"

Leighton said, settling and grabbing a handful of popcorn from Craig.

A comfortable silence fell in the room as we turned our attention to the movie. It was cute, and I found myself quickly drawn into the characters whose lives were playing out without so much as dialogue. A few minutes in, however, I could feel tears pricking my eyes, and I attempted to mask wiping them by rubbing my eyes and yawning.

It was futile; by the end of the opening credits, I was openly weeping and felt like my heart was breaking.

"What... kind of children's movie is this?" I asked between sniffles.

"A damned good one." Az replied gruffly, turning to wipe his face on his shoulder.

Joey wrapped his arm around my shoulders and gave me a comforting squeeze. "Don't worry, Sweetheart. It won't stay like this." He reassured me with a small kiss to my temple.

"Are you over there crying, Az?" Leighton snickered as he sniffed his nose.

Az grabbed a throw pillow he'd placed beside the couch and lobbed it at Leighton with a glare.

"As if you're not, L. You get misty every time we watch this movie." Craig said, not even bothering to wipe the tears that had tracked down his cheeks.

I looked around at all of them and laughed. "Who would have thought, the big bad Horsemen are a bunch of big babies. I'm adding that to the list next to nerds with guns."

"It's an effective emotional scene, good at what it does. There's no shame in responding to it." Craig answered with a shrug. "It's what makes it a great movie."

"If you assholes are done, can we shut up and watch the damned movie now?" Az snarled.

Pressing my fist to my mouth to suppress a giggle, I settled between Az and Joey, giving my full attention to the movie. The guys' commentary petered off as they each became engrossed.

I became aware of the feeling of being moved first as I came back to consciousness slowly. The feeling of strong arms holding me pulled me out of the haziness of sleep into a panic. My first instinct was to make an escape. As I wriggled and pulled away, the arms around me gripped tighter.

"Hey, woah! Settle down, Love or you'll make me drop you. It's just me." Az's voice in my ears quieted the alarm bells going off in my brain.

"Az?"

"Open your eyes, dork, and you'll see it's just me."

My eyes flew open before narrowing on his face. "Did you really just call me 'dork'? Are we twelve?"

"I'm not the one panicking before I've even opened my eyes to assess the situation. I'd say: if the shoe fits, wear it," he said with a smirk.

"Well, excuse the fuck outta me *Az-hole*. I'm sorry I'm not as used to being shot at and having my house blown up as you seem to be. It makes sense I'd be a little jumpy." I hissed.

He had the good sense to look contrite and sighed softly as he carefully opened the door to my room and carried me inside.

"I know, Love. I'm sorry... I was only teasing you. You shouldn't have to get used to those things." He said softly, setting me on the bed and stepping back.

Shifting to get under the blankets, I let my eyes wander back to Az as I settled. "I never would have guessed before tonight that you had such an ooey-gooey center."

"I told you once before, the guy you've known isn't who I really am at heart." He sighed, moving toward the bedroom door. Pausing at the threshold, he looked over his shoulder at me. "Besides, the best candies have a liquid center if you suck on them long enough."

I shook my head at him and yawned. "Oh, so you *are* twelve. Get out."

"Goodnight, Love." He chuckled before slipping from

the room and closing the door behind him.

My pulse thundered in my ears, and my hands shook violently as I struggled to keep hold of the gun Az had given me. The man had appeared out of nowhere and was squared off with my last protector. My feet were frozen to the spot, time slowing as Az and the intruder traded blows.

Do something! I mentally screamed at myself, but my body refused to comply. In a blink, Az was grappling with the stranger, fighting to gain the upper hand. Any chance I'd had of saving us both was lost. There was no way I could risk taking a shot without potentially hitting Az instead of my actual target.

Fear gripped my throat tight as Az's legs were taken out from beneath him. My eyes were glued to them as the man pulled Az to his knees.

"Looks like your protector isn't a very good one, girlie." He said, giving me a lecherous grin.

Like a rubber band pulled too far, I snapped. Somehow, one of my stilettos was in my hand, and I suddenly threw myself toward the man while screaming Az's name. The sting of his hand didn't register until moments before I hit the floor. As if guided by a universe stacked against us, another man materialized behind Az, a gun pointed at his head.

Tears streamed down my cheeks as the newcomer barked out an order to the other intruder. I couldn't make out a single word between the ringing in my ears and the sensation I was slowly slipping free of my body to watch at a distance. One blink... I was on my feet. Two blinks... I was moving toward Az and the man who'd clearly orchestrated the attack on the manor. Three blinks... I was glancing at Az, still on his knees. Four blinks... I lifted the gun and fired.

I jolted awake, my heart pounding a violent staccato against my chest. My breaths came in pants as my eyes roved wildly, trying to take in my unfamiliar surroundings. A panicked scream caught in my throat just as I realized where

I was. Leighton's family cabin, tangled in the bedding, and covered by a thin sheen of sweat. Even though I recognized where I was, I couldn't shake the lingering terror of my nightmare. The air in my room seemed too thin, and every shadow felt like it hid the next threat.

Sitting up, I untangled myself and swung my legs over the side of the bed. I needed... I wasn't sure, but I knew staying in my room wasn't it. I padded quietly across the floor, cracked the bedroom door, and peeked out. The cabin was quiet. That was good. I wasn't in any condition to face any of the guys. Taking a deep breath, I stepped from the room and silently slipped from the cabin.

When we'd first arrived, I'd caught sight of a small lake with a dock a few yards away from the house. It seemed like the perfect place to pull myself together. I winced at the gravel as I walked, regretting not taking a moment to put on shoes, but I wasn't in a hurry to go back inside, so I pressed on. A sigh of relief slipped free once my feet found the smooth wooden planks of the dock. Making my way to the end, I sat down and let my feet dangle in the water while I leaned against one of the rail posts.

I closed my eyes and tried to control my breathing further by focusing on the peaceful sounds of the night around me and taking my breaths in counted measure. My hands were still shaking, but after a few minutes, I could feel some tightness in my chest release slightly.

"Can't sleep?" Craig's voice startled me, and I jumped hard as I tried to turn. I let out a yelp as I felt myself start to slide off the dock. Fortunately, he was fast enough to grab my arm and stabilize me. "Easy! It's too cold for you to take a late-night swim."

I gasped for breath. The hard work I'd done to bring myself back to a calm level was wholly shattered. "I would... say thank you, but if you weren't out here sneaking up on people, I wouldn't have needed it," I said between gasps of air. Craig chuckled lightly and sat down next to me.

"I wasn't trying to sneak up on you. I guess you didn't hear me call out to you as I was walking up."

"Obviously not." I bit out and flinched at how hard it came out. I took another deep breath and sighed heavily. "Sorry. What's got you up?"

"We're taking turns checking on things through the night, and it's my turn. What about you? It's a bit late for a stroll." His brows were knit together in a look of concern as he assessed me.

I thought for a bit about how to answer him. I knew if I told him I was having nightmares, it would worry him... and that information would make its way around all of them. I didn't want to give any of them another reason to worry. But, on the other hand, I knew these things had a way of eating a person up if they didn't talk about it. I'd seen it in the women who brought their children to the youth center. And I doubted it would be easy to find a therapist who knew how to deal with this kind of situation, given we were holed up in the middle of nowhere.

"It's the nightmares, isn't it?" he asked, his eyes studying my face as my mind weighed my options.

"How...?" I stuttered out.

"Bunny, what's happened is a lot for anyone to take in. Nightmares are kind of part and parcel with the territory. It's not an easy thing to kill a person, even someone who deserves it." His voice was soft and even a little cautious as if he was speaking to a frightened animal.

"Is the only thing the five of you do sit around and discuss what I'm up to?" I hissed, unsure why I was so angry at his obvious concern. "It's like I'm living under a fucking microscope with the five of you dissecting every little thing I do."

"It's not like that... It might have started out like that, but you know as well as I do that the situation has changed. You're important to us, and we look out for our own. And we have to do that as a team." He explained, choosing his words carefully.

"I'm alive, aren't I?" I snorted. "You five did your job."

Craig shot me an incredulous look before tugging me into his lap.

"Craig... I'm too heavy to sit on you like this." I protested.

"Shut up with that nonsense, Bunny and let me finish what I was saying." He shot back, wrapping his arms around me. "As I was saying, you mean something to us, and we take care of what's ours. Meaning, not just your physical wellbeing but your mental, emotional, and everything in between."

"Don't make it dirty." I huffed.

"I'm not Leighton," Craig chuckled. "But that does remind me. I never answered your question."

"Huh?" I squirmed in his lap, attempting to reposition myself to look at him.

"The rope. I never answered it."

"I know it's a sex thing," I groaned, rolling my eyes. "I'm not *that* out of touch."

He laughed outright at my comment, and I couldn't help the small smile that tugged at the corners of my mouth. "Sometimes, but it's not just that. It's... it can be hard to explain. Can I show you something?"

I nodded, and he shifted us slightly to pull something out of his pocket. He rocked and moved us to where his back was against the post. I frowned as I realized it was a length of rope coiled up in a neat bundle.

"I thought you said this wasn't a sex thing. I'm really not in the mood right now." I raised an eyebrow and looked at him suspiciously. He rolled his eyes and used the small coil to boop me on the nose.

"Would you just hush and listen? Impatient little Bunny." He smirked as he started to unravel the neat little bundle. "Shibari and other forms of rope bondage can be... intensely erotic, but that's not all it is by any means. And that's not what I'm doing now, I'm not tone deaf."

He gently grabbed my wrist and looked like he was

taking measure of my arm before pulling the rope to its full length. I was surprised by how long it was, considering the small coil it had been when he pulled it out of his pocket. He grasped the center of the rope and wrapped it around my wrist.

"Tell me to stop, and I will, okay?" He ensured I was looking him in the eye when he said it.

"You said it wasn't a sexual thing right now?" I asked.

"Doesn't matter. Consent is paramount even when the activities are platonic."

I let out a derisive snort. "I guess Leighton never got that memo."

"Well, Leighton isn't the one out here right now. Pay attention, Bunny. Now isn't the time to dig into his issues when we're working on yours." His tone wasn't hard, but it had authority in it that had any further snarky comments dying on my tongue. I choked out my assent instead.

I stared at his hands while he worked, looping the lengths around my wrist. There was something incredibly soothing about the feel of his fingers and the silky rope gliding across my arm.

"One of the biggest things about rope that I've always enjoyed is the play between the sense of control and comfort. I find it grounding when I start working on a tie, weaving a pattern around my Bunny–"

"You've never tied me up."

He chuckled and held up my arm that he was weaving lengths around. "That's not entirely true, now is it."

"You know what I mean. Don't be all technical about it." I said with a huff.

"No, you're right. But 'bunny' is what we call rope bottoms. Us tops are called 'riggers', and the people we tie up are called 'rope bunnies.'" He paused and slid his gaze up to my eyes. "And I've thought about tying you up enough that... well, no other name fits now."

I could feel my cheeks heat with a blush at his confession. I tried to think of something to say, but I could only land on a weak 'oh.'

"As I was saying. Working a tie around a bunny, putting them in the positions and harnesses, and even things right down to choosing the colors of the rope. I'm responsible for their comfort and the experience they have while they're in my hands. It gives me a sense of control that lets the rest of the world fall away and focus solely on the work and the bunny."

"That sounds like it means a lot to you... you talk about it so reverently." I said softly.

"It does. When I found my way to this lifestyle, and discovered I had an affinity for rope bondage I kind of dove in headfirst. It gave me a sense of control and purpose that I didn't have when I was younger." He paused for a moment. "Looking back on it now, I got into it way too young. This isn't a world any minor needs to be in. Even if it was something I desperately needed when my own nightmares started."

"You have nightmares?" I asked, my brow drawing down.

"Not anymore, but I did for a long time."

"Why? I mean, if it's something you're comfortable talking about anyway."

Craig stiffened for the briefest moment before blowing out a breath. "My old man was an abusive piece of work." He started. "It was bad enough when he was sober, but more often than not, he'd come home reeking of liquor, and the smallest thing would set him off. My mother took the brunt of his anger; most of the time, she sent me running to the center to beg Mrs. McMillan to let me crash there."

"That must have been awful." I replied gently, squeezing his hand in support.

"It was. It got worse when I was about fifteen or so. I couldn't stand leaving my mom at his mercy. Every time I stood up to him, he turned that anger on me. One night, I'd decided I'd had enough. Me and my mom weren't going to be his punching bags anymore. So, I waited up for him to come stumbling home from the bar and took the metal baseball bat we kept by the door to him. I knew if I stopped before I killed him that he'd kill us when he was back on his feet, so I just... didn't stop."

I sucked in a sharp inhale, stunned by his confession.

"Anyway," he said, shrugging a shoulder as if to shake off the weight of it. "I had nightmares for a long time after that. Sometimes, he'd come back and beat me bloody in them; others, I'd relive that moment like I was watching a monster take me over." His voice dropped to a whisper. "He was my first kill and that took something from me I didn't get back until I found rope play."

"I'm sorry you went through that." I whispered.

"Me too, but it shaped who I am. It took time and finding ways to cope, but I found a new normal. I know it feels like you'll never recover from everything that happened at the manor, but you *will* find your new normal, too." He tucked the ends of the rope artfully into the swirling gauntlet he'd tied around my forearm.

He released my arm so I could turn it around and look at his work. The ropes swirled over each other and created an almost endless look. But more than that, I was calm and no longer needed to struggle with my brain. I looked from the gauntlet to him and found him observing me. I couldn't think of anything else to do but pull him into a hug, with no words that felt right for the moment.

"I promise you will, and all five of us will be here to help while you do."

CHAPTER SIX

Victoria

"Rise and shine, Princess." Az called from the doorway.

Grumbling, I rolled over in the bed and pulled the blanket snugly to my chin. The soft light streaming through the window and the grainy sensation behind my eyelids told me it was too early to be up after my late night.

Footsteps drew closer, followed by the blanket being torn off me. "Come on, Princess. Up and at 'em."

"What the fuck, Az-hole?" I screeched, bolting upright and attempting to snatch the blanket back. "What happened to the nice Az who called me Love and tucked me into bed?"

"I knew you were going to be a brat about today's planned activities, so we're back to Princess." He smirked, looking way more rested than he had any right to be,

"I'm not in the mood, Az. Give me my blanket back and let me sleep."

"No can do, Princess. We're training, so get your fine ass out of bed, put on some workout clothes and meet me outside."

I shot him a murderous glare as he backed out of my room with the blanket still in his hand. The smug smirk painting his lips made me want to punch him right in his perfect face. The irritation and lack of covers were enough to get me out of bed and to the closet Lacey had stocked in my size. Dressing quickly in a pair of yoga pants and a loose t-shirt, I slipped on socks and sneakers before making my way to the kitchen.

"Nope," Az chuckled, snagging my arm just before I could slip into the kitchen and snag something to eat.

Craig shot me a sympathetic look before turning his attention back to the ingredients lining the counter.

"I'm up, the least you can do is let me get a cup of coffee." I grunted.

Az turned so that he was standing before me, his hand still on my arm as he looked down at me.

"The people after us–after you–aren't going to wait until you're well rested, caffeinated, and fed to attack. I'm not doing this to make you miserable. We want to make sure you can defend yourself properly."

"He's right, Sweetheart." Joey piped in from somewhere behind me, causing me to startle. "If you can defend yourself at your worst, you're more likely to come out on top in a fight."

"*Et tu, Brute*?" I whined, dramatically placing the back of my hand against my forehead, causing the three of them to chuckle before Az guided me toward the front door.

I glared at him as he led me down the front steps, Joey close behind us. It was too damned early for this nonsense, and the Az-hole hadn't even let me grab a cup of coffee.

"I know you like to run, so we're going to warm up with a run around the lake." He said with a vicious grin.

"Nobody likes to run." I retorted.

"I like to run," Az shrugged.

"You're a freak of nature." I deadpanned.

"Maybe you should have let her get some coffee." Joey chuckled behind us, earning a smile from me and a glare from Az.

"You should *totally* listen to him. He is the only one without a bullet hole, after all. He's the smart one of the bunch.

Az scowled at me. "No, *Craig* is the smart one of the group. Joey's just a better shot."

"Get good." Joey responded, amused.

"Enough banter." Az sighed, slapping me on the ass. "Time to get moving, Princess. The longer you take, the longer it is before you get that coffee and some breakfast."

Az took off jogging into the woods toward the lake as I

wrapped my mind around the daunting task of running at this time of day. Joey gently nudged my shoulder to get me moving, and I set off at a slow pace, glaring daggers into Az's back. Joey silently kept pace with me as I worked to navigate the underbrush.

The extra strain of navigating the undergrowth of the forest floor only added to my sour mood as we jogged around the lake. I had decided I was going to have an attitude with Az for the rest of the day for this.

"Who decided we were jogging around the lake?!" I shouted as I narrowly avoided a root sticking out of the ground. "There isn't even a trail here!"

Az turned around to look at me without slowing his pace and continued to jog backward. Which was infuriating. "It's not *that* bad, Princess. It's a decent game trail. At least you're not fighting all the brush that could be here."

"Oh, fu–" I started to curse him when my foot caught another root, and I began to hurtle forward. Before I could hit the ground, Joey grabbed me by the arms and pulled me back to my feet.

"Easy there, Sweetheart." He murmured, holding onto me as I stumbled a few more steps before regaining my balance.

"I'm gonna murder him." I grumbled, causing Joey to laugh.

"You'll have to catch me first, Princess." Az called over his shoulder.

Somewhere between fifteen and twenty minutes into the jog, but what felt like forever, I could only glare at Az's back as I struggled to keep going. Risking a glance toward the lake, I wanted to plop down on the ground and give up. We were barely a third of the way around the damned thing, and the guys were still going strong.

Az continued to taunt me while Joey offered words of encouragement to keep me going. By the second mile, I was sweating, my breathing was ragged, and I was ready to give up and murder them both. I'd toss their bodies into the God damned lake to save myself the trouble of burying them. While I plotted how to take both of them down, my pace slowed to a walk.

"Hey, let's take a breather!" Joey called out to Az's rapidly fading back.

Noticing we were falling behind, Az circled back. His eyes scanned over me, looking for signs of distress.

"What do we need a breather for? The Princess looks fine, and we're almost done."

"Fuck. You." I huffed out between gasping breaths as I braced my hands against my thighs. "Do I look... Like I'm... built... To run... Three miles in the... *fucking woods*!?"

"You look like you need to work on your conditioning and that's what we're doing, Princess. So, get your ass moving before I bend you over and spank it right here and now." Az shot back.

Without a word, I lifted a hand and flipped him off.

"Conditioning isn't going to happen in one run. She's done really well for it being her first run around the lake. She's gonna walk the rest of the way back." Joey interjected, leveling a stern look that didn't leave much room for argument.

Grateful for Joey putting his foot down, I heaved myself back upright, deciding then and there that once I was showered, caffeinated, and fed, I was gonna blow him because he deserved a reward.

"You've earned a blowjob for that," I said, patting Joey's shoulder before walking the game trail, leaving both of them in stunned silence behind me.

"What the fuck." I heard Az say.

"Catch more flies with honey, bro." Joey's amused response made me smile. He had a noticeable spring in his step when they caught up with me.

The rest of the hike around the lake passed in silence. The scenery was gorgeous, even if I would have preferred still being in bed. Once the cabin came back into sight, I couldn't stop myself from jogging toward it, coffee and breakfast just a few yards away.

"Not yet, Princess." Az called out as he ran to catch my arm and redirect me.

"The first chance I get to turn you over to the enemy, I'm taking it." I growled as he led me around the side of the cabin rather than inside.

"You'll thank me for this when you're able to defend yourself no matter the circumstances." He replied. "Besides, if you behave for the rest of our training, I might just reward you, since I know rewards are on the table now."

I rolled my eyes at him as we slowed to a stop. Along the side of the cabin were several burlap sacks filled with who knew what, a few pads strapped to the nearest trees, and several thick branches cut down to staff size.

"What is this? Are you training me to be a fucking ninja?" I scoffed.

Az placed his hands on his hips and stared at me. "Lift the bags, Princess."

"*Lift the bags, Princess.*" I mocked, moving to the first sack.

"Really? Who's twelve now?" Az snapped at me.

A chuckle to our side drew my attention to Joey leaning against a tree, shaking his head as if we were petulant children. "For future training sessions, everyone gets coffee to start."

"That's why you're my favorite," I said, turning my attention to the filled, tight-knit burlap in front of me.

Squatting down, I worked my hands under the sack and attempted to lift it. Whatever the Az-hole had filled it with was heavy, causing me to grunt as I struggled.

"What did you put in these? Your fucking ego?"

"It would take more than one sack to hold my ego, Princess." Az smirked. "But if you're having trouble with a little rock and dirt, I'm happy to help you out if you ask nicely."

"Fuck. You." I grunted. "I'd sooner go inside and ask Leighton for help."

"I heard that!" Leighton called out, poking his head out of the window above me, causing me to drop the bag.

"Fuck my fucking life." I groaned as Leighton clambered over the windowsill and dropped down beside me.

"Need some help?" Leighton asked gently, coming to stand beside me.

"No, she doesn't. She's got to do it on her own, or she'll never build the conditioning she needs." Az cut in before I could respond.

I stifled the urge to give Az a grateful look. He didn't deserve it after the morning's events, even if he had just saved me from dealing with Leighton.

"Come chill over here, L. We can supervise so that the Az-hole doesn't run her into the ground in the name of 'conditioning.'" Joey said, patting a spot between the tree roots he leaned back against. Looking far more comfortable than he should have with all the hell I was being put through.

After everyone was settled, I struggled to lift the bags I was absolutely sure were filled with Az's attitude and ego based on their heavy weight. I attached them to the hooks they'd strung from the limbs. But I still wasn't allowed to rest once I'd accomplished that.

Az ran me through the strikes and punches he'd started teaching me back at the manor, and I fell into a rhythm with the movements as it came back to me. Joey continued to offer words of encouragement from the sidelines, and Leighton would offer points on form. Once, he even pointed out a weak spot in Az's stance, resulting in me landing a very satisfying blow to his ribs. I started looking for that opening every time we ran through the cycles, but his more seasoned experience meant I could only use it once. And my focus on that backfired and ended up with me in the dirt.

"Good," Az said after I completed the latest cycle. "Now let's see if you can manage these maneuvers while dodging."

He motioned for Joey and Leighton to move behind the bags I'd hung earlier, instructing them to swing them with varying force before stepping behind the third bag.

"If you don't feel confident striking and dodging, just focus on being aware of your surroundings and not getting hit. The rest will come as you get more comfortable with that." Joey said reassuringly, probably because he could see the bewildered look on my face.

"When did this become part of the plan?!" I sputtered as I looked between them, taking positions behind the bags.

"What did you think you were hanging the bags for? Funsies?" Az said, exasperated.

"Torture seemed more up your alley, actually." I shot back.

"You'll thank me for this eventually, Princess. Now, get your ass in position." Az barked, causing me to jump and stand roughly in the center of the three bags.

On Az's signal, the other two started swinging their bags in my direction. As I grew more comfortable dodging and avoiding impact, they increased the force and tempo while varying their swings, keeping me off-kilter. I'd just narrowly avoided the bag Az shoved in my direction when another slammed into my back, sending me sprawling across the uneven ground. My arm scraped across a small batch of roots, and I hissed as blood began to dot the rough scratches.

"What the fuck, Leighton?" Joey bellowed. "How could you expect her to dodge that one? She's still learning!"

"It wasn't like I was trying to hit her. I fucking stumbled when I let go of the bag, dickwad." Leighton retorted. "The ground out here isn't exactly the best for keeping your footing."

"What kind of weak ass excuse is that? You fight people in the mud for fun." Joey snapped back.

I watched, clutching my arm to my chest, as Leighton turned on Joey, a vicious look painting his face. He grabbed Joey's shirt in his fist and pulled him close, saying something too low for me to hear. Whatever it was caused Joey to clench his fist as if ready to swing on his friend.

"Just go inside, L," Az interjected. "We're about done anyway, and someone needs to let Craig know there's a fire-spitting Princess expecting breakfast."

Leighton huffed, shoving Joey back as he let him go before stalking around the side of the cabin.

"Well, that was fun." I snorted. "Did I hear someone say this hell is nearly over?"

"Run her through a cooldown, Joe, and then she can head inside. I'll make sure she has everything for a bath, so she's not crippled by aches tomorrow." Az said, ignoring me.

Joey ran me through an easy cooldown with stretches before we made our way into the cabin.

"Go clean up, Sweetheart. I'll make sure breakfast is ready, and then you and I can discuss my reward." He winked, lightly pushing me toward my room as he went to the kitchen.

Az was still in the en suite bathroom when I arrived, frowning over two bags of Epsom salts.

"If you think I'm taking a bath, you're out of your fucking mind. I have no desire to sit in my own filth."

"I didn't expect you too, Princess. This is for soaking your muscles *after* you shower."

"Uh, I'd say thanks, but you're the reason they need a soak Az-hole. Now, if you don't mind getting the fuck out so I can shower, that would be great."

"Oh, no. That's not how this is going to work, Princess." His tone darkened as he stalked toward me.

My protests died in my throat as he tugged my shirt over my head before stripping me down the rest of the way. Leaving me fully nude and totally confused, he leaned over the tub and turned the water on.

"You did good today. I thought I'd reward you for it." He smirked, something else I couldn't quite catch playing behind his sly smile.

The temperature in the en suite ratcheted up as I caught on to his meaning. Licking my lips, I tugged at the hem of his shirt.

"Not yet." He chuckled, holding my hand firmly as he tested the water temperature. "Let's clean you up first."

"Az-hole." I pouted, letting him guide me into the tub and under the spray of hot water.

Closing my eyes, I luxuriated in it, letting it soak me through before I felt the heat of him at my back. The soft pop of a bottle opening reached my ears before I could turn around. The scent of vanilla cream filled the small space just as Az's fingers began to work it through my hair. I let out a soft groan as he worked it into a lather, massaging my scalp as he did.

"Rinse." He ordered. And damn if I didn't obey for the first time all morning.

As I rinsed the shampoo from my hair, another soft pop echoed, followed by the scent of my white strawberry body wash. Az instructed me to add conditioner to my hair as he worked my soap into a lather on the loofah before he set to work washing my entire body.

Snatching the detachable shower head from its hook, he rinsed me top to bottom before pulling me against his chest. His leg slipped between mine as he forced my legs apart. I barely noticed his thumb flicking the dial on the shower head before the jet spray hit my clit, causing me to jolt.

Az's arms banded around me tightly, helping me to keep my balance as he continued to assault my sex with the spray. My fingers dug into the skin of his forearms as he drove me closer and closer to the edge.

"Fuck," I whimpered. "God, please don't stop."

Az chuckled darkly, jerking the shower head away and placing it back where it belonged. A whine of protest slipped free just before his fingers slipped inside me. The heel of his hand pressed against my clit as he thrust his fingers in and out. My soft moans grew louder and more wanton as he used his hands to fuck me senseless. My legs trembled with each stroke, the pressure low in my belly steadily rising, ready to crash over me. I threw my head back against his shoulder, barely able to control my body with my impending release, and he stopped.

"That's for acting like a fucking brat all morning." He whispered darkly in my ear as he withdrew. "Orgasms are for *good* girls."

My mouth dropped open in shock as he climbed from the tub and wrapped a towel around himself.

"Maybe you'll behave for training tomorrow." He smirked before slipping out of the en suite.

"Fucking *Az-hole!*" I called after him, throwing my loofah at the door he'd just disappeared through.

"Don't you dare finish it yourself," He called out. "Or else the next time will be even worse!"

That settled it; I was definitely going to fucking kill him.

CHAPTER SEVEN

Leighton

It seemed like the more I tried with Victoria, the more I fucked up. I doubted she would forgive me anytime soon after hitting her with the bag. For a moment, I'd thought Joey and I were going to come to blows over it because of his reaction. Even though it had been an accident, I still saw it as a learning opportunity for her. Our enemies weren't going to go easy on her, so really, I was doing her a favor with my fuck up. He couldn't protect her from everything, as much as I wished the five of us could. The manor had proven that much.

Shaking my head to clear away the strange thoughts like an etch-a-sketch, I grabbed Rinaldo's laptop from my shared room with Az. If they were going to act like assholes about me being involved in training, I could at least get started with Craig on cracking the stupid laptop. Craig was still in the kitchen, plating up breakfast for *ma petit démon* and the two stooges outside.

"What's up, L?" he asked, looking up from the counter.

"I bring presents." I grinned, waving the laptop in the air.

"Is that what you managed to steal from Rinaldo's place?"

"Yep. The paperwork I stole was bust. Nothing we can use to figure out who's pulling the strings, but I can't get into this hunk of junk to see if my little field trip was worthwhile."

"Just because you don't know how to use it properly doesn't mean it's junk," Craig said with a smirk.

"Yeah, yeah." I replied. "I tried to get into it last night, but apparently his password isn't his dead wife's name or his mistresses."

Az stomping past the kitchen drew our attention for just a moment. I couldn't help but grin at the irritated look on his face.

"Let's take this back to my room where we're less likely to be disturbed. I got the computer system Lacey brought for me all set up last night. I needed to check on our cameras at Temptat!on anyway."

I followed Craig into the room he shared with Joey, plopping down on Joey's bed. The temptation to mess up his perfectly made bed ripped through me, but I forced it aside to take care of business. As much as everyone thought I was a loose cannon, I could be serious when needed.

Craig pulled out some wires and hooked the laptop to his system. "This will take a bit for John to bust down the door for us, but we can check on the club while we wait."

"John?"

"Password cracking program called John the Ripper." Craig replied. "We just say 'John' for short."

"Like how I call these bad boys, Killer and Leftie?" I asked, holding my fists up.

"No... not even remotely the same thing. But good try." Craig said, raising an eyebrow.

"Don't listen to him, Leftie," I whispered. "He just doesn't understand us."

"Should... I leave you guys alone?" He paused. "Actually, if you and Rightie need some alone time, go to your own room."

"How dare you insult Killer?" I gasped. "Don't worry, Killer, you're still one of my favorites."

"Jesus fucking Christ. Can we get to work or are you going to romance your fists the rest of the day?" He turned from me back to his setup that dominated his side of the room. "Even I know you're not this crazy. Psycho and schizophrenic aren't the same thing."

I shrugged, letting my hands drop. "Do your techy mojo, my good sir."

"It'll take Optiview a second to boot up, and we've got a lot of footage to go over." He mused as the application came alive on screen.

"Is there a reason we're not going over footage from the manor, and focusing on the club? Feels like one would be more pressing than the other." I mused.

"For starters, we killed everyone at the manor. It's not like we missed anyone we need to track down. But I also didn't have time to grab my backup drives for the manor security system. Everything we might have had was either left behind or, more likely, destroyed when you threw a fucking grenade in the mix."

"Well, how was I supposed to know blowing up our enemies was a bad idea?" I pouted.

"You win some, you lose some, L." Craig chuckled. "Temptat!on is our best bet to sniff out anybody poking around where they shouldn't be. At least until I get us set up to access Victoria's voicemail."

"Giddy up, then. I'm getting bored."

The security footage from the club loaded on Craig's monitors. Everything was normal to the point of being dull. Our men had a handle on things in our absence. As time dragged on, watching the footage play out in fast forward, I couldn't help letting out sighs of abject boredom, earning eye rolls and glares from Craig. I was standing to leave when I recognized Bitch Barbie on the screen showing the back entrance of the club, the timestamp on the video showing it was a couple hours before our guys would show up to open.

"Hey, run that back on normal mode my guy." I spoke. "With volume if you have it."

"Of course, I have sound, Leighton. Who do you think I am?" Craig scoffed.

I moved to his side and leaned closer to the screen as he replayed the section at normal speed.

"We shouldn't be doing this, Tiff." A woman I recognized as the lead enforcer for the Golden Devils said. "If this gets back to Barb, we're both in deep shit. She doesn't take acts of war lightly."

"Those bastards vanished into thin air with Victoria, Mel. What else am I supposed to do?" Tiffany shot back, her hands working the lock on the door in an apparent attempt to pick it. "The manor is blown to shit, but she wasn't there in the rubble."

"And you expect to find what here, Tiff?" Mel asked.

"Probably nothing, but since I can't get close to their home, this is the best shot I have at figuring out where they took her."

"Casadei might think he's cock of the walk, but he's not dumb enough to stash anything in their public club. You know that. You're not thinking with your head here. You can't let emotions take the lead like this."

"If you're not here to help me, Melissa, then just leave. No way in hell am I losing track of her when she's been set up as a honey." Tiffany hissed.

"Fine, move. You're not getting anywhere with those abysmal lock picking skills, and I should probably be first in the door to make sure you don't get your high-profile ass shot."

We watched as Melissa Byrne took over, expertly picking the lock to the club's back entrance. She pulled a gun from her waistband and moved inside, ensuring the coast was clear before motioning for Tiffany to follow her. Craig followed them on the cameras to Az's office. Tiffany immediately began tearing the place apart while Melissa guarded the door.

"Good thing we don't actually stash anything there," I said. "But Az is going to be pissed when he finds out about the mess Bimbo Barbie left."

"I'm more concerned about why she's referring to Victoria as a honey." Craig replied. "We all know what that means in our world."

We watched as she moved in and out of different rooms of the club and finally came to the booth that was reserved for us. She frantically searched all around the booth, presumably looking to open our panic room.

"What exactly are you hoping to find in a booth? She's not gonna be under the table." Melissa asked, crossing her arms impatiently.

"There's a panic room here. I just... don't remember how they opened it." Tiffany grumbled as she slid her hand along the seat.

"Well, if that's true, knowing those five the only way you're getting in there is with a bomb. And before you say anything, that isn't happening, Tiffany."

Tiffany floundered around the booth for a little while longer before giving up. Just as they began to make their way back toward the rear exit, John gave off a notification sound.

"John smashed down the doors on Rinaldo's laptop." Craig said, tearing his focus from Tiffany and Melissa leaving the club.

"Where are we supposed to start now that we have access?" I asked, eyes still pinned on the screen with the club security footage.

Craig's fingers tapped a fast tempo on the laptop's keys, his face pinched as his eyes bore into the screen.

"For such an ancient bastard, he was smart enough to keep this thing relatively empty from the looks of it. Best guess, if we're going to find anything, it's in his email."

"Well, don't keep me on edge here. Open that shit."

Craig pulled up his Outlook messages as well as the calendar and began to scan the emails he found.

"Nothing particularly helpful." He mumbled as he cross-checked different appointments with the calendar. I leaned over his shoulder and read the one he'd left off.

"Looks like he got around quite a bit for an old man... I think I'm going to need eye bleach for what I just read." I gagged and moved away from the computer. "Just tell me if you find anything useful, I'm not doing that again."

Craig just chuckled as he continued his work. I don't know how he had the stomach for it if there was more of Rinaldo's *interests* in the messages. After a few minutes, he waved me back over.

"Got a couple things here. They're older emails, so it took a bit to find. This first one is to what looks like a burner email. I tried to ping it back to its host but that's not going to be possible. The contents though..." Craig trailed off as I started to read over his shoulder.

...Honeys have been sold. Transaction went smooth and was uneventful. Looks like the younger Humphreys girl is finding her footing in the game. Something to be aware of...

"Is he talking about Tiffany?" I asked, already knowing the answer.

"I would assume, there aren't too many Humphreys running around that Rinaldo would take the time to mention to whoever this is." Craig said. "That's twice now that she and Honeys have been connected... The question is, why?"

"I knew that bitch was suspicious from the jump. We got along too well for her *not* to be dirty." I replied. "The thing not adding up is the Devils. They don't normally traffic like this, so what the fuck are they up to?"

"Your guess is as good as mine. The Devils aren't really lining up to fill the street in on their business. All we have to go by with them is past experiences, and we both know, that's not something to bet on."

Craig struck a few keys, and the printer not far away came to life, spitting out the emails that we were currently looking at.

"And this is the other email that leaves me with more questions than answers." He scrolled a bit further down and brought up another email. "This one isn't a burner."

"Abrams.Theodore@Bristolandabrams.net ... He was

the friendly one at Daddy-o's shitty dinner. What about it?"

"Read it, dumbass. You'll see." Craig said, without any malice.

Mr. Marino,

We appreciate your extremely generous donation to our charity fund and dedication to improving the cause. We've arranged a brunch with the young Ms. Bristol to finalize the details. You'll find the outing as a calendar attachment.

We're also arranging a special gift for you as a token of our appreciation. I do hope that you'll find it to your liking. You can expect it delivered within the week.

"Signed, Theodore Abrams..." I trailed off as I finished reading the email. "I don't see what's such a big deal about this one."

"Check the date." Craig said simply. I looked at it and wracked my brain, but nothing came to mind.

"What about it?"

"Think back, that was about a week before there was supposed to be another kidnapping attempt. We had that footage from Gary where they were planning it, and *I* was supposed to take the fall for it."

"Man, I miss Gary." I pondered. "But yeah. I remember now. You're welcome for my interference with that one, by the way."

"If this is what it reads like, why send one communication from a burner email, and another from an identifiable one?" Craig mused aloud.

"Fuck if I know. That's your area of expertise. It could just be a way to throw off anyone who got access to this, for all we know." I said, rubbing my temples. Trying to sort this shit out was starting to give me a headache. We should take this mess to the others and see if they have any ideas.

Craig printed off this email chain as well, then slid back over to his system and pulled back up the footage from

Tiffany's break-in. He printed off a still of her face, clear as day, and then did some sort of tech wizardry to save the significant bits to a flash drive that could be plugged into the entertainment system in the den.

"I'll find Joey and fill him in so he can prepare *la petite démone*, you finish your magic, and we can reconvene after lunch."

CHAPTER EIGHT

Joey

I made my way to the kitchen while Victoria headed for her room. Craig and Leighton were nowhere in sight, but three plates of food were sitting on the counter. Moving to pour myself a cup of coffee, I stood at the counter sipping it as I ate my breakfast. By the time I'd finished, I caught sight of Az wearing a grin and looking like the cat that ate the canary as he headed toward the nook where Rich was. I gave it a few beats before realizing Victoria wasn't making an appearance. Grabbing another cup of coffee and one of the remaining plates, I headed toward her door, fully expecting to find her splayed out on the bed in a state of satisfied bliss.

"*Orgasms are for good girls.*" Her voice carried to me mockingly as I gently pushed open her door. "What a fucking Az-hole. I should show him and fuck everyone else while he has to watch. Dick. An Az-less orgy would serve him right."

"Well, I volunteer as tribute," I said with a chuckle as I watched her stomp around the room. This wasn't the state I expected to find her in, but it was entertaining.

Her head whipped toward me before her eyes narrowed on the food and cup in my hands. "You brought food. You're a God, I swear." She smiled, sauntering toward me to take them from my hands.

I beamed at her and stepped into the room. "I just pay attention, Sweetheart," I said as I closed the door.

She sipped her coffee and moaned in satisfaction before setting the plate and cup on an empty nightstand. "I recall owing you a reward."

"I'm not turning you down, but you should eat before it gets cold."

"Meh, it's already cold." She shrugged, moving in front of me and dropping to her knees.

I felt my stomach muscles tense in anticipation as the look on her face went straight to my cock. I took a deep breath to steady myself and brushed an errant curl away from her face.

"You don't have to do this right now, Pet..." My voice trailed off as her fingertips brushed against my stomach when she reached for my belt. "But I will say, you look so pretty in this position."

"When do I do *anything* I don't want to do? Now hush and let me give you your reward for being a *good boy*."

I couldn't help the smirk that crossed my face at the praise she gave. It would have been off-putting with anyone else, but I with her couldn't think it was anything but adorable. She batted her eyelashes at me with a little smile that said she knew she was toeing the line. I gathered a fistful of her hair and pulled her head back to look up at me.

"I'll let you have that one... this time." I said, my voice dropping low as my need built.

She looked up at me through her lashes, her tongue flitting out to wet her lips as her hands reached for my belt again. She was undoing the buckle when the door opened behind me, causing me to glance over my shoulder.

"Well, don't stop on my account." Leighton grinned, leaning against the door frame.

"Oh, for fuck's sake." Victoria groaned, throwing her hands in the air. "Does *nobody* knock anymore. Jesus fucking Christ."

"You can keep going. I don't mind." Leighton replied as she angrily stood, shooting him a glare over my shoulder.

"And you can drop fucking dead. A girl can't get any peace with you five."

"Hey-" I started.

"Nah, I don't think I'm gonna drop anytime soon, *ma petit démone*, not even for you." Leighton shot back before giving me his full attention. "I need a sec, Joey. Leave the hellcat here so we can talk."

Leighton shoved off the door frame and strolled away, only the slight tense of his shoulders giving away that he'd taken Victoria's words harder than he'd let on. I stepped away from her, adjusting my belt, and gave her a stern look.

"That was uncalled for, Victoria." I said flatly. "Drop dead, really?"

She blinked her surprise a few times before narrowing her eyes at me.

"He did me wrong, *Joseph*, and you know it." She snapped, her tone vicious.

"And I know that, I'm not taking that away from you." I responded, softening my voice. "And since then, he's saved your life more than once and has been working just as hard as the rest of us to figure out what's happening to you. He did wrong, but Leighton's.... Well, he's trying. You gotta give him the space to try."

"I know," she sighed, her shoulders slumping forward. "But that doesn't make it easy. You guys keep telling me he's different, that he doesn't know how to apologize like a normal person, but that doesn't mean my mind can automatically reconcile the way he did me with his fucked-up versions of apologies. It shouldn't be *this* hard for him to just say the words 'I'm sorry' and mean them."

I stepped close to her, tilting her chin up so I could look her in the eye. The fire was gone and had been replaced by shifting and conflicting emotions. I brushed a thumb across her cheek and kissed her briefly before stepping toward the door.

"I know, Sweetheart. Have some patience, he'll get there."

"Yeah, yeah. Fuck you for being right. Now go do whatever gangster shit he needed you for. I need to reheat my food." she said, waving me off.

I gave her a wry smile and left her to feed herself. I turned and saw the guys gathered around Rich's nook and made my way to them. Leighton was reclining on the pullout next to Rich, smiling like nothing was amiss, even though I hadn't missed the tension in his frame when Victoria had lashed out at him. Deciding that was an issue for another time, I turned to Az.

"Just so everyone is aware, Az is responsible for the Princess's shitty attitude today. Apparently 'orgasms are for good girls.'" I announced, making finger quotes in the air.

Az smirked and shrugged. "I'm not wrong."

"Well, if this isn't the math mathing." Leighton spoke contemplatively. "We really need to work out a schedule, so I know when you're gonna be an Az-hole and piss her off."

Craig cleared his throat just as Az opened his mouth to retort. "Can we get down to business. We need to discuss this before she decides to come out of her room so Joey can fill her in on what to expect."

I moved to one of the empty folding chairs one of them had clearly gathered around Rich and sat, motioning for them to proceed. Craig went over everything he and Leighton had uncovered in a hurried whisper, but my attention kept being drawn to my brother. Rich was clearly out of it, his eyes glazed as he leaned back against the pillows that propped him up.

"You paying attention, Joey?" Craig asked.

"Yeah, just wondering if Rich is gonna keel over on us or not." I mumbled.

"I'm fine." Rich replied gruffly, causing me to arch a brow at him.

"As I was saying," Craig continued. "You need to break it to Bunny that we have her best friend on video breaking into the club and referring to her as a honey and a suspicious email from the man she considers her uncle. We don't want her blindsided by this, especially not in her current mood."

My eyes flicked to Az; he was holding the print off of

Tiffany's face, glaring at it as if it would be enough to make her drop dead on the spot.

"After that dinner she brought a Devil to, I'm not surprised she's making moves with us gone." He spoke. "We should call Phil to bring her in and question her."

"As much as I'd love to play with Bitch Barbie, you sure that's the right call right now?" Leighton asked.

"I'm as surprised as anyone about the fact that I agree with L here," Craig said. "Despite the fact that we came out on top, the last showdown was..." he trailed off, gesturing to everyone but me, "rough on all of us."

"I'm fresh out of machetes at this point, too." L shrugged.

"No, you're not, and we all know it." Az said matter-of-factly.

Leighton clutched his chest with a dramatic gasp. "How dare you insult my honor!" He chortled.

"*Anyway...*" Az said, rolling his eyes. He looked down at the picture of Tiffany and considered it for a moment. "You're right; we need to play smarter this time. I'll need one of Leighton's burners to contact Phil. We'll put a tail on them for now."

"Oh. My. God. Did the Az-hole just admit that someone else is right?" Victoria said, causing us all to turn and look at her.

Az rolled his eyes before nodding at me to take Victoria aside. Standing from my chair, I moved to take her by the arm and gently led her to the front porch.

She looked at me with concern as I shut the door behind us, shifting uneasily.

"Joey, what's happened?" Her voice shook slightly, her doe eyes taking in my face. I sighed and scrubbed a hand across the back of my neck.

"We found some evidence..." I trailed off, not knowing how to put it to her gently.

"Just tell me."

"It's not quite a smoking gun, but it doesn't look good, so we wanted to prepare you for it before we laid everything out." I took a steadying breath before continuing. "We have some evidence to suggest that Tiffany and Theodore may be involved in what's been going on with the Jackals and possibly what happened with Rinaldo." I finished, making sure to stay deathly still in the event she wanted to lash out.

"That... that can't be right." She frowned. "Tiff and Uncle Theo wouldn't...."

"You'd be surprised what people can and will do Sweetheart," I replied gently. "I think the only way you're going to be able to wrap your head around this is to see what we found for yourself."

Victoria squared her shoulders and took a deep breath. "Show me."

When I led her back inside, the others had already set up in the den. Craig was standing by the television with a sympathetic look on his face. Az and Leighton stood off to the side, wearing shockingly similar expressions to Craig's.

"Rich nod back off?" I asked as I guided Victoria to the couch.

"Yeah," Craig replied. "She ready for this?"

"No, but I suppose it's better to rip the Band-Aid off than sit here wondering why you five think my best friend and uncle are out to get me." She answered somewhat sullenly.

Craig shot her a look of understanding before moving to play the footage from the club. I didn't have to look to know that all four of us were studying Victoria closely, monitoring her for her reaction. She remained surprisingly stoic, her back straight and expression blank, as Tiffany's break-in played out on screen. I cringed on her behalf when Tiffany called her a 'honey,' instantly regretting not explaining the term before we'd come back inside.

"Is that it?" Victoria asked as the screen went black.

"There's more," Az replied, moving to hand her the printed emails.

She read them silently, her eyes flying across the page as she flipped through them. When she'd finished reading, she carefully sat them on the couch beside her and turned to look at us.

"I take it '*honey*' means something I'm missing here." She said, in a tone so matter of fact I was sure we'd broken her. "And it's clear that Tiffany is involved with *something*, but the only thing that seems like evidence of something nefarious is Uncle Theo promising Rinaldo a gift. The foundation doesn't do gifts."

"A honey is a woman being trafficked." Leighton spoke, biting the bullet for all of us. "Your friend Barbie is involved with known Golden Devils and attended some sort of trafficking exchange with the Jackals. I'd say *that* is pretty nefarious."

The room stilled, waiting to see what Victoria would do with Leighton's information. Tension rolled off her frame in waves, but she stayed still. Leighton looked like he was preparing to defend himself from an attack. For the first time I could remember, he didn't seem like he was going to enjoy the confrontation.

"I know this all looks bad, but Tiffany is involved with Georgialynn, who's entire life's work is outreach to impoverished and battered women. Those two things don't really mesh." Victoria said finally.

The four of us exchanged a loaded glance, wondering if we should break it to Victoria who Georgialynn really was. Before we could decide, Leighton spoke up.

"Georgialynn is a gangster." He deadpanned. "She's a Golden Devil through and through. Friendship tattoo and everything."

"We saw it at the dinner," I said in a rush before she could respond. "It was definitely the Devil's Mark. Though, they aren't generally associated with trafficking, it's true–"

"The only things we know for sure about the Golden Devils is that they have their hands in a lot of things, and they play everything close to the vest." Az cut in. "There are still some inconsistencies, but the point is that this doesn't look good."

Victoria sighed heavily, scrubbing her hands over her face. "It's been nothing *but* inconsistencies since the Gala fire. None of this makes any sense to me. If Tiffany is a Devil, trafficking women, how does Uncle Theo play into this? His email is strange, but it's not exactly damning evidence either."

"For this to make sense, you'll need a little bit of context." Craig spoke up, stepping back toward the entertainment center. "We... uh... While..."

"While I was rotting in jail, we had an associate tailing you when we thought you were responsible, and he brought us this," Az said shortly.

"Don't worry, it wasn't the kinky kind of stalking. He didn't steal your panties or anything." Leighton snickered before releasing a sad sigh. "I miss Gary."

"Who's Gary?" Victoria asked.

"He's dead. And you didn't even know him, L." Az responded.

"When a man gives you his hand, you take it!"

"He didn't give us his hand." Craig sighed, pulling up another video. "The Jackals sent it to us after they killed him."

"Semantics. Now roll the tape." Leighton snapped his fingers into finger guns and plopped onto the loveseat.

I couldn't help the smirk on my face at the brevity, but it only took a look at Victoria's tense control over her expression to be a sobering reminder that this was heavy for her. The video started, and he tried to fast-forward to the relevant part, but when she saw herself on the screen, she called for him to just let it play.

He looked at her cautiously before backing it up and letting the cut-together video play in its entirety. Her conversing with Lenny Moretti at the Gala before the fire broke out, the slides of photographs with her surrounded by Jackals' members. And finally, the video of the Jackals' street thug, whom Leighton called Sanso, whining about having to take a beating for one of the kidnapping attempts they were going to make on Victoria and pin on Craig.

None of us really paid attention to the video as it played; we were watching her take in the evidence that had led us to her doorstep in the first place. We pointed out the members of the Jackals as it played when it was relevant, but otherwise, the room was silent.

"Well... that definitely explains some things as to why you were all so convinced I was a criminal mastermind. But... how does this relate to Uncle Theo?" she asked as the video concluded.

"The conversation between Sanso and the Jackal we couldn't name happened about a week before Theo sent his email to Rinaldo about having a gift for him." Craig answered, switching the television off.

"Right. But the original kidnapping attempt was at the Gala during the fire. This was all after that–"

"And there was the attempt outside the shop, and one at the fight, and we can probably assume the shootout at the club was one, and the one at the house," Leighton counted off the various kidnapping attempts on his fingers, as he lounged casually on the loveseat. "And we can't forget the big showdown where the manor went boom."

"The manor wouldn't have 'gone boom' if you hadn't thrown a grenade *indoors*." Victoria snapped and raised a hand to cut Leighton off when he started to say something. "But point taken. There's been several attempts. But, again, those don't point to Theo without some heavy mental gymnastics."

"It's one thing to not understand, Princess, it's another to be willfully ignorant." Rich's voice came from behind us, gruff and tired. We all turned to find him leaning heavily on his cane for support. He looked frustrated and pained as he leveled a grave look at Victoria. "All of this circles back around to you being offered as a gift to Rinaldo and an expected delivery time. Just because we've thwarted all their attempts and they've had to keep trying doesn't mean that they didn't expect to deliver you each time. And Theodore was promising a gift that the foundation doesn't give. We can only assume, at this point, that gift was you."

CHAPTER NINE

Victoria

The guys watched me closely like they thought I would break apart at any second. That would have probably been a normal response to the information they'd dropped on me, but I was just... numb. I didn't have room to process that my best friend and the man I'd considered an uncle could be behind all the shit that had happened since the gala fire. Tiffany was chaotic enough that I could *almost* see her getting involved in something so dangerous. But Uncle Theo... He was my safe harbor. He'd stepped in on more than one occasion when my father failed to be 'fatherly.' To the point that I'd sometimes found myself wondering what life would have been like if he'd been my father instead.

I found myself going through the motions of the day. My mind was so preoccupied with trying to sort through what had become of my life that I couldn't even recall what had occurred at any given point throughout the afternoon and evening. The lack of ache in my stomach meant I'd eaten. The fact my muscles weren't seized with aches and pains meant I'd probably moved around quite a bit. Still, beyond that, I couldn't recall anything in particular, not even climbing into the soft bed I found myself lying in.

The guys' hushed voices carried through my door, just enough to provide an indistinct lullaby for me to drift to sleep before I jolted awake again. My heart hammered against my chest in the pitch-black room; my body was once again covered in a thin layer of sweat. My fingers reached for the rope gauntlet I'd hastily thrown back on at some point, fingering the silky threads as I worked to ground myself after yet another nightmare. The manor attack haunted me, but now Tiffany and Theodore had joined the fray, taunting me in my dreams as I fought to save myself and Az.

I needed to move. The longer I lay in bed staring at the dark ceiling, the more my thoughts spiraled. Throwing the blankets off, I swung my legs over the side of the bed and stumbled toward the door. The lake seemed as good an option as last time, but I desperately needed something to soothe my parched throat first. It was painfully dry, leaving me to wonder if I hadn't been screaming in my sleep, even if I knew that one of the guys would have woken me if that had been the case.

I hooked a left into the kitchen to get some water, intending to quench my thirst, and then sneak outside. I was so lost in my head that I collided with Rich, standing just inside the archway, leaning on his cane. I jumped back as he wobbled, stumbling forward and catching himself on the counter. He hissed sharply from the sudden movement, and the sound immediately pulled me out of my thoughts.

"I'm so sorry! Are you okay?! You shouldn't be up!" I said in a rush as if apologizing, checking on him, and chastising him were trying to happen simultaneously, but I only had one mouth to get through them.

"Relax, Princess. I'm alright, no worse for wear than when I walked in here. And I can get around enough to get my own water. I wish you'd all stop fussing over me like I was an invalid." He said gruffly as he turned to face me. His patience had been short when we checked him over since we arrived, but it was easy to see that it took him a lot of effort to do things independently. The immediate danger might have passed, but we all knew he wasn't out of the woods yet.

"You just... Here, I'll get it." I stepped around him to the cupboard to get a couple glasses and filled them from the tap. "You want ice?"

"That's not necessary, this is fine." He said, leaning against the counter and propping his cane next to him. "Can't sleep?"

"I haven't slept well since we got here. Not as well as you have been." I said with a weak smile in an attempt at humor.

"Hard to stay awake on the pain meds Doc gave me." He said, with a shrug, returning a weak smile of his own. "No one sleeps as well as me after those."

"The snoring is a dead giveaway," I laughed. "I can hear you all the way in my room."

"I don't snore!" He exclaimed indignantly, immediately grimaced, and grabbed his stomach.

"Easy there, big guy," I said gently, "and you definitely do. It's like you're rubbing your good sleep in all our faces." I chuckled softly.

"Well, take a few bullets, a gut shot, and Leighton's ass blowing you up, you'll sleep great too." He replied dryly.

It was my turn to grimace. "I'm sorry I got you guys into this mess. I know you caught the tail end of the others showing me, well... everything. It really is my fault you're all mixed up in this mess and wounded." I sighed.

"Not all of us are wounded." He offered with another shrug. "And we'd have been in this mess whether it had been you or someone else who was their target." He paused, looking contemplative for a moment before continuing. "While you were the person they kept trying to get at, we were always going to take the fall while the Jackals tried to clear the board of players."

Tears welled in my eyes, threatening to spill, and I wiped my hand over my eyes hastily. "Let me help you back to bed. I need to step out and get some air." I said quickly to cover the sudden rush of emotion.

He raised an eyebrow at me as I stepped closer but didn't move away from his spot as he looked me over. "In the middle of the night? Alone?"

"We're in the middle of nowhere and it's not like anyone looking for us knows we're here. Unless you're worried about a bear or something snagging me, I'm good. But last I checked the bears are supposed to be settling in for hibernation. With everything going on in my head right now, I'm liable to murder the bear."

Rich rolled his eyes, and in his classic fashion, he gently pinched the bridge of his nose. "Princess, no one knows we're here aside from Lacey, her crew of movers, and anyone else she may have told."

"But Leighton seemed pretty sure she wouldn't give us up like that." I interrupted.

"Lacey plays by her own set of rules. She may not give us up now, but give her the right incentive, who knows what she'll do. And even if she doesn't, we don't know her crews, and we can't guarantee how secure Leighton's precautions have been when he reaches out to her. Craig is one of the best tech wizards out there, but we're not the only crew with a tech genius."

Even though his tone told me he wasn't trying to pick a fight, I couldn't help but feel boxed in by his words. It was just one more thing added to the maelstrom slowly overtaking my mind. I was so tired of everything, so completely overwhelmed by how in over my head I was, that his sentiments thrust me toward the edge of my fraying self-control.

"But–" I started.

"Princess, even if we trusted those who knew we were here to be the only ones, it's not foolproof. You can't get careless now, you have to be smart about things."

"You barely started being able to get up and move around, and you're already back on your bullshit, Rich. I'm going for a walk, I need to clear my head. I need some air. So, unless you want to chase me down as I walk out the door, I guess there's nothing you can do about it except bark." I snapped at him harshly, surprising myself with the malice that dripped from my words.

He pulled himself up to his full height and stepped away from the counter with some difficulty, swaying gently on his feet for a moment. The struggle didn't detract from the intimidating presence as he pinned me to my spot with a look of anger and exasperation.

"Listen here, *little girl*, you need to be done with this childishness. It's time to put on your big girl panties and realize that there are real consequences to the stakes here. You'll have to forgive me if I'm thinking ahead to ensure that the *narrow* escape we made with our lives, and those who didn't make it out, wasn't in vain." He snapped, sneering at me, stepping closer to me with every point he made until he stood directly in front of me. "One would think, *Princess*, that you'd have learned how severe that is, considering you know what it is to take a life now."

I froze; his words were like ice water thrown in my face. I narrowed my eyes at him, noting the blaze burning through the glassiness from the drugs in his eyes. I forced myself to keep my tone level, even as tears fell unbidden. "I don't see why you care so fucking much what happens to me. Seems to me you'd have been just fucking fine if you'd left me to sort this shit out on my own once you realized the Jackals were the ones trying to set you up."

His eyes locked on my face as I cried, and he sighed before running a hand through his hair. "Baby girl, you can't be serious... You know why we stuck around. I know you do, somewhere in the turmoil of your mind."

"Do I?" I demanded, lifting my chin defiantly. "Joey and Craig, sure. They might have found a reason to come around. Az got there eventually. Hell, even Leighton has his twisted fucking obsession that would have had him climbing in my bedroom window at night. But you? We've had a moment here and there, but this? This is what we have most of the time. There's *nothing* that should have stopped you from making the call to cut your losses and deal with the Jackals without me. You're the boss; they would have listened if you said 'go.'"

His gaze softened, and he smiled at me as if he found what I said funny. He shook his head. "They would have fought me tooth and nail, is what would have happened, silly girl.

Best case scenario? They would have been sneaking off to see you safe..." He trailed off as if catching himself before saying something further. "Worst case? It would have been a full mutiny."

"Great, so you decided to stick around to make life easier for yourself. Do you not see how you proved my point here?"

"It absolutely does make my life easier knowing that you're safe, Baby girl. Look..." He said, wiping away a few of the tears that had spilled onto my cheeks, "I'm sorry. I was too harsh. I know this hasn't been easy on you, this isn't the world you belong to, but it's found its way to you anyway. They–we have to know that you're okay. We don't blame you for what happened, and we made the choices we wanted to make. I just... I need you to listen to us right now. Until we get things sorted out."

There was something so incredibly tender in how he spoke and looked at me. It spoke volumes to the simple terms he was dancing around, and something about it broke my heart just as much as it warmed it.

"I'm so sorry–" I started, but he grabbed my chin and leaned down so that he was just scant inches away.

"Stop." He said firmly before he claimed my mouth with his.

As much as I wanted to give in, the inferno burning behind his kiss was more than just passion. His skin was on fire with fever, causing me to break the kiss and jump back.

"Oh my god! Rich, you're on fire!" I exclaimed, putting my wrist on his forehead to recheck him.

"You're not wrong..." He slurred, blinking hard in what I assume was an attempt to wink.

"We need to get you back in bed. Come on, I'm not going to fight you on this. You're burning up with fever." I grabbed his arm and put it around my shoulder, knowing that if he went down, I would be powerless to stop it, but I still tried to support him as he swayed on his feet when I stepped away.

"You're such a good girl for Daddy." He murmured,

almost incoherently.

"Thank you, but now I need Daddy to help me get him back to bed. Come on, I'm not gonna be able to drag you." I said, feeling the panic rising in my chest as he became more unsteady on his feet.

The distance from the kitchen to his little nook wasn't far, but it felt like it took every ounce of strength I had to get him to wobble across the den and lie in bed. And when we got there, I couldn't do much but unceremoniously dump him in the bed. But as I was trying to get him to lay back, he held onto me and tried to pull me down with him.

"Stay, Babygirl." He grumbled quietly.

"I'll be right here, Daddy, but I need to get some help for your fever. I'll be right back." I said, gently prying his hand off my arm.

"Don't be long. I've been dreaming about having you to myself for ages." Rich said, his voice drifting as he started to trail off into something incoherent.

That line stopped me in my tracks momentarily, and I just looked at him. It was hard to believe under all his machismo and authority, he'd been anything but annoyed by my presence. But I couldn't consider his words; my brain snapped back into action, and I turned to the nearest bedroom door.

I pounded on the wooden door hard enough to make my hand ache. I was rewarded with a perplexed Leighton opening it. Az was close behind him, looking just as groggy after being pulled from sleep.

"What's wrong, *ma petit démone*?" Leighton asked, rubbing the sleep from his eyes.

"Something is wrong with Rich." I blurted out in a panic. "He's burning up and becoming incoherent. I think.... No, I know... He needs a doctor."

CHAPTER TEN

Leighton

I shot Az a worried look before turning my attention back to Victoria. Guiding her gently away from the door, I pulled her close as Az slipped by us to check on Rich.

"He's burning up," Az said loud enough for me to hear. "And he's muttering absolute nonsense."

"Wouldn't Ma love her? Come on, Joe, you know I'm right." Rich spoke as if to highlight Az's words.

"Shit. I'll call Lacey."

"Not Harrison?" Victoria asked, barely containing the panic laced in her tone.

"No, Lacey already knows we're here and she has the resources to take care of Rich. As much as we all respect Doc, we can't risk it. Why don't you go wake the others while I make the call."

She looked from me to Rich and took a step toward the bed. "I should be here. He's sick and…" She trailed off, searching for something to use as a reason to stay by Rich's bedside.

I thought momentarily, trying to think how Joey or Craig might approach her since she found their presence comforting. I reached for her slowly, gently, and turned her to face me. I chucked her under the chin and gave her what I hoped was a reassuring smile.

"He's going to be okay, *ma petite*. We're going to get him help, but we need to make sure the others know what's going on. Do that for us?"

Her bottom lip trembled, but she nodded silently and moved across the room toward Craig and Joey's door. I blew out a breath, satisfied that I'd managed to emulate my friends well enough to get her moving, and turned back into my room. Absently, I rubbed my knuckles against my chest, the expression on her face stirring hope I didn't know I was capable of. Stowing the thought for later, I raced to the nightstand I'd claimed and retrieved one of my burner phones.

"Do you know what time it is?" Lacey hissed when she finally answered our coded ring system.

"Rich needs a doctor." I replied, ignoring the thinly veiled venom in her tone. "Get your ass up and get one here."

I could hear movement on her end of the line and the hushed whisper of her voice as she soothed whoever was in her bed back to sleep. "I'll be there as soon as I can."

"Make it faster, Lacey." I shot back, ending the call before she could reply and moving back into the den. "Help's on the way," I said to nobody in particular.

Joey sped out of his room so quickly that he nearly slid across the floor. "What's wrong with my brother?" he asked as he approached his bedside.

Rich's unfocused eyes landed on Joey, and his face became childlike. "It's not fair Dad, I told him he had to ask to use my stuff!"

"What?" Joey said, looking at Rich with confusion.

"Is he hallucinating?" Craig asked, following behind Joey a moment later, a laptop in his hand.

"What the fuck is happening?"

"If someone will tell me his symptoms, I might be able to narrow down what's going on while we wait for help. So, is he hallucinating?" Craig asked again.

"If y'all are smart, you'll stay away from Mrs. Bristol's daughter. You're asking for trouble following her around like whipped puppies." Rich all but shouted, rolling his head in Az's direction. "She's too young for you, she's only ten." He continued squinting his eyes as he tried to focus. "I'm looking at you in particular Az."

"He's definitely hallucinating." Craig said, typing away

on his laptop while Az shifted awkwardly and took a keen interest in the floor when Victoria turned to look at him.

"This feels like a front row seat to a replay of y'all's childhoods." I chuckled, trying to lighten the mood.

Victoria stepped forward, pushing past the others to check Rich's temperature with her wrist. In a sudden moment of semi-clarity, Rich grabbed her arm. He jerked her onto his lap roughly, burying his face in her neck and inhaling deeply.

"The things I want to do to you, Princess." He said just loud enough for the rest of us to hear.

I was beside the pullout in two short steps, plucking Victoria from his grasp. "Now's not the time, big guy. You couldn't handle her in your current condition." I chuckled.

"Bunny, why don't you grab some Tylenol from the bathroom and a glass of water?" Craig spoke. "We can at least start dealing with his fever." He waited until she was out of sight before his face fell into a grim expression. "So, I know WebMD is always death and doom, but it's looking a whole lot like Rich might be turning septic. I hope Google is wrong, but nothing else makes sense with the symptoms we're seeing."

"His wounds looked fine when I checked this morning." Az said. "Granted, the bastard fought me over taking a look, but I didn't see anything to point toward infection."

"I've been shot and maimed enough to know that there's not always external signs." I interjected before Craig could respond. "Rich is a pin cushion of bullet wounds, any one of them could have abscessed without us noticing."

Az made a noise and nodded his head ever so slightly toward the direction of the bathroom just before we heard her footsteps padding quickly across the floor, so we let the subject drop for now. She would hear it from whatever doctor Lacey brought. Still, I imagined the rest of the group were of the same mind, not particularly interested in being the bearers of more potential bad news.

She gave him a couple of Tylenol and one of his pain pills and gingerly helped him with the water so that he could swallow them. He continued to mumble unintelligible things, carrying on conversations in his mind that none of us were privy to. There was little we could do but wait and hope what we'd given him worked. Joey and Az worked him out of his sweat-soaked shirt while the rest of us paced around, checking the time.

A knock at the front door sent me racing to answer it. Lacey stood outside looking annoyed, and I stepped back to allow her inside. An older man stepped in behind her with a black leather bag, and another younger man followed him.

"He's just over there," Lacey addressed the men, pointing toward the nook.

I waited until the pair moved away and roughly grabbed Lacey by the arm. "What the fuck are you thinking bringing some random dude with you? Are you trying to get our location leaked?" I whisper-shouted as I leaned into her space.

Lacey frowned, pushing my shoulder to force me back. "You asked me to bring help. If you didn't want it, you shouldn't have called."

"I asked for a doctor, not whoever the fuck was warming your bed when I called." My anger caused my voice to rise above the hushed tones I was aiming for. "I'm starting to think you're trying to get Victoria killed and us with her."

"Honestly, Leighton, get control of yourself." She replied, shaking her head and turning to move toward the nook.

I seethed momentarily as I watched her join the group around Rich's bed before following her. She sidled up to his bedside and sat on the edge across from the doctor, who was busy taking Rich's vitals.

"Looking a little worse for wear there, big guy." Lacey crooned, brushing her fingers against Rich's shoulder.

He turned his unfocused gaze toward her and smiled tenderly. "I've had worse. What happened to Daddy? When did I become 'big guy', Princess?"

Lacey's brows knit together in confusion. "Well, when

did you start calling me 'princess'?"

Rich chuckled and groaned at the movement. "We've called you Princess since we met you, Tory. You sure *you're* okay?" He said lightly before slipping back off into unconsciousness.

Lacey stiffened, barely contained rage flitting across her face as Az stifled a laugh. Standing in one smooth motion, Lacey schooled her features before excusing herself from the room. I shot the guys an amused look. Being called by Victoria's name was the least of what my sister deserved, and we deserved a second to revel in that.

"Is something funny?" Victoria asked, her gaze flitting between us all in confusion.

Joey shook his head, smirking, before squeezing her shoulder. "I'll tell you later, Sweetheart. Just know we're not laughing at Rich."

Looking toward the doctor one last time, I slipped away from the others to follow my sister outside. She was standing on the far end of the porch, her arms crossed in front of her chest, scowling toward the door.

"Ah, did whittle wacey get her feewings hurt?" I cooed, barely able to contain my glee.

Her entire demeanor shifted as if she were a shark sensing blood in the water. Uncrossing her arms, she plastered a saccharine smile on and stalked toward me.

"Did someone get booted from the harem?" She drawled.

"What the fuck are you on about?"

"Awe, come now LeLe, the only reason you'd be out here attempting to gloat is if your precious *Princess* has shut you out. She did give the impression the last time I spoke with her that you were the last man she'd turn to for anything, let alone comfort in her time of need."

"Fuck off, Lacey. You don't know what the hell you're talking about." I gritted out, anger coiling tight in my chest.

"What did you do, anyway, that got you banned from her bed?" Lacey smiled viciously.

"What's going on between any of us and Victoria is none of your business. You're the last person I'd seek relationship advice from." I spat.

Lacey leaned back, her eyes raking over me as she pursed her lips. "Interesting. You think you're in love with the spoiled thing, and you've done something that's left you on the outside pining away like a poor, lost lamb."

I cocked my head at my sister, considering whether or not she was worth breaking my one rule. As much as I enjoyed causing pain, I'd never hurt a woman who wasn't willing or an immediate threat that couldn't be handled another way.

"Poor, broken Leighton. Such a sad, lost, hollow little puppet even after all these years." Lacey crooned. "Obsessed with another woman who will never want you the way you want her. If only you were a *real boy* and could feel things like they do."

"Stop telling me how I feel." I hissed, clenching my fists by my side.

"Why? It's not as if you could figure out how you feel on your own." She snapped. "I warned you; I won't deal with another Angelica incident."

Her gaze flicked over my shoulder as she finished her sentence, causing me to turn my head to see what had drawn her attention. Victoria stood just over the threshold, guilt painting her face. It was enough to tell me she'd heard enough of the conversation to know she was intruding. I tried to relax my face into a reassuring smile. Whatever she saw there caused her eyebrows to raise in alarm before she hurried back inside and closed the door. My shoulders slumped in defeat, knowing I must have scared her.

"You know I'm not responsible for what our mother did, Lacey so why the fuck are you doing this shit to me?" Victoria's reaction left me not caring how my sister would weaponize my words against me.

"I'm trying to protect you from yourself, LeLe." Lacey sighed, her face softening.

"I'm not a child anymore. I don't need your protection." I replied, turning and stomping toward the door. Glancing over my shoulder, I called back to my sister. "I used to think that being like you and our parents was just who I am, but I'm starting to wonder if it wasn't you that stunted me."

Shoving the door open, my eyes popped open in surprise as Victoria stumbled back, a sheepish look on her face.

"Sorry, I shouldn't have been eavesdropping," She muttered as I caught her arm to steady her. "If it makes you feel better about it, I didn't hear everything, and it offered me a much-needed distraction from what's happening over there."

"Are you offering me an olive branch, *ma petit démone*?" I chuckled, leading her back toward the nook.

Victoria looked up at me, studying my face. I could see the gears in her head turning as she worked out how to answer.

"I think I'm starting to realize why you are the way you are." She said finally. "But I still haven't decided if that means an olive branch. I'll let you know when I do."

Before I could respond, she slipped into Joey's arms and turned her gaze to Rich. He was still unconscious, but now there was an I.V. line in his arm, and the younger guy was jerking a painting from the wall to hang the bag on the exposed nail.

"I have good news, and I have bad news." The doctor spoke, addressing all of us. "It appears your friend here is turning septic. It's easy enough to treat, but if we want to ensure that he doesn't get worse, he will need more than antibiotics, pressors, and I.V. fluids."

"Whatever it is, Lacey will get it for us, Doc." I interjected.

"It's not that simple, son. The nurse and I will need to reopen his abdominal wound and evacuate the abscess that I believe to be the cause of his situation. Unless you all are willing to have him transported to a hospital, the procedure itself poses serious risk since this isn't exactly a sterile environment."

"We're not taking him to a hospital. It's too risky." Az confirmed.

"Hey, now wait a fucking minute. Is the risk of someone finding him there anymore than the risk of having him have surgery in a fucking cabin in the woods?!" Joey exclaimed, pulling away from Victoria as he turned his attention to Az. "You can't just decide that!"

"I can. With Rich indisposed, I'm the one that makes those calls."

"And *I'm* the next of kin. I'm the only one who can make his medical decisions while he's indisposed." Joey snapped.

"This isn't a democracy Joey, and you know damned well next of kin means fuck all in our line of work. You don't have to like it, but do you really think with everyone looking for us, risking *another* shootout, this time in a fucking hospital while Rich is in surgery, is wise?" Az bit back.

"If he dies, Casadei, it's on *your* head. You can explain how he died to Ma and Pa." Joey growled at Az before turning on his heel and storming from the cabin.

Victoria stared after him in bewilderment, and I sidled up next to her. "You don't want to be here for this anyway, *ma petit démone.* Go check on your guy and keep him from doing something he'll regret."

She gave me a surprised look as if she was blown away by my perceptiveness and nodded. Shooting her a wink, I turned her back toward the door and gave her a gentle push to get her moving. Turning back to face the bed, I subtly shifted to block her view if she decided to do something stupid, like look back.

"Fellas, I didn't mean we'd do the surgery in the bed." The doc spoke, "I need a flat, clean surface to work on."

"Dining room table it is." I shrugged. "Come on, Craig, let's bleach the fucking thing before we move him."

We wiped the table down with clean water before finding the bleach and dousing the table and the surrounding area. I stepped away while Craig was wiping up the excess to find something to cover the floor. It took a minute, but I found some old painter's plastic in a closet. I came back and started laying it out under and around the table while Craig moved the chairs away.

We'd barely finished cleaning and preparing the space when Az yelled for one of us to come help him move Rich into the dining room. It took the three of us to carry him easily from his nook and lay him out on the table.

"Fuck, dead weight is heavy." I said absently after we'd finally gotten him in position on the table.

Az cut his eyes to me with a narrowed side-eye. "Really, L?"

"That's... not how I meant it to come out," I said after realization dawned on me. We were all tense, and I was doing my best to try and be aware of what might make it worse.

"This isn't going to be pleasant without anesthesia, boys. You may have to help, so I need everyone to scrub up. We can do our best to keep it as clean as possible." The doctor said matter-of-factly as he started the seemingly overly complicated process of washing his hands.

We mimicked what he'd done after he finished and took up ready positions around the table in case we were needed. The younger guy, I'd finally realized must be a nurse, had done as thorough a job as possible disinfecting Rich's wound and the tools the doc would need and was now placing them on the table beside Rich. Grumbling about the lack of gloves, the doc moved to his side and picked up his scalpel, dragging it along the line of stitches in Rich's abdomen.

No sooner than the doctor had started cleaning away the abscess–that had become sickly apparent as the scent of infection filled the dining room–Rich came to sudden consciousness and started screaming. He started squirming, yelling, and trying to stop the pain that he didn't understand.

"Little help here boys." The doctor said; somehow, his voice was still as calm as it had been when examining Rich before.

Az and Craig flew into action to pin his arms away from

his body while the nurse held down his legs.

"Watch the door, L. Make sure Joey doesn't come running in here with a gun." Az shouted over Rich's screaming. "The last thing we need is him dropping me while I'm holding his brother still."

I snickered at the image that called to mind. "He's not going to shoot you. But he still doesn't need to see it." I said as I moved to the door.

"Victoria doesn't need to see this shit either." Craig added offhandedly as he struggled with Rich's attempts to flail against his hold.

I bit back the urge to tell the doc to work fast as Rich's screams became the background music to the doctor's movements. Taking in the sweat starting to bead the doc's brow, I realized it was going to be a long fucking night.

CHAPTER ELEVEN

Victoria

As much as I wanted to stay by Rich's side, I knew I couldn't stomach watching him be cut open. When Leighton directed me to go to Joey, I was relieved. For someone so out of touch with how ordinary people expressed themselves, he seemed to pick up my need for an out without me ever uttering a word. After the things I'd overheard Lacey saying to him, I could almost understand why. If his own sister berated him the way she did, it could only be something she had learned from their parents. My chest tightened at the thought of the sort of damage that kind of upbringing would have caused a child.

Packing away the conflicting emotions vying for my attention, I made my way outside. Joey was on the front porch pacing. The light that spilled from the cabin when I opened the door illuminated the tension in his body, and I could just make out the way the muscles in his jaw clenched. As scared as I was for Rich, I knew what Joey was going through must be several times more intense as Rich's brother.

"Hey." I said softly, slipping into the same headspace I'd used hundreds of times when dealing with women and children at the center.

Joey's eyes snapped to mine, and he huffed out a breath. "Hey, sweetheart."

Moving to stand in front of him, I wrapped my arms around his waist and leaned my head against his chest. The tension in his body eased slightly as he relaxed into my hold.

"He's going to be okay," I said, knowing I couldn't really make that promise. "Rich is... Well, he's a stubborn bastard is what he is, but that's exactly why he's going to pull through."

Joey made a noncommittal noise before moving us to lean his back against the porch railing. Neither of us spoke, not wanting to voice our fears aloud. We stayed like that, seeking comfort in each other's arms, the night air thick with unspoken worry and the muffled sounds of movement inside the cabin.

The first scream caused us to jolt apart. Joey stepped toward the cabin door, and I caught his arm, urging him silently to stay. He looked at where I held him, the soft light spilling from the cabin windows casting his face in shadows. The need to go to his brother rolled off him in dangerous waves. If he chose to ignore my pleas, there would be nothing I could do to stop him.

"Don't..." I whispered.

"I can't do this." he said before pulling his arm from my grasp with a pained roar. "This isn't how shit was supposed to go. I can't just leave my brother in there to suffer."

"You're not in any state to help him, Joey." I replied softly, placing my hand on his chest. "If you go in there, what exactly do you hope to accomplish?"

He raked a hand through his hair, tugging at it roughly. "I don't know. Something. I can't just stand here doing nothing."

"Come on," I said, sliding my hand from his chest to take his hand. "Walk me to the lake. Standing out here listening to what's happening inside is only going to tear you up more and there's nothing you can do for Rich right now."

Joey's shoulders slumped forward, and he sighed, letting me gently pull him toward the steps. "I'm sorry," he mumbled. "I should be comforting you right now instead of you being the one holding me together."

"That's not how relationships work," I said as I continued to lead him toward the lake. "They're not one-sided like that. Besides, it's kind of nice in a weird way to not be the only one losing their shit for once."

We made our way to the lake, walking in silence to the end of the dock before sitting down. Joey pulled me into his lap as he leaned against the wooden post, his legs stretched across the dock toward the opposite post. I pushed away the urge to protest about being too heavy and shifted so that I could wrap my arms around him and lay my head on his shoulder.

"You need a distraction." I said as his arms wrapped around me tightly.

"I don't think I can focus on anything else right now."

I pulled away just enough to study his face. "I know I haven't exactly handled all the craziness that's happened very well, but I do know from my work at the center that distractions can be helpful even when you think they can't."

"I don't wanna burst your bubble, Sweetheart, but I'm not a kid anymore."

"I know, but I didn't just work with the children. The center may be a safe space for the kids of South Sacona, but that's not all it is. My mother taught me that sometimes the best way to help those kids is to help their parents first."

Joey considered my words for a moment before blowing out a puff of air. "Alright, what did you have in mind?"

"Tell me something about your childhood," I replied, relaxing back into him and laying my head on his shoulder again.

"What do you want to know?"

"Well, Az and Craig told me about meeting me at the center as kids and knowing you all pretty much grew up there, I suspect you have a story as well."

Joey chuckled lightly, the sound vibrating through his chest and into my side. "It's ironic that you want to know if I have a memory of you from the center."

"What do you mean?"

"You had a little bit of a hero complex even then." He replied. "The first time we met, you acted first and thought later."

"Don't keep me in suspense." I laughed, poking him in

the chest. "Tell me."

"Well, I was a pretty small kid." He started with a shrug. "When Rich or the others weren't around, some of the bigger kids liked to pick on me. I lost count of the number of scraps I got into trying to defend myself and prove I could hold my own. I don't really remember what started it that day, but a group of them had me surrounded in the play yard. The guys were inside in the gym and had kicked me out for being a pest."

"I can't imagine them ever kicking you out for that."

"How many sixteen-year-olds do you know that aren't assholes? And me being nine years younger than him, it's only normal he wouldn't want to hang out with me at that age." Joey replied. "It's not unusual for siblings to be tighter as adults than as kids. Anyway, they'd kicked me out of the gym, and I'd gone out to the play yard. Six or seven kids that liked to bully me had me surrounded and I knew I was about to get my ass beat."

"That's horrible." I gasped. "Where was Mrs. McMillan or my mom?"

"Most likely handling something inside. The center didn't have much staff back then and they couldn't be everywhere at once." Joey shrugged.

"So, what happened?"

"Well, I was preparing to defend myself as best I could when this cute little six-year-old you came storming up to the group. You stomped yourself right through the other kids and stood in the center of them with me and demanded to know who was the one that started the shit. I was sure I was about to get beat half to death when you picked out the biggest boy of the group and stood toe to toe with him. You weren't big enough to get in his face, but you gave it your best effort to look big. You started screaming about telling your mother, and he wouldn't be allowed back if he didn't leave me alone and the look on his face said he was about ready to swing on you instead of me."

"Oh my God, I remember that." I gasped. "I was on the

swings when I saw them corner you. That boy had just been picking on me before that. When I'd told my parents, my father told me the only way to stop a bully was to stand up to them. When I saw them going after another kid, I just lost it. I don't remember him trying to hit me though. I just remember them running off after I yelled at them."

"That's adorable." Joey said, smiling softly as he tucked an errant strand of hair behind my ear. "He didn't get the chance to swing on you because while you were yelling at him, some other kids had run inside to get my brother. Rich was a big guy even as a teen, so was Craig. Az wasn't as big, but he had a mean streak a mile wide. The bullies tucked tail and ran as soon as the guys showed up."

"I don't remember them being there, and I think I would have noticed a group of teenagers swooping in to save the day." I said, searching my memories for Joey's explanation. He chuckled a little, leaning his head back on the post.

"Well, that's probably because they weren't standing there when you turned around. You'd given the classic 'That's right, you better run' yell, complete with shaking your tiny fist, after our bullies had scattered. Rich had just rolled his eyes and went back to the gym. By the time you turned around and pulled me after you to play on the swings, they were gone."

"You know, my father took me out for ice cream when I came home that day and told him that I'd run those kids off and stopped them from picking on you," I said. "I thought I'd come home the conquering hero."

I got taken by a fit of giggles as I thought back to myself standing up for Joey. I was now picturing a young Rich, Craig, and Az standing behind me, staring down the other kids while I, in my bravado, had thought I'd run them off. This version definitely made more sense than mine. Joey started chuckling, and it wasn't long before we were both laughing so hard I could feel the prick of tears in my eyes.

It felt good to laugh. It probably wasn't as funny as all that, but we'd latched onto the humorous idea like a life preserver thrown out to us in the ocean of tension. After a few minutes, we'd settled down into chuckling quietly before it died off into something adjacent to comfortable silence as we looked out over the lake.

"We should probably check and see how things are going." Joey said after a time, staring at nothing in particular. His mind was already back in the cabin with his brother, and I could hear the concern back in his voice.

"One of the guys will come and get us." I said softly. "I know, I want to be in there too. The doctor needs space to work, and we don't need them worrying over our states while they should be focusing on Rich."

"But–"

"If we were in a hospital, we'd be in a waiting room. Try to think of it as the same thing here... except the view is better and the smell of cleaning chemicals is absent." I offered matter-of-factly. Joey looked at me like he wanted to argue, but instead, he sighed heavily, leaned his head back against the post, and stared up at the sky.

"You're right. You're becoming surprisingly level-headed these days and I don't think I much like it right now." He said, without any malice to his sarcasm.

"Well, I was fairly level-heading before my world got up ended... but, if it helps, once Rich is back on his feet, I'll probably be storming out of the cabin in response to whatever crap he's giving me again and I'm sure you'll be sent to chase me down." I shrugged with a smirk. He snorted and gave my hair a gentle tug.

"Once we're through with all of this, I think we'd both enjoy me chasing you down through these woods."

"We'll just have to make sure it's *not* on a day that Leighton's sister visits... I feel like that's the last thing any of us will need for her to walk up on." I groaned. "I'm not sure what problem she has with me."

Joey lifted his head and looked me in the eye with a smirk. "She'd have to care about someone to have a real problem with them, and none of us are sure she actually has the ability to care about anything. I wouldn't take it too close to heart."

"She didn't seem to like everyone laughing at her inside. That would make me think she does actually feel things." I said, "What was all of that in there about anyway?"

Joey snickered at my question, making me raise an eyebrow impatiently. "I did promise an explanation, now's as good a time as any I guess." He shifted under me slightly and glanced back up at the cabin. "We met Leighton when the Horsemen didn't even have a piece on the board yet. We were just a bunch of kids trying to figure out the game. I ran into him while I was doing some street job for Az, trying to prove to my brother that I could run with them and hold my own."

"You didn't start the Horsemen with them?" I asked, a little surprised.

"To his credit, Rich tried really hard to keep me out of it. He didn't want me to go down the same road he was on because... well, you don't really need intimate knowledge of organized crime to know it can be blood-soaked and dangerous." His voice turned contemplative as he stared into space.

"I doubt your parents were on board with that." I mused.

"They weren't. I mean, it took me weeks of wearing Az down to get my first job because *no one* liked the idea.

"I can't imagine it taking Az weeks to do *anything*. Not if you made it a point to irritate him. He's kind of been snap first ask questions never." I laughed lightly.

"Sweetheart, you might be adept at getting under his skin, but you haven't even broken the record for getting him to explode yet. That belongs to me." He smirked, looking pleased with himself. "But in all fairness, Az is Rich's second in command for a reason. He's only easy to get to when you know how. I was the group's kid brother, no one wanted that for me. When the Horsemen started turning a profit, Rich set our parents up in a nice suburban area. He paid for their house outright, and makes sure they don't want for anything..." His voice trailed off, sounding pained.

"He told me a bit about your mother once... It's hard for me to picture him like that, sometimes, but it's easy to see that taking care of you guys is a priority for him." I said, silently hoping that we could keep his mind out of the cabin. "But I'm not sure... what does this have to do with laughing at Lacey?"

"I'm getting there. Just trying to give you some context," he huffed. "Anyway, I finally got to Az enough that he gave me some bullshit street job. I don't even remember what it was now... the only thing that stuck in my memory is my run-in with Leighton. I think I ended up stepping on his toes for something he was doing. It ended up in a street fight."

"Somehow, I'm not surprised by that at all." I snarked.

"Some things never change, Sweetheart. But back then, Leighton's fighting style was feral, and instinct based. He still is, but he's got some discipline and training now. It was rough, but because he wasn't as skilled as he is now, he was bad about leaving himself open. Eventually we called it a draw because we were both exhausted and bleeding. I'm pretty sure I had a couple broken fingers." Joey stopped and started chuckling, thinking back on the memory. "And the wildest part about all of it, was that as we sat on the curb, he turned to me and offered to share his beer and candy bar. He said I was scrappy, and he liked me. Surprised was a bit of an understatement, but I mean... I was beat up, I wasn't going to turn down beer and chocolate. We've been friends ever since."

I couldn't help but join in Joey's chuckling as I pictured the two boys sitting on a dark street, deciding that they were best friends after beating each other up. Leighton offering him beer and candy was the most 'Leighton' thing I'd ever heard. I had to resist asking again what this had to do with everyone laughing when Rich had used my name when talking to Lacey.

"We hung out all the time, and eventually we kind of took him in. And with Leighton's help, I was able to get my own spot in the group as a Horseman. After a few years, Lacey came looking for Leighton. She's resourceful, so it was only a matter of time from when their parents had tasked her with finding him that she would track him back to us. Leighton, I'm sure you can guess, told her to fuck off and he wasn't going."

"I don't imagine that went over well with her." I surmised.

"No, it didn't. Lacey fucked Rich instead." Joey sneered.

I choked out a laugh of disbelief. "She didn't!"

"She absolutely did. In all fairness to Rich, though, we weren't in a great spot, and he'd been pretty stressed out. From what he told us, he'd come stumbling in from drinking away his troubles at the Spotted Cobra, and she was waiting for him in his bed. Honestly, I can't say I blame him. She's a pretty woman, and she was willing and available... and none of us knew she was a fucking psychopath," he paused. "Well, except L. And I doubt Rich bothered to ask first.

Anyway, this kicked off what's been the last decade or so of him politely dodging her every time he sees her and her trying to get him back in her bed every chance she gets."

"She's still chasing him around after just a one-night stand?" I asked, surprised.

"Oh, no. It happened more than once. But every time it does happen, Rich is down and out, stressed over something, and probably drunk. She's definitely not his type, but I mean... good for Rich I guess, because that's gotta be the best she's had. It's been something like two years, and she's still stuck on him like a stubborn tick that's got its head buried under the skin."

"It's weird to know she's so desperate given how easily she can flip her 'human' switch." I murmured.

"I suppose bedding four of the five men makes you a better woman." Lacey spoke, startling both of us. "Personally, I prefer my affairs to be one at a time."

I eased myself from Joey's lap and stood up, shoving aside the urge to slap her. She wasn't worth it.

"It's not an affair when all parties involved are consenting." I snarked back.

"Well, maybe not *all* parties." She scoffed, pretending to study her nails under the soft light the moon provided. "Rich doesn't seem to be falling for you spreading your legs open to anyone who wants to get between them."

I felt Joey's hand on my shoulder as he stood behind me. "Sure, Lacey. That's why it was her name coming out of his mouth earlier and not yours." His tone was stern, icy.

"He's entitled to his mistakes," Lacey replied dryly. "It's my bed he'll be crawling into when he's healed. He has better taste than you and my darling baby brother. Specifically preferring not to bed whores."

The air whooshed out of my lungs, and my thoughts began to race. If she was taking jabs about Rich being in her bed in the future, that had to mean he was okay. Still struggling with the urge to smack her smug smile off her face, I forced myself to speak.

"Are you here to let us know the surgery went well?" I asked, barely keeping the bite of anger out of my tone.

"No thanks to you." she replied, glaring daggers at me. "The doctor is getting him situated to rest now, but he was only ever in this position because of you. If his little lackeys weren't obsessed with what must be a loose pussy by now, he'd never have been injured."

The second of relief of knowing that Rich was okay was replaced instantaneously by a combination of my anger at myself, Lacey's words, and the stress, fear, and worry that had been building since the Gala fire. The flood of emotions snapped my composure like a rubber band pulled too far. My vision narrowed on her, and before I'd even acknowledged the thought, I had one hand tangled in her black hair, jerking her head backward as my other fist collided with her nose.

Lacey screeched and reached her clawed hands out to attack me, but I used one of the takedown maneuvers Az had taught me to take her to the ground. My voice hit my ears as if from a distance as I straddled her and continued to slam my fists into her face until there was a satisfying crunch beneath them. Some distant part of me knew I was overreacting, that this wasn't a *normal* response, but the more primal drive to snuff out the woman beneath me rode me hard. I barely even registered moving my hands to grip her throat; I was so intent on ending her.

Arms banded around my waist as I continued to hiss and snarl some semblance of words. The sudden pressure of Joey at my back seemed to ease the enraged haze that had taken me over entirely, and I slowly came back to myself. My chest heaved with my ragged breaths, and I became aware of the stinging cuts and scratches that Lacey had left on my face and arms.

"That was hot as fuck." Leighton spoke. "Probably the hottest thing I've ever seen."

My eyes never left Lacey, though I could see Leighton moving toward us in my peripheral. She swiped her hand across her face before gingerly touching her broken nose as she worked to get her feet back under her.

"Agreed." Joey said, his voice was hoarse and husky in my ear. I could feel his agreement pressing against my back.

Lacey stood the rest of the way, turning to face Leighton. "You're going to get this one killed just like the last one. But this time, at least, the bitch deserves it." She hissed, shoulder-checking him as she stormed past him toward the cabin.

CHAPTER TWELVE

Victoria

The doctor gave us a rundown of Rich's condition once we arrived back inside the cabin. Lacey was, thankfully, nowhere in sight. She'd climbed into her car straight away and sped off into the night. Even as my body shook from the adrenaline crash, I couldn't find it in myself to be sorry for what I'd done.

Leighton was strangely quiet as the doctor informed us that the surgery had gone well even without anesthesia and informed us there was something off about how quickly Rich had turned septic. The doctor said it shouldn't have been possible unless the person who patched him up originally hadn't used sterile equipment. He'd prescribed some antibiotics that he said Lacey was having delivered and gave us strict instructions to keep the area clean. Joey hovered by the head of the pullout where Rich had succumbed to unconsciousness again.

Craig guided me to my room, insisting that I needed to get some sleep as the doctor finished instructing the others on how to use the remaining I.V. bags of fluids and medication. I crashed as soon as my head hit the pillow. For the first time since Rinaldo attacked the manor, I didn't have nightmares.

My good mood the following day was buoyed by the fact that Az hadn't come crashing through my door demanding an early workout. Between a good night's rest and a day off from his Az-hole drill instructor mode, things felt like they might just go right for once. I should have known it was just a fluke.

A single day off was all that Az allowed. He didn't care whether I had nightmares or not the night before, waking me at the crack of dawn like some sort of 'roided up farm cock. He did concede to letting me have coffee before torturing me with a run around the lake and his increasingly intense training methods.

For the most part, I kept my complaints to a minimum. While it was absolute insanity to be up so early and work as hard as he pushed me, the incident with Lacey had allowed me a sort of catharsis. I found myself chasing that release during training since that was the only release Az was letting me have right now. It wasn't entirely his fault since everyone was still reeling from the near miss with Rich, but it didn't help.

About four days after the doctor had operated on Rich, I found myself outside training with Az. Craig and Joey were attempting to mother hen Rich inside, and Leighton had been successfully avoiding me. Az caught one of the bags we'd been practicing dodges and punches with and stilled its swinging.

"That's enough for today, Love. You're going to injure yourself if you don't learn when to stop." Az said.

"I can do more, Az. I'm not an idiot. I *do* know my limits."

Az sighed and shook his head. "I've been in the game long enough to know what you're trying to do here, Love. While I'm happy to see you finally taking your training seriously, I know from experience that the release you're chasing right now isn't what you're going to get if you keep pushing yourself like you have been the last few days. All you're going to get is a torn muscle and a sour attitude. We have enough injuries and pissy crybabies dealing with Rich."

Movement off to the side caught my attention, and I noticed Leighton trying to sneak by. "Leighton, tell him he's being stupid," I called out.

Leighton froze, his eyes widening almost as if he were a deer caught in headlights as they flicked between me and Az. "I, uh... You should do whatever Az said." He said, moving backward.

"What the fuck, Leighton?!" I shouted, moving toward

him as he took another step back. "Since when do you just agree with Az?"

"Now, I guess." He shrugged. "I've got shit to do, Victoria, so I don't really have time for your spat with Az."

I looked at Az, stunned by Leighton's reaction to me, but like a fucking coward, he raised his hands and turned to head to the front of the cabin. "I'm not sorting your Leighton problems for you, Love."

I glared at him before the sound of a twig snapping pulled my eyes back to Leighton. Narrowing my eyes on his slowly retreating back, I stomped across the uneven ground. "What the fuck is your problem, Leighton? You've been avoiding me for days, and now you're turning down the opportunity to get under Az's skin?"

Leighton whirled around and stared at me with narrowed eyes. "Really, *Princess*? You spend weeks antagonizing and actively avoiding me, and when I finally give you the space you seem so desperate for, you aren't happy with that either. Do you want to be the pot or the kettle in this analogy? You don't get to spurn my attention and then decide you want it when I take the hint."

"I was wrong, okay!" I yelled, balling my hands into fists at my side. "I don't understand why you are the way you are, but after hearing your own sister speak to you the way she did, I thought..."

"You thought what?" Leighton demanded. "That I was a broken toy you could patch up and then I'd magically become someone like Joey or Craig? Because I won't."

I blew out a heavy breath, letting my shoulders slump forward. "I know that. But I also realized I was expecting you to act like them when that's not who you are." I pinched my lips into a thin line as I decided whether or not to lay my thoughts bare for him to do what he would with them.

Leighton threw his hands in the air with a groan, clearly impatient with my silence. "I don't understand you."

"Right back at ya, Leighton." I shot back. "But I think...

After what I did to your sister, maybe we aren't as different as I thought. Maybe I *want* to understand you."

Leighton's face softened, and he ran both his hands through his hair. I'd never seen him look so unsure of himself.

"Taking a few well-deserved shots at my sister doesn't make us the same." He said softly. "If this is you trying to make yourself feel better about that, just don't. I don't want your pity because of what you overheard either."

"That's... That's not what this is, okay. We didn't get off to the best start to begin with, and then afterward... I fucked up by deciding that what I had seen from you was all there was to you. Obviously, there's more to it than that. I was doubly wrong because when things got difficult for me to cope with, I decided to take it out on you because you... You keep a part of yourself locked up and don't let anything get to you. You're different, and I needed to make you my villain because of the mistakes you'd made with me before."

"I tried to show you that I'm sorry for what I did." Leighton lamented. "I did the only things I know how to do to show you that."

"But you never just said the words, 'I'm sorry', Leighton." I replied. "In what world beside your own is taking me to a fight and having me paint Az's car supposed to be interpreted as apologies? That's not how people like me work."

"Because in my world, people don't say 'I'm sorry'. If they do, it's usually a ploy and it doesn't go beyond the surface. You apologize by *showing* someone you mean it."

"I'm not from your world, Leighton," I said, my voice on the verge of yelling.

Leighton stalked toward me, narrowing his eyes. "But you are, Victoria. We grew up in the same circles but different cities. You should know better than anyone here that 'I'm sorry' means *nothing*."

I drew back a step as if I'd been hit. Meeting Lacey had caused me to realize that Leighton Laurent was not just some kid from South Sacona who shared a name with *the* Laurents, but he was one. I'd lumped him into the same background as the rest of the guys, with what little I did actually know. He was, in fact, from the same world I was.

My upbringing in the upper class wasn't the standard; my parents had been attentive and present. They cared about me and not just because of our reputation or for appearance's sake. But I'd had to learn the rules of the games the upper-class children played all the same. And Leighton was right. Apologies were often hollow and bereft of any genuine regret for the actions that made them necessary. More often than not, they were coerced by parents who wanted to sweep whatever the altercation was under the rug before it could damage the family name.

Leighton studied me closely as I processed the information, re-evaluating things that I'd made my decisions on without the knowledge of who he was.

"You... have a point," I said slowly. "I concede that apologies are worth their weight in air for as much meaning as they carry. But how was I supposed to know that's what you were trying to do without you telling me?"

He tucked an errant strand of hair behind my ear, his eyes never leaving mine. "For whatever it's worth to you, *ma petit démone*, I *am* sorry. It never occurred to me that you wouldn't recognize me for my family name. If it had..." his voice trailed off, and he shook his head. "No, I probably still would have tried to show you that I was sorry the only way I know how."

"How about, for future reference, if you're doing something as an apology that you let me know that's what you're doing. Not Joey, or Az, or Craig trying to explain you to me. How about *you* explain you to me when I need an interpretation."

"Deal," he replied, his face splitting into a grin. "Can we start over now, because I've been dying to know what led to you kicking my bitch of a sister's ass and Joey won't tell me."

"Yes, Leighton. Fresh start as of now." I said, smirking at

his comment.

"Great! Pleased to meet you, I'm Leighton. Now, tell me what happened." He grabbed my hand, shaking it for a second as he re-introduced himself, and then led me to the porch and sat me down. "I *need* the tea."

I gave him the play-by-play of what had gone down on the dock with Lacey. When I got to the part where she called me a whore and blamed me for what had happened to Rich, I had to physically pull him back to the porch to finish my story. He was still stewing over it when I reached the part where he'd arrived, and Lacey made her comment to him.

"The second we don't need her for supplies here, I'm going to kill her." He seethed. "Unless you want dibs."

"Your sister is a piece of work, but I don't think we really need to kill her for being a jealous bitch." I shrugged. "What I want to know is what that Angelica stuff was about."

"That's... I don't think that's a conversation for... ever."

I reached over and took his hand in mine, giving it a gentle squeeze. "I'm not going to force you to tell me, Leighton, but I'd like to know what it was that caused you to somehow disappear in a three room cabin the last four days. Not even the other guys really knew where you got off to. I asked."

"Technically the cabin has eight rooms if you count the bathroom, dining room, kitchen, den, and laundry." He responded simply, avoiding my eyes.

"Alright, I'll take the hint," I said gently, "I'd heard Lacey say enough about it that I have an idea of what happened. I would rather know from you, than drawing conclusions based on what she said. But, like I said, I won't push."

Leighton sighed and plopped down next to me on the porch steps. He stared at the ground for a while before he answered.

"No, you're right. I should get it out in the open between us. That way it can't be used as a weapon against you anymore. Just... promise to keep an open mind, okay?"

"I promise."

"In case you haven't noticed before, I can get... obsessive." He chuckled dryly. "When I was about fourteen or fifteen, I met a girl. Angelica was different. She wasn't raised like us. Her parents weren't old money society types. Don't get me wrong, they were loaded. Almost enough to put my family to shame, but they were *new* money. She was... nice to me, but not in the way everyone else was." He paused, going silent for several minutes.

"Hey, it's okay." I assured him. "I promised I was going to listen with an open mind."

Leighton took a deep breath, keeping his eyes on the ground. "I think it was the first time I'd ever experienced *genuine* kindness. My parents are... Well, you've met Lacey. They don't exactly show any feelings if they have any. So, when Angelica showed me friendship, I thought she *liked me* liked me. I fell for her in the way that young kids do, y'know. It was a whirlwind of emotions I didn't know how to deal with. My parents didn't approve, of course, and told me to stay away from her. So... I kind of, sort of started stalking her and showing up in her bedroom in the middle of the night. I didn't know I was scaring her until it was too late. One night, watching her sleep wasn't enough. I wanted to be closer to her and I climbed into her bed."

"Did you..." I started gently, causing his head to snap up.

Leighton gripped my hands in his almost painfully. "No. I wouldn't do something like that. I just wanted to lay beside her. I didn't touch her, but that didn't matter. I fell asleep and when she woke up, her screaming brought her father running. I don't really know what happened between him threatening my life before calling my parents and the day I came home to my mother calling me and Lacey into the basement."

"That's awful, Leighton. I'm so sorry." I murmured.

"Just... that's not the worst of it." He replied, easing his grip on my hands. "My mother had Angelica chained in the basement when Lacey and I got down there. I tried. I need you to know I tried to get her out of there, but my mother hid the keys, and there was no way I could rip the chains from the basement floor. My mother watched me struggle and beg for her to let Angelica go, and the longer she let me go on, the more hopeless I felt." He stopped and took a deep breath. Standing, he started pacing, wringing his hands as if he were trying to work up to saying more.

"She waited until I *knew* there was no way out of it and ordered Lacey to lock the basement door before chaining my ankle to the floor too. My mother told me that they'd warned me. That her and my father had told me to stay away from Angelica. She made sure I knew it was my fault, that she was '*sorry*' for what had to be done. And then she slit her throat in front of me. She left me chained in the basement with Angelica's body for two days before she had Lacey clean up the mess and let me out."

"Jesus Christ, Leighton." I gasped, bolting up from the steps and moving to wrap my arms around him. "It wasn't your fault. There were so many other ways your parents could have handled that. Your mother being a psychopath isn't your fault."

"Yeah, well, like mother, like son." He snorted.

"From what I've seen, you're nothing like that." I said firmly. Leighton snorted again, and I held up a hand to shush him. "I'm serious. Sure, you're–"

"A lunatic." He interrupted.

"I was going to say understandably fucked up..." I huffed at his interruption. "But you're not like *that*. Look me in my eyes right now and tell me you'd murder an innocent girl for no other reason than she was afraid of something most people would be afraid of when they don't understand."

Leighton stared at me for a long time, his brows knit together, but he said nothing. Instead, opting to shake his head in silence.

"See? You're not like them. You don't hurt people like that." I said. "You, like the others... you may not be good guys. But you're not *bad men*."

"I am like them though." Leighton frowned, looking away. "My mother, my sister, even my father, none of them feel *anything*. It's how I know that I'm the same, because I don't feel things either."

I scoffed at him. "Leighton..." I said gently, pulling his face back so I could look him in the eye. "That has to be... the dumbest fucking thing I've ever heard you say."

Leighton almost looked like he was going to start laughing for a second before he just shook his head and stepped back from me.

"I'm serious! You're trying to convince me that you don't feel anything. If anything, everything I've seen points to you feeling things deeply, and intensely. You just... were never taught what to do with them. So, it was easier to compartmentalize them, if I had to guess."

"Oh yeah, when did you turn into a shrink? You're not the girl that Phil is seeing, are you?" Leighton said with a laugh.

"Who is Phil?"

"Oh, he's... never mind. You'll probably meet him eventually."

I rolled my eyes and pushed against his chest. "Okay, you need proof. How about when you were the one who steadied me during the shootout at the club because you were one of two in the group who didn't read my fear as an act."

"Well that–" He started, I held my hand up again to shush him.

"Or when you beat a man to death for trying to kidnap me after Joey stepped away. Or when you told my father point blank that you'd never let anything happen to me when he was trying to berate you all for the machinations of whoever started this whole mess. I know you were the one who left condoms all around the house like some adult version of an easter egg hunt too."

"Well... you can't be too careful."

"Yeah, but you did that knowing that you and I were on the outs at that point. Just guessing here, but you'd been needling between me and Az hoping we'd deal with our shit when it didn't directly benefit you in any way. And between you and Joey, you two believed that I wasn't a fake or a liar before anyone else in the house." I said, putting my hands on my hips. "You keep trying to say that you don't feel anything. I don't believe you for one fucking second. You might not know how to *deal* with it, but that doesn't mean it's not there, Leighton. And you'll be a lot better off when you stop lying to yourself about why you do the things you do."

"Fuck," He groaned. "It makes me hard when you dress me down, *ma petit*. If you don't stop, I might end up in love with you."

"You already are, idiot. I knew that the moment you beat a man to death with your bare hands for me." I smirked, turning to head into the cabin.

He muttered something about not understanding women and followed me inside. Movement to the right of the door caught both our attention, and I saw Az, Joey, and Craig sitting on the floor, crowded around a cracked window.

"Enjoy the show, boys?" Leighton laughed.

"What the hell are you three doing on the floor?" I asked.

"They were eavesdropping, the nosy bastards." Leighton answered as they all three scrambled to their feet, looking sheepish.

"Well, Az said we couldn't go outside because you two were having it out." Craig shrugged. "It's not like we have a whole lot else to do for entertainment if we're not allowed outside."

"They're going to say next they were just making sure you didn't murder me." Leighton grinned, waggling his brows.

"Oh, man. I gotta take this." Az spoke, pulling a cell phone out of his pocket that definitely *wasn't* receiving a call at that moment.

"Ope, yep. Me too." Joey added, leaving the room in a hurry.

My eyes narrowed on the device in Az's hand. "You

fucking *Az-holes*, why do you have phones but I'm stuck in the dark ages?"

CHAPTER THIRTEEN

Victoria

"Craig," Az said, "Why don't you explain the phone sitch to the Princess."

"Pussy," Leighton laughed as Az slipped around us to the front door.

Craig let out a long-suffering sigh. "We all have burners to handle business, Bunny." he started, scowling in the direction Az had fled. "Until we know *who* is behind this mess, it's not exactly smart to give you free reign to call people. You wouldn't intentionally give away our location, but with Tiffany and Theo's connections, it would be easy for them to trace the call."

Leighton leaned forward and dropped an arm around my shoulder. "If it makes you feel any better, Rich doesn't have a phone either."

"He's barely gotten back to staying conscious more than not," I snorted. "So, no, that doesn't make me feel better."

"Well, maybe when we get everything settled, we can get you in with Phil's therapist to talk about it?" Leighton chuckled.

"Who the fuck is Phil? You keep mentioning him."

"He's one of our most trusted guys, if one of us can't do something he usually does." Craig answered candidly.

"So, he's a mobster that sees a therapist. Maybe the five of you should get an appointment." I deadpanned.

"She's... I mean, I'm sure she's very good at her job. But–" Craig started, stumbling.

"He dips his wick, if you know what I mean." Leighton

said in a loud whisper.

"So, there'd be lots of conflicts of interest going on." Craig finished the explanation.

I shook my head in annoyance. "Can we circle back to why I'm not allowed to have a phone. Like, good for your guy or whatever, but this feels suspiciously like being kept prisoner *again*."

"It's not that you're not allowed one, Bunny. It's just... we have to be extra careful right now. We're not at our best game, and the burners we have were ones we could get our hands on quickly when we made a run for it." He paused, looking at me earnestly.

"But they're burners. Aren't those supposed to be untraceable? That's the whole reason to have them, isn't it?" I protested.

"Burners absolutely can be tracked. That's why I brought so many." Leighton replied, his face startlingly serious. "We only call people we can trust. I'm sure Craig can tell you all the why's and how's of tracking burners if you really want them."

"He's right. Sure, they're good about offering some anonymity on the surface, but it's not foolproof. Anyone with the skill and equipment can track them using call records, location tracking, stingrays, or surveillance. Even if they're not tracking things on our end, they can also track the activity for people that we might call and put two-and-two together. It's a matter of risk reduction to have a few on hand, but not so many that we can't keep an eye on them all." Craig explained simply as if it were common knowledge.

"So, what you're saying is with all your big-brain-techy skills, you can't set up a phone for me to call my father? My best..." I trailed off as the memory of what they'd shown me came to mind. "Have any of you even bothered to let my father know I'm alive? He must be worried sick."

Craig and Leighton shared a look that I couldn't decode. But before I could call them out on it, Craig gave me a sheepish look and took my hand.

"I have been working on something, but I didn't want to say anything until I was finished with it. It's not a phone, but it's what I can do with what I have here." He led me into his room and sat me down in the chair at his desk. He turned on his system, and I had to blink with the light of several monitors coming on at once. After a couple seconds, he pulled up what looked like an old-fashioned dialer.

"You can't call people from this, but I have set it up where you can get into your voicemail specifically by dialing your number. You know how to get into it from calling that way, right?"

I looked at him like he just asked me a question in tongues. "Why would I have ever needed to know that?"

By the way his lips twitched, I could tell he was keeping his answer to that question to himself.

"Neeeerd." Leighton, from the doorway, laughed out loud.

"L, how old are you? Twelve?" Craig said, without any menace. "If you're not going to be helpful, go away."

"How am I supposed to help with this?" Leighton asked, seemingly with genuine curiosity.

"You can't. So, go away." Craig said with a grin.

"Thanks for ruining my dick joke." Leighton pouted, flipping him off and sauntering out of the room.

"So, as I was saying before I was so *rudely* interrupted," Craig said loud enough for Leighton to have heard it, then turned back to me. "With this, I've set it up where you can call your own number and get into your voicemail."

"But I can't call other numbers?" I asked, a little annoyed.

"Nope. If another number is dialed, it will terminate the call before it can go out. Pay attention, Bunny. Call your number, and when your voicemail picks up, hit the star key on the number pad here," he said, pointing to the star key; I rolled my eyes at his over-explaining but stayed silent. "Then you'll put in your voicemail pin, and it will let you check your messages. *If* there's anything concerning, important, or time-sensitive in there, come and let one of us know."

"Okay, cool. Easy enough to remember." I said simply and then looked at Craig expectantly. He looked back at me as if he was waiting for me to say something else.

"Tag out, bro!" Leighton called from the doorway. "You're hogging her."

"Thank you for this, Craig. Now," I said, looking between him and Leighton, "shut the door on your way out, please."

"But we just made up!" Leighton pouted.

Craig shook his head at him, forcing him to step back just enough to leave the room and shut the door. Given the way we'd found Craig, Joey, and Az eavesdropping earlier, I suspected the pair would be listening on the other side of the door. But having it closed gave me some semblance of privacy.

Taking a breath, I followed Craig's instructions and let my voicemails begin to play through.

"Honeybee, where are you?" My father's voice rang out, laced with worry. *"The news said the manor was on fire. Please, call me. Let me know you're alright."*

I frowned to myself as the options at the end of the message played out. I didn't recall there being *any* fire in the manor when we took off in the dead of night after Rinaldo's attack.

The following voicemail was timestamped ten minutes later. *"I'm on my way to the manor. Please. Honeybee, call me back."* My father's voice was strained, and I could hear the soft purr of an engine.

There were several short 'Call me' messages timestamped within the time it would have taken him to make it to the manor. Each was slightly more frantic than the last before there was a several-minute break in timestamps.

*"They're.... God, Honeybee, please. I need to know you're okay, the emergency workers are bringing **bodies** out of the manor. They won't,"* he choked out a sob. *"They won't let me close enough to know if one of them is you."*

"Victoria! Where are you? Your father just called asking if you were with me?" Tiffany's voice rang out in the next message. *"If those guys have done something, please just call me. I can help you, whatever it is."*

"Jellybean, where are you?" Uncle Theo's voice was next. *"The police won't tell us anything other than you weren't in the manor. Hugo is losing his mind with worry. Please, call us."*

"Honeybee, I am begging you. Call me. I need to know you're really okay. They... they said they didn't find you in the manor, but nobody has heard from or seen you. I shouldn't have trusted those men to take care of you. I'm-" The message abruptly ended.

"Tory, I swear to God bitch, if you don't call me back, I'm going to be so pissed. Everyone is freaking out. Your dad is calling a press conference. He thinks the guys took you to hurt you." Tiffany practically shrieked.

"Jellybean..." Uncle Theo's voice again, tearful and despairing. *"Jellybean, please. If you're okay, you have to find a way to let us know. I don't... You have to be okay. You **have** to. You're all I have left. I can't... Please..."* After that, there were no more words, just Uncle Theo sobbing before it cut off.

"Gentlemen, at this point, I'm assuming that you have my daughter, and you're not letting her have access to her phone for some reason. If she's okay, I implore you to let her let us know that. And gentlemen..." My father paused, taking a deep breath. His voice was shaking, but his tone was firm. *"She had **better** be okay. If she isn't, if you've done something to her, the consequences will be **severe**."* There was some shuffling on the line, but just before it cut off, *"Find my fucking daughter."*

I almost hadn't caught it; I'd had to replay the message to make it out. It almost sounded like someone else entirely, despite being my father's voice. It was cold, hard, and demanding as if he was giving someone an order he would accept absolutely no argument for.

I don't know when I started tearing up while listening to the people who meant the most to me begging for some contact and reassurance that I was okay. My chest swelled, and

I felt almost warm at my father's message to the guys. But it broke my heart that they were all left without any knowledge that I was alive and... that there was a possibility at least one of them was lying.

Tears streamed down my face as I played through the next several days of messages. They were all similar to the ones I'd already listened to, though there was a heightened sense of panic and urgency in everyone's voices. I listened to each one over the course of the next half-hour or so before I'd finally reached the last message. Steeling myself to have my heart broken even more by their distress, I pressed play.

"It's time for you to end your tantrum, Victoria." Benson's voice played through the speakers in jarring contrast to the other messages. *"You've had your little fun running with those criminals. It's time to come out of hiding and come back to where you belong."*

Benson launched into a spiel about how I was wronging him, and I couldn't help tuning out his self-important droning until he said something that caught my attention.

"You opened a door when you ran off with those thugs, Victoria. Now they're not the only ones that think you belong to them. But we both know you're mine. If you don't end this pathetic little game of yours, I will come for you myself. And I've got some friends that will help me find you."

It wasn't his words that chilled me; it was the tone in his voice. He'd always been an arrogant prick, but this was beyond that. Benson *knew* something he wasn't giving away in his voicemail. Something he knew I should rightly be terrified of. Before I could replay the message to search for any clues about what it might be, the door burst open behind me, causing me to jump.

"First thing I'm doing when we get back to Sacona is murdering that prick." Leighton snarled, moving toward me with a predatory gaze, but as he got closer to me, something in his expression softened, and he dropped down to my level and pulled me into a reassuring squeeze.

"Run that one back again, Bunny. There's something there." Craig said, following in behind him.

"Let me go for a second, Leighton." I said softly, tapping his back.

He shook his head and did a bunny step to the side so that we were shifted, and I was able to reach the keyboard.

"Nope. I feel like you need this, so work it out." He said gently.

"...Alright, fine. Whatever makes you feel better, Leighton." I suspected he needed it more than I did, and I couldn't help but smile a little as I craned my neck to look over his shoulder and hit the key to replay the message.

"We'll talk about who needs this later, *after* you've had your fill." He snickered.

Craig shushed us sharply, and after a few moments of listening, he reached around us to stop the playback.

"Leighton, let her go so she can get out of my chair. I need to analyze this message, and I want to run down if there's anything to his vague threat here." Craig said absently; his voice was all business, and he spoke to us without looking as he tried to wedge himself between us and his desk.

Leighton pulled back just enough to glance at Craig before letting me go and taking my hand to pull me from the chair.

"Yeah, sure. Come on *ma petit*. I'll give you all the cuddles you need to deal with this emotional load in the den. Craig… sick 'em big dog."

CHAPTER FOURTEEN

Craig

I was only vaguely aware of them leaving as the door shut behind them when I took my place at the desk. Leighton and I had been leaning against the door while Victoria listened to her messages, and when Benson's played, it hit us both square in the chest. When we got the opportunity, we'd probably have to draw straws to see which of us would have the privilege of strangling the life out of him if Leighton didn't sneak off to handle the bastard first.

I pulled the number of origin for his voicemail to start my work. The caller ID traced it back to Gold City Associates, a reasonably large hedge fund in Sacona. I opened a tracer program and pulled the ANI information just to confirm that it was the actual origin. Once I'd done that, I saved the audio file and ran it through a filter just to check for anything that might stand out.

The voicemail itself didn't provide any additional information other than Benson was not only an abuser but an idiot. Even if the person he was dealing with didn't have our resources, he made a threatening call to a woman from his workplace and didn't do anything to hide it. I pulled information on the company that the call came from. It took about thirty seconds to figure out that the owner of Gold City Associates was his father, and most of the partners and higher-ups all shared the name 'Prescott.'

"Well, here's why he wasn't worried about it. The whole staff are nepo hires." I snorted as I pulled the information on the company to fill out intel about Benson. I'd be pulling it all at some point, anyway, so I might as well get it now. I filtered through the information and started a digital dossier on Benson, knowing it would be requested, and began plugging in the information about his company that had been easy to find. I started a web scraper, tapped into an algorithm I'd built, and set it to work with a few inputs about what I wanted it to look for and compile in the dossier. I manually added what I'd already found since I had the information at hand.

While I was looking at the 'employees' page on the Gold City website, taking down the names of the nepotism staff, I found myself staring at the picture of a man in a suit that caused a record scratch moment in my brain. He bore a slight resemblance to Benson and had the same last name, but peeking out from the collar of his overly expensive suit was a bright red tattoo of a spider lily. I quickly added the name 'Trey Prescott' To the scraper and algorithm when alarm bells started going off in my head.

Once I'd set my programs to do their jobs and filed what I needed to, I double-checked that my security programs were open and set for what I needed to do next. Benson's threat had caused an itch in my brain, and I had a twisting feeling in my gut that it was more than just bravado. Opening Tor, I navigated to a forum that I knew would have the answers if there were any to find. I filtered through irrelevant threads until I landed on one that couldn't have been more obvious if it had tried.

Missing Asset, Assistance needed, Honey Reward.

I'm reaching out on a matter that's become more than a mere inconvenience. We have a situation with a missing asset, its name is Victoria Bristol, for those who will be doing the background research. Now, I won't bore you with the details and assume most of you will have heard one version of the story or another, but she's managed to run off with the Boss and Underbosses of the Horsemen.

As you can imagine, this isn't your run-of-the-mill

disappearance. This Honey has become more trouble than she's worth, and we need to rectify the situation before it gets further out of hand.

*So, here's the deal: we need boots on the ground. This isn't just for made men or affiliates; this job is for **anyone** who can get it done. If you can track down our Honey, extract her from the Horsemen, and remove them from the board, you will be generously rewarded.*

And when I say generously, I mean you're free to keep her and do as you please, no additional charge. I don't have to spell out the perks here. This isn't just about the money; it's about sending a message. If you have the skills and desire, we want you on this.

I've attached an image of the asset below and additional contact information for whoever finds her to claim their reward once we've verified the work is done.

The stakes of the game are high, and time is of the essence. And remember, gentlemen, discretion is key. Ghost in, ghost out.

4r4chnOWr417h

The twisting feeling in my gut from earlier turned into a boiling rage the more I read. There were thread replies, and it looked like every bit of street-walking criminal scum had decided they were in on the game that ArachnoWraith had put out. Everyone from made men to local drug dealers, with a few disgustingly enthusiastic responses about the proposed reward.

I didn't realize I was white-knuckling my coffee cup until I heard the ceramic crack and felt the dripping of the hot liquid onto my leg, though I couldn't really be bothered to care at the moment.

I knew this user, or at least knew of him. His work was a little rough around the edges, but we had professional respect in these spaces despite being on opposite sides more often than not. I wonder if he knew that he'd signed his own death certificate when he made this post.

I knew it wasn't likely to work with the setup I had on hand, but I would be remiss if I didn't attempt what I could to actually find Wraith with what I had. I worked my tracers, and it didn't take long for it to become apparent that it wasn't going to go anywhere. Almost as quickly, a message showed up from my newly acquired prey.

VO1DPH453

So, I'm getting pings that you're trying to find me. I'm going to guess you're trying to play the big hero here, considering you have something that doesn't belong to you.

You're supposed to be the best, right? Some master at extracting assets and slipping through the cracks to find vulnerabilities. But I have to say, I had a much-needed laugh at these derisory attempts. Tracers? Really? It's like watching a blindfolded mouse in a maze, thinking it's on a mission.

I'll make this easy for you. You're not going to find me unless I want you to. You should really just give up that honeypot you're carrying around and save yourself the trouble. Die with some dignity, at least, rather than chasing your own tail trying to find me.

But hey, if you're not going to do the smart thing, you can keep playing detective. We can bury you with the participation award when all is said and done.

Tick-tock, VoidPhase. Tick-tock.

It took everything in me not to hit something because my workstation was the only thing nearby, and I needed it. My jaw hurt from the way I was clenching it. It was obvious bait, but I knew that even without my complete system, I had enough here to keep us safe from any attempts they made to find us. I might not have found him, but he wasn't going to track me down either, so we were in a digital deadlock until I got home. After a quick breather, so I didn't break my keyboard, I started my response.

You must feel like one of the big kids right now, puffing out your chest and making threats and promises you can't deliver on. Cute.

You are correct that I don't have you yet; I find myself working at a slight disadvantage. You have some time, but I promise you that it is running out. I will find you.

So, keep playing your games and talking your talk, but I want you to remember something while you're sitting behind your security thinking you're untouchable. Your words are the death rattle of a man who's forgotten that no matter how good you are, there's someone better. I'm that someone. You won't be able to touch me or mine, and when the dust settles, you'll find out just how deep the waters are that you're in.

Be seeing you real soon, Wraith. Enjoy your last days.

I closed the window and started transferring my files to my tablet when I heard someone come into my room and shut the door. I turned to find a flustered and haggard-looking Rich leaning against the wall.

"You look like shit, Boss." I said flatly. He raised an eyebrow at my tone but didn't comment on it. "You need something?"

"Just needed... I don't know, a place to hide? Victoria will *not* quit mother henning me. She damned near followed me into the bathroom when I went to take a piss, for fuck's sake." He groaned, leaning his head back against the wall. As sour a mood as I was in, I couldn't help but start laughing at him.

"Well, you aren't known for being the most reasonable when it comes to taking time to heal, you almost died a few days ago, and during *that* process you all but confessed your undying love to her. How would you expect her to act?" I leveled an amused gaze at him.

"I did no such thing." Rich huffed. "And I expect her to let me be when I ask her to. Not whatever the hell she's been doing the last hour."

I snorted in response. "Okay, Boss. Whatever you gotta

tell yourself to keep the colors pretty in your world." There were times that I wanted to hit Rich over the head with a mirror to make him take a real hard look at himself. But he didn't need a head injury, too. I held up my hands to indicate I was done needling him about Victoria. "... Actually, I do need a favor regarding Bunny. I have some news that I need to bring the guys up to speed on, and I know we promised that we'd be keeping her in the loop, but..."

"That bad... What's going on?" Rich asked, his brows knitting together in concern.

"Rich, it's a fucking free-for-all back home." I said, checking my transfers so I could show him the forum messages and fill him in on everything I'd found. The more I explained, the angrier he looked. By the time I was done explaining, he looked like he was ready to kill every single criminal in Sacona that was likely going to be in on it.

"Yeah, the Princess definitely doesn't need to know about this while we're out here. It's not something we can keep from her forever but... for now." He grated out. "We'll tell her when we have to turn the streets into mortuaries when we get back. What was the favor you needed?"

I smirked at the irony of the favor I was about to ask. "I know you ducked in here to hide from her for a bit, but I need you to go ask her for some help and get her out of the cabin. Tell her... I don't know, tell her you want to take a walk around the lake or something because you need to start moving around more, and you're going stir crazy. She'll buy that, and it'll mean I can fill the others in on what's going on back home. And..." I stopped myself from finishing the rest of the sentence that would have ended with 'maybe it will help you get your head out of your ass.'

"And?"

"... And it will make her feel like she's helping. You know she blames herself for the position we're in, so feeling useful would be good for her." It was the first thing that came to mind, and it wasn't a lie either. We all knew that she blamed herself, and it didn't matter that we'd all tried to tell her that it wasn't her fault and that she had no reason to feel any guilt.

Rich looked at me through narrowed eyes before heaving an audibly annoyed breath. "You owe me, Dougherty. You don't understand how maddening this is."

"Personally, I think I'd rather enjoy having Bunny follow me around for the day. It'd be–"

"I'd really rather not know, thanks." he said, opening the door to my room and slowly making his way back into the cabin proper.

I followed him out, tablet in hand, and stood back with a smirk as I watched Victoria bounce over to him and fuss about him over-exerting himself and remind him that it was time for his medication. He groaned and glared at me as he worked himself up to asking her to escort him outside so he could get some fresh air.

The smile that split her face was beaming, and it made my heart squeeze pleasantly to see her so happy. Then it immediately dropped into my stomach as I remembered that I was to be the bearer of some really shit news to add to the top of our dumpster fire of a situation that she was still in danger.

As soon as the front door shut behind Rich and Victoria, I rounded on the guys, who had been just hanging out in the den.

"Find anything on that slimeball?" Leighton glowered, noticing the tablet in my hand. "Please tell me you found an excuse for me to castrate him."

"There was definitely something to the threat he made on that voicemail." I replied. "Someone has decided to play a game of for keeps with, Bunny. Whoever takes us out, gets her as their prize."

Az and Joey let out twin snarls of rage at my statement.

"Oh, goody. I get to go on a spree." Leighton said with a vicious grin.

Az opened his mouth to speak just as a notification chimed on my tablet. Holding my hand up to signal for him to wait, I opened it. Horror and murderous rage to rival Leighton's sadistic whims tore through me.

"What is it?" Joey asked, muscling his way to my side to read over my shoulder. My hands were shaking when I handed him my tablet without a word. I didn't have the ability to form coherent sentences, so it was better to just hand it over. Between what I'd discovered in my room with this new information, my even-tempered mind was being washed out by anger that was reaching apoplectic levels.

Joey hissed angrily as his eyes scanned the screen, and the sneer that contorted his face was reminiscent of the way he looked when he entertained 'guests' in our basement. I took my tablet back when I noticed him gripping it hard enough that I was worried he might snap it. It was comforting knowing that I wasn't alone in the sentiment, but I still needed my limited equipment to work.

"You two gonna share with the class, or shall we just sit in here in suspense?" Az snapped, eyeing us impatiently.

"Benson is a dead man." Joey said flatly.

"Yes, we've established that fact. Care to tell us the reasons we're adding to the list of why?" Leighton prodded.

"How about the fact that he put her in the hospital a few months before she left him? He beat her up bad enough that a police report was filed, but apparently nothing was done about it because, as we all know, he's still walking around a free man." Joey answered, growling.

Leighton went eerily still, his jaw working for a moment before he spoke. "Tell me every injury I'll be replaying in technicolor on that piece of shit."

"You're going to have to share this one, I think." Az said, his tone low and simmering as he motioned for Joey to continue.

"He broke her arm, bruised her ribs, she had some pretty extensive bruising actually. Face, torso, larynx..." He paused while he let that sink in. "Fucker was trying to kill her." He hissed angrily.

"I thought you said she told you their split was amicable. That's not fucking amicable." Az snarled as he started to pace the floor like a caged animal preparing to strike.

"Clearly, perhaps we should have her look up the definition of the word." Joey responded.

"Hey, being angry at this shit-stain of a person is one thing, but we're not going to turn that on her." I snapped, not really at them but to catch their attention. "We don't know how the split went down, and whether she chose to downplay the trauma or sweep it under the rug entirely is not something I want to hear anyone blaming her for." I slid a harsh look between Az and Joey to make my point clear.

I couldn't blame their runaway emotions, but if it was going to spiral, they needed to make sure it was spiraling in the right way. I'd learned enough in my younger years about how victims came to look at their circumstances. Leighton hopped up and grabbed the tablet in the moment of quiet, scanning it over as if he were committing the details to memory.

"So, what else was it that you came to tell us?" Az asked after a bit. I raised a brow at him before realization dawned, and I snagged the tablet back from L.

"Hey!" He whined.

"We both know you've already got what you need, now you're just stoking the fire." I shooed him away and pulled up everything else I'd found. "So, there wasn't anything *in* his voicemail, all that said was that he was brave enough to make the threatening call from his work phone. Which isn't surprising, considering the entire company's upper levels are staffed by his family members..." I trailed off, handing Az the tablet so that he and the others could all see what I was detailing.

"What's unusual about that? If we had to make a dossier on all the nepo babies in Sacona's upper class, we would have to rent out a house just to hold the files." Leighton chuckled at his own joke.

"Trey Prescott." I said flatly. Az swiped a few times, and I didn't even have to do any further prodding for them to catch it. All of their gazes slid up to me. "Yeah."

"Welp, I've seen all I need to." Leighton said darkly, moving toward the door.

"Agreed." Az stood, straightening his shirt and following Leighton's direction.

Joey and I shared a quick glance before I dropped my tablet, and we both moved to get in front of them.

"Move, Little Brother." Leighton said in a low tone, biting out the nickname our men had given Joey.

"You wanna go, L, you'll have to go through me." He growled in response. When Leighton's muscles tensed as if he would hit him, Joey's hand fell to the gun he had in his holster.

"We'd be doing the world a favor and you both know it." Az snapped.

"And you're acting like idiots who let their brains slide out their ears and onto the floor." I retorted. They both looked at me like I had grown a second head, and they were debating which one to punch. I rolled my shoulders and grabbed them both by their shirts. "Come here."

I moved them several paces away from the door before they pulled out of my grip, complaining. I pushed them toward the open archway that led into the kitchen.

"Go look out that window and tell me what you see." I said, pointing at one of the windows in the kitchen that faced toward the back of the cabin, where Rich and Victoria would be somewhere around the lake. They looked at me stubbornly and didn't move, staring at me as if they were trying to stare me down.

Joey groaned loudly and stalked forward, grabbing Leighton by the ear and pulling him toward the kitchen. They made it another few paces before L got free.

"Ow! Damn it, Ma, alright! I'll go look. Ain't shit out there." He grumbled petulantly.

"What do you see?" I asked again.

"The lake, and the woods." Leighton snipped.

"And?" Joey asked, flicking him on the ear.

"Boy, I swear—"

"And?" I cut him off.

"Rich and Victoria coming up from the back of the lake. He's leaning on her a bit, but he seems to be doing okay moving around." Leighton said finally.

"Do you think that either of you running off to squash a bug back in the city is doing them any fucking favors? Removing half the able-bodied people here if something happens out here at the cabin, *or* having something happen to yourselves because you're running into a situation you have very little information on. Either of those things sound very bright to you boys?" I deadpanned, crossing my arms over my chest. "You both got bigger brains that that bouncing around in those thick skulls."

Leighton and Az looked like they wanted to argue with me, but they knew I was right. Az grabbed a glass off the counter and threw it at the wall.

"Feel better?" Joey asked with a sigh.

"No. That motherfucker is walking around breathing air he doesn't deserve." Az snarled.

"We agree." Joey nodded. Joey and I exchanged another look, and an almost animalistic grin split Joey's face. It was good we had such an understanding.

"When the time comes, we'll see he pays for every slight, every insult, every injury. He'll pay for every breath he took that he didn't deserve. We just have to bide our time until we can do that without taking risks to people we need to keep safe." I said, hoping the pair of hotheads wouldn't continue to raise problems about it.

Leighton leaned against the archway, his arms crossed. He looked like a kid who had been told he couldn't have a toy and was debating being understanding or throwing a fit about it.

"When we're done, you can serve that worm to her on a fucking silver platter." I offered. Leighton stared into space for a moment before finally nodding his agreement and moving away from the threshold to the kitchen.

"There won't be enough left when we're done."

CHAPTER FIFTEEN

Victoria

Rich was breathing heavily and leaning on his cane when we made it back to the cabin's front door. Our walk had only been about a quarter mile, there and back, by my estimate, but it had done a number on him. It was almost alarming to see him look so weak, even knowing what he'd survived between the manor and the impromptu surgery in the cabin kitchen to save his life.

"Do you..."

"I'm fine." He barked. "I can manage getting myself inside, Princess. I'm not an invalid." If looks could kill, the glare he shot me would have dropped me on the spot.

I worried my bottom lip between my teeth as I watched his cane wobble under his weight as he used his free hand to open the door. The stubborn asshole was going to end up face-planting the floor if he wasn't careful.

"See," he huffed as the door swung open. "Just... fine..."

"Whatever you say," I replied, rolling my eyes and waiting for him to move inside before I followed. If I mentioned how winded just opening the door had left him, he'd probably deny it anyway.

Craig was already ushering Rich toward his nook when I stepped inside. The other three were standing in a semi-circle facing the door. Their faces were painted with varying shades of rage, and Az looked like he was on the verge of having a stroke. I'd never seen his face so red, and there was a vein pulsing near his temple.

"Uh... You guys alright?" I asked cautiously.

"I thought you said shit with that bastard ended amicably?" Az snarled. "Do we need to give you a rundown of what amicable means, Princess?"

My brows shot up to my hairline. "What the fuck are you talking about?"

"Benson." Leighton snapped. "The son of a bitch that put you in the fucking hospital."

"Wha– how do you know that?" My voice was nearly breathless from the shock.

"Did you think Craig wouldn't find that when he went digging into the bastard's voicemail?" Leighton asked, cocking his head to the side as he glared at me. "He doesn't half ass his work, Victoria. When he digs, he *digs.*"

"What happened between me, and Benson is not any of y'alls business." I forced my voice to remain steady. "It's not open for discussion."

Az stalked toward me, anger rolling off him in waves. "It *is* our business, Princess. The sooner you learn that, the better off you'll be."

"Fuck you, *Az-hole*. It's not like any of you are lining up to tell me about your exes." I hissed.

"I did though," Leighton spoke so softly I barely heard him from where he stood as I glared at Az.

"Hey! Az, you need to put that shit on ice. We already talked about it." Joey snapped, stepping between me and Az.

"She needs to–" Az started, but Joey stepped forward and shoved him in the chest, causing him to stumble back a few steps.

"She needs to get some air while you take a fucking chill pill and remember what we agreed on. You're absolutely right," Joey growled out before turning on his heel, grabbing me by my arm, and pulling me toward the door.

I nearly stumbled keeping up with him, and he didn't slow down until the door slammed behind us, and we were off the porch. When there was a bit of distance between us and the house, he stopped abruptly, turned, and hugged me tightly.

"Thanks for that." I murmured, wrapping my arms around his waist and burying my face in his chest.

"I know, Sweetheart." he said softly, kissing the top of my head.

We stood there until it became apparent that Joey wouldn't let me go until I pulled away. His body molded to mine like a comforting shield. Heaving a sigh, I broke his hold and stepped back.

"I appreciate you not letting Az and Leighton push about this." I spoke.

His brows knit together slightly as he rubbed my arms. "They... were harsh about it, but Sweetheart, they're angry *for* you, not at you. That's the first thing I need you to understand."

"It's ancient history though. What happened doesn't matter now." I shrugged. "It was only the one time, and I left not long after. Benson didn't put up a fight when I did either. My history with him just isn't relevant to what's going on now."

He listened to my explanation patiently, but I could see the warring emotions on his face. I'm not sure how he was so much more emotionally intelligent than the rest of the guys, but I was glad for it. He shook his head as I finished.

"Once is once too many, Sweetheart. There is absolutely nothing you could have done that would warrant having that kind of response."

"Well, I mean... Az was pretty dead set on murdering me at one point, so...."

"Two pretty stark differences in those situations. Firstly, Az wouldn't have *brutalized* you. Even when he wanted to kill you, he never put his hands on you like that. And secondly, Shit-stain was your boyfriend when he hurt you. Az was a stranger who thought you were a rival mobster."

"Total mobster material right here." I snorted, pointing both thumbs at myself before putting on my best scowl.

Joey stared at me with a deadpan poker face for a

minute until I got anxious about my little joke before his lips started twitching, and he burst out laughing.

"You're too cute." He said as he got air between laughs. Once he'd composed himself, he booped me on the nose. "Though, you show some promise after how you handled Lacey. Might have to start calling you Bruiser instead of Princess."

"You better not go back to calling me Princess." I gasped in mock offense and slapped his chest. "Do that and I'll *show* you 'Bruiser'."

A low growl sounded from his chest, and he raised a brow. The step he took toward me had an entirely different air, and I felt my pulse quicken.

"Is that right?" he asked, almost menacingly.

A flush bloomed across my entire body, and I took a step back from him and placed a hand on his chest.

"I... Uhm... Well..." I tried to find words to backtrack, and my brain returned nothing.

Joey grinned savagely before leaning in and kissing me on the cheek. As fast as his mood had shifted, he was himself again.

"Sweetheart, you're not scaring anyone. Your adorable little threats are just an invitation I'm not sure you're ready for right now, *Pet.* And don't forget, you owe me."

I took several deep breaths to steady myself, my mind playing images of how he'd hunted me in the woods of the manor. I needed to pull myself together before I rose to the unspoken challenge in his words. He was right that now really wasn't the time, but that didn't stop me from needing to change my panties when I got back into the cabin.

"Now, let's work on making your threats carry more weight. You handled yourself as well as anyone could have asked during the assault. Actually, given the situation and your lack of training, you did really well keeping yourself and Az alive; most people in your shoes would have froze." Joey chose his words carefully as he spoke, evident in how he watched my face to make sure he wasn't triggering me somehow. "However, the next time you have to pull a trigger to keep yourself alive, you might not be at point-blank range. It's time you learn how to use a gun properly."

"Next time?" I balked.

"We're going to do everything in our power to make sure there isn't one, Sweetheart, but after the manor. Well... We'd be foolish not to train you for a next time just in case."

"Joey... I don't know. I don't think I'm comfortable with this. I don't–"

"As much as I wish it wasn't necessary, that's not the case. We're not in a place anymore where hand-to-hand training is going to cut it." He touched my face and gently caressed my cheek with his thumb. "The most important thing is keeping you safe, and part of that is teaching you how to keep yourself safe if you need to. We'll go at it slower if needed, but we have to do this. It... It'll help all of us sleep better."

The idea of having another gun in my hand didn't sit well, and my stomach turned. The logical part of my mind knew Joey was right, but the rest of me was screaming against it. Flashes of the invasion at the manor assaulted my mind. The yelling, the gunfire, the explosion... Fuck. Whether I liked it or not, I was neck deep in a world I wasn't familiar with. I knew that if I didn't get brought up to speed, then more people would die trying to keep my inept self alive. And if I died, then all the shit we'd all been through would be for nothing.

When I finally pulled myself from my thoughts enough to notice my surroundings again, I realized Joey had led me to sit in a chair they guys had pulled from storage in the last few days. He pulled the small table and another chair they'd brought out at the same time so that they were in front of me and sat, placing his gun on the table between us.

"I'm not going to have you shooting yet. I think the best place for you to start after everything is just getting used to the gun." He spoke. "I want you to watch carefully as I take this apart and put it back together, because I'm going to have you do that when I'm done."

I nodded, my eyes falling to the weapon sitting between us.

"Guns need to be cleaned to function well. If you know how to take it apart and put it back together, cleaning it will be easy for you. I expect you to maintain your weapons better than Az does." He smirked. "Unlike that asshole, I'd be pretty upset if yours jammed or backfired on you. If I have to use yours and they jam, I'm taking it out of your ass, Sweetheart."

I snickered at the thought of Az injuring himself because of his own arrogance. "Agreed."

"Good." He smiled back. "Now watch, then repeat."

I watched closely as he took his gun apart, talking me through what he did before slowly putting it back together and handing it over to me. Joey had made it look so simple when it was anything but. It took several attempts with him offering guidance as I worked before I got the thing back together without missing the spring piece. Joey patiently told me all the names of the gun parts as I worked, but he may as well have been speaking a dead language for all they stuck.

"Sweetheart, how do you expect the thing to fire if you keep forgetting to put the firing pin and spring in?" he asked gently.

"The what? Why are there so many springs?!"

Joey released an exasperated sigh and visibly cringed as he picked up one of the pieces I'd managed to leave out in my latest attempt. "You need all of this that you've left on the table, but this one makes the gun go bang."

"Yeah, well, if I don't file a 990-T for the youth center we lose our 501C3 status." I snapped.

"What?" he asked, his face pinched in confusion.

"Exactly." I huffed, crossing my arms.

"I think that's probably enough for today." He mumbled as he made quick work of taking what I'd done apart and putting things back together correctly.

"Show off," I mumbled, rolling my eyes as I stood and

moved to the cabin door. I was frustrated, and while I knew it wasn't anything Joey had done, it didn't really matter. I stomped into the house, through the den, and into the kitchen. The other guys weren't anywhere to be seen, and more's the better for it. I didn't want to deal with them or their attitudes while I was in one myself.

I got a glass of water because it was all I could think to do once I got into the kitchen. I didn't know what to do; I wanted to stomp around. I gulped down the water and set the glass down too hard. I noted the time on the stove and told myself I should probably get some food. I was probably hangry.

Opening cabinets and closing them again, I couldn't think of anything I wanted to eat. The more I looked, the more irritable I got until I was slamming cabinet doors. I slammed the last one so hard that it bounced back and narrowly avoided it colliding with my face. I whirled around when I heard an amused snort from behind me.

"Is your tantrum making you feel better, Sweetheart?" Joey asked, leaning against the kitchen wall with his arms crossed.

"No." I snapped, turning away from him.

"Awww, poor thing. Little miss brat ass in a bad mood?" I could hear the grin on his face, and it grated on my nerves.

"Fuck you." I huffed and stomped into the dining room.

I hadn't made it more than a few steps into the dining room when I felt a hand in my hair before being jerked to a stop and pulled back. My back collided with Joey's chest, and I felt his breath on my neck.

"Wanna try that again, Pet?" His voice was a low growl in my ear that sent shivers down my spine.

"Oh, did you not hear me?" I snarked, trying to jerk away from him but succeeding only in having his grip tightened in my hair. "I said, 'fuck you' Joey."

He inhaled deeply as if taking in my scent and chuckled darkly in response. It was my only warning before I was turned sharply and pushed back against the wall, causing me to yelp in surprise. He pushed up against me and caged me in with his body, one hand still gripping my hair and forcing me to look him in the face, the other holding my hip tightly.

"That's what I was hoping you'd say." He grinned, a predatory excitement rolling off of him. "Seems my pretty pet has gotten herself in a bad mood and forgotten her manners..."

"Wait... I..." Heat bloomed through my core, and I felt the flush rushing across my skin again under the weight of his hungry gaze.

"Gonna try and walk it back now that I've called your bluff, Pet?" He tsked and smirked at me. "What happened to all your tough talk, hmm?"

I sneered at him, struggling against his hold, but my voice was dead in my throat.

"You've had a bad attitude for a while, and I think you're long overdue for an adjustment." he said, his voice dipping low as he leaned his head down to brush his lips against the corner of my mouth.

I turned my face to complete the kiss, parting my lips in an invitation that he readily accepted. I moaned into his mouth, encouraging him to deepen the kiss further. Just as I felt his grip on my hair loosen slightly, I pulled his bottom lip between mine and bit down.

He jerked back with a growl, but instead of anger on his face, it was lit up with pure excitement. He grabbed me by my throat and pushed me back into the wall, his deep brown eyes glinting a dark promise.

"Since you seem so desperate to misbehave with your pretty little mouth, I've got a much better way for you to put it to use." he said, stepping away from me and pulling back on my hair until I had no choice but to follow his lead. His other hand on my shoulder pushed me toward the floor until I was kneeling in front of him. "You're so beautiful on your knees, Pet."

Somewhere between the kitchen and now, my entire mood shifted, and I was practically salivating as he undid his belt, and I reached out to finish undoing his pants. He slapped my hands away.

"No. No touching until I tell you." Joey's voice was deep and dark and hit me straight in my core. I could feel how slick my thighs already were in anticipation. He took his time removing his belt and slowly undid the button on his pants. It was agonizing, and my hands twitched with the want to intervene.

After what felt like ages, he finally sprung free from his pants; I licked my lips and shifted. He hadn't released his grip on my hair, so I knew I wasn't moving until he did. I looked up at him and saw him just staring down at me with an amused little grin.

"If you try to bite me again, Pet, I'm going to make sure you're so sore that you won't be able to sit down for days," he said with a little raise of his eyebrow. I nodded eagerly, shifting again, wanting to be let go. "Use your words."

"Yes."

"Yes, *what*?" he asked, giving me a little jerk.

"Yes... *Alpha*." I said slowly, tasting the honorific on my tongue.

"Good, now open your mouth." I complied, and he released his tight hold on my hair, allowing me to move.

I licked my lips again as I grasped him and sized him up with my eyes. It had been a long time, and I hoped I could take him the way I desperately wanted to. I licked him hesitantly, running my tongue across the head and swirling it lightly. He sucked a sharp breath in and groaned. The sound emboldened me; I gently sucked his head into my mouth, working my tongue in gentle swirling motions as I took him in slowly.

"Fuuuck..." He breathed as I started bobbing on his cock, setting a slower pace to start until I found my tempo. His grip on my hair tightened again, but not so much as to restrict my movement.

I snaked my hands up his legs and dug my fingers into his thighs as I sucked him off, reveling in the sounds he made and that I was the one pulling those noises from him. Flattening my tongue against his length, I worked up to a faster rhythm until I was testing myself on how much I could take all at once. My name fell from his lips alongside a string of curses, and he pumped himself into my mouth a few times before pulling out and stepping back.

I groaned unhappily and reached for him and grasped at nothing before he pulled me back up onto my feet. He pushed me back against the wall and started ripping me out of my yoga pants and clothing. I couldn't be bothered to care when I heard seams pop as he pulled my clothes off of me.

He fell on me in a fury, his mouth exploring my body and leaving a new trail of bite marks across my torso. One hand played with my nipple roughly, and the other sought out my center. I cried out when two fingers slipped inside me without any preamble. I felt him grin against my skin.

"You're already soaking, Pet." He growled in my ear as he worked his fingers inside me, his thumb working circles around my clit. My head fell back against the wall. Desperate wasn't a strong enough word to describe my need for relief. Az's continued denial of my satisfaction had done a number on me, and it didn't take long before I was panting under Joey's ministrations and clawing at his back as he pushed me closer to my climax.

"Fuck, Alpha... Please, don't stop." I bit the words out between gasps of air, arching my back and digging my shoulders into the wall as I closed in on the edge of my orgasm, my nerve endings lighting up as my core tightened.

Not a second later, my eyes flew open as he slipped his fingers out of me and removed his hand.

"What. The. FUCK?!" I nearly screamed, digging my nails into his shoulders so hard they likely broke the skin. He groaned deeply, a little smirk playing on his lips.

"Settle down, Pet. We're not done." He led me over to the table, haphazardly kicking the chairs out of the way and pushing the few things littered about the table away. "Up."

I eyed the table, a little unsure that it would hold my weight. When I didn't move to follow his command, Joey's palm cracked harshly across my ass, making me cry out.

"I–" I didn't have a chance to say anything further when he lifted me by my hips like I weighed nothing and slammed me down on the table. I squeaked out my surprise.

"I don't generally like to repeat myself, Pet. Don't make me do it again." He snarled, pulling me to the very edge of the table. I instinctively wrapped my legs around his waist and my arms around his shoulders. He teased me with the head of his cock for a bit until I was all but whimpering and pleading for him to finish what we'd started.

He gripped my hips as he slammed into me to the hilt, causing both of us to groan with satisfaction. My eyes fluttered as he stretched and filled me so deliciously. When I opened them, a slight movement over Joey's shoulder caught my attention. It took a second for me to be able to focus, but when I did, my gaze fell on Leighton.

He was standing in the doorway to the dining room, leaning against the frame with his arms crossed. He didn't move or make any noise; he was just watching us. His eyes were dark and hungry, and he had his lower lip pulled between his teeth. I could see the outline of his hard cock in his pants as he took in the scene before him.

We locked eyes at the exact moment that Joey snaked his hand between us and rubbed his thumb in circles around my clit. The dual sensation caused the nerves in my body to burst like fireworks and my head to spin. Something about having Joey fuck me senseless on the dining room table while Leighton watched me lose myself to the feeling was a heady mix that made the already overwhelming sensation feel so much more intense. I wasn't breathing so much as I was just consistently moaning and begging Joey not to stop.

My orgasm hit me like a fucking train, and there was no stopping the scream that tore its way out of my throat. Leighton never broke eye contact with me. His only movement was to adjust himself as I rode the waves of my climax. Joey wasn't far behind me, digging his fingers into my hip and his pace sputtering slightly as he finished.

As Joey and I panted, coming down from our coupling, Leighton stepped back from the doorway, licking his lips. He gave me another once over, dragging his thumb across his bottom lip before he was gone just as quietly as he'd arrived. I stared at the spot for a moment longer before returning my attention to Joey.

He touched my face gently and kissed my forehead and the corners of my mouth. I trembled slightly in the after-glow.

"You okay, Sweetheart?" he asked, still panting slightly.

I huffed a weak laugh and smiled, still floating in a satisfied haze. "Better than okay. You have no idea how much I needed that."

He gave me a knowing look and chuckled. "I had an idea. And besides, you deserved it. Orgasms are for *good* girls."

CHAPTER SIXTEEN

Victoria

The rest of the day passed in a satisfied haze. At some point, Craig had made lunch and we'd eaten at the dining table. The smirks on both Leighton and Joey's face drawing images of Joey's face twisted in pleasure, and Leighton's hungry gaze to mind. Somehow, I'd managed to eat my meal without drawing attention to the fact that my mind was replaying the erotic scene from mere hours before.

Az hadn't bothered to eat with us, his anger still radiating off him in waves when he stopped long enough to grab his plate. Even after Joey's method of relaxing me, I didn't have the patience to seek him out and demand he get over himself. He'd managed to revert to the version of himself I'd met at the manor. It was a resoundingly '*him*' problem as far as I was concerned.

After lunch, Craig disappeared back into his room saying he had more work to do and Leighton settled into the den, sprawling out on the loveseat. I helped Rich back to his nook, making sure he took his medication before joining Leighton. He eyed me warily as I positioned myself on the couch, tucking my feet beneath me, but he didn't seem to be angry with me anymore.

I pretended to focus on the movie he'd put on, trying to ignore his constant glances in my direction. I thought I was doing a good job of it until he paused the movie and cleared his throat.

"You could have told me, ya know." He murmured. "I told you about Angelica."

I wasn't prepared for the hurt that laced his tone. "I-I'm sorry," I replied, guilt weighing on me.

Leighton frowned and moved to sit beside me on the couch. "I'm going to murder that bastard the first chance I have. Just so you know." He said, reaching out and tucking a stray curl behind my ear. "If I thought I could slip away from here long enough to take care of him, I'd already be gone. I can't, not without risking everyone's safety, but I want you to consider it done. That shit stain will never touch you again."

His tone was so matter of fact that I burst out laughing. Of course, Leighton would announce his plans to murder Benson like he was stating the sky was blue. It was just such a *'him'* reaction.

"You're not demanding that I leave him alone, so I'll take that as consent." Leighton nodded with a grin.

"I suppose this means I should offer to murder your mother." I wheezed between laughs causing Leighton to fall into his own fit of giggles.

"I think walloping on my sister was plenty *ma petit.*" He chuckled, pulling me closer. "You don't need to add my mother to your nightmares on my account."

I pulled away just enough to poke him in the chest. "Told ya you have feelings."

Leighton grabbed the remote and pressed play on the movie. "Hush and watch the movie."

We spend the rest of the afternoon and evening watching films, stopping only when Craig emerged from his room to feed everyone dinner. Joey joined us after our evening meal and I found myself sandwiched between him and Leighton, the warmth of their bodies lulling me to sleep as night fell outside the cabin.

"We should get you to bed, Sweetheart." Joey said, startling me awake as he shifted to help me up from the couch.

"Mhm, yeah." I mumbled. "Let me just check on Rich."

"Rich is fine. I got him his evening meds and he's been out cold for the last hour." Joey replied, guiding me to my room. "You, on the other hand, can't keep your eyes open. You need some sleep before Az puts you through another hellacious training session in the morning."

"Maybe I'll just put murder the Az-hole on my to-do list."

I murmured letting Joey lead me into my room.

"I have a feeling you'd regret that one," Joey smirked, flipping back the bedding and gesturing for me to climb into the bed. I gave him a sleepy growl in response but allowed him to tuck me in. "He might piss you off, but I'm pretty sure arguing is the love language between you two."

"I don't love that fucker." I grumbled, flopping onto my side to get comfortable. "He's too mean."

I heard him chuckle softly but my eyes refused to open again. "Yeah, alright Sweetheart. Sweet dreams." He whispered somewhere close to my ear before I felt him kiss the top of my head. I didn't hear him leave the room before sleep claimed me again.

My chest heaved as panic gripped my throat. Az was bleeding, on his knees with a gun pointed at his head. Some part of my mind knew this was just my memory, but I was trapped reliving it all the same. Weight slammed into me, a loud bang ringing out as Az's head jerked back. A scream tore from my lips and my eyes shot open.

"Leighton?" I asked, my eyes focusing on the man pinning me to the bed as reality began to replace my nightmare.

"You were screaming." Rich grunted, causing me to turn my head toward the door.

"Wha-" My brows dipped down as I took in Az, Rich, Joey, and Craig standing just inside my room, the door barely on the hinges. "Did you break down my door?"

"You were screaming like someone was trying to murder you." Az huffed. "We had to make sure you were alright in here."

"There isn't even a lock on the door... You could have just... opened it." I frowned.

"Well, since we didn't swoop in to save you *properly*, next time we'll just hope it turns out for the best then." Az snapped, turning on his heel and disappearing into the den.

"I'll always come to the rescue, *ma petit*." Leighton smirked, kissing the tip of my nose.

I rapidly became aware of the fact that he was splayed

out on top of me, holding my hands together at the wrists above my head.

"Can you get off of me?" I asked, arching a brow at him.

"You nearly slugged me when I got up here. I'm not moving until I'm sure I'm not gonna be k.o.'d." He smirked. "Besides, I like it here."

"I'm going back to bed." Rich grunted from the doorway. "The rest of you should do the same, meaning you too, Leighton."

"Let me up, Leighton." I said again. "Can you two, I don't know, help me get out from underneath our favorite lunatic?"

"No dice, Bunny." Craig chuckled. "He's your problem now. At least I'll be able to get some sleep without him in our room."

I scowled at him as he nudged Joey and they put my door back where it belonged, muttering to each other that they would fix it in the morning.

"Favorite lunatic, huh?" Leighton grinned, bringing his face so close to mine our noses touched.

"I'm serious, Leighton. Get off of me." I said, ignoring him as I tried to shift my hips to toss him to my side.

"Fine," He pouted, pulling back and releasing my wrists from his grip. "But we're roomies tonight."

"That is a complete overreaction and wildly unnecessary, Leighton." I grumbled, and shifted my hips again, successfully knocking him off of me before I moved from the bed. "I'm just going to grab a drink and go back to sleep. I don't need a babysitter in case I have another bad dream."

It wasn't fair, but I was still reeling from the nightmare, and Leighton's presence was grating on my last nerve. Instead of doing as I asked and leaving me alone, he was behind me before I reached my damaged door.

"Jesus Christ, Leighton! I can get water by myself." I snarled. "I'm starting to understand why you freaked out Angelica so much." I regretted the words the moment they left my mouth.

Leighton grabbed my wrist and spun me to face him, his face twisted in a pained expression as his nostrils flared.

"Yeah. Well, I'm starting to see why you're having such a blast slumming it with gangsters." He bit out.

Without thought, my free hand reared back and I slapped him hard enough for his head to jerk sideways. Slowly he turned his head back to look at me, a vicious grin on his lips. Leighton released my wrist and placed his hand around my throat with enough force to slam me into the wall behind me.

"Do that again," he purred in a dangerous tone, bringing his face a hair's breadth away from mine. "I liked it."

My core clenched with need and my thighs pressed together involuntarily. I swallowed roughly around the pressure of his hand on my throat causing him to smile.

"It shouldn't surprise me that you like things a little rough." Leighton said, his lips brushing against mine as he squeezed my throat tighter. "You were made for me, *ma petit.*"

A whimper of need clawed free from my throat at his words. Leighton gave me a knowing smile, his eyes darkened by his blown pupils, and stepped back.

"Would you like to play with me, *ma petit demoné?*"

"Yes," my voice was breathy and barely a whisper when he released my throat enough for me to speak.

"Strip and wait for me on the bed." He ordered, slipping toward the ensuite bathroom.

I did as he said, anticipation heightening my arousal as my mind whirred with the possibilities of what he had in mind. He returned just as I positioned myself, seemingly random items in hand. My eyes narrowed on the metal alligator hair clips and scissors he held.

"Wha–"

"Don't worry," He said with a dark grin. "I won't hurt you more than you'll enjoy."

Fuck if that wasn't the hottest thing he'd ever said to me, even with my mind railing against the idea that pain had any business in the bedroom.

Ignoring my inner turmoil, my eyes tracked Leighton as he moved to my closet and grabbed a sheet before systematically cutting it into long strips while he held the hair clip between his teeth. Once he was satisfied with his work, he stalked toward me dropping the clips on the nightstand before grabbing my wrists together in his hands roughly and jerking them over my head. I gasped as he set to work using the strips he'd made to secure me to the headboard.

"I thought Craig was the one into tying me up." I laughed breathlessly, feeling a small bite of pain in my wrists as I pulled against the makeshift restraints.

"These are so I don't hurt you more than intended." he replied seriously as he tugged the strips checking they were secure. "I'd tell you to stay, but you're not going anywhere now."

"L-" before I could get his name out he stuffed a balled up strip of sheet in my mouth, booped me on the nose and made his way to the door.

I worked my tongue against the material trying to push it out so that I could scream every obscenity I knew and then some after him. All I succeeded in doing was lodging it more firmly in my mouth. As if called by my mental tirade, he returned with two long, white emergency candles. Setting them on the nightstand beside the clips, he raked his eyes over me and started to strip. Every curse I'd been thinking fled from my mind as he revealed himself to me, inch by delicious inch.

His eyes moved to my legs as I slammed them together, desperate for any friction, and he chuckled darkly before climbing on the bed and wrenching them apart. Without a word, he eased himself down until he was between my knees before licking and biting his way toward my aching core. My breath hitched as he hovered just over where needed him. My hips bucked toward him in a silent plea, the sheet around my wrists burning as I strained against them.

Leighton clucked his tongue before moving to my left hip and biting hard enough to bruise. Somehow that only turned me on more. Giving me a knowing look, he worked his way up my body with a trail of bruising bites that he soothed with his tongue before moving on. I was practically thrashing on the bed with need when he reached my breasts and pulled back just enough to grab the hair clips from the nightstand.

"Rap your knuckles on the headboard twice if this hurts

too much, *ma petit,*" he commanded before pinching one of my nipples roughly.

Leighton lowered his head and continued his ministrations, sucking my other nipple into his mouth, nipping at it until it was a taut peek. Releasing it, his skilled hands clamped the metal hair clip in place of where his teeth had been moments before and I moaned against the material in my mouth. Kissing his way to my other breast, he repeated the action. The bite of metal into the sensitive skin set my skin ablaze.

He sat up, leaning on his heels between my thighs and smiled. "Fucking beautiful."

I lifted my hips toward him, so lost to my need that I didn't notice the pain from his makeshift restraints any more. A pleased smirk settled onto his face and he leaned over me again, this time grabbing one of the candles and lighter. My eyes were locked on his face as he lit the candle and waited for wax to start dripping down the sides.

"Remember, two raps on the headboard." He said absently before tilting the candle and dripping a trail of burning wax from my stomach to my core.

My back arched off the bed when the hot wax hit my throbbing clit and my core clenched around air. Leighton continued to drip the wax down my thighs with one hand and thrust two fingers inside me with the other. He wasn't gentle, his eyes dark with intent as he roughly slammed his fingers into me as the other continued to leave trails of wax on my thighs and abdomen, pushing me to the brink.

"Come for me, *ma petit,* so I can give you what you really want." He commanded.

My orgasm ripped through me like a lightning bolt causing my entire body to arch and tense. Before I had even come down, Leighton sheathed himself to the hilt. My legs wrapped around him of their own accord, my heels digging into his muscular ass to press him closer. He groaned in pleasure and bit down hard on my shoulder. The slight sting had my core clenching around him again.

"I can't be gentle." He gritted out as he began slamming

into me.

I clung to him, moaning around the cloth in my mouth. Each thrust sent me hurtling closer to my second release. Leighton snapped his hips forward causing my eyes to roll back as his piercings pressed against my inner walls, and then bit the fleshy part of my breast. I screamed, the cloth strip doing nothing to muffle the sound as the pain from his bite mingled with the pleasure of his thick cock pumping into me. My vision blacked out and I came harder than I ever had in my life just as Leighton's hips stuttered, my sex gripping him so tightly he softly cursed under his breath.

My body collapsed against the bed, my eyes fluttering closed. The mattress shifted as Leighton moved to undo my hands and stand from the bed.

"Stay," I murmured.

"I'll be right back, *ma petit.*" He assured me, kissing me sweetly on the lips.

I drifted in and out of consciousness until he returned and I felt the metal clips being removed from my nipples. Cracking my eyes open, I watched him through my lashes as he set them on the nightstand before using a warm wash cloth to gently wipe away the wax he'd poured on my body. When he reached for my wrists with a frown, I fully opened my eyes and looked at him, confused.

"What are you doing?"

"Shhh. I'm taking care of you." He replied. "I never wanted to do this for someone before, I always just let the professionals deal with it, but with you...."

Sucking air through my teeth, I hissed as the sting of antiseptic hit my wrists before he slathered some sort of ointment on them before wrapping them in gauze. His lips pinched together as he looked down to my neck and then the breast he'd bitten. Following his gaze, I realized he'd bitten me hard enough to break the skin.

"Fuck." He whispered. "I'm so sorry, *ma petit.*"

"Why? You told me what to do if I wanted it to stop." I replied gently as he worked to cleanse and bandage the wounds.

"I hurt people." He sighed. "I hurt *you*."

"You didn't do anything I couldn't handle, Leighton. Besides, I *enjoyed* it. Maybe it makes me as twisted as you, but I'm kinda into this whole being marked up thing you and Joey seem to have going on when it comes to me."

Leighton paused bandaging my breast and looked at me. It was clear from his expression he was searching for something in my expression, but I meant what I'd said.

"Let's see how you feel about it in the morning." He said finally with a tight nod of his head.

He finished securing the bandage over the bite mark he'd left before helping me under the blankets and climbing in beside me.

"What are you doing?" I asked as I worked to get comfortable.

"This is what the kids call snuggling if I'm not mistaken." He laughed. "Now hush and take my post-sex-snuggle virginity, *ma petit.*"

I snorted in response, but let him wrap his arm around my waist and pull me close. It didn't take long for the heat of his body to lull me back to sleep, this time without the nightmares.

It was nearly noon when I finally rolled out of bed the next day. The side Leighton had been on was cold, but I wasn't surprised even with his insistence on staying the night. I used the bathroom, brushed my teeth, and splashed cold water on my face before dressing quickly, fully expecting Az to be in a pissy mood about me sleeping in. Instead, I found all five guys seated in the den playing Yatzee. Leighton and Joey both had a self-satisfied look on their faces and I wasn't sure if it was because of the game they were currently playing or the ones we'd played together.

Az was the first to notice me as I crept closer to them, intent on checking over Rich even though he was settled into the loveseat playing with the others.

"Afternoon, Princess." He said with an evil grin.

"Oh no, I know that look, Az-hole. Whatever punishment you have in mind for me not working out and training today, stuff it up your ass. If you wanted me to do any of that you could have woke me up."

"You were dead to the world, what did you want me to do? Pour a bucket of ice water on your head?" He smirked, making it clear he was teasing me.

"Don't act like you didn't consider it." Rich drawled.

"He could have tried, but I'd have gutted him before he got to you *ma petit*." Leighton grinned, hopping up from his seat next to Rich and sauntering toward me.

He drew to a stop in front of me and gently grabbed my arms, bringing them up to inspect my wrists.

"What are you doing?" I asked.

"Damn it, Victoria. You didn't change the bandages. I left clean ones right beside your toothpaste so you wouldn't miss them." He all but growled at me.

The energy in the room shifted so fast you could almost hear the record scratch as it happened. A few seconds later Craig, Joey, and Az were standing shoulder to shoulder with Leighton and looking me over.

"What the fuck do you mean *bandages*, L? What did you do?" Az growled at him.

The way Leighton's shoulders tensed told me he was still unsure how I felt about it, so I spoke before he could respond.

"Nothing I didn't enjoy. Hell, maybe you could take a few pointers because he at least knows how to make me cum." I snarked, warmth spreading through my chest at the soft smile that spread across Leighton's face as his shoulders relaxed.

The feeling in the room shifted again, even more quickly than the first time. Joey started laughing out loud, and clapped Leighton on the shoulder before going back to the sitting area. Az raised an eyebrow and a slow, evil smirk crawled across his face.

"Is that right, Princess? Duly noted." He leaned forward, close enough to where our faces were just inches apart before booping my nose. "When this comes back to bite you in the ass, I want you to remember that statement."

"Do you mind? I'm trying to take care of her wrists."

Leighton said, shoulder checking Az out of the way.

All four guys' gazes snapped to Leighton wearing matching expressions of shock.

"Bro, you should close your mouth. It's not cute." Leighton laughed at Az before turning his attention back to my hands.

I snickered at his remark as he produced a tube of some sort of cream and new gauze from his pockets and set to work rebandaging the rope burns and slight tears in the skin from the strips of sheet he'd used as restraints.

"Jesus Christ, L. What did you use as restraints?" Craig asked, his eyes narrowing on my wrists before he jerked it out of Leighton's grasp.

"I cut up a sheet." Leighton shrugged.

Craig snapped his gaze up to Leighton's face, his eyebrows raised in surprise. "You did *what*? Leighton! That's not a good restraint! Not even factoring in the way it's going to hurt the skin with resistance, knots slip. What would you have done if it had gotten too tight to untie?! Did you even have any safety shears for emergencies?"

"Bro, you don't need a hairline when you can get your eyebrows that high." Leighton laughed. "Besides, I had scissors."

Craig slapped Leighton on the back of the head, hard enough to make his head snap forward. "You had scissors... We're gonna have a whole conversation about this. And what are you even putting on these friction burns?"

"No idea. Whatever I stole out of your weird little stash of rope in your top left draw." Leighton grinned, thrusting the tube toward Craig. "I'm done with it for now though, so you can have it back."

"Is nobody gonna mention how fucking weird it is that *LEIGHTON* is doing aftercare?" Az asked, looking between me, Craig, and Leighton.

"You're not supposed to point out *good* behavior as weird, Az. It makes it hard for people to continue doing it." Joey said, his tone amused.

"I know our first time is the time that shall not be

discussed, but what's so weird about him rebandaging my wrists anyway?" I asked.

"I... have a tendency to leave damage in my wake," Leighton said hesitantly.

"It's normally something that one of us or a doctor has to patch up. It's just... unusual to see the change is all." Craig added gently, seeming to not want to come across as critical of his friend.

"It's hard to do something you've never been taught." I replied, softening my gaze as I looked at Leighton. "Maybe all you needed was someone to teach you."

CHAPTER SEVENTEEN

Az

A few days after we'd all busted down Victoria's bedroom door and Leighton's sudden interest in aftercare the following morning, I woke with a strip of condoms in my hand. Glancing across the room to Joey's bed, I noticed he had been gifted the same thing.

"What the fuck." I grumbled, sitting up and dropping them on the nightstand. "I guess that explains Leighton's little sanitary products trip to town that wasn't actually needed."

"Can you shut the fuck up, Az? I'm trying to sleep." Joey mumbled, completely unaware of Leighton's gift in his hand. He rolled over in his bed and as he did, he managed to smack himself in the face with the strip of unwrapped condoms. "The fuck?"

I snickered as he shot upright in his bed, staring at them for a moment before shooting me a dirty look.

"Thank Leighton," I shrugged. "I would have given them to you like a normal human being."

"At least we're protected from anything you four picked up somewhere." Joey snorted, tossing his strip aside before settling back into his bed. "Pregnancy wasn't really a concern with her IUD."

I considered thumping him on the head for a moment and setting the record straight about how clean I was, but Craig's cursing drew my attention. Not bothering to put on a t-shirt, I padded my way out of our room and found Craig scowling at Leighton.

"You couldn't store them somewhere else? You had to block my workspace?" Craig yelled. "There's fucking closets and the laundry room with plenty of space for your weird ass costco trip."

Leighton poked his bottom lip out in a mock pout. "I thought you all would be happy about my presents."

Craig's yelling had woken everyone and I nearly lost it when I heard Rich muttering to himself about not needing condoms and turned to find a tower of boxes built on either side of his pullout.

"Merry Fuckmas everyone!" Leighton cackled.

Before any of us could respond, the crash from the remaining hinge on Victoria's door giving up when she attempted to open it caused us all to whip around. She stood in the doorway holding a large box of condoms and staring at the door on the floor looking flushed, frustrated... and kind of adorable.

"So... does anyone want to tell me why there are condoms where my tampons are supposed to be, and lined up in little rows on my bathroom counter?" She said, stepping over the door and into the den. "As much as I... appreciate the utility, I don't think anyone would use this many before they expire."

"It's Fuckmas!" Leighton grinned, making jazz hands by his face. "You get a condom, and you get a condom, and everyone gets a condom!"

Victoria rolled her eyes and pitched the box toward Leighton. He ducked, causing it to narrowly miss him before it pelted the side of my head.

"What the fuck?" I asked, raising a brow.

"I'm not in the mood for your shit today, Az-hole. You know I was aiming at Leighton so don't be a dick about it."

"First of all, *Your Highness*, I did not-a-god-damn-thing. You hit me with a box of condoms, pretty sure 'what the fuck' is an appropriate response from any sane person." I said, crossing my arms over my chest.

"Oh, like you haven't been stomping around here with a permanent scowl on your face and a pissy ass Az-i-tude ever since you got shitty with me about Benson."

"Ohhh, I need some popcorn. Mom and Dad are gonna fight it out." Leighton cackled.

"Nope, not doing that. Come on, L. You need to unbury my workspace." Craig said, grabbing Leighton by the arm and dragging him into their room.

"Awww, come on Craig! You only get action like this on pay-per-view!" Leighton whined as Craig pulled him into their room and shut the door behind them.

"If you two are going to argue, take it outside." Rich grunted. "I've got nowhere to go."

"Unless Az is ready to apologize for being his usual dickish self, I've got nothing else to say about the matter." Victoria huffed, turning toward the kitchen.

My legs ate up the distance between us as I followed her into the kitchen, reaching her just as she made it to the coffee pot. "Who said you get to decide when we talk about this shit, *Princess?*" I demanded.

"Me. The person it actually happened to." She deadpanned.

I reared back as if she'd slapped me. When I'd seen the medical records showing what Benson Prescott had done to her, I'd been too angry to think clearly. I wanted nothing more than to storm from the cabin, hunt the bastard down, and inflict every injury he'd given her times two. It was one of the few times I actually agreed with Leighton's stab first ask never attitude. Unfortunately, I hadn't been able to contain my anger enough to speak to Victoria with a clear head.

Sighing heavily, I raked a hand through my hair. "I'm sorry."

"Yo– What?" She said, turning her head to give me a suspicious look. "Who are you and what have you done with Az. An alien imposter right? Because Az doesn't apologize."

"I've apologized to you before, don't be so dramatic, Love." I snorted. "And I *am* sorry. I wasn't angry at you and the way I handled finding out what that dead bastard did to you wasn't okay."

"I need a lottery ticket." She chuckled, cracking a small smile before turning her attention back to the coffee pot.

"I'm serious. I... I don't mean to lash out when I get angry, but when I've got nothing to do with it then..." I trailed off, trying to make the words come out right.

"I get it, you need therapy. Maybe you should ask Phil to recommend his therapist." Victoria shrugged.

"How the fuck– No, nevermind. Not right now. But, sure, everyone needs therapy, I get it. Are you gonna keep tossing barbs at me or are you going to let me apologize and work things out with you?"

"That depends entirely on whether or not your apology is a good one." She replied, pouring her cup of coffee before turning to lean her backside against the counter.

I stood there for a second wanting to argue further, but then another thought crossed my mind. Strolling over to where she was leaning against the counter, I took her cup from her hands and placed it on the counter before I grabbed her by the hair and put my hand over her mouth.

"Then, *hush*, Love. Let me get through it." I crooned.

The wet warmth of her tongue against my palm caused me to roll my eyes at her. When she realized I wasn't going to react further to her bratty behavior, she narrowed her eyes at me.

"Proceed." Her voice was muffled by my hand.

"Not sure what you thought that was going to do," I said, amused. "You're not my first brat, Love. I'm not afraid of a little tongue." I licked my lips and gave her a pointed stare before I gave her hair a sharp tug and released her.

She settled back against the counter and picked up her mug, looking so flustered and adorable I had to back away to lean against the opposite wall in the kitchen so I wasn't tempted to further derail the conversation.

"As I was saying, before you so rudely interrupted me," I paused a second, the look on her face telling me she wanted to say something but she didn't. Good girl. "Love, I wasn't angry *with* you. I was angry *for* you, and I didn't know what to do with it. There wasn't anything that I was doing that felt like it was working it out of my system knowing that bastard was walking around. He might be breathing borrowed air, but he's still breathing."

She sighed into her coffee mug before turning to sit it

back on the counter. "It happened *once*. Aht," she raised a hand to stop me from speaking. "Joey already gave me the 'once is once too many' speech, I don't need it from you too. But I *do* need all of you to understand that when I ended things, there was no fighting. He let me walk without so much as a word, probably because he was afraid that one time would be leaked if he didn't. The why of it doesn't matter so much as that I got out, I am... well I was safe until whoever decided to drop me in the middle of this mess, played their hand."

I fought my urge to tell her that she was safe, because she wasn't. We knew that more than she did because we hadn't filled her in on everything Craig had dug up. I took a deep breath and stared at the floor trying to find my next words. "We're going to do our best to make sure you're safe, and that we teach you whatever we can to keep yourself safe even if we aren't around. None of us can promise that, and we know it, but we're going to do our damndest."

Victoria eyed me carefully as I spoke, but thankfully she was letting me find the words on my own. "Yes, once is once too many, but I'm sure you knew that even without Joey's input. We all know Prudence helped a lot of women escape situations like that. Hell, she even tried with Craig's mom. It... didn't work out the way any of us wanted it to."

"You're going to have to explain that a little more. I'm not quite following what my mother attempting to help Craig's mom has to do with me, or why her work with battered women is even relevant." She frowned, her tone making it clear she was genuinely confused trying to follow my train of thought.

"The whole story... isn't mine to tell, but suffice it to say that Prudence's work with battered women was very relevant to Craig's home life. But she wasn't cooperative when Harrison showed up. It was a shit show... and it left me feeling powerless. Useless. We could only help Craig pick up the pieces as best we were able to when it was over." I trailed off, trying to find my way back to the present from the images of a young Craig's life that flashed in my mind.

"When we saw what was in that report..." I trailed off

again, taking a deep breath to steady myself. "It didn't matter that it was just once, and that it was a while ago. It happened, and there's nothing I can do about it from here. Those same feelings from back then came rushing back."

When I looked up, Victoria was looking at the floor. Her brows were drawn together and she looked remorseful and ashamed. I strode across the kitchen and tilted her head upward to make her look at me. I could see the tears pricking at the corners of her beautiful brown eyes and my heart broke for the sight of them.

"Don't do that, Love," I said softly, gathering her up in my arms. "What happened to them, and to you, wasn't anything you should feel guilt for. It's not your fault, so don't you put that on yourself."

I pulled back to look at her and I wiped away a few of the tears that fell on her cheeks when she shook her head.

"It's not that," she sighed. "I know it's not my fault. I'm angry with myself for not considering that you guys would have known how helpless it leaves you when there's nothing you can do to stop it. If the son of a bitch wasn't dead already, I'd have wanted to kill him myself. Even knowing he couldn't hurt them anymore, I was still so angry."

"We don't always get to take care of the bad guys personally." I replied, a little stunned at the realization that Craig had told her about his dad.

"You're right, we can't. But... we have to find a healthier way to deal with these angry outbursts before it leads us to not speaking for days on end." She said, stepping out of my embrace and wiping the remaining tears from her face.

"I can think of a few things we can try..." I smirked. She rolled her eyes in response and slapped my chest hard enough that it stung a little. "You're just making an argument *for* those things."

"That's not what I meant... and I need a little break anyway. I was thinking something more along the lines of putting our enemies in the ground so we're not trying to kill each other." She said simply.

I raised a brow and stared at her for a long moment.

When did our little rich girl start getting so cold-blooded?

"Well, we don't have all of our stuff so we'll have to do it the old fashioned way... but we could always slay dragons and kill bandits in the meantime." I offered. "It's not as viscerally satisfying, but it comes in a close second."

A few hours later we were gathered around the table at a set up that reminded me of how we played the game when we were kids. We used notebook paper for not only character sheets, but to construct quick grids as battle maps. We used things like loose change, a soda can tab, the plastic ring off the milk jug, a bottle cap, paper clip, and a pencil eraser as our miniatures.

Victoria had shown a good deal of interest in the process of running the game, and after giving her a little pep talk and assuring her that she didn't *need* to know much more than she already did to run a game effectively, she decided to give it a shot. Things were slower in a few places since she wasn't as well acquainted with the rules and she didn't have her own systems in place for keeping track of the various things happening between the characters, the npcs, and in combat. But she recovered from her stumbles well when she had to stop and look something up.

It was also nice to take a break from running the game, despite having to bite my tongue a few times to not tell her how I would have called one thing or another. I'd given her the premise of a one-shot I'd run the guys through years ago, and told her to change whatever she wanted about the characters and story, and that if she struggled with anything, I would be happy to help. She knew any of us would, but she did really well for someone new to the game, much less to being behind the screen.

"Good work guys!" Victoria praised us as she cleared away the change from the grid that had represented the group of giant rats we'd been fighting.

"Is anyone in need of any dire healing at the moment, or can we wait for a short rest when we're out of the tunnels?" Craig asked us as a collective, he'd chosen to play a Cleric for this mini game we were running. We didn't have enough tablets to go around to use our usual characters.

"As long as we don't run into anything on our way out, I think I'm good," Joey responded.

"We cleared the tunnels out as we moved through them. Unless we missed something on the way in, there shouldn't be anything *left* to give us issues." Leighton said, sounding almost like he hoped we had missed something.

"Are you wanting to rest here, or start making your way back?" Victoria asked.

"We'll work our way back. I, for one, look forward to being out of these fucking tunnels." I stated before telling her I was gathering up my things and heading back the way we had come. The guys indicated that their characters fell into step behind me.

"Great. What's everyone's passive perception?" She grumbled, flipping through the papers she'd started to accumulate behind the makeshift screen we'd set up for her with a few of Craig's binders.

".... Why?" Joey asked hesitantly. She flicked her gaze up at him, and let it sweep across us before smirking.

"Don't worry about it," she said simply. I couldn't stop the grin that split my face. *Devious little thing.*

The boys were tense, and stayed that way as she occasionally rolled a die as we made our way back down the labyrinth of abandoned tunnels. The group let out a collective sigh of relief as the hole we'd entered through came into view.

"As your party emerges from the ancient labyrinthian tunnels below the brewery, the stench of dead rats still clinging to your clothing, you find yourself back in the main aging cellar where you'd started. Gundrik, the stout dwarven owner you'd received the job from appears to be pacing at the foot of the stairs as you approach. The flickering light of lanterns casts dancing shadows on the wooden barrels stacked around the room, and the air is thick with the scent of fermenting ale. Gundrik approaches, his eyes narrowing as he takes in the state of your party. Curiosity and relief mix in his features." Victoria narrates for us. "'By the beard of Moradin!

You did it then, cleared out those filthy rats?' Gundrik asks, eyeing your battered weapons and tattered clothing."

"Aye. And not to be rude, but can we get somewhere that's above ground before we continue this little chat? I'd like to smell something besides stale air and rat stink." Rich grumbled in character, indicating that he started moving upstairs without waiting for anyone to respond.

"'Oh, aye. Yes, let's get you gents a little more comfortable and we can discuss your reward.'" Victoria responds as Gundrik, trying to make her voice low and gruff. Her effort is adorable, and I'm again struck with just how naturally she seemed to take to the narrative since she'd seemed to find her footing.

There is a bit of banter back and forth as we move the scene along, she shuffles a few papers, looking for other notes she'd made at some point.

"Gundrik gestures toward a large wooden table in the center of the room, laden with parchment, quills, and tankards. 'Let's talk reward, then. I'm not one to part with my gold easily, but I reckon you've earned something for your troubles.'"

"I'd fucking say. The job we ended up on didn't exactly match the one you *gave* us." Rich said gruffly, narrating his character flopping down in a chair in irritation.

"I'm going to put my hand on Rich's shoulder, and step just in front of him to address Gundrik. 'Ah, Gundrik, my good man. What my friend here *means* to say is that the job turned out to be quite the adventure. Not only did we clear your cellar of those pesky rats as agreed, but beneath your brewery lies a forgotten labyrinth of tunnels filled with ancient dangers!'" I say with flourish. I chose to play a bard this time around, enjoying reprising the role of the party face whenever it's needed.

"Gundrik narrows his eyes at you, you can see concern and surprise on his face, and he motions for you to continue," Victoria notes.

I consider how I want to spin the story. "'We braved the depths of these long forgotten tunnels, discovering several nests of giant rats that would make even the most seasoned adventurer quiver! They were harrowing battles. But your brewery is now safe and secure. We exterminated every nest we uncovered and made sure there were none left to bother you.' I pause for a moment, taking in the large tasting room around us that showcases all of Gundrik's work. 'Truly, it was an honor to assist such a talented brewer in preserving his art.'" I finish my little performance, looking to Victoria to see how she'll have her own character react.

She's looking down at what I would assume is his character sheet, and you can almost see her brain working on how to properly proceed.

"'Well, son, that's quite the tale you've spun for me. And while I appreciate that you've done this, we both know that it's not just out of the kindness of your heart. I assume you'll be wanting more reward than was offered on the job call.' Gundrik crosses his arms and looks at you expectantly." She says.

"'Straight to the point. I like that in a business relationship. We understand that you may not have been aware of the extra challenge the tunnels and rats posed, but be that as it may, it *was* an extra challenge. And a little extra compensation would go a long way in showing that you take care of those who take care of you.'" I counter without giving anything specific. She's gotta learn to pivot what she'd expected.

"Make me a… persuasion roll." She asked, a little pause as she remembered which one to ask for.

"Do I get advantage?" I asked, hopefully.

"What makes you think you would?" She asked me flatly, her eyebrows furrowing in confusion.

"I told that story really well!" I explained. I knew it wasn't something I'd get advantage for, but I wanted to keep her on her toes.

"No, I don't think so." She said, rolling her eyes.

"But! We deserve an extra reward!" I argued.

"Keep arguing with me and I'll make you roll with disadvantage because Rich's character was being rude to start with." She returned sternly, pinning me with an authoritative look. It made my dick twitch.

I raised my hands in surrender and clattered the single d20 we had across the table, did some quick math and hissed at the roll. It wasn't the lowest, but it wasn't very good.

"I'm going to give him Guidance." Craig interjected, handing me a d4. I rolled it and added it to my total.

"16," I finally offered.

"'Alright then, you've proven yourselves in the face of unexpected challenges. Here's what I can offer you,' Gundrik declares, a thoughtful glint in his eyes. He moves to a large bar at one end of the room and rustles around a few things, and his arms are laden down with things as he returns. 'For a job well done in the face of unforeseen circumstances, here's a purse of 200 gold. Spend it wisely, friends.' He places down a sack, the sounds of clinking coins echoing around you. 'And a few other tokens of appreciation that you may find useful. You're welcome to enjoy free drinks at my brewery whenever you pass through these parts. Consider it a brewer's boon. The finest ales and meads are yours for the taking, on the house.' He hands you a small parchment with his stamp and the words 'Gundrik's Boon' on it."

"'If I'm not working the tasting floor, whoever will be knows what these are. Also, if you ever find yourselves interested in the art of brewing, I'll share some of my expertise with you. 'Tis not an offer I make to just anyone, and you never know what you might find in the process that may be useful on your travels.'" Victoria narrates animatedly.

"Just one more thing..." I start, trailing off at her withering look.

"Aye?" She says in character.

"You got somewhere we can clean up, dwarf? The wizard stinks of burnt rat and I'd hate to see it permanently stained into your nice furniture." Leighton says with a laugh.

"Oh... right!" Victoria chuckles. "Yeah, he shows you to the upper floors of the brewery, he has a small apartment up there for when his work keeps him over, and he invites you all to clean yourselves up and rest before you head out."

We make small talk and banter for a while longer while our characters are going about their resting activities, before we wrap the game up for the evening. I sat back in my chair looking around the group, and sensing for the first time in a long time the release of some tension that had hung around all of us just like the imaginary stink of burnt rat.

CHAPTER EIGHTEEN

Leighton

Watching Victoria DM our session caused a tightness in my chest that didn't fade. Even after we all went our separate ways for the night, I couldn't shake it. Usually, I could sleep through Craig clacking away at his keyboard, but instead, I tossed and turned, the strange pain growing stronger. When I heard the others moving around the following day, I was convinced I needed a doctor.

Craig was still working at his computer with his headset on when I finally gave up and climbed out of bed. Strolling from our shared room to the kitchen, intent on finding some aspirin since I'd read somewhere that helped with heart attacks, I saw Joey and Az talking quietly by the coffee pot.

"Morning," I mumbled as I moved toward the cabinet where the aspirin was stored.

"You look like shit." Az snarked, the pair looking me over as I rustled through the cabinet.

"Fuck off," I retorted, digging around for a few more moments before coming up empty. "Where the hell is the aspirin?!"

"What do you need aspirin for?" Joey asked.

"I'm having a heart attack." I shrugged. The pair looked at each other and then back at me, eyes wide and brows furrowed.

"What?!" Joey exclaimed, alarm evident in his tone.

"What... Wait, having a heart attack?" Az sounded more confused than alarmed, turning to look at me fully. "You don't look... Why do you think you're having a heart attack?"

"Az, if he *is* having a heart attack... taking the time to ask about it might be a bad idea." Joey said, moving to grab his phone from his pocket.

I sighed heavily and turned to face both of them. "Well, my chest feels funny for starters. It feels too big and tight, and it's oddly warm. And I've got, like, bubbles in my chest and stomach." I paused to rub my knuckles against my breastbone. "I can't focus, I slept like shit because it started during DND and hasn't stopped. So, yeah, if you don't mind. I think I need a fucking cardiologist stat."

Joey and Az listened intently, their facial expressions shifting as I described my symptoms. When I finished, they shared another look, which lasted what felt like forever. Just as I was about to ask if they were still on this planet with me, they both burst into laughter so hard that Az gripped the countertop, and Joey doubled over, clutching his legs.

"I didn't know me *dying* was so damned funny." I huffed.

"I..." Az started, pausing to wipe tears from his eyes and catch his breath. "I seriously cannot *wait* to tell everyone this story." He looked at Joey with a wide grin. "Do you wanna tell him, or should I?"

"L... Buddy, no..." Joey paused to straighten his posture and catch his breath, his wheezing making it hard for him to talk. "Bro, that's not a heart attack, but I do know what it is. You might want to have a seat for this." He said, gesturing toward the dining room.

"This is serious guys. Just fucking tell me so I can make sure my affairs are in order before I drop dead." I demanded.

Az had gone back to chuckling behind his hand, motioning for Joey to continue since he didn't look like he could get through saying anything.

I shot Az a dirty look. "Thanks for the concern Az-hole. I didn't think you'd take my impending death so well. Know what, fuck both of ya, I'm going to grab my phone and call for the doc." I grumbled, starting toward the kitchen door. Az burst out laughing as I finished my statement while Joey grabbed my arm.

"L, you're not having a heart attack." Joey said, his grin mocking my concern. "We're very sure you're not going to die because of what's going on."

"Well, stop being so fucking cryptic if you're so certain and tell me what you think is going on." I snapped.

"You're having *feelings*, Leighton, not a heart attack. Most people would call what you're experiencing 'affection'." Joey said, his grin twitching like he would start laughing again.

"Feelings? *Feelings?* You take that back right now!"

"Not happening. That's what's going on. I know, it's a shocking diagnosis, but I'm sure you'll come to terms with it in time." Az said, his shoulders shaking with barely contained humor.

"Unfortunately, L, feelings can be terminal." Joey added before laughing hysterically at his own joke.

"Yeah, they can. Especially when they're attached to the Princess." Az added. "Depending on how she's acting at any given time, it *might* end in you dying."

I slumped back against the counter and ran my hands through my hair. "Fuck, you guys are serious." I breathed.

Joey quirked a brow and looked me over. "You look like you really did get a diagnosis of something. Feelings, especially things like affection and love, are generally considered positive things, L."

"Considering my history with this sort of thing, I'm not really sure about that," I replied quietly.

With that, the humor from moments ago seemed to vanish from the room. The guys shared a look again before turning back to me, looking like they were settling in for a long conversation.

"Leighton, your past might color how you see something, or how we handle things... but it doesn't have to repeat itself. You aren't the same you, and Victoria is not Angelica." Az said, his tone serious but not hard.

"Maybe, but I still don't know how to do this shit anymore than I did back then." I replied.

Joey moved back to the coffee pot and poured two mugs full, motioning for us to follow him through the door to the dining room. Az grabbed his cup off the counter and followed while I brought up the rear, shuffling my feet.

We sat around the table, Joey sliding the warm cup of

coffee toward me as I slid into my chair.

"The reason you don't know what to do, or how to approach it, is because after what happened you never *tried*. What happened was painful, so if you never got close to someone again, that would never happen again." Joey said carefully.

"Alright, Dr. Drew, consider this me calling into the loveline." I snorted. "Tell me what I'm supposed to do about it then. I know she likes my dick, but beyond that, I got nothing."

"I doubt I'd take his advice, he wasn't even a relationship therapist. He does addiction medicine." Az snorted.

"Addiction, feelings. Same diff." I shrugged. "Now tell me what the fuck I'm supposed to do about it."

Joey sighed slightly as if my logic were childish. "First off, let's not tie your emotions to your dick. That's not going to end well for anyone involved. Relationships based purely on sex have a time limit before they fizzle out."

"I mean, that's always been the goal before. Get what I want and get out." I replied, cringing at the thought of Victoria bailing on me. My chest squeezed painfully with the thought, and I rubbed my knuckles roughly against it. "Are you sure I'm not having a heart attack?"

Az rolled his eyes dramatically. "If you were, then by now you'd probably be dead and we'd be digging a hole in the backyard."

"Az, you can make fun of him later, right now we're doing a thing. Or, you can go." Joey said a little sharply. "What caused that reaction, Leighton?"

I blew out a puff of air. "Circle of honesty is a no judgment zone right?"

"Of course," Joey said simply, shooting Az a stern glare as he said it.

"It was the thought of *la petit* leaving. It's not like my other fucks, I always wanted them to leave."

"Well, you obviously don't want things between you and Victoria to fizzle out and for whatever this budding relationship is between you to end. The idea of people we care about leaving is generally painful. I know it's new territory, but this is normal, L." Joey said softly, still sounding like he was choosing his words carefully.

Taking a moment to digest his words, I turned to look at Az. "How did you make her like your cantankerous ass back?"

Az leaned back in his chair momentarily, staring down into his coffee cup as if looking for answers in the black liquid it held. "Honestly... I'm not sure she does. We get along sometimes, but at others, it's like she'd rather scratch my eyes out than look at me. And sometimes the feeling is mutual."

"Don't bullshit a bullshitter, Az. You two fight like Joey and Rich's parents. I've seen it." I snorted.

Az laughed, but there wasn't much humor in it. "I doubt it's anywhere on the same page. Dawn and Ian bicker like a married couple who love each other but they've been around each other a bit too long. Victoria and I... at times we barely tolerate each other."

Joey arched a brow at Az. "Yeah, no. Ma barely tolerates Pa sometimes too. Or did you forget Christmas when Pa got her a vacuum? Lucky for us, Ma has good aim or we'd have all been dodging vacuum parts."

"I'm pretty sure she dumped the old canister on his dinner when she made his plate. His ham was looking a little dusty." I laughed.

Az let out a long-suffering sigh. "Anyway, it's not the same. The Princess would just as soon slit my throat as hop into my bed and you both know it. Besides, we're getting off topic here, this is about Leighton."

"Listen, I don't enjoy thinking about my parent's sex life," Joey paused to shudder in disgust. "But you just described what it was like watching them get along growing up."

"I was there, remember? I know they bickered, and sometimes it was bad... but I've never seen two people look at each other with adoration the same way they do. Life makes things hard, but there isn't anyone who's met them who can't say that even after all this time they aren't disgustingly in love with each other." Az said, his voice had an edge of sadness to it. "It's not that way between Victoria and I. Okay, I'll give you that maybe we aren't actively on opposite sides anymore, but

I'm not in love with her any more than she is with me. I don't... I don't quite know what this is, but it isn't that."

I snorted at about the same time that Joey sighed. Apparently, sorting out how we feel about these *feelings* wasn't something I was the only one struggling with. I guess, at least, there was company in this hell.

"Whatever you say, bro. We can sort that out later." Joey offered before turning back to me. "Leighton, uncertainty, and fear can come in the same package as affection and care. Especially when past experiences with those emotions are tainted with pain. Everyone who's ever been hurt experiences it to some degree, even if it's not in the 'likely tied to complex PTSD' way that you do."

I blinked a few times as I took in his words. He said them with such confidence that despite my instinctual response to argue with him trying to psychoanalyze me, I couldn't find any words to refute him that didn't sound childish or stubborn to me. I could feel myself open my mouth and then close it when no words would come out.

"Look at Joey, being all well-adjusted and shit." Az said with a smirk, though the humor sounded a little forced.

"Listen, don't go poking fun at me just because I'm one of the more emotionally intelligent men in our group. It's not my fault you guys are playing catch up here." Joey fired back warmly, with no judgment in his voice or face.

"Okay, Dr. Joseph. Now that we've established that you are in love with *la petit **and*** emotionally 'healthy'," I air quoted healthy, "let's get back to what I'm supposed to do about these *feelings.*"

Az chuckled and leaned over to poke Joey in the shoulder. "Yeah, while you're all psychoanalytical over here. You're obviously so in love with her, it's oozing out your fucking ears, Casanova."

Joey barked a full laugh, throwing his head back as it escaped him. After a little bit, he settled down and wiped a tear from his eye. "It's hilarious you think you did something with that. Of course I am. But the difference between me and you two idiots is that I'm aware of it, and it doesn't bother me." His words were so simple and direct that neither Az nor I had any immediate retorts. "*And*, I suppose another key difference is that when I need to talk to her about us, I ***do***. I don't bitch out about it."

I don't think I'd ever had a conversation with Joey that had left me speechless as often as this one had so far, and I didn't think I liked it any. It felt like this little upper hand would go straight to his head, and we'd never hear the end of it... but well, Joey wasn't really like that. It took me a second to realize he was still talking, so I pulled myself out of my internal bitch session. He was staring past me, looking like he was trying to find the words he needed on the wall behind me.

"To answer your question, Leighton..." There was more emphasis on my name than felt necessary, but I didn't interrupt him. "What you do about it is *talk to her*. It's normal to take time to sort out your feelings, and acknowledge what they are and what you want to do about them. It's healthy and will give you a place to approach the situation and understand what you want and need. But after you've done that, you talk to her. Go to her honestly and openly. It might not mean that everything will end with roses and picnics, but it's a lot better than pretending it's not there when everyone around you can see it. You're not being fair to either of you by doing that."

The sound of a throat clearing behind me caused me to turn in my seat. Rich was hovering just inside the dining room, his gaze locked with his younger brother.

"Just in time to be lectured huh, *Daddy?*" I smirked, Joey's last line making sense now that I knew who was behind me.

Rich grunted, a sneer painting over his face as he moved through the room toward the kitchen. "I have no idea what you're talking about. I just need coffee."

Craig strolled into the dining room behind Rich and glanced around at us. "Oh, good. We're all here. We need to talk about calling the doc in."

Az leaned back in his chair and pinned Craig with a look. "Don't tell us, you're having a heart attack too?"

Craig gave him a double take as he slid into a seat at the

table. "What? ...No. Who had a heart attack?"

"Nobody is having a heart attack," Rich said, shooting Az a puzzled glance as he slowly crept toward the kitchen doorway. "And we don't need a doctor, Craig. I'm healing up just fine and there's no reason to call someone to poke and prod at me some more."

"Let's just agree to disagree on that point." Craig said. "I didn't mean a doc just for you anyway. I was digging through Victoria's medical records some more and she's due for her birth control."

"You were what?" Victoria's shrill voice rang out around the dining room as she entered.

"Been nice knowing ya, bud." I smirked at Craig.

"Why the hell were you digging into my medical records, *again?*" She demanded, closing the distance to the table in a few short, angry strides.

"I-,"

"No, I don't want to hear it. Wasn't it enough you already dug once. You couldn't stop yourself from snooping further into things that are *none* of your business? I expect this shit from Az, hell, maybe even Rich, but you, Craig?"

I didn't miss Joey's flash of a smug smile as Craig narrowed his eyes at her and squared his shoulders.

"First of all, Bunny, don't ask me a question and then get shitty with me before I can answer it." His tone had a warning that caused Victoria's eyebrow to quirk up. "Secondly, *yes*, I did continue to dig into your history, associations, voicemails, phone records, and medical records. Because if you need a reminder, we aren't out here in the woods on vacation. We're hiding out because people keep trying to *kill you*. And you hid the fact that your abusive ex could be one of those people. Not to mention that you also hid those threatening text messages from Rinaldo–"

"Well, I didn't–"

"I *know* you didn't know who they were from. Doesn't change the fact you were getting them, and chose not tell us. I could have figured out who was sending them ages before we found out if I'd had time. At almost every turn, *Victoria*, you have taken it upon yourself to keep important information from us that could have helped keep all of us safe. So, *yes,* I've been digging."

I leaned toward Joey and whispered in a conspiratorial tone. "Oh, mom and dad are fighting again."

"And before you go on about how this particular information isn't my business, considering that you're sleeping with almost everyone in this room, I'd say it concerns us just as much as it does you." Craig finished, crossing his arms over his chest and looking at Victoria like he dared her to argue further. He was angry, but something else tinted the look on his face and the tone of his voice, and it was apparent he wouldn't let her lecture him over doing his job. I'd have to shake his hand when the tension in the room wasn't so thick; I didn't know he had it in him.

Victoria stood, rooted to the spot, her arms crossed in front of her chest and her face an angry shade of red. "For your information, I noticed this morning that I was due for my shot and was coming in here to tell someone."

"I think that's my cue to leave," I said, scooting my chair back to stand.

Victoria pinned me with a stare, stopping me in my tracks. "No, stay, since this clearly has to do with all of you." her gaze shot to Rich. "Most of you, rather. I need more than just my birth control. My period is fucking late."

Everyone in the room froze, staring at her with wide eyes. The only sound you could hear was Rich's feet shuffling across the floor as he chose that moment to slip from the dining room into the kitchen, wisely escaping the storm that was about to explode into the room.

"How late?" Az managed to get out before clamping his mouth shut, a muscle in his jaw twitching.

"A little more than a week. It wasn't something I'd noticed because of, well," Victoria motioned broadly at all of us, "everything. But before all this, I was like clockwork, so..." She trailed off, leaving us to fill in the blanks for ourselves.

"I actually have just the thing for this." I interjected, hopping up from my seat. "Be right back."

"Don't tell me you have a test, and just *because...*" Victoria stated as I left the room.

While I couldn't really explain *why* I'd thrown it in with the entire condom aisle, I had picked up a pack of tests when I went on my shopping spree for Fuckmas. Ignoring Victoria's voice trailing after me, I made my way into the communal bathroom and dug under the sink.

"Yes!" I cheered as I pulled out the bulk box of pregnancy tests. I all but ran back into the dining room, holding my prize over my head. "There's eight in here. Maybe take all of them?"

"Leighton, that's not how it works." Joey said, a humorless chuckle following his words.

I scowled at him. "I know that, I just meant if she pees on all of them then we know for absolutely sure."

Victoria sighed and took the box from him. "That wouldn't tell you anything more than one will right now. But... thank you for your foresight."

Joey cleared his throat, seeming to return to earth since she'd announced she was late. "Go get something to drink, Sweetheart. I guess it's better to go ahead and get it done since I'm pretty sure we have to wait for a result anyway."

She nodded and shuffled off into the kitchen, her steps seemed as heavy as the air in the room did. Seemed like no one really knew what to do.

The tight, warm feeling in my chest returned as a grin spread across my face. "So, who gets to name the kid?" I asked in a hushed whisper after she disappeared through the doorway.

After a few moments, we heard the sound of her setting her glass on the counter harder than necessary, and irritated footsteps retreating from the kitchen before the bathroom door slammed.

"Well, I guess we should address the elephant in the room." I said, leaning back in my chair. "We're all cool sharing her right? I mean it seems obvious since she has four baby daddies now, but I wanted to check."

"Oh my fucking god, Leighton. Really?" Craig sighed, scrubbing his hand over his face.

"What? It's a serious question. They say it takes a village to raise a kid, and I for one, don't think we need to have fighting over our woman tearing apart our village." I shrugged.

"That's... surprisingly insightful, L. I know I have no issues with our polyamorous situation. I mean, I feel like if we did it would have already been starting fights. It's not like we can't all hear it when she's... spending time with someone." Joey said, again speaking slowly to make sure his words were chosen carefully.

"I mean, I know y'all can hear when she's with me," I smirked. "If I don't put something in her mouth, she'll scream the house down."

"Yes, yes, Leighton. Should we all applaud you now?" Craig said, rolling his eyes.

"Hey, you're welcome to watch next time." I shrugged. "I enjoyed the show she put on, on this very table, with Joey."

"On the table?!" Rich's gruff voice from the kitchen called out. "Fucking really?"

Joey's response was to simply grin and shrug as if to prove his point that he was entirely unbothered by our unconventional arrangements.

"Is this really the elephant in the room you think we should be addressing?" Az spat out. "Did all of you forget that we're fucking gangsters? We steal, we kill, we manufacture drugs and weapons. Do *any* of you think that we're fit people to be raising a child in all this? What the fuck is wrong with all of you?!"

We all turned to stare at Az, and based on the looks Joey and Craig wore, it seemed like we were on the same page, having been expediently sobered up by his outburst.

"What the fuck are we going to do if she is pregnant? It wasn't a few minutes ago Craig was just laying out all of the bullshit going on in our lives right now, and the fact that people keep trying to *kill her*! Do you fucking assholes really think that we're the type of people that just get to have that house with a yard, a dog, and 2.5 fucking kids? When they aren't physically in danger, there's nothing about our life that lends to raising well adjusted fucking people!" Az was nearly yelling now, taking breaths in big gulps, his eyes bugged out. He was throwing himself headlong into a panic attack.

"Az, bro, slow down. You're gonna make yourself pass out if you keep that up. We don't even have an answer yet..." Craig said, placing a hand on Az's shoulder to reassure him. "Stress can cause being late too, there's just as much chance of one as the other."

"What do we do if it's not though?" Az said breathlessly.

"We'll do what we have to. It won't be the easiest thing in the world, but we'll figure it out." Rich said as he hobbled back into the room, his voice sounding far away as if he were wrapped up in his own thoughts despite not quite being part of the menagerie.

"Everyone can breathe." Victoria's soft voice grabbed our attention as she came back into the room. "It's negative, so there's nothing to figure out."

CHAPTER NINETEEN

Victoria

I stared at the ceiling above my bed as the early morning light filtered through my bedroom window. Yesterday had gone from awkward to worse. I wanted to be reasonable and understand why Craig thought it was okay to dig so far into my medical records that he felt the need to discuss my birth control with the guys instead of me. Still, the subsequent lecture I'd received from him only heightened my anger. The rollercoaster of emotions from the pregnancy scare didn't help matters.

A derisive snort slipped free as I recalled the scene I'd walked in on in the dining room to announce the test was negative. If I'd thought I was freaked out about the possibility of a baby with these guys, Az put me to shame. It took several minutes for him to calm down from his panic attack after I'd told them I wasn't pregnant. He still didn't seem like he had himself pulled fully together when he stormed from the cabin, refusing to look at me afterward. I felt awful that he didn't feel like they were the type of people who could ever have those things in life, but was I so bad that the thought of figuring it out wouldn't even cross his mind? Everything he'd said was true about our current situation, but it didn't mean it didn't hurt to hear.

"I don't want a kid with you either, Az-hole." I huffed to myself, shifting in my bed to get more comfortable.

I stewed in my anger for a while longer until it became clear that nobody was coming to retrieve me for what had become our daily routine of coffee, and then the guys pushing me to my limits with workouts and hand-to-hand or weapons training. Throwing the blankets off violently enough for them to slide onto the floor on the opposite side, I swung my legs over the edge and stormed from my room. Aside from Rich's snores coming from the nook, the cabin was eerily quiet, almost like the other guys weren't even there.

"Fuck all of them," I muttered and made my way to the kitchen to make my coffee. I nearly ran face-first into Leighton as I stepped into the room.

"There you are!" He grinned brightly. "I was wondering if I needed to come wake you up or not."

"Yeah, let's go with not. It's going to be a while before any of you guys are allowed in my room again." I snapped as I moved past him.

Leighton's smile dropped into a pout. "What did I do, *ma petit?*"

"It's not just you. It's *all* of you. I mean, I totally get that it's not ideal. Hell, I don't think you could write worse timing if you tried to. But, you guys didn't have to have such a *strong* reaction to it. Fuck." The words tumbled out of me in a rush when I started talking.

"Naming it was too far, noted." He nodded curtly.

I raised a brow and looked at him, slightly astonished. "The fuck?"

Leighton raised a hand and scratched the back of his head, giving me a sheepish look. "I mean, I kinda thought Bodhi was a cool name, but I also thought I was having a heart attack when I woke up yesterday, so I guess it makes sense you'd have hated the idea of me picking a name."

"You know what, I don't even know what to say to that, Leighton." I chuckled softly and sighed. "I... appreciate that at least *someone* didn't completely melt down about Schrodinger's baby." I reached for the coffee cup I'd claimed as 'mine' and poured myself some. I'd need it to get through what would likely become more of *these* conversations.

"Schrodinger," Leighton said thoughtfully as he moved toward me and crowded me against the counter. "I like that for the future, baby momma." he grinned, gently booping my nose.

"Immediately, no. Nope. Absolutely not. You can either

go back to calling me *petit,* or you can use my name if that's the other option." I said, eyes widening in equal parts horror and resistance. I considered the rest of what he said for a moment. "And there's no way in hell that Schrodinger would even make the list."

"I'm very confused. Weren't you just angry with me because you thought *all* of us were against having a baby?" he frowned, shaking his head. "Now you're upset about the name I picked out for both of you?"

"It's complicated, okay?" I huffed out a long breath. "It's... uugh!" I stopped again, not sure how to proceed. "I know it's–"

Pounding on the front door cut me off, followed by Rich's half-asleep shouting.

"We don't want to buy a fucking vacuum!" He bellowed from the nook, causing Leighton to burst out laughing.

"We'll finish this conversation later, *ma petit.* I believe the doctor has arrived," he said after stifling his laughter. Shooting me one last grin, he strolled from the kitchen to answer the door.

I followed a little behind him, taking a long drink of my coffee since I figured it would likely be cold when the doctor finished with me. I'd never had a house call appointment and didn't know what to expect. As I shuffled into the den, I saw Az's sleepy shuffle out of the bedroom, rubbing his fists into his eyes.

"Are there really door-to-door people this far out?" He grumbled unhappily.

"Not at all," Joey said, clapping him on the shoulder from behind before stepping around him and out of the room. "Somebody just woke Rich up mid-dream, apparently."

"He dreams about vacuum salesmen?" I snorted, drawing Az's gaze to me.

Az's eyes dragged over my body from head to toe, and he visibly cringed before stepping back into the room he shared with Joey. He shut the door, not hard enough to be considered a slam but hard enough to make a statement.

My upper lip curled, and my face twisted into a sneer as I flipped the door off. I didn't have the energy to deal with

Az's latest tantrum right now, but I wasn't going to just let it go. Joey shot me an apologetic look and moved to the nook to make sure Rich was fully awake, just as Leighton cleared his throat to make introductions.

"*Ma petit,* this is Phil," he started, gesturing toward a man in his mid-forties who wouldn't really stand out in a crowd. "And this other guy is a doctor."

I smiled at him as Leighton introduced us and extended my hand. "Nice to meet you Phil. Joey told me a little about you."

"High praise coming from the boss." Phil smiled, gently shaking my hand. "Between you and me, he's the one with his head on the straightest. The rest of them need a little work." He said in a not-so-subtle stage whisper. I liked him immediately.

"You're telling me. Maybe you can give me the number of your therapist and I can start leaving it around the house until they get the point." I grinned back at him.

"I'm not sure they're her type," he frowned. "But she can probably give them a referral."

I raised a brow, unsure of his implication, before my attention was drawn to Leighton and Joey as the dam broke, and they both burst into a fit of laughter. Rich was grumbling about being surrounded by smart-asses, and I felt like I'd walked into an inside joke I wasn't aware of. Before I could press them for an answer about what was so funny, the doctor cleared his throat.

"If we could move this along. I have other patients to see later today." The man awkwardly shifted his medical bag to his side. "Rich, if you would, I'd like to check your injuries over first and then we will deal with the lady."

"Excellent, I have time to finish my coffee before it gets cold," I mumbled to no one. I strolled back into the kitchen to give the doctor space to do his work. I could hear the murmur of Joey, Leighton, and Phil talking in the den and the soft, pained grunts from Rich as the doctor poked around on him. His wounds had healed up really well since being cleaned out, but the one on his gut was still a bit tender. I had to give the man his due; he rarely complained about it despite all he'd been through.

I'd finished my first cup and was rummaging in the cupboards for something quick to eat when Joey came to retrieve me.

"Doc figured you'd be more comfortable in your room. It's not ideal for a full check over, but he insisted you'd need full privacy." Joey said softly as he guided me to my room.

A clean white sheet had been thrown over my bed, and the doctor, whose name I still didn't know, stood just inside my room, waiting beside a dining room chair that had been moved for him. As soon as I stepped inside, he moved to shut the door in Joey's face and turned to me.

"I'm Doctor Nolan." He said gently. "I understand you need birth control, but I wanted to speak with you before we do anything. Is that alright?"

"I mean, sure." I replied, somewhat confused.

He motioned for me to take a seat on the bed and moved the chair to the end of the bed. I took my place at the end of the bed and waited for further instructions.

"I know the guys out there are paying me so you may not be comfortable being truthful with me, but I want to stress that if you are in danger, I *will* find a way to get you out of here."

I smiled softly at him, touched that he would put himself at risk if I were in some kind of danger... well, *more* danger than I've been in so far. I fought back the curve at the corners of my lips and drew my brows together.

"Well... yeah, I would say that I'm in danger."

Doctor Nolan was on his feet in a flash. He moved to my door and leaned his ear against it, listening for a moment before turning back to face me.

"I have enough medical supplies in my bag that, if you're comfortable, we can make it seem as if you're having a medical emergency and need a hospital immediately. Their man brought me here blindfolded, so I need him to get you out. I'm always prepared for something like this when these gangster sorts call me, so it should be no problem getting you out of this cabin. Once we have you in the hospital–"

I hopped off the bed and approached the ranting man

with my hands raised. "Woah, woah, woah there Doc! Take a deep breath, I was just messing with you a little. I might be in danger, but it's definitely not them. The guys out there are the reason I'm still alive. I didn't mean to send you on a spiral."

"You're sure?" He frowned, studying my face for any hint of deceit. "Like I said, I *will* get you out. You don't have to cover for them if you truly aren't safe here."

I thought of what would calm the doctor back down and felt the bright red flush stain my face. "Doc... uhm. You're here to give me birth control, right? I don't... think that... I mean, does that really scream 'in active danger' to you?"

Doctor Nolan let out a heavy breath. "It's not uncommon in these... situations for the woman to be forced against her will. But, if you're certain that you don't need me to get you out of here, I'll let the matter drop for now."

"I assure you, Doc, it's all consensual. We just had a bit of a scare, and now we need to make sure that we don't have to worry about that going forward."

"The elder Mr. Innocenti made me aware of the scare, as you put it." the doctor nodded, seeming to finally believe me as he led me to sit back on the bed. "He was rather insistent that we place an IUD today, but this is your choice. I brought several options with me. We can renew your shot, Mr. Dougherty informed me that was what you were currently on. I have a few months worth of Apri, which is a pill. I wouldn't recommend either as you have no idea how long you will be here, nor will I be able to provide you with a different type of pill if you react poorly to the Apri. I also have everything we need to place an IUD or the implant. While I cannot stress enough that what we do today is *your* choice, given your circumstances, I would recommend the implant."

I considered all of the choices he'd presented me and tried to keep my mind from wandering as to why Rich thought he had the right to tell the doctor what kind of birth control I would take at this point, but that was a subject for a different time.

"Is there a specific reason you'd recommend the implant over the IUD?"

"Is this really the environment you'd want me inserting something into your cervix?" The doctor deadpanned. "Look, I am happy to do whatever you choose. If you want a hysterectomy, I'll sort out how to get it done. But neither that or inserting an IUD in a cabin that can't exactly be properly sterilized is something I'd recommend."

The way he said it made my question seem silly once he'd answered it.

"Alright. Well, I don't want to run the risk of running out and being unable to get more… So let's go with the implant. If I want to revisit the other options, can I look you up once we get back to civilization?"

"I'll leave you my card before I go." He smiled, patting my knee gently. "Lay back on the bed, and if you have a preferred arm, stretch that out a bit above your head."

I did as he asked and nodded along as he explained the process, potential side effects, and healing complications. He was very thorough in his explanation and made sure he left space for me to ask any questions.

"Alright, you're going to feel a pinch, but otherwise, it shouldn't be very painful. If it is, let me know. And it will take a little getting used to afterward, but soon it should be something your brain just ignores." He said as he leaned over me. He turned my head away before he gripped my arm. I started to ask him why, but it was cut off by a groan as I felt the pinch in the sensitive skin of my underarm. Then I remembered it had always been obvious that 'pinch' meant something entirely different to doctors than the rest of the population.

"That does it. You're all set." He said after putting a bandage on the injection site.

"I appreciate it, Doc." I wiggled my arm as I sat up and smiled at him. He gathered up his things and handed me his card before moving to the door.

"Now, if you need anything or experience any complications I named, please give me a call." He reached to open the door, and as he did, he turned to look at me over his shoulder. "And as a reminder, that will take a few weeks to be fully effective. Make sure you have a backup form of contraceptive to prevent any more 'scares'."

He opened the door and jumped back as Leighton tumbled to the ground in front of him, apparently leaning so hard on the door to hear that when it moved, he couldn't catch himself.

"No worries about that, Doc. We're all set!" Leighton beamed up at the other man from the floor.

"Leighton! Really?!" I yelled and threw a nearby pillow at him. "We're gonna have to work on our boundaries!"

To his credit, Doctor Nolan simply shook his head and stepped over Leighton, leaving us alone in my room.

"I mean, the guys and I talked about it and we're all okay with the sharing, so I'm not really sure what you mean about boundaries *ma petit*." Leighton said, lifting himself up from the floor before launching himself at my bed.

"My boundaries, Leighton! Just because you guys all had a little kumbaya session and decided you don't mind passing me around, doesn't mean that you get to go stomping around on *my* boundaries!" I yelled.

"It's just the doctor," Leighton replied. "He kinda *needs* to know you're having safe sex. That's like his whole job. And I wouldn't really call it a kumbaya session, we had to make sure all the daddies were on the same page. Even Rich, who's dumber than me and won't admit he wanted to be the daddy."

I stared at him and very seriously considered how difficult it would be to remove his head from his shoulders. Then I remembered *who* I was looking at and stomped over to my door and opened it.

"Get out, Leighton," I said softly.

"Aww, come on baby momma. I'm just trying to make sure we're one, big happy family." He pouted, pushing himself up on his elbow where he'd landed earlier on my bed.

"You know what, fuck it. Make yourself comfortable." I paused as I noticed him light up and grin at me. "Stay as long as you want. *I'll* leave."

I stepped out into the den and slammed my bedroom door. A couple of pairs of eyes turned to look at me. I heard the start of Rich saying something before I decided I needed more space and stomped through the den, opened the door to let myself onto the porch, and slammed that one behind me, too.

I heard Rich's muffled yell from behind me, asking Leighton what the fuck he did as I stormed around to the back of the cabin where the bags were set up. I picked up a rock, moved away from the house, and drew my arm back.

"Men. Are. So. FUCKING STUPID!" I yelled, launching the rock toward the tree that held our training bags as hard as possible.

A second later, I heard a yelp of surprise and pain followed by Az's voice. "What the fuck?" he bellowed. "LEIGHTON you better not have been aiming for me with that rock, asshole!"

I heard the faint "Not it!" coming from my room where I'd left Leighton. I started to apologize because I hadn't seen him standing there until he turned around to look at me. The way his whole body flinched away from me with a nearly disdained look made the apology on my lips twist into unbridled rage.

"You!" I said, pointing at him as I started stalking toward him. His eyes were wide as he looked all around me as if he was looking for an exit from the situation. "Don't you even *think* of running off, you fucking coward."

At that, his wide eyes narrowed on me, and he crossed his arms over his chest. "What the fuck did you just call me, Victoria?"

"You fucking heard me, but let me say it a little slower so you don't miss it. *Coward.*" I formed the syllables so slowly it was almost painful to say, glaring at him the whole time. "You've been avoiding me since yesterday; looking at me like the sight of me causes you physical pain. And that was after you made a whole speech during yesterday's scare that sums up exactly what you think about having any kind of future with me."

His stern glare softened slightly, but he didn't say anything.

"I am so beyond over this hot and cold bullshit with you,

Az! You promised we were going to do better about talking. You *promised* you were going to stop running from me and look at you. You barely made it a week, and you're already doing it again! I realize that the news was shocking, but if it was that fucking painful to consider, then what is it that you fucking want from me?!" I don't know when I started screaming, but I didn't feel inclined to stop.

"This isn't about us." He shot back. "I fucking *murder* people for a god damned living, Victoria. Is that the sort of man you really want to raise a child with?"

"Do you think that fact was something that was lost on me while I was standing in the bathroom, staring at the fucking test for three solid minutes of silence and waiting to see what comes next?! Az, I *know* what the fuck you all do." I scrubbed my hand through my hair in irritation. "For fuck's sake. I fucked Joey in the woods, on the ground, after he *beat a man with a golf club and slit his throat*. And you know what?! Your hands aren't the only ones dirty here. I *murdered* a man to save your life, you fucking IDIOT!" My throat was starting to hurt, but none of the words were coming out at normal volume. I just couldn't make them.

Az stalked toward me, tension radiating from his body, until he'd crowded me back against the side of the cabin. Bending his head down until our noses nearly touched, he spoke, his voice barely above a whisper.

"I know I allowed you to end up in a position that you had to *destroy* yourself to save my worthless life. I can hear your screaming every night when your guilt over it creeps into your dreams. And there's not a damned thing I can do to change any of it."

There was something so earnest in his words the screaming anger seemed to bleed out of me. Left in its wake was the sting of pain, knowing that he'd recoiled so hard from the idea, even though part of me knew it wasn't all about who it might have been with.

"I'd do it a hundred times over, you know that, right? I wouldn't change anything because the alternatives mean that you wouldn't be here for me to be angry at. I'd rather be at your throat than at your funeral," I whispered.

Az angrily slammed the side of his fist against the cabin wall before rearing back and scrubbing a hand over his face. "You shouldn't have to make that fucking choice, Victoria. You should be running galas and happily ignorant about the world the five of us live in. You're too good for any of us, but especially me. You *deserve* someone that leaves no doubts in your mind that you and any kid you decide to have are safe."

I felt the tears prick at the corners of my eyes and tried desperately to blink them away. It felt like he was about to break up with me, and I hadn't even figured out what we were yet.

"If I were a better man, I'd send you on your way the moment we get rid of whoever put you in this mess to begin with. But I'm not a good fucking man. I'm hot-headed and selfish, and I can't stand the thought of anyone outside of this cabin claiming you as theirs, even if it means they can give you what we can't."

"You keep saying all these things about what I should have and what I deserve, but isn't it my choice? Who I choose to figure out all of life's bullshit with isn't something that you get to decide for me based on what you think I need. Have you even stopped for a second to consider what I actually want?" I demanded.

"Of course, I fucking have!" Az shouted. "God damn it, Victoria, I've thought about every second of every day since I realized *you* weren't pulling the strings. I can't *not* think about it, and worry if you're going to wake up one day and realize you should run very far and very fast in the opposite direction of us because I fucking *love you,* damn it!"

The moment the words left his mouth, he pulled back just enough for me to see the stunned expression on his face. It likely mirrored the one on my face as we settled into a stunned silence.

"If..." I paused and wet my lips, uncertain of quite how to continue. "I'll understand if you didn't mean that... so if you want to take it back, you can."

Az looked at me momentarily as if I'd grown a second

head. "Of all the things between us I wish I could take back, telling you I love you isn't anywhere on that list. Though I'll admit, the timing is pretty shit."

I couldn't help it when a smile split across my face, and I started laughing. It felt good as it bubbled up from my chest.

"I feel like that's become one of our relationship's defining traits. Shit timing." I chuckled, and Az let out a bark of laughter before we both leaned against the side of the cabin, giggling and trying to catch our breath.

"Yeah, you're right. Our meet cute was a fucking fire," he snorted.

"Should have been a sign. But if you're happy with our dumpster fire, so am I." I grinned.

Az leaned his head against the side of the cabin and slipped his hand down to take mine. "Let me know if you still feel that way when we're fighting again in a couple weeks."

Lacing my fingers through his, I squeezed gently. "You know I don't think I want to hear you call your life worthless anymore. I don't take too kindly to people talking about the man I love like that. We still need to talk about how you reacted to the pregnancy scare though. That was not okay."

"I know." he sighed, gently squeezing my hand back. "That was an entirely me thing. I just need some time to sort my shit out."

"I understand, and I appreciate you talking to me." I said softly, burrowing my face into his neck. "And the next time we're standing in the backyard screaming at each other, just remember that I *do* love you despite the fact that you're such a pain in the ass. Alright, babe?"

"Nope, don't like that. It's Sir or nothing," Az chuckled as he leaned down and kissed my lips softly.

"Yes *Sir*," I snickered. "Fucking Az-hole."

CHAPTER TWENTY

Victoria

The sound of the front door broke the spell we'd fallen under. Az gave my hand another gentle squeeze and pushed off the side of the cabin.

"Why don't you head inside and find something to eat. I'm sure Craig is up by now and cooking. I need to speak with Phil and see them off." He smiled softly.

The mention of Craig was like an arrow straight through our happy little bubble, bursting it around me and allowing all the irritation from the night before to come rushing back in. As if sensing the sudden shift in my mood, Az glanced at me, the corners of his lips pulled down slightly.

"Hey, don't be too hard on him, okay? Craig was just doing what he does best to try and make sure we can keep you safe. That shit he found about Benson, it hit him harder than he let on."

"When did you become so insightful, Mister Miyagi?" I snorted.

"If you haven't noticed, I'm actually a pretty sharp guy. Until a certain irritating princess gets in my head and makes me crazy." He laughed. "Seriously though, I know you're used to Craig running to you with every little thing like the lovesick pup he is, but when he gets a lead on something, he doesn't stop to think. He just latches on like a dog with a bone until he's got everything he can find."

"Two dog references in one go? I'm not sure that's a really flattering comparison."

"Well, they don't call him the 'Bloodhound' in his weird

tech circles for nothing." Az shrugged as we turned the corner of the cabin and moved toward the porch.

"Alright, well..." I considered my words as we stopped at the porch and squeezed his hand before letting it go. "I promise not to hit him in the head with a rock before we start arguing, how about that?" I chuckled and planted a quick kiss on the corner of his lips. "Go tend to your stuff."

"How about you just don't throw any more rocks, period." He snickered as his hand moved to my back, and he gently pushed me toward the door. "I'll be inside in a bit; go get something to eat before you hulk out on everyone else because you're hangry."

Phil and Doctor Nolan were standing to the side of the door as Az motioned for me to continue inside. The Doctor, to his credit, raised an eyebrow in question as if to ask if I were sure I was okay and remained silent. I gave him a slight smile and nodded my farewells as I moved past the men into the house. Phil, however, barked out a laugh, and I could swear I heard him ask Az if he just wasn't man enough to handle a hangry woman as the door closed behind me. Shaking my head, I made my way back to the kitchen in search of food.

Craig wasn't in his usual morning spot at the stove. Part of me was disappointed. I'd gotten used to seeing him cooking breakfast for everyone daily. The thought alone made my stomach growl, demanding to be filled, and I silently cursed the bastard for all but training me to expect a five-star restaurant meal in the morning. My rumbling stomach only seemed to make me angrier at him as I ripped open the cupboards to find something to eat.

Ripping open each cabinet, I became increasingly frustrated as I found nothing more than ingredients for various meals. I was ready to find a rock to throw at Craig for not including anything quick and self-serve on the grocery runs when I finally came across a ten-pack of mini-cereal boxes. The sugary marshmallow cereal wasn't to my taste, but I was starving, and it would have to do.

"Thank God for Leighton's childish taste in food," I mumbled to myself as I tore open the pack and snagged two of the mini boxes to pour into a bowl.

I ate quickly, some of my anger subsiding alongside my hunger. By the time I'd finished and rinsed my bowl in the sink, I was a little annoyed that Az was right about me being hangry, even if I'd go to my grave without telling him he was right. Craig still hadn't made his way to the kitchen, and I was starting to get a little worried about him. Deciding I should deal with the lingering hurt and anger from his digging, I made my way to the room he shared with Leighton.

My mind bounced between being angry and worried. It wasn't like him to not have come out of his room yet, and I couldn't help but wonder if he was alright in there. I paused outside the door, wondering if I should knock in case he was still sleeping, when I heard the soft clacking of keys on his keyboard.

"Craig, I think we should talk about–" I started as I pushed open the door, only to see Craig jump so hard that he almost slid out of his chair.

"*Jesus*, Bunny! Don't sneak up on a man while he's working. That's a good way to get shot in our line of business." Craig yelped as he righted himself. I raised an eyebrow at him suspiciously as I moved into the room.

"What's got you so focused over there? I hope you're not doing what I think you're doing..." I trailed off, closing the distance between us and craning my head so I could see around him at his laptop screen. I caught enough of the title to send my temper through the roof again before he slammed his laptop shut.

"Bunny–" Craig started as he eyed me carefully.

"Are you fucking *serious*, Craig?! You haven't done enough at this point?" I crossed my arms over my chest and narrowed my eyes as I pinned my glare on him.

"Before you run off with your assumptions, maybe–" He started again, moving toward me slowly with his hands raised.

"First, you dig up my shit with Benson and lay it out for everyone to see without talking to me about it first, and *then*, you decide to announce to the house that I need more birth control *again* without talking to me first. What now? Maybe you could just save time and print out your bullshit tabloid article and hang it in the den where everyone can read it!" I found my voice starting to rise again. Part of my brain, somewhere in the back, had the passing thought that I was never a yeller until these men decided to walk into my life and stomp on every single one of my nerves. "Here's a headline for you, in case you fucking missed it. Benson Prescott spotted with bombshell blonde at Avante Bella having a cozy dinner. Has he finally ditched the Bristol Heiress? Spoiler alert, it was me that dropped his ass, and the blonde was his cousin Dahlia! So, before you go announcing the trash to the world, maybe it's good to remember that you shouldn't believe everything you read on the internet."

Craig looked at me with an impassive expression before backing up to his desk again and opening his laptop. He pointed at a man's picture that struck my brain as vaguely familiar and sighed.

"This guy, Bunny. I was looking for information about him. He's related to Benson and mentioned in the article." He deadpanned. "I couldn't care less about what the rest of the article has to say, I just needed what was relevant to Trey."

I felt my anger deflate as if it was a balloon that Craig had stuck a needle in. My arms fell to my sides, and I couldn't think of what to say, so I just stood there looking between Craig and his laptop. Almost as infuriating as his actions was his calm demeanor and steadfast logic. I opened my mouth, closed it, tried again, and still nothing.

Okay, fine, maybe this wasn't all that bad. But I'd had stuff to talk with him about before I even came in here, so...

"My point still stands!" I snapped, putting my hands on my hips. "Even without this stupid tabloid article. You still put my information out to the rest of the group without even talking to me. You went digging into my past without telling me you were doing it!"

I found my footing again as I continued on. Craig's shoulders dropped, and he put his hands in his pockets and looked at me as if he were merely waiting for me to continue.

"Of everyone in the house, do you have any idea how blind-sided I was to find out that the largest invasion of my privacy that's happened to date came from *you*?! I could have handled it from almost *anyone* else!" I wanted to yell about it, but as I kept talking, my voice started to return to a normal volume. Looking at him patiently waiting as I ranted was quickly taking the wind out of my sails a second time. Why the fuck was it so hard to stay mad at him. "Why are you so fucking calm all the time? I came in here ready to fight about this."

"Bunny... If you want to fight, go do it with Az." He said simply. "I'm happy to *discuss* things with you, but if you want to fight, you'll have to do it with someone else because I don't do that."

I stared at him for what felt like a ridiculously long time, unable to produce a response to that. "What kind of gangster doesn't fight about stuff?" I snarked eventually. It felt lame even to me as it came out.

The corner of his lips quirked slightly, but his passive expression didn't shift. "You know why, Bunny. But don't mistake the fact that I won't argue with *you* for the fact that I can't do what needs to be done when it comes to my job. And don't mistake my job for who I am, I told you once... We weren't always gangsters."

I fell into a stunned silence again, feeling all of the pent-up frustrations and emotions just seep away from me and be replaced by guilt. I shifted my weight from one foot to another, trying to figure out where to go from here, knowing I'd fully put my foot in my mouth.

"I'm sorry, Craig... I didn't even think about... I really came in here acting like an Az-hole." I said with a heavy sigh.

"It's really okay, Bunny. Honestly, I should have told you

I was digging, and I'm sure not feeding you this morning probably added to your irritation with me." He replied with a slight smirk.

"It definitely didn't help," I responded with a mock sneer. "I ended up reduced to eating a single serving box of children's cereal I found in the back of the cabinet."

Craig's smirk deepened slightly, and he moved toward me, pulling his hands from his pockets to place them gently on my shoulders. "I can't promise you that more things about you you'd prefer we didn't dig into won't come up while I'm doing my job, Bunny." I opened my mouth to interrupt, and he narrowed his eyes at me. "But I can promise that I will come to you with anything that I find *before* I discuss it with the guys. We can decide together what's actually important and relevant for them to know so we can keep you safe, as long as you agree to accept it if I say that something you'd prefer to keep to yourself is absolutely necessary to share to keep you safe. Deal?"

I pursed my lips, considering whether or not to accept the deal Craig was offering.

"How about this? Why don't I tell you what I was looking for specifically just now and what I've found so far? You'll be the first one in the house other than me with that information." Craig offered.

"Okay, sure. That sounds…. fair." I replied, allowing him to guide me to sit on the side of one of the beds.

Craig slid his computer chair over in front of me and sat down with his open laptop facing me.

"This guy," he started, tapping on the man he'd pointed out earlier. "Is Trey Prescott."

"I know, he's Benson's uncle and Dahlia's father. I've never met him myself, but Dahlia and I got along well enough I heard a lot about him. Typical upper-class father, too busy for their kid." I spoke. "Kind of a miracle Dahlia turned out as sweet as she is."

"Well, that could be because he's involved with

the Jackals. That's what this tattoo means, Bunny." Craig continued, pointing out the red spider lily tattoo barely visible above the collar of Trey's shirt.

"How do you know? What if he just likes spider lilies, or it has some other significance?"

"Well... Sure, I suppose there could be a chance of that. But it's not just the fact that it's the spider lily; it's in the color and composition of the tattoo as well. All of them have the exact same tattoo, it's how we identify each other." He answered before turning his head to the side and gesturing to a stylized moth tattoo that was a carbon copy of the one on Az's hand. "We all have this one, the Acherontia Atropos... though most people know it by its more common name African Death's-head Hawkmoth. Every man in our ranks gets one once they move from Associate to ranked Soldier."

"And everyone's looks like yours and Az's?" I asked curiously.

"Exactly like them." He replied. "All of our men go to Joey or Az for them, they're actually really good artists."

"I've... never seen them do one the whole time we've been around each other."

"You haven't really met any of our men, either." Craig shrugged. "And we don't let just anyone become a made man in our ranks. Any more questions, or are you ready for me to continue?"

I thought for a moment before I nodded and made a motion for him to continue, satisfied with his answers.

"So, as I was saying. I noticed the tattoo in a company photo and started putting the pieces together to dig further into Trey. From what I can find, his Jackal tattoo got an upgrade about thirteen months ago." Craig pulled up a second photo, doing something on his laptop so the two images of Trey were side by side. "There's more petals in this one, which for these bastards, means a promotion. But the weird thing is he went from Soldier to more petals than their Capos, which means he did something big."

I couldn't help the twinge of sadness that passed over me. Thirteen months didn't mean anything to me, but it was a reminder that my mother had been gone for over fifteen months now.

"You okay, Bunny?" Craig asked, noticing the shift.

"Yeah, just having a moment. It's silly, but hearing you say thirteen months made me think about losing my mom a couple months before whatever *this* means." I answered, waving my hand at the images on his laptop.

Craig sat his laptop on the bed beside me and leaned forward, pulling me into a hug. "I'm sorry, Bunny. Prudence was a wonderful lady; I can't imagine how hard it must have been for you to lose her. You know I'm here if you ever want to talk about it."

I leaned into his hold, taking a deep breath as I considered his words. My father had all but vanished on me after mom died; Tiffany had thought partying to keep my mind off of it was the solution, and I just realized nobody had ever actually asked me if I wanted to talk about losing her.

"That would be nice, actually." I started. "But we can talk about it later if there's more about this stuff with Trey you need to cover."

He leaned back and touched my face softly, gently rubbing his thumb across my cheek. "What I need to do is be here for you." he said, closing his laptop and pushing it away as if to make a point. "Those things can wait until later, you're my priority here."

I puffed out a breath and frowned. "There's not really much to tell. Pretty much everything the police could find was shared on the news. Mom stayed a little late at the center, Dad couldn't get out of some client dinner in time to pick her up, and some stranger saw an obviously wealthy woman and... it was a mugging gone wrong." I started. "They never found the guy. None of us ever thought something like that could happen to *her* even in Southside. Not with how loved she was there, ya know. But it did. For a while I was angry with Dahlia over it."

"Dahlia?" Craig asked.

"Yeah, Benson's cousin. The daughter of the guy you've been looking into."

"Right, I'm just not totally sure I'm understanding what she has to do with what happened to your mom."

"Oh, well she had called earlier in the day to see if mom could stay a little late for her to bring by a donation check. She never showed though, and I may have somewhat blamed her for mom even being in Southside when the mugging happened." The words started to pour from me as I spoke. It was like having someone to talk to about my mother's death was all I needed for the dam to break. "I did run into her about a month or so before the gala. Turned out while I was busy blaming her, she was also busy blaming herself because her car wouldn't start, and her father refused to let her take his to meet my mom. Blamed her driving record and made her call a mechanic, which is no small feat for someone in our circles. By the time she found someone to come out, the news of my mother's attack was already plastered on every news station in Sacona."

"I can't imagine how guilty she must have felt." Craig offered.

"I know," I sighed. "And I'm just the asshole that avoided her because I blamed her for something she had no control over. She wasn't the one that cornered my mom near that alley and then stabbed her to death over some jewelry and cash."

"At the risk of making you mad at me again, I have to tell you, I dug into the coroner's report. We didn't know you then, but we knew Prudence and all five of us wanted to find the guy that did that to her and put a bullet between his eyes. More, but I don't know if you want the graphic details of what we had planned if we'd been able to find anything to lead us to him."

It took me a second to put together why he was bringing up something he'd done before he met me before it dawned on me that he was being honest about it because I'd come in here ready to fight about his digging. I nodded, and when I turned my gaze to him, I blinked several times, realizing my vision had gone blurry from unshed tears during my rambling.

Wiping the few that fell away from my face, I sucked in a deep, steadying breath. "I appreciate you letting me know. I know how tied to the center you guys were; it honestly would have been more surprising if you'd said you *didn't* look into it." I rolled my shoulders to release some of the tension that had built there. "Would it be alright if I said I want to... move on to something else? I really don't want to dwell there anymore."

"Of course, Bunny." He said gently, running his hand over my hair in that soothing way of his. We sat there for a moment in silence, not sure how to shift the topic to something else, when he perked up suddenly. "You know what I realized not long ago?"

"What's that?"

"It's spooky season! Literally the best time of the year. I know that you're used to going to a fully loaded Halloween party, and it sucks we can't do that for you, but we can do the next best thing!" He beamed, a huge grin splitting his face, making him look so adorably excited.

It was infectious, and I couldn't help but feel myself getting excited. "What's the next best thing?"

"Go grab everyone else and meet me in the den. You'll see!" He jumped up and pulled me to my feet before planting a quick kiss on the corner of my mouth and sped from the room, leaving the door open behind him.

CHAPTER TWENTY ONE

Rich

Between Victoria's screeching at Az and then Craig, and the ache in my gut from the doc poking and prodding at my surgical incision, I needed an Advil. And probably a shot. I was on my way to the bathroom to raid the medicine cabinet when I heard her scream Leighton's name. Pinching the bridge of my nose, I slowed to a stop just outside of her bedroom, catching sight of Leighton attempting to build some sort of structure on her bed with boxes of condoms.

"What? You told me I could stay here, so I did." Leighton frowned, his hands working to keep his condom house together.

"Could you two keep whatever this is, down?" I grumbled, startling both of them and causing Leighton to scowl as the boxes tumbled off the end of Victoria's bed. "All of this yelling is giving me a migraine."

"Don't worry, Boss. As soon as you dislodge your head from your ass, she'll be yelling at you too." Leighton said with a wide grin.

"No thanks." I deadpanned. "Just keep the shit down. The rest of us shouldn't have to suffer because you and Az can't keep yourselves from pissing the Princess off."

"I'm right here, ya know." Victoria scowled. "And I actually didn't come in here to fight with Leighton. I was grabbing him, the others, even *you*, because Craig asked me to get everyone to the den."

I raised an eyebrow and looked her over for any indication of what Craig could want. "Did he find something we need to know about?"

"Is this gonna start another fight between everyone?"

Leighton groaned.

"No and no. He said it was something fun. Not that you'd know much about that, *daddy.*" Victoria said as she rolled her eyes.

"Well, he might not... but I know a thing or two about having fun." Leighton drawled, waggling his eyebrows at Victoria.

"And on that note, I'm out." I scowled. "I'll meet you in the den."

I turned on my heel and stalked off to the bathroom, flexing my fist that had been clenched at my side when she rolled her eyes at me. Something about her sass went straight through me; it was all I could do to keep my hands to myself. However, the mental images of bending her over my knee and making her pay for every sarcastic remark or gesture were as enjoyable as they were painful.

I grabbed a couple of Advil, tossed them in my mouth, and washed them down by drinking from the faucet. The sink bowl was too tiny for me to do it comfortably, but I didn't feel like tracking down a pack of disposable cups that should have been in here. I hoped it kicked in before whatever Craig had planned started, but whatever it was would likely be more entertaining than what I'd been doing for the last month while everyone fussed over me as if I was still on my deathbed.

I would be glad when we got the fuck out of this cabin, I mused as I moved back through the den to take a spot on the loveseat further away from the couch. If I had my guess, the four stooges would end up fighting over who sat on the sofa with the Princess. I was mostly healed up, but my gut wound definitely wasn't in a state to be anywhere near all that. One cheap shot and I'd be out for the count and likely be sent back to bed willingly, or they'd carry me if I fought them about it.

The idea of Victoria fussing about and mother-henning me, all worried and considerate, played in my head and almost made me want to move seats. It was endearing, and I'd go to my grave before I ever said out loud that I rather enjoyed the attention. But, it was also infuriating and got under my skin in a way so few people in my life ever had.

And sure enough, the quiet of the den was short-lived as Victoria, Joey, Leighton, and Az all made their way into the room. The three guys were already squabbling about who would sit where. Joey and Leighton started scrambling over each other to get to the couch first, with Joey barely planting himself on one of the cushions before Leighton. Az slipped onto the other side, pulled Victoria down on the center cushion, and tucked her into his side. He murmured something in her ear that made her laugh, and they both shook their heads at the other two men.

Leighton stood up and turned around as if he would sit on the other side, only to narrow his eyes at Az, who had already claimed the spot and was snuggling with the Princess.

"Really?" Leighton whined.

"These pants are Armani. Sure as fuck not sitting on the floor." Az said, shrugging nonchalantly.

"Fine, fuck it. You guys win this time." Leighton said before making the most ungraceful climb I've ever seen from him to move behind Victoria and sit on the back of the couch behind her.

I rolled my eyes before I leaned my head back and closed. I really wanted to be happy for them, all of them... but something about the entire scene struck an irritable nerve with me, and I didn't want to look at it anymore.

The distinctive smell of popcorn filled the cabin a few moments later. We all looked toward the kitchen area as Craig emerged with two large mixing bowls filled to the brim with popped kernels.

He handed one to me, the other to Victoria, and grabbed the remote off the coffee table before sitting on the floor without putting up near the fuss the other two had made.

"Just gonna give up and sit on the floor? Tsk Tsk, Craigy boy." Leighton said in his lighthearted, mocking tone.

Craig barely turned his head before a smirk split across his face. "Why would I fight it? I'm the only one of us that's between her legs right now."

"Craig!" Victoria squealed before playfully swatting him on the head while Leighton sputtered on the fistful of popcorn he'd eaten. Joey reached down to fist-bump Craig while Az patted Leighton on the shoulder to keep him from choking.

I shook my head and cleared my throat loudly. "So... What's the plan, Craig?"

"Right! Well, it's the best time of the year, and since we're stuck here for now, I just thought..." He trailed off as he hit the button on the remote, and the TV sprang to life to display the 'Halloween' movie menu. "What better way to ring in the season than a horror movie marathon! Starting off, of course, with Halloween!"

"Hell yeah!" Joey exclaimed. "Let's watch some gratuitous violence to celebrate the spooky season."

After a round of agreement, Victoria and Az were less enthusiastic than the others. He hit play, and we all settled in for the marathon.

I wish I could say that I'd enjoyed it, I really do. I *tried* to pay attention and watch the movies. But I couldn't keep my attention on the screen. As it turned out, the Princess wasn't too keen on horror, and she made it everyone's problem. Between all her shifting, screaming, whining, and squealing, it was challenging to pay attention to anything but her. But, it was more problematic when the comforting, cuddling, whispering, and canoodling started to calm her down. After the third movie, it was all I could do to not excuse myself.

"I don't know if the Princess is going to be able to get through another one of these without passing out," I grumbled as the most recent flick rolled credits. "Doesn't seem she's got the stomach for it."

"Oh! I have an idea," Leighton chirped. "Lemme just..." He grunted as he clumsily untangled himself from where he was jammed between Victoria and the couch. When he'd finally freed most of his body, he yelped as he promptly fell off the back of the sofa to the floor.

"You good?" Az asked, with not a single hint of concern in his voice.

"Totally intentional," Leighton said as he popped up from the floor, moved around us to where the movies were stacked, and started sorting through the small library until he'd found what he wanted. He was visibly giddy as he put the disc in the player and returned to the couch. Leighton unceremoniously crammed himself back behind Victoria, nearly kicking Joey in the head in the process. Az reached out slowly as he shifted to get comfortable and flicked him in the ear.

"What the fuck, bro?" Leighton barked, rubbing the side of his head.

"Nothing." Az shrugged. "Start the movie, Craig."

"Fucking Az-hole..." Leighton muttered as Craig pressed play. As soon as the menu popped up, Craig groaned loudly and sat back hard enough to make a thunk on the bottom of the couch.

"Really, Leighton? You're gonna make me sit through this a second time? Once wasn't enough for you?" Craig said, heaving a long, suffering sigh.

"The theme is horror night and *ma petit* is getting scared. I figured 'so bad it's horrifying' would fit the theme." Leighton chuckled.

"Raptor Pastor?" Az said, clearly confused. "Is there a t-rex? Because I love a good T-rex. Just call me Az-asaurus." he followed his words up with a poor imitation of a dinosaur screech.

"Immediately no." Joey deadpanned. "You're stuck with Az-hole for life now. Nothing else."

We all agreed vehemently that his nickname was what it was, and he should just accept it, while Victoria sat in stunned, wide-eyed silence as she stared at him.

"What... What the actual fuck was the sound that came out of your mouth?" She said when she seemed to find her voice again.

"A dinosaur sound, duh." Az chuckled. "It's not my fault you never asked me about my favorite dinosaur before now to realize I'm an absolute dino-nerd."

"No, no, it was not. That sounded like a cat that was dying after having been hit by a truck." She retorted.

"Whatever," He shrugged. "Gonna play the movie or what, Craig?"

"I know you've only seen the nerd out to play when we have DnD sessions, but don't get it twisted. He's fully just a nerd." Craig offered with a laugh as he hit play on the movie and settled back between Victoria's legs.

"Fucking nerds with guns..." Victoria muttered quietly with a giggle as the opening credits played. There was a roll of chuckles from the couch before the den went quiet.

What followed after Craig hit play was one of the most ridiculous and painful excuses for a movie I'd ever seen. And I'd sat through Avalanche Sharks, so that was saying something. After a while, I was very close to just going for a walk, considering that would be better time spent than what I was currently being subjected to.

"Guys, listen... I know you put this on for me because the other ones were scary, but... I can't do this. This is fucking painful. It's just *so bad*." Victoria finally said. "It's only been 20 minutes, and I feel like I want to go make a bleach smoothie and put myself out of my misery."

"Thank fucking god someone else was feeling it. I was seriously considering whether or not it would be worth it to shoot the TV to get out of this." Az added, sounding fully relieved.

"It's not *that* bad, guys!" Leighton whined. "It's funny!"

"Yeah, Leighton... about as funny as watching a sack full of kittens drown." Joey groaned, scrubbing his hand over his face.

I chuckled a little at the dramatic way everyone disagreed with the idea of continuing the film that Leighton had picked. I agreed, but I almost felt bad for the little psycho being in that corner all by himself.

"I mean, I'll give you that it's bad. I'm going to be adding it to my list of potential torture methods for future use. But what else is there to do out here?" I offered with a shrug.

"Besides fuck." Joey said, a mean little smirk pasted on his face as he looked at me. Little shit.

"Joey!" Victoria chirped and slapped him on the shoulder, almost mirroring her response to Craig earlier. "You two are supposed to be my mature ones. What's gotten into you guys?"

Leighton wrapped his arms around her from behind and placed his chin on her shoulder. "Pretty sure they're trying to make a point to the guy who hasn't gotten into *you* even though he wants it real, real bad."

"*Leighton!*" Victoria yelped, starting to squirm to get away from him.

"That's not what's going on here," I grunted, cutting her off from scolding him further. I realized that was a mistake when her head whipped in my direction, and her eyes narrowed on me.

"Right, and all those things you said, calling me Babygirl when you came and got me from the Spotted Cobra, telling me I was a 'good girl for daddy' before we had to call you a doctor. None of that means fuck all." Victoria said with a derisive snort.

I bit the inside of my cheek hard to keep myself quiet as I stood from the loveseat. "I'm not doing this with you here, *Princess*." I sneered. "Don't think I'm going to bend just because you got yourself all worked up in knots." I moved away from the living area and toward the front door. I would not fight with her in front of the whole house.

There was a soft oomph behind me just before Victoria stormed past me to block my path. "I think not. It's time we had this shit out, Bossy pants. You're almost as bad as Az with this hot and cold bullshit. You told me you'd been dreaming of having me to yourself for ages and then just what? Changed your mind? Decided I wasn't worth your time since the other's want to share?" Her voice raised in volume as she spoke, and her tiny hand slammed against my chest in an attempt to push me back. "What is your fucking problem anyway?"

The irritated groan I'd wanted to make came out of my chest like a growl as I stared her down, causing her to pull her hand back. "Currently, little girl, my problem is that you are in my way. I *will not* be having this conversation here. Now move, or be moved." I raised an eyebrow at her and looked at the door.

"Fucking try me, Rich." She hissed. "We are going to talk about this."

I grinned meanly at her and shrugged. "Have it your way, *Your Highness*." I said before putting my hands under her arms and lifting, biting the inside of my cheek again because it made my still healing wound feel strained, and setting her down to the side of the door. "I told you, move or be moved." I opened the door and stepped out onto the porch. I knew she'd follow me, but I sure as fuck wasn't about to fight with her in the den.

"Are you *seriously* walking away from me right now?" She screeched before I heard her footsteps stomp onto the porch behind me. "I will never understand you. You say all these things. Things that make me think... maybe. And then you, what, pretend I don't exist because you don't like the idea of sharing your toys? Which I'm not, by the way. I'm a fucking person with real feelings that you keep stomping all over."

I gripped the railing on the edge of the porch and stared at my hands. I was entirely at war with myself while Victoria went off behind me, throwing my numerous missteps with her at my back as if they were bullets. Fuck, might as well have been for how much they stung. I wanted to grab her by the shoulders and shake her, break down and tell her everything, put her over my fucking knee and spank her for her fucking attitude, and run as far from her as my legs would carry me. When the fuck did everything get so complicated? It would have been so much easier if she'd just stick to the others and leave me the fuck alone.

"Rich! Fucking answer me!" She screeched. My headache was coming back.

"What the fuck do you want from me, Victoria?!" I roared, whirling on her. She jumped slightly and took a step back. I sneered and started approaching slowly, crowding in her space. "What are you expecting, huh?" Tilting my head slightly as I stared down at her. I'd almost forgotten how small she was after having spent so long laid up. This was the last way I wanted her to look up at me, but it was necessary for all of us.

"Are you expecting to come out here, yell at me for a while, and have me confess my undying love to you? Are you expecting this to devolve into some whirlwind passion born out of frustration?" A cruel laugh escaped my throat. "If that's what you're looking for, then go read a fucking book."

I could see her lips quiver as she backed up until her back hit the wall, but I knew if I let up, she'd just come out swinging. The Princess was persistent if she was anything.

"These ideas you have floating around in your head? They're daydreams, little girl. They're fairy tales you're telling yourself. You don't even *know* me. Matter of fact, what do you *know* about any of us? We've been subjected to your presence for all of three months or so, and in that time, we've come closer to death than we have the entire time I've run this fucking organization. So, I'll ask you again, *Princess*," I spit the word out like a curse. "What. The. Fuck. Do. You. Want?"

She stood there staring up at me with confusion, pain, and anger painting her beautiful features, and it broke my heart to watch her curl in on herself with every word I said. I waited a moment to see if she had anything to say, and when she didn't, my heart hit my stomach. I hadn't done enough. Fuck. Somewhere inside my mind, I could hear a part of myself screaming at me to stop. At this point, I was just being cruel for the sake of it, to push her away, and it wasn't fair. But that's life. It's not fair.

"Princess, you might have gotten every other member of this house to forget the fact that you were a job to us. But I haven't." I snapped before stepping away and turning my back on her. "Go back in the house, and leave me the fuck alone."

I couldn't look back, staring out at the wooded land just beyond the bounds of the cabin yard. I wanted to, but I clenched my fists at my sides and rooted myself to the spot. If I turned around and saw her face, it might break me. I wasn't strong enough to keep it up if I had to watch her deal with the nails I'd hammered into my coffin.

It wasn't fair, and fuck if it didn't hurt enough that I'd rather walk into the lake and see how long I could sit at the bottom before my name had to be taken off the census... but life wasn't fair. This was for the best.

CHAPTER TWENTY TWO

Victoria

Rich turned his back on me, and I watched him stalk across the gravel drive. Tears pricked my eyes, and my face burned from fighting them back. Huffing out a breath, I turned and slipped through the cabin's open door, keeping my eyes on the ground. As much as I hoped the other guys had scattered during my fight with Rich, part of me knew they'd been listening. I didn't want them to see me cry, not over *that* bastard anyway. Pushing the door shut behind me, I slumped against it, my eyes still pinned to the floor.

"I'm not fucking crying over him." I gritted out as tears spilled over my lashes and streaked down my cheeks. I let out an angry grunt and swiped them away.

A familiar hand gripped my chin tight, and I was forced to look up into Az's face. Concern, anger, and something soft I rarely saw in him warred across his features.

"Rich is a fucking idiot, Love." he said softly.

"An idiot I'm going to fucking murder." I heard Leighton spit behind Az.

Shifting slightly to look around Az, I saw all three of the other guys standing in a loose semi-circle. Joey and Craig looked sympathetic, but Leighton looked on the verge of a coronary.

"You're not going to murder him." Az barked out, not bothering to look behind him.

Leighton moved around Az and gently grabbed my arm, tugging me away from the door. "I didn't mean *actual* murder, Az-hole. But I *am* going to kick that sorry son of a bitch's ass."

Az shifted me toward Craig and Joey, giving them a look as Leighton tore open the cabin door and took off at a clipped pace. "I need to make sure he doesn't actually murder, Rich. What that little psycho says and what he does... well, just... You guys got her while I handle this?"

Craig stepped forward and pulled me into his chest, giving Az a tight nod. Az looked at me as if he wanted to say something and wasn't quite sure catching up with Leighton was the right thing to do.

"Go," I murmured. "I'll be fine. I'm just angry."

Az hesitated at the door for a second longer before moving back toward me and planting a chaste kiss on my temple. "Like I said, Rich is a fucking idiot. A bigger idiot than me."

The corner of my lips tugged up in a small smile as Az headed back to the door, picking up his pace as he exited the cabin and shut it behind him. My eyes still burned with more unshed tears. While I hadn't been lying that I was angry, I was just as hurt by Rich's words as I was anything else. I thought we were getting past whatever bullshit box he was trying to put us in. Now, I wasn't so sure I hadn't misinterpreted everything between us.

"Don't do that," Craig said gently.

"Do what?" I shrugged, attempting to turn and move away from him.

"Second-guessing everything that took you out on the porch in the first place, Sweetheart," Joey said as I turned from Craig and ran face-first into his chest as I tried to pull away.

"Well, looks like whatever I thought was going on was wrong. I mean, he–"

"Is a bigger idiot than any of us thought." Craig cut me off. "Even *if* you were wrong about what you thought was going on between you–"

"And I'd hazard a guess that you weren't as off as you thought," Joey added.

"But even if you were, he was wrong for how he's chosen

to handle it. And if he is too big of an idiot to see what he's missing out on, then it's his loss, Bunny." Craig finished, turning me to look at him in much the same way Az had earlier. Though his touch was tender and the expression on his face almost reverent. He pulled me flush with his chest, looking down at me with a look that all but stole the breath from my lungs as he brushed away an errant strand of hair.

"But *we* see you, Sweetheart," Joey whispered in my ear, causing a shiver to run up my spine as I felt him step into my space, his chest brushing against my back.

My breath caught in my throat as Craig wound a hand in my hair, tilting my head to the side, an opening that Joey capitalized on by beginning a trail of searing kisses from just behind my ear and down my neck. My eyes were pinned to Craig's gaze, and he smirked when a wicked glint passed through his expression. He leaned down and gently brushed his lips over mine before claiming my mouth in a shattering kiss of his own.

It didn't take long before my heart was hammering in my chest, and my mind blanked out with the feeling of their hands and lips on me. When Craig finally pulled away and looked down at me with a super-heated gaze, I could only whimper. I felt Joey smile against the nape of my neck, leaving a little love bite before he pulled away.

"Should we take this somewhere a little more private, Bunny?" Craig asked, raising an eyebrow. It took me a moment before my brain caught up to the fact that he was offering me a chance to say no if I wanted to, and I couldn't help but smile up at him.

"Less likely to get interrupted that way, I'd imagine," I said.

Craig smiled at Joey over my shoulder just before Joey murmured in my ear. "Let's take this to a bedroom so we can show you just how much we appreciate you, Sweetheart."

Joey stepped from behind me, turning me gently toward the door to Craig's room. I could feel myself blush all over as

I moved toward the room. When I looked over my shoulder at the guys, they seemed content standing there watching me. But their heated gazes and predatory grins sent a shiver up my spine and made me move across the den quicker.

I stepped into Craig's room, turning to look again and see if they were still watching me, when my gaze landed on Craig's chest. I jumped back, not having heard them move across the room. He raised an eyebrow at me with a smirk before he circled his arms around my waist and hauled me further into the room. Joey stepped in behind him, shutting the door behind him.

Craig set me down as Joey reached for me, pulling me flush against his chest and slanting his mouth over mine in a kiss that seemed like it would melt me from the inside out. When he pulled away, I found myself in Craig's arms as he did the same. My head started to spin as they passed me back and forth, touching, teasing, and kissing me. I barely registered the tug of my clothing as they set about relieving me of it with each pass. Eventually, I stood between them, panting in just my panties, before they stopped their game of tug-o-war. Having one of them looking at me with that hungry gaze I'd come to recognize had been intense enough, but both of them? It was almost too much.

"Come here, Pet..." Joey's voice was husky, almost a low growl, as he sat on the bed and pulled me down onto his lap, shifting me so I was straddling him. His fingers brushed into my hair and gripped it tightly as he pulled me in for a hard, hungry kiss. I groaned against his lips; the sizzle of lightning shot through my nerves as I felt his stiff cock when he rocked his hips up against me. "I don't think I'll ever get over your taste." He whispered against my lips before he nipped on the bottom one, kissing me like he would devour me.

After a few moments, I jumped slightly when I heard Craig clear his throat. I pulled back, looking at him, though my vision wasn't quite wanting to focus.

"Don't get me wrong, it's hot as fuck to watch Bunny get

all worked up, but..." Craig trailed off.

"Jealous?" Joey remarked playfully, smirking.

"You know I am," Craig answered, sounding equally amused.

"Awe, Pet... Craig's jealous of all the attention you're giving me," Joey whispered, brushing his lips across my ear and making me shudder. "We can't have that. Why don't you give him some?" He nipped my earlobe, sliding out from underneath me in a way that left me kneeling on the bed.

I looked up at Craig as he moved toward me, as he slid into place on the bed, and pulled me against him. His grip on me was firm, and his kiss was almost desperate, like a man starved. I pulled his lower lip between my teeth and bit gently as he rolled and pinched my nipple, which left us both moaning. Suddenly, I felt Joey's hands roaming over my body, teasing and touching everywhere that Craig's weren't. The sensation was... almost overwhelming. I jumped slightly when his fingers brushed against the outside of my underwear, nearly giving me some of the friction I was craving, but not quite.

"Oh... Pet." Joey crooned, stretching my nickname out like he was tasting each syllable. "You're ruining these pretty panties. They're already soaked for us."

Craig broke the kiss, his chest heaving slightly from his heavy breathing.
"Sounds like she doesn't need them anymore then. Let's fix that." His eyes never left mine as he spoke, and I couldn't help but bite my bottom lip and blush. Joey pulled me back toward him with my upper arms, and Craig grabbed me by my knees to pull my legs out in front of me. In one swift motion, he had my panties off and thrown over his shoulder. Craig gave me another hungry once over, licking his lips as he stared down at me. "You look good enough to eat, Bunny..."

Joey's hands slid down my body, his fingers tracing teasing patterns along my sides until he reached my thighs; he gripped them a bit roughly and pulled my legs open, causing

Craig to growl low in his chest.

"Let him enjoy the view, Pet." Joey murmured in my ear. He kissed the sensitive skin behind my ear before scorching a trail down my neck kissing, sucking, and nibbling.

I jumped when Craig gripped my thighs, kissing and nipping at them while Joey's hands moved back to my breasts, and his mouth continued to tease at my neck and shoulder. I rolled my hips, feeling a desperate need for friction and pressure riding me, and I couldn't stop the whimper that escaped me. Both of them chuckled appreciatively.

"Do you want something, Bunny?" Craig asked innocently, looking up at me from between my thighs. The view was sinful. I narrowed my eyes at him, but when I tried to move my hands to his head, a firm grip held my arms in place with an amused chuckle.

"This much teasing ought to be illegal, boys." I rasped out.

"Awe, poor Pet." Joey said, and I could feel his smirk against my shoulder.

"Such an impatient Bunny..." Craig crooned before pushing against my belly to make me lean further into Joey. I moaned loudly, and my eyes closed when I felt the pressure of Craig's tongue teasing around my entrance. A fist in my hair forced my head to turn to the side as Joey kissed me, taking my lips in a way that consumed me. Craig's tongue circled my clit and had me mewling and shuddering between them. I could already feel the pressure building, that tension coiling with every overwhelming sensation. After a while, I couldn't even tell whose hands were whose; they were everywhere. Craig was relentless as he chased down my climax, and Joey swallowed every moan and cry with his kiss.

I arched my back hard, tearing my mouth away from Joey's kiss to cry out when Craig slipped two fingers inside me. He crooked his fingers as he worked them inside me. Joey held my elbows behind my back, whispering into my ear and kissing my neck as Craig continued to play me like a well-practiced instrument.

"That's it, Pet. Let's see how pretty you are when you let go. Show us how beautifully you scream." Joey growled in my ear, and it was like he reached out and gave me a little shove to push me over the edge that Craig had me teetering on. I threw my head back into Joey's shoulder and cried out as my back bowed and my hips rolled against Craig's fingers and mouth. "Good girl, yeah, just ride it out. Feel good for us."

Craig didn't let up until I was a shaking, whimpering mess in Joey's arms. He leaned up on his arms, a look of pure lust written across his features, and that was all it took for me to feel that electric tingle in my spine again. These boys would be the death of me, I thought as he crashed his lips into mine. I could taste myself on his tongue, and something about it was erotic as fuck.

Leaning forward, I pushed him back until Craig was sitting on his knees. Giving him a once over, with a look thrown over my shoulder at Joey.

"Seems you boys are wearing too many clothes for my tastes," I crooned.

"Are you sure, Bunny? We wanted to make you feel good, you don't have to–" Craig started.

"Get naked. Now." I said impatiently, earning a swift slap to my ass from Joey. "Please?"

"Better, Pet." Joey stated, amusement lacing his voice.

I don't think I've ever seen two men undress as quickly as them. A flurry of fabric later, and the three of us were pressed skin to skin, and it felt like heaven. I pushed Craig back into a similar position as before, looking up at him through my lashes to see him watching me with dark eyes. Behind me, I heard the sound of a condom wrapper being ripped open. Craig gathered my hair in a fistful and tilted my head back slightly.

"If you want us to stop, just start hitting Craig's leg if you can't get your safe words out, okay?" Joey asked, though it was more of a statement.

"Yes, Alpha." I answered.

"Safe words." Joey demanded.

"Yellow for a break, red for stop." I groaned, anticipation coiling in my stomach like a spring.

"Good girl..." Craig crooned. I licked my lips as he pressed his cock closer to my mouth before darting my tongue out to taste the tip. He hissed in a breath as I ran my tongue across his head, swirling it around him before I leaned forward slightly to close my lips around his head and suckle. Behind me, Joey massaged my hips a moment before gripping them firmly and slowly pushing his cock inside me.

Almost in unison, they entered me. It was fucking dizzying as they each became fully seated. They were slow and tender as they moved to start with, and all I could do was breathe and relax. I moaned around Craig's cock as Joey pumped inside me and hit that sweet spot that had my body singing for him. Soon, the bedroom was an orchestra of heavy breathing, grunting, and strangled moans as they chased their releases with me.

Craig's fist in my hair was tight enough to almost hurt, but it was a sweet contrast to the pleasure of Joey's fingers as he leaned forward and played with my clit as he stroked into me. I was fucking helpless in their hands to be anything other than used, and I was fucking loving it.

"Always knew... there was a pretty little... dirty whore in there waiting for us." Joey bit out as he picked up the pace. Something about that went straight through me, like a lightning bolt to my pussy. I groaned hard around Craig as my body tensed.

"Oooh shit! Do that again; I think she liked it." Craig groaned as the sounds from my throat vibrated on his cock.

"I could tell." Joey's voice sounded strangled, and they both started to pick up the pace as they chased their release. "Do you like that, Pet? Knowing that you're our little whore to play with?"

Oh fuck... Joey slapped my clit as he said it, pistoning into me as Craig rocked into my throat, and if I could have screamed, I would have when I came. It hit me like a freight train, and I could have sworn I almost blacked out. Craig and Joey held me up when my arms started to shake beneath me, their thrusts becoming erratic, and their breaths gave way to grunts and growls as they followed me over the edge. I moaned at the feeling as I swallowed Craig and clenched around Joey, greedy for what they offered.

We collapsed in a heap of limbs and exhaustion on Craig's bed. I was dizzy and didn't feel like I could move. The boys looked down at me, each with a tender smile as they adjusted me to lay on the pillow, with Joey tucked in behind me.

"I'll get us some water, and then someone is scooting over or we're taking the pile to Bunny's bed so there's room." Craig's voice barely registered since I was already starting to doze.

"Bring a straw so we can get her to drink without moving... looks like it might be a minute before she can do that again."

"Fuck... both of... you." I got out as I found my voice, causing Joey to laugh.

"Oh, Pet. We just did that." He chuckled.

CHAPTER TWENTY THREE

Leighton

Rich was testing the limits of my loyalty, and I didn't like it one bit. Worse, I didn't understand *why* him telling *ma petit* that she was just a job had me itching to beat him bloody. It wasn't any of my business if he liked her or not. Still, I found myself storming from the cabin, jumping over the steps instead of walking down them as my eyes scanned the tree line in search of him.   Whatever these sensations roiling in my chest were, they were nothing like the obsessions I'd had in the past.

A feral grin split my face as I caught sight of his white t-shirt amongst the vivid colors of fall leaves. Breaking into a jog, I raced after him, weaving through the trees and jumping over the underbrush. As soon as I caught up to him, I grabbed him roughly by the shoulder and jerked him to face me, my free hand balling into a fist and slamming into his gut, causing him to double over.

"Oh, shit." I said, remembering he was still injured as his mouth gaped open and shut struggling to pull in air. "I forgot you're not healed yet. You need to hurry the fuck up an heal already so I can thoroughly kick your ass. Me and you," I said, jabbing my finger towards each of us to punctuate my words, "we're in a fight."

"Leighton!" Az called out somewhere behind me as Rich stared up at me with rage filled eyes where he was still doubled over holding his stomach.

"I said I wasn't going to fucking kill him, Az-hole!" I hollered back, looking over my shoulder to watch Az pick his way toward us. "You didn't have to follow me out here like a fucking nanny to make sure I behaved myself."

Az scowled as he reached where I stood, muttering something under his breath before he moved around me to help Rich right himself.

"You can't tell me he didn't deserve to be hit." I said, crossing my arms over my chest.

"Why the fuck did you even hit me?" Rich demanded, finally catching his breath.

"You know why, fucker." I snarled. "And the second you're all healed up, I'm finishing what I just started and wiping the mat with your sorry ass."

"I see," Rich said evenly. "This is about the *Princess.* Christ, she has all of you so pussy-whipped you can't see the forest for the fucking trees."

Az's fist shot out and connected with Rich's jaw, causing Rich's head to jerk sideways. I couldn't help the cackle that escaped me. Fucker deserved it. Az glared at Rich as he shook out his hand, almost like he was daring him to say another word.

"Maybe you needed the murder nanny," I snorted.

"This is the shit I'm fucking talking about!" Rich snarled as he rubbed his jaw. "Since when have we come to blows over a piece of ass, huh? When the fuck did you boys start taking sides that weren't *ours*?! She's a fucking distraction! And it's going to wind up getting someone killed!"

"You shut your whore mouth!" I shouted, possessiveness clawing at my chest. "She's *mine*," Az shifting his weight drew my gaze to him, "Fine, *ours*. And that makes her side our side. She *killed* for us, that makes her ours."

"He's not wrong, Rich. If she was one of our people, she'd already have gotten her mark because she saved my ass. And you'd do well to start treating her with at least that same kind of respect. Right now, you're worse than I was when all this started. You're just being cruel for the sake of it, and we're better than that." Az growled, sounding like he was trying to find an even tone but not quite getting there.

"*I'm* being cruel?" Rich scoffed. "I'm not the one who's forgotten why this started and why we're still here. It's the rest of you that can't seem to remember there's someone gunning for all six of us. Too busy sticking your dicks in her every chance you get. Reminding her that she is, and always was, just a job isn't being cruel. It's being honest."

"Did you get brain damaged when the manor blew up?" I asked before busting out laughing at how absolutely hilarious his words were.

"Are... You have got to be fucking kidding me." Az snapped. "Who the fuck even are you right now, Rich?"

"I'm the head of this family and you'd do well to remember that." Rich replied tersely.

I laughed even harder, doubling over as I tried to catch my breath and get control of myself. "This guy. He's a fucking riot."

"That can change..." Az said, a dangerous seriousness in his tone. "You're making yourself fucking useless at this point. Acting like plans can't change. Newsflash, you fucking idiot. They did. They've been changed a long goddamn time, and you need to figure out how to roll with it. She is *ours*. She earned her right to be here. It wasn't even that long ago that even *you* were killing for her while she was killing for us. Every single one of us was in the shit trying to get out and it's not her fucking fault it went sideways. Just because you don't know how to handle your feelings, refuse to admit them to even yourself, doesn't change any of those facts."

I flung my arm around Rich's shoulders. "We're still in a fight, but I know a few things about not understanding feelings. I'm thinking of taking Phil up on his offer for his therapist's number, you should come with me."

Rich shrugged my arm off of him and stepped a space away from me. "All of you seem to keep forgetting the *Princess* isn't made for this world. When the dust settles and she's safe to go back to her ivory tower, she'll leave us all in the dust and never look back. The only question is how much fucking damage she's going to leave in her wake."

"How fucking childish..." Az sighed, running a hand through his hair. "Do you think that we're the first people to run the risk of someone leaving us? When it's over, if she wants to leave, then she will because we'll respect her choices enough to let her go."

"I-" I started.

"*Yes*, you would. Because we aren't going to keep someone with us against their will."

"I licked her, she's mine till death do us part." I huffed, scuffing the toe of my shoe in the dirt.

"That... is not how marriage works, Leighton." Az rolled his eyes before turning back to Rich. "So, what if she leaves? Sure, that shit would hurt like hell. But how well-versed are we in heartbreak? *All* of us. Hell, most of us are more prepared to deal with that than we were to realize that there was something there. Life will go on, and so will we. But there is absolutely no fucking reason for you to act the way you did because you're creating situations in your head that you have no way of knowing. She wasn't made for this world, but so far, she seems to be finding her way with more grace than any of us did."

"Speak for yourself," I mumbled again.

"Do you not hear her fighting in her sleep? Replaying the bullshit, she's been through over and over in her mind when it's at its most vulnerable." Rich said, but his voice was losing its heat, coming out almost sad.

"You think we don't hear it? One of us is always there, soothing the nightmares away when they happen. And which of us hasn't dealt with some kind of nightmare that follows us around? That comes with the fucking territory! I've gotten up from my own nightmares to find you already at the coffee pot because yours didn't let you sleep either. I've never seen you so absolutely stuck in that you refuse to admit when someone has done well in our ranks. You haven't even gotten your own head out of your ass enough to talk to her, to figure out where her mind is at. Everything about the shit between you two, hell, all of us, it's all what you've created in your own fucking head because you are too stubborn to acknowledge that you have feelings for her that run just as deep as ours." Az stared Rich down, his arms crossed over his chest.

Rich raked a hand through his hair and tugged at his curls so hard I thought he was going to rip out a bald patch. With a low growl, he stalked toward Az until they were standing toe to toe. I struggled against the urge to clap my hands together in excitement for the fight that was coming.

"It's my fucking fault!" Rich bellowed. "Is that what you want to hear? That it's my goddamned fault she's here, that she was ever in a position to kill someone, that she had to watch us beat and kill a man for information, that she's having fucking nightmares? If I'd just had a little goddamned more patience and dug just a little deeper, we'd have known Rinaldo was behind the gala set up. We would have been fucking *prepared* to take the fight to them and end this, all without ever crashing into her fucking life."

"She's not all sunshine and light like you think." I frowned. "Like knows like, and deep down, she's got the same darkness in her we all do. Only something vicious could take me to task the way she does." I couldn't help the smile that curved my lips at the thought of how she came at me every time I made her mad.

I spotted the curl to Az's lip, and he nodded in agreement. "You've got this idea in your head that she's something she's not. Rich, she's not some wilting wallflower who is going to faint when things get hard. Hell, eventually, she probably won't even need rescuing."

"She did hit Az in the head with a rock, that was pretty impressive." I shrugged.

"How did you know that? You weren't even there?" Az asked.

"I may have been spying out her window. Or not, who knows?" I snickered, causing Az to roll his eyes again.

"Of course you were. But... to be fair, she didn't know I was there because she was just throwing things."

"Still counts."

"Can the two of you stay on fucking topic here? Or are we done with the 'bitch at Rich' hour?" Rich huffed. "My point still fucking stands, she wasn't made for this world. She shouldn't *have* to change who she is to make herself fit. It's fucking selfish of any of us to expect her to."

Az stared at the ground for a moment; Rich's words seemed to make him play something out in his head that had his lips curling up in a tender smile that wasn't usual for our hot-headed Az-hole.

"I don't care what the rest of you guys do, but it's like you don't even know me, Rich. Selfless is not in my wheelhouse." I said dryly.

"I... said the same thing to her not long ago, actually. We were fighting, because of course we were, and I told her that she deserved better than what we could offer. If I was a better man, I'd let her go. Shit, if she was smarter, she'd run for the hills the first chance she got. She shouldn't have been put in this position to watch us do what we do, or be dragged down into it herself..." He trailed off a bit, that tender smile finally reaching his eyes. I'd have to give him shit later about going soft on us.

"What Loverboy here is trying to say," I interjected. "Is she's a big girl, and it's her choice what she does. I heard her tell him that herself."

Az shot me a look like he was wondering what else I heard, so I grinned at him and winked. I'd overheard their entire argument and make-up session against the cabin, but I wasn't telling him that yet.

"The little eavesdropper here is right. She is adamant that she's here by choice, and it's not ours to decide for her who has space in her life or in her bed. You're just holding onto shit that wasn't your fault, or hers. At this point, Rich, you're making a fucking fool of the both of you, and you're being a bigger idiot than I've ever known you to be. I don't know what you need to do, but eventually, you need to realize that if you wanna come out of this without having done more damage than we came here to do... realize that you're the one stomping all over what could have been, and you'll have to take the result up with the mirror."

"Shit, even if you don't wanna tell her, because sometimes that woman even scares *me*," I said, forcing a shudder. "At least be honest with yourself about it. I have, and let me tell ya, it's a whole lot better than thinking you're having a heart attack."

Rich rubbed his hand over his face with a groan. "What you two chucklefucks don't seem to understand is that what I feel, hell what I *want* with her doesn't fucking matter. You say it's her choice to be here, well that's a dumb fucking choice. We. Will. Ruin. Her. The kindest thing we can do for her is walk away from her if she won't walk away from us once all this is over."

"If you think that any of us, even *you*, are gonna be able to–"

The shrill sound of my phone ringing in my pants pocket interrupted Az. Scowling, I tugged it out of my pocket, and my frown deepened as my sister's name flashed on the screen.

"What Lacey?" I demanded when I answered the call. "I'm in the middle of important shit right now about feelings."

"You're- Never mind, I don't have time to deal with whatever weird shit you're into right now. The Jackals know where you are. One of my inside men just reached out to me. They are on their way to you now. If you don't want to get killed over that bitch, you need to leave now."

"Fuck! Ok, I've gotta go. Call her a bitch again, I'll stab you in the throat next time I see you. Byeee!" I said, hanging up the phone and looking at Rich and Az's confused faces. "Jackals en route, boys, we gotta roll."

CHAPTER TWENTY FOUR

Victoria

I was curled against Joey, teetering on the edge of oblivion, so blissed out that I'd barely registered Craig leaving the room to get everyone water. Joey trailed his fingers up and down my spine, driving me closer to sleep when pounding on the door jolted me back to reality.

"We have to go, now!" Az barked, throwing the door open wide.

I let out a squeak of alarm, tugging the blankets up to cover myself as I sat upright. Joey released his hold on me and narrowed his eyes at Az.

"What the fuck man?" He asked.

"We've been found. We have to go." Az replied. "Get dressed, don't bother grabbing anything. There's not time."

"Fuck," Joey muttered, running a hand through his hair as he scrambled from the bed and pulled his pants on.

He dressed with one hand, using the other to hand me my clothes from the floor. I dressed quickly, wondering why we were on the run... again. Leighton's family cabin was in such an isolated area it didn't make any sense to me that someone could have found us. I'd barely tugged my shoes on before Joey was pulling me into the chaos outside of Craig and Leighton's room. Craig barreled past us without a second glance, heading straight for the computer set up on his desk. I didn't have to ask to know that he was either planning to take it or destroy it so whatever work he'd done while we'd been in the cabin couldn't be found.

"How did your sister know we've been found?" Rich

demanded, standing in the center of the open space and staring Leighton down.

"It's Lacey." Leighton shrugged. "She has people everywhere. You really didn't think my family held onto their power and status through legal means only, did you?"

"How do we know she's not the reason we've been found?" The words left my lips unbidden.

Leighton turned his head to look at me. "Lacey is a massive bitch, but she wouldn't endanger me. Being a Laurent means something to her."

"If it was her or one of her men, we'd have been found already." Rich added. "The only person it could be is Phil."

Leighton's head snapped back toward Rich; his eyes narrowed. "Don't you put that on Phil. He may be Joey's guy, but he's fucking loyal. And the closest any of us has to a second in command."

A coat draped over my shoulders, and I looked up to find Az behind me. "Can we table this for now? We don't have time to argue over who may or may not have betrayed us. Since we don't have a vehicle, we're on foot until we can steal something, and I'd rather not get caught up in another shootout."

Craig chose that moment to emerge from his room. There was a hint of sadness in his expression that made me wonder if it was aimed toward the lack of computer equipment, he'd brought with him. Before I could stop myself, I let out a barking laugh at the fact that my guys were, indeed, nerds with guns. They all shot me puzzled looks before springing back into action.

"There's a bag with snacks and bottled water by the door. I loaded it up since it's gonna be awhile before we make it to town."

"Didn't Leighton make the trip there and back in a day?" I frowned as I was shuffled toward the cabin door.

"I took the roads, *ma petit.* That's not an option this time. We need to stick to the forest, so we don't risk running across any Jackals. At least until we can get our hands on a car."

I murmured a soft 'oh' and let the guys lead me from the cabin into the thicket of trees just beyond the gravel driveway. Leighton took point, leading us deeper into the forest, while Craig and Joey each walked beside me. Az and Rich flanked us from behind. We walked in silence as night fell. The darkening forest gave me the chills, my mind providing unpleasant images of wild animals or even monsters from horror films popping out to eat us alive. I'd been so caught up in my wild imaginings that I hadn't noticed I'd slowed down until Az's hands landed on my shoulders from behind.

"Leighton, hold up a minute." He called out softly, causing Leighton to double back toward us. "Victoria needs a break."

"No, I'm good. We can keep going." I protested even though my feet were screaming for me to stop. I shuddered at the thought of stopping on my account and getting caught by something or someone hunting us through the forest.

"It's not just for you, Sweetheart." Joey offered. "L is about the only one of us used to this kind of hiking since he grew up doing it. And Rich is still injured."

"I'm fine." Rich's gruff voice piped in, close enough to make me jump.

"Well, I'm not." Craig huffed. "The three of us didn't get a chance to hydrate and refuel before we were out the door. Why do you think I brought snacks?" I could barely see the duffle bag as he lifted it off his shoulders and dropped it to the ground.

Rich muttered something about thinking with dicks under his breath as he brushed past me and found an overturned log to settle onto. Az gave me a gentle nudge in the same direction as Joey moved to help Craig distribute water bottles and bags of goldfish crackers. I'd barely settled onto the other end of the log when Leighton plopped down beside me, making it bounce, and threw an arm around my shoulder.

"We should probably come up with a new plan instead of hoofing it into town like this." He spoke. "At this rate we won't have a car until midday tomorrow and I don't think it's a good idea for us to be out here traipsing through the woods with the vermin on the hunt."

"Vermin?" I asked, lifting my feet from the ground like a mouse would run over them at any moment.

"He means the Jackals, Bunny." Craig replied, settling on the ground and taking a long pull from his water bottle.

"What did you have in mind?" Rich asked.

"We're not too far from the highway, two miles at best. I say we catch a ride."

"The only people who might be on the road this time of night are the same people we're trying to avoid, L." Az spoke.

Leighton moved his arm from around my shoulder and pressed a button on the watch he was wearing, illuminating the area. "Nah, if we move fast, we can catch the second shifters going home for the day."

"I highly doubt anyone is going to stop for the six of us." Joey interjected.

"No shit, that's why I'm suggesting we have *la petit démone* do the stopping for us." Leighton grinned just as the light from his watch went out.

"I'm-"

"All you gotta do is flag someone down, we'll do the rest." Leighton cut me off. "We can assume any cars going southbound are safe since we're a day's drive north of Sacona. The Jackals don't exactly have any reach this far, so they'll be coming from home."

"This is a horrible idea." Rich muttered, causing me to scowl at him in the dark.

"We're not hurting anyone, right? Just catching a ride?" I asked.

"Leighton wants to use you to carjack someone." Az said bluntly. "But other than leaving them stranded on the highway, no, we won't be hurting anyone unless absolutely necessary."

I sucked my bottom lip into my mouth and worried it between my teeth as the others finished their snack and bottled waters. The idea of leaving some stranger stranded on the mountain highway as we drove off toward safety in their car didn't sit right with me. Neither did the possibility of the Jackals finding us and doing whatever it was they planned to do with us.

"I'll do it," I said softly as Craig gathered all the trash into his duffle bag. "Under one condition."

"Name it." Joey said.

"We call the person we carjack a ride home."

Leighton chuckled and clapped his hands like a gleeful child. "Perfect. We should get moving though. Don't want to miss our chance."

We picked our way quietly through the forest, trusting Leighton to lead us in the right direction. I nearly laughed out loud when he insisted we all hold hands so nobody got separated, but he had a point. Even traipsing through the dark forest for hours wasn't enough for our eyes to fully adjust to the overwhelming darkness that swallowed us up. I didn't realize how tense I was until soft light from the highway started filtering through the trees.

"Ok, so, we're gonna hang back out of sight, *ma petit.*" Leighton said, drawing to a stop just inside the tree line. "You go down and flag down the first car you see coming from that direction." My eyes followed his hand as he pointed to the left. "Keep them talking long enough for us to get to the car and then we'll take things from there."

"Got it," I replied with a quick nod before moving to pick my way to the edge of the road.

I stopped just at the edge of the road under a streetlamp and waited. There wasn't a car or headlights in sight in either direction, or I began to wring my hands together in front of me, wondering if we'd have been better off sticking to the original plan. Just as I was about to give up and beg the guys to just keep hiking through the forest toward town, a pair of headlights appeared in the direction Leighton had told me we needed.

Nervous energy coiled through my gut, and my hands began to shake, but I waved them in the air anyway. As the lights drew closer, I took a step out onto the road, desperate to get them to stop. Even though they were coming from the right direction, the one Leighton had been confident would be safe, I felt too exposed. I gasped in relief as a tan minivan slowed to a stop beside me.

"You okay, honey?" A woman's voice called out as the passenger side window rolled down.

"I..."

"Are you lost?" she asked as I stepped closer to the vehicle.

"Uh, yeah. I was out walking, and it got dark and I have no idea where I am." I managed to get out.

"Do you know where you came from? I can call for someone if you need me too." the woman frowned as I moved close enough to grip the door where the window was rolled completely down.

"If you could take me into town that would actually be great." I replied, hoping like hell the woman wouldn't take off and leave me standing in the middle of the road.

I could feel her eyes roaming over my face for a moment before the sound of the automatic door locks echoed in the night. My hand reached for the door handle just as the driver-side door jerked open, and Leighton was illuminated by the interior light coming on. The woman and I had both been so focused on each other that neither of us had noticed him moving from the trees and behind her van.

"Get out of the car." He barked; a gun pointed at the woman's face.

I clamped down on the urge to make him lower his weapon. The sliding door beside me slid open, drawing my attention to the others. Joey snagged my hand from the passenger door and pulled me beside him, ushering me into the back. A gasp slipped free as I registered the car seat buckled into the middle of the second-row seat.

"Oh, God. She has a baby," I hissed.

Az climbed in after me, looking over my body at the infant seat. "Empty. Kid's not with her."

"Get out of the fucking van," Leighton ordered, his voice harder than I'd ever heard it.

"Please, I'll do what you want. Just don't hurt me." The woman blubbered, the sounds of her struggling with her seatbelt filling the vehicle.

My eyes shot to Leighton as the others climbed into the van. The terrifying look on his face was enough to make me wonder if he truly intended to hurt the woman after promising me he wouldn't. Sobs racked her thin shoulders as she clambered out of the driver's seat onto the empty highway. As if on cue, Rich climbed into the front passenger seat, pulling a gun from his waistband and pointing it toward the woman while Leighton took her place behind the wheel.

"Call a ride," Leighton said coolly, tossing a brick phone at her through the window before slamming his foot on the accelerator and tearing off down the highway.

My stomach twisted violently, and I swallowed hard, tamping down the urge to vomit. Joey's hand rubbed my back in a soothing motion as he made soft shushing noises.

"It had to be done, Love." Az spoke from the back row of seats. "We'll find her information and make sure she has a new car seat and gets her vehicle back or replaced if we have to ditch it."

"It had to be done, Bunny." Craig murmured from behind me, his hands tangling through my hair as his fingers gently massaged my scalp.

"I told you she wasn't cut out for this shit." Rich huffed in the front passenger seat, causing any guilt I'd been feeling to turn to irritation at his presence.

"Yeah, yeah." Leighton retorted, waving his hand as if to erase what Rich had said. "Where we heading now?"

"Home." Rich said. "We hid out and nursed our wounds, now I think it's high time we remind the Jackals we aren't to be fucked with."

CHAPTER TWENTY FIVE

Az

We ditched the minivan in favor of an SUV halfway back to Sacona. I'd made it a point to dig through the glove box for the registration so I could follow through with my promise to Victoria. As soon as we were home and situated, I'd make a call to have the woman's van returned.

No longer on foot, we arrived home late the next evening, ditching the SUV on the outskirts of Sacona and having our closest crew pick us up. Victoria was dozing with her head on my shoulder when we pulled into the driveway to our mansion. Not wanting to wake her, I eased myself out of the vehicle and carefully gathered her into my arms.

"You can put her in my room if you want." Joey said quietly. "I'll bunk with Craig for now."

Giving him a nod of acknowledgment, I followed Rich into the house and made my way across the large open space that made up the living room and kitchen, heading for the stairs next to Leighton's bedroom. Victoria didn't stir at all until I laid her on Joey's bed and began gently removing her shoes.

"Whe-"

"Shh, go back to sleep," I whispered as she stretched across the king-size mattress. "You're safe."

She mumbled something incoherent and shifted just enough for me to put the blankets over her before she was out again. I studied her sleeping form for a moment, wondering how I ever thought she could be behind everything that had happened before turning back toward the door. When I made it back downstairs, Rich, Leighton, and Joey were seated at the large round dining table, and Craig was at the coffee maker.

"We need to discuss what to do about Phil." Rich spoke as I settled into an empty chair at the table.

"I'm telling you, Rich. It's not Phil." Leighton barked. "He's too loyal to be our mole."

Rich scrubbed a hand over his face and let out a long-suffering sigh. "He's the only one that makes sense, Leighton. He was in charge of finding the mole and turned up nothing, and then our location was leaked right after he brought the doc to us."

"Are we sure it wasn't a leak in Lacey's organization?" I asked as Craig moved to the table and sat a cup of coffee in front of me. "She seems to have players everywhere. Any one of them could have ratted us out."

"It doesn't make sense for them to wait as long as they did if it were one of her lackeys." Rich replied, his shoulders slumping forward. "We were in the cabin for a little more than a month and we saw her people maybe twice that whole time."

My eyes moved from each of the men at the table, landing on Joey. He was fidgeting, his eyes on the table, and his lips pulled into a tight frown. Phil had been his number two almost as long as he'd been part of the horsemen and practically taught him everything he knew.

"We should check in with our people now that we're back." I said, tearing my gaze away from Joey. "For the most part, they've kept me up to date while we were gone, but I'm sure there's small shit that didn't seem pertinent to share during the check ins."

"I think that's a good idea." Rich replied. "We should all get some rest, and we'll get to work first thing in the morning. I think it's best we handle business in pairs for a while, though. Craig can go with me, Leighton and Joey, you two already manage the streets so just make sure you have each other's backs out there. Az-"

I already knew where he was going. "Yeah, yeah. I'll be on

babysitting duty. There's some paperwork from the club I need to deal with anyway. I can handle it from here."

"Get some sleep, boys. We'll touch base over dinner tomorrow." Rich said, pushing his chair back and rising from his seat.

I took a sip of the coffee Craig had given me before moving to dump it in the sink and rinse my cup. When I turned back toward the table, Craig was gone, but Joey and Leighton appeared to be having a silent conversation. Neither of them were taking the accusations thrown Phil's way well, but there wasn't anything to be done about it. Shaking my head, I made my way upstairs to my bedroom.

When I woke the next morning, Craig was already in the kitchen cooking breakfast. Snagging a cup of coffee, I leaned against the counter next to the stove.

"I know that look," I said, noting the frown on his face. "Not up to running with Rich today?"

"It's not that," Craig started. "After everyone went to bed last night, I did some more digging since I have my full setup now."

"And?" I pressed.

Craig turned off the burner and moved the pan of scrambled eggs he'd been cooking to the back of the stove before he turned to me. "I didn't find a whole hell of a lot, yet, but what I did find made it pretty clear that Victoria's so-called bestie is deep in the skin trade."

"So, the email to Rinaldo wasn't a one off? We kind of figured that, didn't we?"

"Yeah, but it got me thinking. After the shooting at Temptat!on she called Rich by his full name. If she were just some street level player, she wouldn't have known that. It's not like we run around announcing our government names to every player we meet."

I took a moment to consider what he'd said. "You think she's a bigger player than we initially thought."

"I don't know, man." Craig sighed and started plating the

eggs. "It's the only thing that makes sense, but I can't figure out how the hell we missed it if she's a major player."

"None of the pieces we've managed to gather have made any damned sense since the beginning." I offered. "But, we do know she's been running with the Devils; she could be a recently made woman for them. It would explain why she flew under the radar for so long."

"Still leaves the question of what the hell the Devils are doing working with the Jackals and why it seems like they've teamed up against us."

"All we can do is keep looking for the answers and have faith we'll find them." I replied just as Rich strolled into the kitchen, Joey and Leighton right behind him.

I snagged a plate from the counter and made my way to the table, receiving a dirty look from Craig in the process. Nobody talked as we settled in around the table and Craig brought over everyone else's plates. We were halfway through our silent breakfast when Victoria appeared, making a beeline for the coffee pot. Rich scowled at his plate as she passed by him, and I fought the urge to kick him under the table.

"We should get moving." Rich grunted out, dropping his fork and letting it clatter against his plate. "We'll meet back here for dinner."

"Where are we going?" Victoria piped in, causing Rich to turn an angry glare in her direction.

"*We* aren't going anywhere, Princess. You're here with Az." Rich scoffed, raising from his seat and motioning for Craig to follow him.

Victoria took a sip of her coffee and glared at him over the lip of her cup.

"Don't be mad, *ma petit.*" Leighton grinned, bounding from his seat to give her a chaste kiss on the cheek. "It's just gangster stuff, you're not missing anything important."

Rich huffed in annoyance as Joey and Craig moved from the table at roughly the same time to put their dishes in the sink and turned to head for the door with Leighton behind them. I watched Victoria set her cup down, and smirk to herself before she pushed off the counter.

"Wait a second!" She called after them, causing all four of them to freeze, but only three of them turned around. "I can't believe you all forgot something." She said, putting her hands on her hips as she approached them all with a small smile on her face.

I smirked as I watched her give Leighton, Joey, and Craig a kiss before stepping back and telling them to have a good day, promptly followed by flipping Rich off when he scoffed and headed toward the door. When she turned to look at me, I just shook my head.

"Brat."

"What? Don't tell me the concept of a goodbye kiss is foreign to you." she said innocently.

"It wasn't the kisses, Love." I chuckled as she moved back toward the counter to grab the plate Craig had left for her.

"So, what's the plan for today? I could really use a phone to call my dad and T-," she shook her head, "Er, just my dad and let him know I'm back."

"No dice, Love. We can't let anyone know we're back in town until we have all our ducks in a row. So, *I'm* going to grab my laptop and settle on the sofa to get some paperwork done, and you can watch T.V., explore the house, whatever you want as long as it's inside and not a phone call."

"I can respect that you guys have to get your feet underneath you since we just got back... but it's my dad. He's probably worried sick, and we haven't been able to say anything to him since we ran. *And* he hired you guys to look out for me. I don't know what the harm is in letting him know I'm safe." She fired off her points at me like rapid fire; her arms crossed over her chest.

"I'm not saying you can't ever call him. Just not today. I *will* make you a deal, though. There is one person I know you can trust implicitly that you can call."

"And that person isn't my father because..." She retorted

with an annoyed expression.

"You can call Mrs. McMillan," I replied, choosing to ignore her attitude. "If you absolutely need your dad to know you're safe right this second, she can pass the message for you. She hasn't held down the center as a neutral zone this long by blabbing things she shouldn't."

"Ugh, *fine.*" she pouted, holding her hand out. "Phone."

I chuckled at her, dialing Mrs. McMillan's personal cell before handing Victoria my phone. "Don't even think about leaving my sight while you're on the phone, Love. You may not understand the need for secrecy right now, but that doesn't mean I'm gonna make the mistake–."

"Hey, Mrs. McMillan!" Victoria said into the phone, and she rolled her eyes at me before turning away, but she didn't leave the room.

I settled into the couch and flipped on the T.V. and tuned out the conversation but kept my peripheral on her so she couldn't wander out of the room without me knowing. After about ten minutes, she handed me my phone back, with a scowl on her face.

"Just so you know, the five of you are in deep shit with Mrs. McMillan." She said, swatting me upside the head. "She told me to give you that."

I rubbed the side of my head and watched her stomp back upstairs, waiting long enough to hear the door to Joey's room slam shut before I went to retrieve my laptop and get to work. We spent most of the day just existing under the same roof. I worked on all the paperwork I needed to catch up on, while Victoria only seemed to surface to find something to drink or eat. She'd finally decided she was bored enough to share space with me on the couch when Rich and Craig strolled through the front door. Craig was scowling so hard at the back of Rich's head; I wondered if he was hoping to develop telekinesis and drop the big man on the spot.

"Rough day?" I called out, closing my laptop and setting it on the coffee table.

"A waste of fucking time, actually." Craig replied, dryly.

"Why don't you go upstairs, *Princess.*" Rich said, a hint of irritation in his tone. "This conversation doesn't pertain to you at all."

Her eyes narrowed at him, and she opened her mouth to speak.

"Hey," I said gently, reaching out to grab her hand. "I know he's being a bit of a hard ass, but that's Rich in boss mode. Why don't you go on upstairs and if it turns out anything he needs to discuss with us does pertain to you, I'll fill you in later?"

Victoria's eyes widened for a fraction of a second as if surprised I could be reasonable. "Uh, sure." she murmured and pulled her hand from mine before heading for the stairs, only pausing long enough to flip Rich off once more for good measure before she stomped out of view. If Rich's scowl got any deeper, I wondered if his face would get stuck that way.

As if on cue, Leighton and Joey appeared in the front door, both of them looking suspiciously relaxed after a day getting their teams back in order. Not bothering to wait for Rich to start barking out orders, I made my way to the kitchen table and took a seat. The others all followed suit.

"So, who wants to fill me in?" I asked.

"Today was a waste of my time and skills." Craig popped off. "I should have been here going over anything new my programs popped up instead of listening to Rich give his 'I'm the Boss' speeches."

"Yes, because I was just standing there stroking my ego," Rich huffed, "I didn't see you complaining when we had to go put down the upstart fucking with Leighton's street guys, and deal with the other punk that had got it in his head we weren't coming back. We don't need small fish making power grabs at the best of times, but sure as fuck not now."

"What upstart?" I asked.

"Just some punks that thought they could encroach on my territory. Like little roaches." Leighton answered. "Nothing we couldn't handle, but there were enough of them we needed to call in Rich and Craig to squash the issues."

"Anything we need to head off before the news gets a hold of it?" I asked, looking at Rich.

"Nah, Craig wiped the camera footage and we really only hurt a few of them. Once their leader had a bullet between the eyes, they were shitting their pants begging us to have mercy." Leighton laughed.

"They were mostly just kids trying to swim in the deep end before they're ready." Craig said, his mouth twitching into an amused smirk. "Kind of reminded me of us when we were young."

"I take it everything else is in order then?" I asked, looking around the table for any of them to fill me in on the rest of their day.

"Mostly," Joey said before sharing a loaded look with Leighton. "Couple of shipments got mixed up and I still need to track one down, but otherwise my end is solid. L and me are gonna head back out after dinner and see if we can't track it down."

I narrowed my eyes at the pair, something about the look he shared with Leighton not sitting right with his explanation. It wasn't necessarily unusual for him to take L to hunt down leads, but when he did, whatever he was hunting down was important enough for him to give us details of the shipment. I looked between them, trying to decide if I wanted to say something or just let sleeping dogs lie.

"So how are things on the legitimate side? Anything we need to know?" Rich said, interrupting my thoughts.

"Nothing to say really, since they're actual businesses, I pretty well stayed on top of things while we were gone so the only thing I had to do was catch up on the paperwork I wasn't around to fill out or sign." I shrugged.

"If that's all, I'm going to check my systems and see if anything new has been caught by my programs and start digging through the other shit I couldn't get through at the cabin. It's gonna take me most of the night since *somebody* insisted I play backup today. Y'all might wanna order pizza or something." Craig said, standing from his seat and heading for the stairs.

"Fuck yeah. Greasy pizza." Leighton whooped; fist-bumping Joey as Craig disappeared upstairs.

"Y'all call in the order. I've got a little bit of paperwork to finish still." I laughed, shaking my head at them before moving back to the living room to grab my laptop.

CHAPTER TWENTY SIX

Leighton

"You ready for this?" I asked Joey.

"Yep," he replied, checking his gun before holstering it under his jacket.

We'd spent the day dealing with our teams and re-establishing the chain of command, not that it took much. Our men had taken care of business as if we'd been there the whole time we hid out in the cabin. But that meant Joey and I had time to discuss our plans for the vet.

The doctor who dealt with Rich's abscessed wound had made it pretty clear the only way that could have happened so fast was if the wound had been tampered with in the first place. None of us had been allowed back when the vet patched Rich back together after the manor assault, so it seemed pretty obvious he was the cause. While Joey handled business at one of his warehouses, I'd posted myself up in his office and called the vet's receptionist, Tisha.   The petite brunette was waiting for us at the back entrance of the office when we pulled into the lot.

"The kennels are empty like you asked. Robert is in his office finishing up his notes for the day." Tisha's nose crinkled in disgust as she said the vet's name. "Make sure that bastard knows I had a hand in this. I can't fucking believe he tried to fuck this up for all of us. The extra you guys pay us pays for me to have in-home health take care of my grandmother, so I don't have to put her in a home."

"You did good, Tisha." Joey said with a polite smile. "You can rest assured that you will still be taken care of, but you need to get out of here so we can get to work, yeah?"

Tisha nodded and murmured something I didn't quite catch before she made a beeline for her car and was gone.

"Let's see if Bob is still taking walk-ins." I chuckled as I moved to open the door and held it open for Joey, motioning for him to go ahead. "Age before beauty."

"I'm younger than you." Joey rolled his eyes and moved past me; I eased the door shut with a small click so we wouldn't be announced before we were ready to be.

We made our way to the back office in near silence. The door was open already, revealing Robert hunched over his desk, scribbling notes into an open file. Joey strolled into the room, and I followed behind him, slamming the door. Robert jumped, his head snapping up from his paperwork, his eyes wide as they landed on us.

"You scared me half to death." He scolded. "But it's good to see you boys. I hope Rich is recovered."

I snorted. "Yeah, big man is doing just fine." I said, letting a manic grin spread across my face.

"Well, since you two are standing here, clearly fine, I think it's safe to assume you brought Craig for me to patch up this time." Robert smiled weakly, standing from his desk and moving as if to slip past me for the door. "I'll just grab some supplies and you can meet me in room one."

Joey put a hand out and shoved the man backwards. "Not so fast there, *Bob.*"

The vet stumbled back, slamming into his desk fear and worry warring for dominance on his face.

"Yeah, Bob. We need to discuss a few things."

The man struggled to school his features and regain his composure, his voice cracking slightly when he spoke. "What can I help you boys with? Anything you need, you know I've got you covered."

"Aww, damn it. I forgot my bag." I sighed. "You wanna get him situated while I gather some stuff up?" I asked Joey, ignoring the vet.

Joey nodded at me, and I jerked open the office door and skipped down the hall. I could hear Robert struggling against Joey behind me, and the loud grunt from Joey hitting him in the gut as I made it to the back entrance. Not wanting to miss any of the fun, I ran to the SUV we'd taken off our men when we got back into Sacona and snatched my black duffle from the back. By the time I made it to the exam room where Joey had taken the vet, it was clear I'd missed something entertaining from the growing wet spot on Robert's crotch.

"Man, you weren't supposed to start without me." I whined, dropping the duffle bag in the plastic chair against the wall of the room.

Joey shrugged, turning to look at me. "You didn't miss much, Bobby-boy here is just a little bitch. But I'm guessing that's not *new* information for anyone."

"He pissed himself, man, I can *see* it. You can't tell me you didn't do at least a little something to cause that." I scoffed, unzipping the bag and digging around for the rope to tie up Robert.

"Listen, I had to control the slimy bastard somehow, and you left the bag. *All* I did was put my gun in his mouth and tell him to behave. I didn't even hurt him yet!"

"Eww, you let him get his nasty germs on your gun." I grimaced, finally finding the rope and pulling it from the bag. "Hey, why does this look like Craig's? Did you steal it from his room?"

Joey rolled his eyes at me. "Of course, I didn't steal it from him. What do you take me for? I told him I needed some rope, and he's so annoyed from his day following Rich around that he told me to just take what I need and get out."

"Well, for starters, I take you for a criminal." I snickered.

"P-p-p-please, what is this about?" Robert chose that moment to open his mouth. "Whatever it is, I'm sure we can make it right."

"We'll get to you in a fucking second." Joey snapped, hitting him upside his head with his gun. "You wanna tie him up or do you want me to? And another thing, I might be a criminal, but I wouldn't steal from family."

"Yeah, yeah. You go ahead and tie him up," I said, passing Joey the rope. "You know how to knot Craig's fancy shit better than I do."

While Joey went to work tying up Robert, I started pulling our tools from the duffle bag and laying them out on the counter. Glancing at the vet, I decided he wasn't scared enough by the things we'd brought, so I started tearing open the drawers and cabinets looking for the tools of *his* trade.

"Man, why do you have a mini potato shooter? What the hell do you use this thing for?" I asked, holding up a random piece of veterinary equipment I'd found in the cabinet.

The doc just whimpered as Joey was tying him to the chair, we'd sat him in. I turned around and raised a brow expectantly. Joey hit him upside the head again.

"He asked you a fucking question, Bob. I suggest you answer the man," Joey growled.

"I-it's a balling gun for giving medication to livestock. Sometimes, I make house calls outside of town." Robert blubbered.

"Well, that's boring." I sighed, tossing the thing aside. "I was hoping you'd have the good tools in here, but whatever. We'll make do with what we have."

"Please, why are you doing this?" the man cried.

Ignoring him, I ran my fingers along the knives and other tools I'd laid out, taking my time deciding which one to start with. After a few passes, I settled on a small, silver switchblade. Grabbing it, I turned to face Robert, his face paling at the feral grin I wore as I advanced.

"Before we forget, Trisha said to let you know she helped. She's a good egg, that one." I laughed before stabbing the blade into his thigh. "Start asking the questions, little brother."

"There's really only a couple that are important. And I'd suggest you think real hard about whether or not you're being honest with us." Joey said slowly, his voice dropping into that false calm he took on when he worked. "Who put you up to it, and what exactly did you do?"

"What– I don't know what you're talking about!" Robert stammered.

"Oooh, wrong answer Bobby-boy. Try again." I laughed, pulling the knife out of his thigh, twisting it as I did, and handed it to Joey. "Your turn!" I said cheerfully.

Joey considered him for a moment, before dragging the blade across the man's bicep in a shallow stinging cut.

"Please," Robert cried. "I don't know what you're talking about. Whatever it is, it has nothing to do with me."

"You think he's dumb or just forgetful?" I mused, moving over to the counter to grab a pair of pliers.

"I think he thinks we're dumb. Honestly, it'd save us all a lot of time if you just started talking."

"Oh, but I like doing it this way. It's a lot more fun." I cackled, grabbing the tip of the nail on his index finger with my pliers and pulling hard enough to tear it from the nailbed.

Robert screamed in pain, but still played dumb when we asked him our questions again. Realizing he was going to let us play with him, we set to work. Joey made shallow cuts along the man's arms, eventually grabbing a pair of scissors to cut away his bloodied polo shirt and start on his chest. I focused on ripping out each fingernail one by one, before moving on to taking his fingers one knuckle at a time as I hummed random jingles to myself. Every so often, we'd ask our questions again, and each time Robert only begged us to stop hurting him.

"Wow, tough nut to crack this one." I snickered, positioning my custom cigar cutter over his remaining thumb. "Kinda weird for a guy who pissed himself over a gun."

"Maybe he likes it." Joey huffed, dragging his blade across the man's collarbone.

"Oh! I might have a solution for that!" I grinned, using my cigar cutter to take off his thumb before bouncing over to the duffle bag and grabbing my mini torch. Moving back to

Robert, I turned the torch on and held it to his bleeding nub. "Man, why does burning flesh smell like food? It's making me hungry."

"I mean, it does kind of smell like burgers on the grill." Joey chuckled.

"Bah dah bah dah dah," I started another jingle kicking off in my head. "I'm in love with her." The new ending I'd given the jingle caused me to jolt fully upright and freeze. "Huh."

Joey paused his work and turned to look at me before he started laughing. "Just figure it out, huh?"

I turned my head slowly to look at Joey, my eyes wide. "I don't know what to do with that. Should I call her right now?"

Joey chuckled, his face softening in amusement. "She doesn't have a phone, Leighton. And... maybe telling her about it while we're working. Do you think that's how she'd want to hear it?" He said slowly as if he was going to let me piece it together.

"I mean she was into you working Colin over, so maybe?" I shrugged.

"That was a physical thing, L, fueled by adrenaline. I wouldn't tell her I loved her after a torture session. It deserves... a little something more than that."

"If you boys will just tell me what you want to–" Robert whimpered, his voice broken.

"Hold on a fucking second. Can't you see we're having a serious conversation here, *Bob*?" Joey snapped, flicking the man in the ear.

"You haven't told her. I know you haven't. There wasn't really a lot to do at the cabin besides eavesdrop. Az is the only one that's told her, so maybe I should ask him for advice." I said, picking up the conversation like we hadn't just been rudely interrupted.

"What? When did– No, that makes sense. Let me guess, they were fighting?" Joey smirked.

"They're always fighting, so yeah. But Az just put it out there like it was nothing. Meanwhile, I've been having daily heart attacks that *none* of you have taken seriously." I paused, frowning. "Well, I guess they weren't heart attacks after all and I can stop taking aspirin, but still. I don't know how to do this shit, man."

Joey leaned against the chair Robert was tied to, resting his elbow on the man's head. "L, we told you it wasn't a heart attack. Why were you taking aspirin? God, you're goofy." He said with a grin. "And as for how to do this... it doesn't come with a manual, my guy."

Remembering the mini-torch I was still holding against Robert's nub; I pulled it back and studied the flame for a second. "Be better if it did," I sighed, waving the torch around as if to gesture to myself. "I mean, have you met me? Killing, maiming, that I can do, no problem. But up until recently I was pretty sure I didn't have any kind of feelings at all. Now..."

"Well, you'd be the only one who thought you couldn't feel. But... I get that it's easier sometimes not to. Honestly, it's been a world of adjustment for all of us in our own ways, I guess." Joey paused, considering some thought in his head for a while. "So, when you think about telling her you love her, what do you imagine you're doing?"

I considered his question for a minute, letting my mind mull it over, before it settled on one image, and I grinned. "Well, in a perfect world, we'd be torturing someone together. Maybe hookup in their blood after."

Joey rolled his eyes. "L... bro. No. Does *anything* about Victoria say that she'd be into that?"

"Dude, you saw her kick my sister's ass. *Ma petit* may like to pretend she's an angel but there's a reason for that *démone.*" I shrugged.

"I know. There's something in her that's a bit... vicious. But even still, she's not... how do I say this? She's not a sadist, L. That's all your wheelhouse. You wanna tell her you love her, you gotta meet her on her court."

"Damn it, thinking about her vicious streak gave me a boner." I grumbled, reaching down to adjust myself. "Now I'm in love with her *and horny.*"

Joey threw his head back and laughed. "Well, I'm sure you'll think of something to–"

"Please, no!" Robert wailed. "I'll tell you everything, just please, don't let him…"

It was obvious what the man was insinuating, but the fact that he was finally willing to talk led me to letting it slide. Instead, I leaned into his assumption, grabbing my crotch roughly and taking a few steps toward him as I grinned maniacally.

"You already know what we want. We've asked you so many times I've lost count." Joey said coldly, stepping away from the man so I could crowd his space.

"Fine, okay, fine. But please, keep that psycho away from me!" Robert wailed. I raised my hands and stepped back before motioning for the man to continue. "Trey Prescott sent his goons after my family. Said you boys were going down, but if any of you showed up here alive, to end you or else. I didn't have a choice." the man sobbed, fat, ugly tears streaming down his cheeks.

"Poor little Bobby-boy, don't you know you always have a choice?" I cooed, waggling a finger at him. "Unfortunately for you, you chose wrong."

"Tsk, tsk, Bob… You could have told us that someone was leveraging your family against you. How long have you worked for us? You know we would have kept you and your family safe. We take care of our own." Joey said, if you didn't know him it might have sounded like he was remorseful. I knew better.

"I did the only thing I could think to do! Rich is a strong man, I knew he'd stand a chance, but I had to do something. So, I used soiled equipment when I patched him up. It wasn't something I thought would actually work, but it was enough to get them off my back." Robert said in a rush, trying to justify his actions. "Please, I just want to keep my family safe."

"Oh, I'm sure your family will be just fine." Joey said

slowly. "But when you said goodbye to them this morning before you left, I hope you made it count."

"Should have come to us, Bob." I sighed, parroting what Joey had already said once as I stepped away from the vet. "But you tried to kill his brother, so my hands are tied. Nobody can help you now."

Robert, sensing that our time with him was coming to a close, started to struggle against his bonds and scream at us. It was always amusing to watch a person go through all the stages of grief right at the end of a torture session, trying everything from anger to bargaining. Bobby-boy here was no exception.

We let him thrash about like a fish out of water for a few moments before I saw Joey shift out of the corner of my eye. The sharp pop of his silenced pistol sounded just a split second before Bob stopped moving, blood trickling down his face from the entry wound.

"Fucking coward..." Joey murmured as he holstered his weapon.

We didn't bother moving the body, leaving it tied in the chair we'd put him in as we gathered our gear up and slipped from the building to grab the gasoline cans from the back of the SUV. Joey took one end of the building while I took the other and we systematically doused the whole place before meeting outside.

"You wanna light this bitch up, little brother?" I asked.

"Would be my pleasure." Joey grinned, lighting a pack of matches and tossing it down onto the gasoline fuse we'd poured ourselves. We watched to make sure the building caught like we wanted it to before turning back to the SUV. As we got in the car, Joey looked at me with a grin. "Also, really L? I didn't figure you'd be willing to go *that* far for the info."

"Dude, I wasn't gonna actually do it. What do you take me for?" I huffed.

"A criminal, L." Joey said, and we both burst into laughter as we pulled away from the inferno that had been the vet's office.

CHAPTER TWENTY SEVEN

Leighton

I'd just finished a sparring session with Joey and was stripping down to shower when I decided I needed to slake my thirst first. Not bothering to cover my nudity with a towel, I pulled open my bedroom door and stopped in my tracks. My parents were standing in the middle of the open-concept layout where the kitchen met the living room.

"Fuck." I hissed, hearing the word echoed by Az to my right on the stairs and Rich behind my parents. Glancing over their shoulders, I caught sight of Rich, covered in soil, standing just inside the entryway, the front door open wide.

"Leighton." My father drawled, looking down his nose at me in the way he always did.

"Father." I bit out, not bothering to cover myself.

"I hear we have another *Angelica* situation." My mother spoke, her shrill voice nearly causing me to wince.

Before I could respond, Az glided down the stairs and intercepted my parents. "Mr. and Mrs. Laurent, we weren't expecting you."

"Yes, well. It seems you *boys* had something to do with our cabin burning to the ground. It was only proper we came to speak with our son about the matter in person." My mother answered.

"Make yourself presentable, son. We have much that needs to be discussed." My father's tone was cold. Not like it had ever been warm in my lifetime. The man was an empty shell of a person, with less feeling than even me.

"Why don't you two have a seat? I'll bring you a drink." Az said, gesturing toward the couch. "Scotch, neat, Alistair and Rosé for your Cicely?"

"That would be lovely, darling." My mother cooed, her mask sliding back into place seamlessly.

I turned back to my room, tuning out Az's schmoozing of my parents, and slammed the door, my mood immediately more sour than it had been in a long time. I started picking through the clothes on the floor, trying to figure out where I'd tossed my workout clothes. Fuck them, I wasn't going to dress for the occasion. Took a little bit of searching, but I found what I was after, dressed myself, and took a deep breath before heading back out into the house proper.

By the time I stepped out of my bedroom, Victoria was seated opposite my parents in the living area. My heart plummeted into my stomach, and I struggled against the urge to snatch her from the loveseat and stash her away somewhere until they went away. If not permanently. Forcing myself to close the distance at a normal pace, I didn't miss the tightness of her smile and the rage burning in her eyes. I'd have to pat myself on the back later for my new emotion recognition skills.

"What do you need to cover the cost of the cabin?" I said without preamble as I eased myself onto the loveseat beside Victoria, noting the drinks Az had grabbed for them sat untouched on the coffee table.

My mother wasn't bothering to hide her disdain about my chosen seat, all pretense of normalcy wiped from her face. I could practically hear the gears in her head turning as she plotted Victoria's murder.

"It's time for you to return home, Leighton. You need to return to the fold and take your place as the Laurent heir."

"Pretty sure Lacey is doing that just fine." I shrugged.

"That role wasn't meant for Lacey, you're the eldest son, it is yours. And it's time you stop playing with your little toys and come home to take it." My father said, sounding bored.

"That's not misogynistic at all." I replied, my tone dripping with sarcasm as I rolled my eyes. "You're the ones who put *me* out. I've built a life and legacy of my own that *you* can't control. Deal with it."

"Oh, don't be so childish, Leighton. That's not what

happened. You just needed a little time to learn to control your *urges*." My mother waved a hand dismissively. "Don't make it out to be more than it was."

I let out a sardonic laugh causing Victoria to tense beside me. "I was seventeen."

"It was a lesson we thought you needed, Leighton." My father replied without an ounce of emotion behind his words. "With recent events, it's clear we need to take another tact with you. We have arranged a marriage for you. You will return home by the end of the week to meet your bride."

I stared at my father for several long moments, trying to keep my composure. Eventually it came rushing out of me as hysterical laughter that had me throwing my head back and my eyes watering.

"I didn't know you had jokes, old man." I wheezed out between cackles. "You guys hear this shit?"

"Alistair, surely you can see how this isn't the right course of action." Rich's steady voice cut through my laughter as he moved from the stairs. It was obvious he'd quickly showered and dressed. All hints of soil were gone from his body, and he was dressed in a smart suit, only his wet curls standing out from his put-together appearance. "Surely we can pay for the cost of restoring the cabin and let this matter go."

My father looked Rich over like he was assessing a bit of crust on the bottom of his shoe, his lip curled up slightly before turning back to me.

"Your father never jokes about matters of business, son. We're quite serious. We've selected a good match for you in station, and she comes from good stock. It's a mutually beneficial arrangement." She said snidely.

"And Victoria Bristol isn't those things?" I challenged, arching a brow.

My father turned his attention to Victoria for the first time since I'd entered the room. "No. Her father may have been of good stock, but she has that unfortunate stain of a mother."

Victoria shifted next to me, curling her hands into fists in her lap. Rich and Az both stiffened, and I was sure the red creeping up Az's neck and face meant he was about two seconds away from strangling my father. I hoped he'd do it. I'd have paid good money to see Alistair Laurent at the end of a blade.

My mother rose from her seat, gently indicating for my father to follow suit. "Next week, Leighton. If you do not return home, there will be consequences." her eyes flitted to Victoria, letting me know just what sort of consequences she had in mind.

I sneered in her direction but didn't respond since anything I said might mean they'd choose to darken our home with their presence even longer. They swept out of the house, and as my father closed the door behind them, it felt like the whole room released a breath we hadn't realized we'd been holding.

"Could have let us know your parents were coming, L." Az snapped, picking up the scotch he'd poured for my father and downing it.

"How would I have done that when *I* didn't even know they were coming?" I said, scrubbing my hand through my hair. "How the fuck did they just walk up in here? I don't see either one of them picking locks."

Rich coughed softly, and we all turned to look at him. I noted that Victoria looked away after a second. He was scrubbing his hand over the back of his neck, looking strangely sheepish.

"That's... probably on me. I was out tending my garden. I'd had to come in a couple of times and figured it'd just be easier to leave the door open..."

"Jesus fucking– Are you serious?! After all your harping, and you just leave the door open to where anyone can walk in?!" Az snapped.

"I was *right there*! It's not my fault Leighton's parents move like fucking ghosts in formal wear!" Rich tossed back.

"They're about as lively as the dead too." Victoria snorted before seeming to catch herself and shifting so her body faced away from Rich.

Joey appeared on the stairs at that moment, glancing at each of us in confusion as he strolled toward the living area.

"Who died?"

"Leighton's bachelorhood, apparently." Az chuckled. At least someone found the situation as humorous as I had.

Joey's eyes got as wide around as dinner plates as he looked between me and Victoria. "Damn, dude! You told her already?! I'm proud of you, man."

"Told w–" pounding on the front door cut off Victoria as I mimed zipping my lips angrily at Joey.

"Richard Innocenti, I know you're in there. Open this fucking door right now!" Tiffany's voice called out, all hints of her party girl persona lacking.

Victoria stood, making a motion as if she'd rush the door for a moment before she stopped herself. She shook her head and turned back to us, a sad sort of expression on her face.

"I don't want to see her. Not after..." Her lip trembled slightly as she moved back toward the kitchen. Az caught her around the shoulders and pulled her close, murmuring something in her ear, and moved her toward the stairs.

Tiffany continued to pound on the door, screaming threats and obscenities loud enough I was glad we didn't have neighbors. I waited long enough for Az and Victoria to disappear from sight before painting on a manic grin and bounding toward the door.

"Malibu Barbie," I widened my grin as I pulled the door open. "What are you doing here?"

"I know she's here," Tiffany seethed, pushing past me and storming into the house. "Victoria!" she screamed before narrowing her eyes at Rich and closing the distance to jab him in the chest with one perfectly manicured nail. "What the fuck have you done with her?"

"She's not here," Rich lied smoothly. "Though, I am curious to know how you knew *we* were."

"How the fuck do you think, Innocenti?"

I closed the door and leaned my back against it, crossing my arms over my chest as I watched them.

"Get that info from your friends with matching golden tattoos?" He said, quirking a brow up.

"I told you the night of the shooting at Temptat!on Innocenti, if *anything* happened to Victoria, there would be hell to pay. And I have just the devils for the job. Now tell me what the fuck you've done with her, *to* her, before I make sure you burn."

"Well, that's enough of that." I chuckled, taking a step toward them, intending to remove Tiffany from the house myself.

"Maybe you should be asking your friends instead of us, *honey.*" Rich drawled.

Tiffany jerked back like he'd slapped her. "You have no idea what you're fucking talking about." She spat, looking like she was about to claw his eyes out. "You can't see the forest for the fucking trees."

"Well, plan on cluing me in?" Rich narrowed his eyes on her, waiting a moment. Tiffany sneered at him but said nothing. "Leighton, the door." He stalked toward the petite blonde and grabbed her around the waist, hoisting her up over his shoulder like she was nothing. I pulled open the door with a flourish, waving at Tiffany as Rich stalked past me.

A few steps from the door, he shrugged her off his shoulder and dropped her on her ass at his feet.

"You bastard, that's going to bruise." She shrieked as she scrambled upright.

"I could have thrown you, I chose not to." Rich shrugged, his voice dripping venom.

"Oh, he definitely wanted to throw you Traitor Barbie." I snickered as Rich strolled past me back inside the house. "You should just be happy it was him and not me."

I shut the door, pulling out my phone to text someone to make sure she left our territory without giving her a chance to respond. As soon as the text was sent, I looked up to find Rich moving toward the liquor cabinet.

"I guess if we had any doubts before, we know the way she rolled with that double speak like a champ, Tiffany Humphrey's is a player in the game."

"Yeah, but is she the one moving the pieces?" Joey sighed, causing me to do a double take because I'd forgotten he was in the room.

"Fuck, maybe *you're* the ghost, Joey. But I don't know, but if the Devils know we're back, we need to get moving on plugging up the hole before they sink our battleship." I replied. "Until we figure that bit out, I'm heading back to the gym. I've got some shit to sort out."

Joey just chuckled and shook his head. "You'd be surprised what you hear when you're the quiet one." He shrugged. "Come on, I'll kick your ass a few rounds if it'll help you feel better. A punching bag isn't gonna stand up to all that childhood trauma."

CHAPTER TWENTY EIGHT

Victoria

I hovered just out of sight at the top of the stairs while Az held my arm, ready to pull me back if I decided to move down them. He didn't let me go until we were both certain Tiffany was gone. As hurt as I was that the woman who had been my best friend my entire life had betrayed me, I was more worried about Leighton's reaction to his parents. It had taken every scrap of my self-control not to claw Cicely's eyes out as she sat on the sofa across from us.

"I wouldn't." Az said softly as I moved toward the stairs. "Leighton isn't going to be in a good place right now. He works his shit out best through violence."

"I appreciate the warning, but I need to do this." I replied. "From the sounds of it, Joey is with him, so I'll be alright. He won't let Leighton cross any lines."

Az studied me for a moment before pressing his lips together and giving me a tight nod. I wrapped my arms around his waist and gave him a quick hug before turning and making my way down the stairs. Rich was still in the dining room, but his back was to me as I slipped past him and moved down the long hallway at the front of the house. My eyes moved to the door that led to the basement as I made my way toward the guys' home gym, and for a moment, I allowed myself to imagine Cicely chained there the way the man Joey had interrogated had been. I clenched my jaw against the shiver of excitement that tickled my spine at the thought and forced myself to continue toward the gym.

Leighton and Joey were locked in a brutal dance on the

mats in the center of the room. I stood just inside the gym, momentarily enraptured by the beauty of the violence playing out before me. Their lithe forms moved with a kind of grace that I'd only seen in ballet. Joey's eyes landed on me just as Leighton rushed forward and wrapped his arms around Joey's waist, taking them both down to the mat.

"I'm out," Joey said, tapping Leighton's shoulder.

Leighton muttered something I didn't catch before releasing his hold on Joey and sitting back on his heels. Following Joey's gaze, his eyes found me, and his face split into a breathtaking, feral smile. He helped Joey sit up and leaned forward to whisper something in his ear that had Joey's eyes darkening as he gave me a similar smile.

"I think I just had a better idea on how to work my shit out." Leighton said darkly, his eyes raking over me.

"Yes," I breathed, not sure exactly what I was agreeing to as a shiver of need tore through me.

Leighton stood up and offered Joey a hand up. Once they were both on their feet, they were moving toward me. I had the distinct impression of watching two predators advancing on their prey as they moved.

"We have an idea, Pet." Joey said, his voice pitched low and taking on the growling tone I'd come to recognize.

"What did you have in mind, Alpha?" My voice was breathy as I batted my lashes at him.

Leighton choked on a laugh before shaking his head and bumping Joey with his shoulder. "Yeah, *Alpha*, what are we going to do with *la petit démone?*" His voice dropped to match Joey's tone as he spoke.

Joey reached out and tucked a stray strand of hair behind my ear, causing me to shiver. "I think we should play a game. What do you think, Pet? Would you like it if we hunted you down and worked out Leighton's *issues*?"

I nodded vigorously in consent, my words trapped in my throat.

Joey clicked his tongue and narrowed his eyes at me.

"Now, now, Pet. You know the rules, you have to use your words."

I cleared my throat, trying to get myself to make some kind of sound. "Yes, I... Yes, *please*."

"Listen to that... She says please so sweetly." Leighton chuckled as he moved toward a row of cabinets on the wall. I watched through heavy-lidded eyes as he pulled them open and grabbed a hunting knife before opening a small drawer and producing two condoms. I squeaked out a laugh, causing him to look at me over his shoulder.

"What's so funny, *ma petit?*" he asked.

"You just... you have them stashed *everywhere*."

"I like to be prepared." He replied, turning to move back toward me and Joey.

Joey held up a hand to him to stop, "Not that one," he tilted his head toward the hunting knife. "She's not ready for the full extent of your brand of play, L. The blade needs to be dull."

Leighton squinted at him for a moment as if he were turning the words over in his head. With a shrug, he turned around, placed the hunting knife back in the cabinet, and grabbed a smaller, ivory-handled blade.

"Where should we do this?" Leighton mused as he moved toward us again.

Joey rubbed his chin thoughtfully. "We have the orchard Rich bought for Ma. It's not far, and nobody knows it even exists, so we'd be able to safely play there."

"Perfect, let's go." Leighton grinned, snagging my hand and pulling me behind him as he headed from the gym.

Before I knew what was happening, we were loaded into a small sedan. I almost laughed at how easy it had been for the pair of them to get me out of the house and on the road without any of the others realizing. I was quickly brought back to the moment as we drove toward the outskirts of town by Joey's voice.

"Do you remember your safe words, Pet?" he asked,

glancing at me in the rearview mirror.

"Yes. Yellow for slow down, red for stop."

"Why is it always the stoplight method?" Leighton mused. "Why is it never a word like pumpernickel that's not used in normal conversation?"

"Because who is going to remember *that* in the heat of the moment? The stoplight is short and easy to remember." Joey answered.

"Okay, but it's so *common*. Like if I said I love that red on her, everything would stop because of a compliment. Nobody is gonna be confused if you yell out pumpernickel."

"I seriously doubt *anyone* mistakes that for safe word use. Normally, they're said on their own when they're being used..." Joey considered for a moment. "I've never had anyone safe word *ever* while using it in a sentence."

"Whatever man, my points are valid, but *fine* we'll use the damned stoplights." Leighton pouted. "It's not my fault your kinks are too tame to toe the line of needing a damned safe word anyway."

Joey shook his head and returned his focus to the road. We'd driven maybe ten minutes before we were turning off the main roads onto a gravel path that led deep into a grove of apple trees.

"We're here." Joey smiled as he eased the car to a stop.

The guys got out of the car almost simultaneously, and as Joey came around the front of the car, Leighton handed him a small foil packet containing a condom before he pulled open my door. I scrambled out of the car to find myself backed into it once Leighton shut the door behind me.

"Do you trust me, Pet?" Joey asked as his hand slid across my hip.

"You know I do," I whispered.

"Good girl," he crooned. "What do you do if you need to use one of your words?"

"Yell loud enough that you can hear them." I breathed out, my heart was already pounding in my chest hard enough that I could feel it through my whole body.

Leighton's hand slid across my other hip, pulling my attention to him. "We'll give you a head start, *ma petit*. Get as far as you can, so the game can last."

"Count of three," Joey said, pulling me off the car and positioning me in front of them. "Three..." he whispered in my ear.

"Two..." Leighton said, in the other. There was a long pause that had me shuddering, waiting.

"*Run.*" I heard their voices bite out simultaneously.

I tore away from them, the tightly packed dirt giving slightly under my feet. My head swiveled from side to side as I searched for anywhere I could hide among the tidy rows of trees. Realizing that there wouldn't be anywhere to take sanctuary from my guys, I began to zig-zag through the orchard, hoping to slow them down with my erratic movements.

My heart pounded in my chest, and my breaths soon became shallow pants as a small trill of fear heightened all my senses. They'd promised me a head start, but they hadn't told me how much of one I'd get, and it only served to drive my anticipation higher. I risked a glance over my shoulder to see if they'd begun their hunt, only to find more empty rows of apple trees.

Laughter rang out in the empty orchard from somewhere behind me, and I picked up my pace. There was a sinister edge to the sound that made my core clench and wetness pool between my thighs. A sound similar to a crow cawing echoed to my left, startling me and causing me to zig to the right.

The quiet peace of the orchard was broken suddenly by the sounds of mimicked bird calls. Leighton and Joey had found a way to communicate without speaking as they hunted me, and I soon found my footsteps slowing as they closed in. Sweat trickled between my breasts, and my chest heaved as I worked to catch my breath. I couldn't see them, but I could *hear* them getting closer as my eyes searched for a way out.

"I'm coming for you *ma petit*." Leighton's voice rang out somewhere behind me, urging me into motion once again.

"You're gonna have to move faster than that if you want to stand a chance, Pet." Joey's gravelly tone echoed from my right.

I shifted to the left, weaving through the trees as they resumed making bird calls around me. It was like they were everywhere and nowhere all at once as they managed to keep themselves hidden and moving around me unseen. My eyes landed on a weathered shed in the distance, and I gulped down air, picking up my speed as I raced toward the possibility of sanctuary. I was so focused on my new goal that I didn't catch the movement in the row of trees to my left.

Arms snaked around my waist, throwing me off balance as they brought me to an abrupt halt. "Got ya," Leighton crooned in my ear, his breath against my skin sending shivers down my spine.

He turned me to face him, and I caught sight of Joey stalking toward us through the wide space between the rows. My breath caught in my throat, and I squeezed my thighs together against the rush of need that washed over me at his expression. Leighton's lips quirked up in a smile, and he backed me into the shed I'd thought would be my safe haven before pulling his knife from his pocket.

The dull blade kissed my throat before he trailed it down toward my breasts. Leighton licked his lips and dipped it just below my collar, his breathing growing heavy. The sound of fabric ripping tore through the orchard as he jerked the dull blade through the center of my shirt.

"Fuck," he groaned, pressing his hips forward so that his erection pressed against my thigh through the material of our jeans. "What I would give to see you bleed."

Joey made a low warning sound in his throat. "No, L. She's not there, so you're going to have to play *nice*."

Leighton growled like a feral animal but nodded in

assent. Still holding the knife in his hand, he grabbed the ragged edges it had left of my shirt and pulled them apart, ripping it open. The cool fall air tickled my skin, and my entire body trembled.

"Please," I pleaded.

Leighton smiled and dipped his blade between my chest and bra, jerking it through the material so hard it pulled me slightly forward as my breasts fell free. Without a word, he tossed the blade aside and leaned down, wrapping his lips around my nipple. My head tilted back against the shed, and I let out a soft mewl. A rough hand on my other breast drew my attention to Joey as he edged his way in next to Leighton.

"Get her on the ground." He barked out.

Leighton released my nipple and stepped back. His hands trailed down my waist and legs until he was kneeling in front of me, gripping my ankles. With one hard tug, he pulled my feet out from under me, and I was falling. Joey reached out and eased my body to the ground, shooting Leighton an angry look as he did.

"I said, play *nice* L." Joey growled.

"This *is* me being nice." Leighton snapped back, moving his hands to the waistband of my jeans. "*Ma petit* can handle it."

"We don't want to break our toys before we even start playing with them." Joey said protectively.

Leighton bared his teeth at Joey, his fingers deftly unbuttoning my jeans and pulling down the zipper before he snatched them down my legs along with my panties. He left them tangled just above my knee and shifted me roughly to my stomach.

"On your knees, *ma petit*." He bit out.

I scrambled to get my hands and knees under me and comply. Leighton's fingers tangled in my hair and pulled my head back sharply as if I were moving too slowly for him. The violence of the action caused my core to clench, and I whimpered.

"Do that again; she's got the prettiest whimpers," Joey growled as he came to his knees in front of me.

Leighton tugged my hair again, leaning over my back and bringing his lips close to my ear. "Tell me how much you like it when I hurt you, *ma petit,*" he commanded.

I whimpered again, mewling in response. Leighton yanked back on my hair harder.

"*Words, ma petit.*" He snapped.

"Yes! I like it. More, *please...*" I barely choked out, forcing myself to use actual words.

I felt the heat of Leighton's body move away from my back and the sudden intrusion of two fingers being stuffed into my aching core. I arched into his hand, crying out.

"I think that can be arranged." Leighton snarled, a feral edge to his words. "I think we should make you choke on Joey's cock while I take what I want from you."

A gush of wetness accompanied his words, and he chuckled darkly. His hand was still tangled in my hair, and my head was pulled back so far it was just shy of painful, but I didn't miss the way Joey's face held evidence of a silent conversation between the two. Leighton's fingers continued to thrust in and out of my aching core as Joey undid his zipper at a torturously slow pace.

Nonsensical pleas fell from my lips along with my wanton moans. I lifted my hands from the ground, letting the hold Leighton had on my hair keep me upright, and reached for Joey. He freed his thick cock and chuckled.

"So needy, Pet." He cooed, shifting close enough for me to stick out my tongue and lick his tip.

"Open your mouth." Leighton said gruffly.

I complied and felt him shift me forward, the ground pulling at my pants still tangled around my knees, before shoving my head forward. I gagged slightly as Leighton pressed my head until Joey's length hit the back of my throat, and my nose smashed against his abdomen. The sound that Joey made was guttural, and I clenched around Leighton's fingers in response. Leighton held me there until my body craved air, and my eyes began to water.

He pulled my head back at the same time he removed his fingers from my aching sex. "Suck." The word was a command, not a request.

I compiled without question, swirling my tongue around Joey and hollowing my cheeks in an attempt to make up for my inability to move my head with the hold Leighton had on my hair. Joey groaned, and I heard the sound of foil ripping behind me, the ache in my core causing my eyes to flutter closed.

"Eyes on me, Pet." Joey barked.

My eyes snapped open, and I looked up at him through my lashes just as Leighton lined himself up with my dripping sex and thrust himself into the hilt. He shoved my head forward with the motion, causing me to gag again as I fought to swallow Joey down.

"That's right, *ma petit. Choke.*" Leighton snarled.

"Hands down." Joey commanded, and I complied immediately, supporting myself on my hands again.

I immediately felt some of the pressure release from my hair. The relief was short-lived in the shift before my head was jerked back again. Joey pulled my head back this time as he started to slowly move himself in and out at the pace he wanted. Behind me, I felt rough hands on my hips, gripping hard enough that I was sure there would be fingerprint bruises as marked reminders. Leighton held me still as he began to move.

My head swam a bit at the overwhelming sense of being fully taken over. I moaned around Joey's length in my mouth, working to swallow him as he picked up the pace. Leighton grunted behind me, digging his nails into the sensitive skin. The sharp bite of teeth in the flesh on my side made me cry out or try to. The motion in my mouth pushed Joey into my throat and caused him to moan loudly.

The boys ramped up their pace almost in time with

each other as they used me to chase down their release. The delicious coil of tension started to tighten in my spine as I arched my back, my eyes fluttering. I was helpless in their hands, completely at their mercy, as they drove me toward the edge. I clenched around Leighton as he pistoned into me. Joey moaned loudly, yanking my hair harder.

"Break for us, *ma petit*." Leighton snarled, thrusting himself impossibly deeper and hitting that place inside me that drove me to near insanity. "She's so fucking close. *Break*."

"Don't hold back, Pet. We want to see you shatter." Joey growled, his grip in my hair tightening.

My entire body tensed, my lids fell closed of their own volition, and fireworks exploded behind my lids. A scream ripped from my throat around Joey's cock, and I felt both of my men's movements stutter. The orgasm tore me open, stealing my senses and bringing me to the brink of oblivion. I barely registered Joey and Leighton's grunts as they reached their own release, Joey spilling down my throat as my entire body went lax.

I felt myself eased gently to the ground as they pulled free and released me. One of them stroked my cheek softly as I lay there with my eyes closed, working to catch my breath.

"Fuck," Leighton groaned. "I didn't mean to actually break her."

Joey chuckled as I mumbled nonsense in my attempt to respond.

"You still in there, Pet?" Joey asked, turning my head to look at him.

"Mmmm," was all I was able to get out.

I felt the gentle tug of my panties and jeans being pulled back into place, and then my body lifted from the ground as Joey pulled me to his bare chest.

"When..." I managed.

"Shh, Pet. I got you." He replied, carefully pulling his shirt over my head.

I felt Leighton's hands join Joey's as they worked in

tandem to get me into Joey's shirt. It felt like a tight hug the way it squeezed my larger body.

"Let's get you home."

CHAPTER TWENTY NINE

Joey

I was smirking to myself over breakfast the day before playing over in my head. I had a few minutes before I had to worry about current events, and playing the events of the night before was more interesting than the droning of news stories as I moved to the dining table.

"Penny for your thoughts, *Alpha*?" Leighton's amused voice pulled me out of my thoughts.

"Fuck you, L." I flipped him off with a smirk. "Don't call me that. Doesn't have the same ring to it when you say it."

"Awe, you wound me." He laughed as he grabbed his plate from the counter. Craig just rolled his eyes at us as he finished cleaning up from cooking breakfast.

"You two seem to be in a good mood this morning. Should I be worried?" Rich drawled as he emerged from the stairs with Az behind him.

"With those two? Definitely." Az snarked, adjusting his tie with a little smirk. "Where's the Princess?"

I couldn't stop the smirk that plastered itself on my face, and Leighton huffed out a laugh.

"Likely still sleeping… she needs the rest." I said simply, trying to school my features when Rich scowled at me before turning toward the coffee pot. *Not my fault you're a moron, big brother.* I thought to myself and rolled my eyes behind his back.

"Our next story is a sad one. A local veterinarian's office, the Sacona Animal Center, burned down last night. Emergency responders were unable to save the building but managed to prevent the flames from spreading to the surrounding buildings.

Fire Chief Michaelson said, quote, 'There were no animals or staff in the building, except for one. It's unusual to see this place so empty, but it's better than the alternative.'" I was so glad for my ability to keep up a poker face when the news started with the story.

"The one victim that was lost in the blaze has been confirmed to be Dr. Jacobs. A tragedy: I know he'll be missed by his patients. Both the pets and the owners had nothing but good things to say about the good doctor."

"Tragic. He'll surely be missed. Our next story when we come back: The sudden influx of drug activity in the Southside. Is this a sign of something more dangerous behind the scenes? More when we come back."

Rich sneered, and I could see the muscle in his jaw twitching.

"Daaamn. Shit's wild, huh?" Leighton said absently. I kicked him under the table.

"What the actual fuck, you two?!" Rich finally yelled, setting his coffee cup down hard enough that I was sure it cracked.

"What? Just because a place burns down doesn't mean *we* did it." I said with a shrug.

"Are you saying that you didn't have anything to do with it?" Rich snapped sarcastically, and I rolled my eyes. He wouldn't believe it even if we *hadn't* done it.

Craig slid into his chair with an annoyed look. "You owe me some rope, Little Brother. When I told you to take what you needed, I didn't know you'd be leaving it in a fire. My shit is not cheap."

I cut my eyes to Craig with a glare, mentally berating him for bringing that up now. Rich crossed his arms over his chest and stared hard at me.

"Wanna try that again, Joey?" He snapped, making me bristle. I hated it when he spoke to me like I was still a child.

"Fine!" I tossed back, standing up and moving to put my

plate in the sink. "So, what if we did, huh? He fucking earned it, and you know it!"

"Do you not think that this will cause retaliation since we know that the vet was on the take from the Jackals?" Rich growled, a vein in his forehead seeming like it would pop any second.

"He was *our* guy, Rich! He was on our fucking payroll, and he tried to kill you. He could have come to us, but no, he decided to be a traitor. As far as I care, he signed his own death warrant." I clipped, throwing my hands up. Bob got what was coming to him.

"To be fair, he knew the risks when he decided to do what he did." Leighton added, surprisingly calm during our argument as he continued his breakfast. "He had to have known if we found out that his number would be up."

"And maybe the Jackals need a fucking message, huh? They keep coming for us, and we've said *nothing* back. It's not a good look, Rich. I mean, for fuck's sake! Victoria's childhood home got *blown up,* and you were nearly killed." I yelled, not understanding why my brother didn't want to stomp them into a grease stain for trying us.

"Leighton blew up the manor," Az said, pouring another cup of coffee. The rest of the guys didn't seem bothered by Rich and me yelling at each other, continuing to go about their mornings. It would have been amusing if I wasn't so pissed off.

"Hey! I only did that because there were too many little roaches to kill by hand." Leighton said, putting his hand on his chest in offense. Az rolled his eyes and moved to the living room to sit on the couch with his coffee.

"You didn't clear this with any of us! You don't know what kind of consequences this could have! In case you fucking forgot, we're kind of in the middle of some shit here!" Rich yelled at me.

"Why the fuck are you angry about us making sure they don't forget who we are!" I snapped back.

"It's not safe! We only just got back home, we're still

putting our house in fucking order, and it's not just us we have to worry about anymore!" Rich roared. "You have to be smarter than the people we're up against and *THAT*," He pointed to the TV as the news logo rolled back on the screen, "was not fucking smart!"

There was a beat of silence after Rich's yelling. I raised my eyebrow at him, wondering if he caught his slip.

"Why is everyone yelling?" Victoria's still sleepy voice rang through the room, drawing our attention. Her hair was still messy from sleep, and the shirt she'd thrown on fit her like a dress, falling off one shoulder. "Is something going on?"

I immediately felt my shoulders relax, and I smiled softly at her. She looked so sweet standing there, still waking up. I wanted to carry her back up to bed and tuck her in. "Nothing's wrong, Sweetheart. Rich is just being a stubborn jackass."

She snorted slightly. "Ah, so business as usual. Well, I'm going back to bed."

Rich's body went rigid, and he scoffed, turning away from her to fill his cup again. Not before I caught the double take, and once over, he gave her. I wanted to flick his ear like Mom would if she were here. *Big idiot*, I thought for the thousandth time.

"Actually, Love." Az stood up, moving toward her. "We all have places to be today, and we need you with someone."

"You could come with us!" Leighton said cheerily.

"Uhm, no. She doesn't need to spend the day with street guys." Craig said flatly.

"Well, I'm gonna be at the warehouse almost the whole day. I'm still catching up on the logistics from when we were gone. Leighton's just riding in with me since he's got some shit to sort out with his guys." I said, perking up at the idea of her coming with us. It might not be as productive a day as possible, but I'd set that paperwork on fire if someone asked me to choose.

"It's up to the Princess." Rich said in a low tone, not turning around. She stared at the back of his head like he'd just done a standing backflip or something.

"Uh, yeah..." She said slowly before she recovered herself. "Yeah, sounds good. Probably better than sitting through meetings with Az or not understanding anything the Craig says." When Craig looked up at her with a smirk, she trailed her fingers across his head with a smile. "Let me get changed."

"We're not done talking about this." Rich snapped at me as she disappeared back upstairs.

"What's done is done, Rich. Want me to take licks for it, then I will when I get home. I have work to do." I snapped back.

"Yeah, bet that's what you're planning on *doing* today." Leighton cackled, dropping his plate in the sink on top of mine and heading for his room. Rich sneered, heading for the garage. I shook my head at the sound of the door slamming on his way out.

A little while later, we pulled up at our main warehouse. It looked damn near abandoned from the outside: faded, run-down, windows boarded up, and in disrepair. Leighton had complained the entire way about some of his associates being skittish since the skirmishes with the Jackals started. Apparently, one was so insistent about being pulled off the street that he was beginning to annoy the soldiers and capos he worked under.

"I get his wife is pregnant, but where the fuck am I supposed to put him? All I got is street guys!" He'd groaned.

I was glad we were finally here. Leighton was like my brother but getting him to understand why someone like that might be nervous was like beating your head against a wall. And could give you a headache just as quickly.

"This... is where you work?" Victoria said, somewhere between disbelief and disgust.

"You didn't expect me to be overseeing guns and drugs in

some upscale place, did you? This place looks unused and is in a mostly unused area of warehouses for a reason, Sweetheart." I smirked as I pulled the car into a small, connected building and cut the engine.

"Not knowing we're even here helps us out if anyone not in the know comes looking." Leighton explained further.

"Yes, I understand the concept, Leighton," Victoria smirked.

We got out of the car, and Leighton started heading to one side of the warehouse to find his boys before he stopped and turned around.

"Almost forgot something." He grinned, sidling up to Victoria and giving her a hard kiss. I leaned against the door and waited, but I couldn't help but laugh after a little while.

"L, bro, you're gonna see her again. Let the woman breathe." I spoke. He flipped me off and continued for a few more seconds before finally letting her go and headed out. She stood there momentarily, looking dazed and flushed as she caught her breath. I had to bite my lip to keep from pulling her back into the car.

"Come on, Sweetheart." I gestured with my head toward the side door and held out my hand for her to take.

"So… you're in charge of production," she said. It wasn't a question, but it did need an answer.

"Yeah, Rich insisted when I joined up because he doesn't want me on the street with Leighton. And before you get any bad ideas about what we do, we might sell drugs, but we don't do it too just anyone. We don't sell in Southside, and we don't sell to kids. Our… clientele is mostly the wealthy of the city." I said, opening the door for her and letting her inside. "Our people are all paid fairly, and I make sure they're provided with safety gear so that they're not exposed to the product they're working with accidentally. I'm actually quite proud of the fact that we beat out most of the factory jobs in the city as far as wages go."

"Somehow… for this city, I'm not surprised that one of

the better factory jobs is for a fucking mob." She said, a hint of pained humor in her voice. I nodded. It was sad, and it probably said something about us that we did contribute to it, but we did our best to ensure our people were cared for. And they repaid us in loyalty. Well... most of the time.

I gave her a short tour of the warehouse, at least the parts I felt comfortable with her seeing for the time being, before we headed up to the office.

It wasn't a big office and didn't have a lot in it. I hadn't skimped on the chairs, so those were comfortable, but since this place might need to be abandoned in a hurry, there wasn't much point in decorating.

She seemed to take a keen interest in my work, and somehow, I felt my chest swell with affection as she looked over my paperwork and asked questions. I could see the wheels in her head turning. Our girl was sharp, and it made my chest swell with pride and affection.

A knock on the door interrupted us, and I let my face fall into a passive expression as I sat up. Victoria moved off where she'd perched her hip on the desk and stood to my side, her hand on my shoulder.

"Hey, boss? I'm sorry if I'm interrupting, but I wondered if I could have a word." A man at the door asked, pulling his mask down. I didn't recognize him until I saw his face.

"No problem, Terry. Come in and shut the door." I nodded. He flitted his gaze between me and Victoria but did as I asked before shuffling to stand before my desk.

"I hate to be the bearer of bad news, but one of our guys... he's skimming." Terry said, his face a mask of disappointment.

"Really? Do you have proof?" I asked, leaning back in my chair to look up at him.

"I saw him dealing, boss. And it gets worse. When I saw him selling, he was in Southside, and it was kids. They couldn't have been more than 15." The other man shook his head slowly and produced the bag of pills from his pocket. They were definitely ours; they even had our tiny moth stamp on them.

It wasn't detailed, but it was enough that we would know if our shit was somewhere, it shouldn't have been. "I got this off the kids that had bought it. Told them that if you five found out, you'd probably have someone talking to their parents personally."

I smirked at his little improv. "Well, hopefully that scared them back home. Alright. Who was it?"

"One of the new guys, Russ." Terry sighed. "Seemed like a bright guy when he started... guess not."

I nodded slowly. I had a vague recollection of the guy. "I appreciate you coming to me with it, Terry. Why don't you head home for the day, huh? Consider it my thanks for this."

"If it's all the same, boss, I need the hours." Terry shifted a bit.

"You'll be paid for the day, now get out of here. Give your wife my best." I said, keeping my face impassive. He nodded and backed toward the door before heading out and closing it behind him.

I let out a slow breath and leaned my head on the back of my chair. "Fucking hell. I really can't afford to lose another guy right now. We had a few people leave already because of this shit with the Jackals, not wanting to be here if they decide to hit the warehouses again. I can't blame them, but if I get any more short-staffed, we won't meet demand."

I pinched the bridge of my nose, causing Tory to laugh.

"You look like your brother when you do that." she said when she'd stopped chuckling.

"Offend me like that again, I dare you." I smirked, giving her a pointed look. She moved to sit in one of the chairs facing my desk and watched me for a second, looking thoughtful. I raised a brow. "Something to share with the class."

"Well... Seems like your problem has a pretty simple solution." she said hesitantly. "I don't want to step on any toes here–"

"Tell me what you're thinking, I won't be upset or anything." I smiled.

"Seems to me like you need to take this Russ guy out back and shoot him. And Leighton's nervous nellie, the expectant father, give him the job since it will be open. Solves two problems at one time. A nervous street guy doesn't seem like an effective one, and you need to keep your team moving." she said, tapping her chin absently as she thought. "Honestly, if Leighton could afford to move the nervous ones to here for the time being, that seems like it would benefit everyone."

I stared at her, blinking slowly. She looked at me after a few beats of silence and scrunched her face.

"What?" she asked indignantly.

"I'm just... surprised is all." I answered.

"Well, it seems like a simple solution to move the nervous people off the street to a place they perceive as safer so they can do effective work. Starting with the expectant father," she said.

"That's not the part of your suggestion that surprised me." I chuckled. "I just didn't expect you to go for the obvious solution after everything that's happened."

"Well, with all the training with guns that you walked me through, it helped a lot. And during our conversations about it... well, I may have learned that sometimes people just need to be shot. If that wasn't the route you were planning on going though–" She rambled, looking a little sheepish.

"Oh no, I was going to shoot him. He's breaking major rules here. First, he's skimming off my product. Second, he's dealing in off-limits territory. Third, he's dealing to kids. He was a dead man from the moment he was caught, it just hasn't caught up to him yet." I shrugged. "It was just a little surprising coming from *you* is all."

"Well... I've been paying attention. I mean, eventually, all this other bullshit we've got going on will end, and I'd rather be useful to you guys than not. I don't want to always be sidelined or doubted when something needs handling, I don't like it there." she said, lifting her chin. My heart squeezed in my chest at her words. I moved around my desk and pulled her up from her chair.

"None of us deserve you, you know that, right?" I felt like I smiled so much around her that my jaw hurt sometimes, but I couldn't help it. I wove my fingers into her hair and kissed her with everything I hadn't said yet. I didn't think I'd ever get over how sweet she was.

When I pulled away, she had that adorable flush on her cheeks I adored so much.

"Stay here, Sweetheart. Why don't you call Leighton and fill him in on your idea? He'll love it. He hates nervous trigger fingers in his people. *He* might be reckless, but he doesn't like his people to be." I said, brushing an errant strand of curls away from her face, stepping away from her, and giving her my phone. I checked my clip as I moved toward the door, more out of habit than necessity. "I'll be right back."

I shut the door behind me, letting my impassive mask fall back into place as I moved out onto the production floor. A few of my people waved as they did their work, but I ignored them. I cut a beeline to my floor manager, who knew what was up when he saw me coming.

"New guy. Russ." I clipped, raising my voice to be heard over the noise of the floor, handing him the bag that Terry had given me. The manager's eyes widened, and he motioned for me to follow him.

We found the guy cutting up and laughing among a few people who worked with him as they headed out the back, likely for a break.

"Russ." I said coldly. Everyone froze and turned toward me.

"Uh, yeah boss?" The one in the middle spoke up. I swept my gaze across the group, doing a quick mental check that there wouldn't be any unintended casualties before I lifted my gun and pulled the trigger. The man was dead when he hit the floor, blood and grey matter leaking from the holes in his head.

I turned around to the rest of the production floor.

"If there is anyone else on this floor that's thinking of

making themselves a little side profit, ask yourself if the cost is worth it when I find out." I snapped. "Someone get this fucking mess cleaned up!"

The floor manager pulled a couple of people off the line who rushed across the floor to move the body until we could get a clean-up crew out to dispose of it. I stalked back to the office. Those who had waved at me previously kept their eyes on their work, everyone having just been who they were working for.

As I approached my office, I saw Leighton pulling Victoria out with a big grin on his face.

"Leighton!" I hollered over the noise.

"Loved her idea, gonna take her out to lunch as a thanks!" Leighton hollered back until I got close enough to talk normally. Well, there went my plans for how to spend the afternoon. Just as well, though, I did actually have work to get caught up on.

"Keep it in the territory right now, alright? Word's got around, and I imagine it's on sight more than usual." I said, leaning in to kiss Victoria before Leighton pulled her away.

"Duh, I'm gonna take her to the club for lunch. I'm reckless, not stupid." Leighton said, waving as the door to the warehouse swung shut behind them.

CHAPTER THIRTY

Victoria

Leighton pulled his bike into an empty space at the back of Temptat!on and cut the ignition. We climbed off and he smiled at me as he helped me remove my helmet and clipped it to his saddlebags.

"I don't know about you, but I'm starving." he said, grabbing my hand and pulling me to the back entrance of the club.

"I could eat." I smiled.

He led me through the back hallway to Az's office. Motioning for me to take a seat, he moved behind the desk and picked up the phone. The short conversation he had, made it clear he was calling whoever was working the bar for the lunch crowd as he placed an order for a couple of chicken strip baskets and fries. After hanging up the phone, he plopped down in Az's office chair and started rummaging through the desk drawers.

"What are you doing?" I asked with a soft laugh.

Leighton shrugged. "Killing time."

We sat in a comfortable silence as we waited for our meal. It wasn't too long before a stocky man in the black uniform of Temptat!on strolled into the room with our food in hand.

"Enjoy, Boss." He smiled, sitting both baskets on the desk and slipping from the office.

My stomach growled as the scent of fried chicken strips reached my nose and I dove forward, snatching mine from the desk. The first bite was perfect, just the right amount of crispy and well-seasoned. I couldn't help the small moan of delight that left me as I savored it.

"I'm suddenly hungry for something else entirely," Leighton spoke, drawing my eyes to him as I stuffed fries in my mouth. His eyelids drooped slightly as he stared at me. "How do you make *everything* so fucking sexy?"

"You're ridiculous," I chuckled around a mouthful of chicken.

"Says the woman making those delicious noises as she eats." he replied, pushing away from the desk and standing. "Come here."

There was something dark to his tone that had my body complying before my mind caught up. Setting my half-eaten lunch on the desk, I rose from my seat and moved around the desk to stand in front of him. His hands went to the hem of my shirt and tugged.

"I need to see all of you, *now.*" His voice took on a gravelly edge that made my pussy pulse with need.

I nodded at him quickly, raising my arms so that he could pull my shirt off. Air hissed through his teeth as his eyes roamed over my exposed torso before his hands went around my body and he unsnapped my bra.

"You have the most perfect pair of tits." he murmured, his hands sliding along my exposed skin back to the front of my body to squeeze them.

He alternated slowly between massaging my breasts with his rough hands and tweaking my nipples with his fingers. I let loose a low moan as my hips jerked forward seeking out friction, my body already coming alive in his skilled hands. Leighton let out a dark chuckle and dragged his hands over my belly to the button at the top of my jeans. He pulled them down so slowly I whimpered. Leighton dropped to his knees in front of me, gently lifting one foot and then the other to help me step out of my pants, before repeating the process with my lace panties.

"Ass on the desk, *ma petit,* legs spread." He barked out.

My breath quickened at his words, and I placed my hands on the desk behind me to help hoist myself up. Leaning back slightly on my palms, I let my legs fall open and stared down at him through my lashes.

"So fucking responsive," he breathed, "Already soaked for me."

"Leighton," My voice came out a plea.

"I got you, *ma petit*." he replied, his hands going to my inner thighs and forcing my legs open wider.

He leaned forward and his tongue swiped from my opening to my clit, drawing a gasp from me. Leighton's fingers dug into the soft flesh of my inner thighs as his tongue swirled around my sensitive nub. My legs bent around his body so that my heels could dig into his upper back, urging him on. He chuckled against my aching core, the sound vibrating against my clit and sending shockwaves through my entire body.

One of his hands moved from my thighs and snaked between us. He slid two fingers inside me slowly, causing me to moan and buck my hips. His mouth and fingers worked in tandem causing tension to pool low in my belly. Leighton flicked his tongue over my clit faster, curling his fingers inside me at the same time, causing me to detonate. My upper body collapsed onto the desk as my core clenched around his still pumping fingers.

"We're not done yet, *ma petit*." he spoke, pulling his fingers from me and gripping my thighs as he stood.

Leighton's eyes were dark and hooded, taking in every inch of me while he stripped completely. Grabbing my thighs, he stepped forward and wrapped my legs around his waist, before positioning himself at my entrance with one hand. He pressed into me achingly slow, letting me feel each one of his piercings as he filled me.

I reached out for him, and any control he'd had before snapped. Leighton began slamming into me so hard the office became filled with the sound of the desk scooting along the floor mixed with my moans. He snarled as he pistoned into me harder and faster, his head snapping up to look at the door. Leighton grabbed me by the shoulders and pulled me upright, leaning forward to whisper in my ear before slipping out of me.

"We have an audience." He snarled, spinning me around and pressing my chest into the desk as he slammed into me again.

A loud moan ripped from my lips and Leighton grabbed my hair, jerking my head up roughly. I caught sight of movement just on the other side of the office door, realizing that it hadn't been closed properly when our food had been delivered. There was a flash of blond hair as whoever was watching stepped back.

"Stop," Leighton barked out, before leaning to whisper in my ear. "Does it make you hot to know someone is watching us, *ma petit*? The way you're choking my cock makes me think I should have them open the door."

I whimpered as my pussy clenched around him. Leighton groaned loudly and picked up his pace causing the edge of the desk to dig painfully into my hips.

"Push the door open further." He commanded. "My girl wants to be watched."

My back arched, taking Leighton deeper, as the door slowly opened another inch revealing half of a blonde woman on the other side. Her chest was rising and falling rapidly, her eyes locked on us. My legs trembled as I felt myself getting wetter. I heard Leighton chuckle darkly as his hand snaked between my body and the desk. His fingers found my clit and my body bucked against him. My body felt electrified as his hips slapped against my ass and his fingers worked my sensitive nub.

"Come for me, *ma petit*." He commanded, pinching my clit.

My vision went dark around the edges, and I screamed, my orgasm washing over me like a tidal wave. I distantly heard Leighton curse under his breath as he swelled inside me and found his own release. He let go of the hold he had on my hair, and I collapsed forward onto the desk, my eyes drifting shut as I worked to catch my breath. Leighton's footsteps sounded through the office and then I heard him speak.

"Pack your shit, you're fired." He snarled, before the door slammed and he moved back to where I was still sprawled across the desk. "Next time someone watches us play, they'll be someone *we* invited."

CHAPTER THIRTY ONE

Leighton

Victoria dressed with a soft smirk on her face. I couldn't tear my eyes away from her, struggling with the urge to tear them right back off of her so much that I stumbled, trying to get my pants back on.

"Enjoy watching me fall for you *ma petite?*" I grinned as she laughed at my near miss with the floor.

She opened her mouth to respond, but the sounds of shouting just outside the office door cut her off. Groaning internally, I motioned for her to stay put as I strolled over to the door and opened it.

"What the fuck?" I shouted as an officer in riot gear pushed into me and barreled his way into the office.

"Hands where I can see them, both of you." he barked out, raising his gun and pointing it at me as his partner stepped into the office behind him. "You, against the wall here. Nice and slow."

"What is the meaning of this?" Victoria demanded as she complied with his order.

The officer ignored her, grabbing me by my collar and turning me toward the wall before slamming me into it hard enough to split my lip open. My hands curled into fists at my sides. I'd had enough encounters with the police to know that giving in to my impulses would only make the situation worse.

"Excuse me," Victoria's voice took on a tone I was familiar with from high society women. "Do you *know* who I am? Officer, I am speaking to you."

"Lady, I don't give a flying fuck who you are. If you don't

get your ass up against that wall so my partner can frisk you for weapons, I will put you in cuffs."

Her face twisted into a scowl, and as much as I wanted to see her let loose on the asshole cops, it wasn't the smartest play. "*Ma petit*, just comply and let them do their job."

"No, Leighton. We have rights." she hissed before turning her attention back to the second officer. "My *father* will have a field day with this. Neither of you will work on any force again once he's through with you." I had to admit, as much as I'd never really been into the entitled high society shit, it was pretty hot when Victoria did it. "My name is Victoria Bristol; my father is *Hugo Bristol*. If you have any desire to keep your job, you will let go of my boyfriend and pray like hell we don't choose to sue for excessive force."

"Your boyfriend here is a known criminal, Ms. Bristol. You're free to go, but we have some questions for him."

"If you think I'm leaving him here for you to violate the rights he has, then you've got another fucking thing coming. He's invoking his right to an attorney *now*. Doesn't matter what questions you have. You will unhand him, and you will wait for his fucking lawyer!" Victoria shrieked at the officer.

"We don't have to wait for his attorney here, *little girl*. We are well within the limits of our position to take him back to the precinct for questioning."

"You haven't even told him his charge, or that he has one at all." Her voice was increasing in octave as she stomped toward Az's desk and picked up the phone receiver. "I highly suggest you remove your hands from him and step outside before I finish this call if you want to keep your fucking badge."

"I just want you to know, one yes to that boyfriend shit, and two, you are so goddamn hot right now, *ma petit*." I grinned, wincing slightly at the pain from my busted lip.

"Not now, Leighton." She snapped, before her attention turned to whoever was on the other end of her phone call. "Regina, it's Victoria. I need you to put me through to my father immediately, please... Oh, I see. Can you put me through to someone else? It's urgent, but I don't want to bother him in court... Yes, thank you."

She glared at the officer who still had me pinned to the wall as she waited for someone else to be put on the phone. It was making me hard again, which was unbelievably inconvenient, not to mention uncomfortable as hell.

"Last chance. Get. Your. Hands. Off. My. Boyfriend." she bit out.

The other officer shifted his weight from foot to foot, his expression growing increasingly unsure. "Maybe you should just let him go, Masterson. We don't have to leave the room, but I can't really risk this job. I've got a baby on the way man."

"Yes, *Masterson*, listen to your partner." Victoria sniped before her attention was pulled back to her phone call, her face paling slightly. "U-uncle Theo... I'm at Temptat!on with Leighton Laurent... No, I don't really know what's going on. Some officers busted into the office where we are and slammed him against a wall... No, they haven't said... Uh uh, no, no charges mentioned yet... Yes, I did. That's why I called; we've invoked our attorney rights..." She paused for a long moment, nodding her head as she listened to Theo on the other end of the line. "Masterson and..." she snapped her fingers at the other officer, and I couldn't stop the gleeful cackle that left me. "What's your name. I need both of your badge numbers as well."

The officer cleared his throat before speaking. "Bennet, badge number three-nine-five-two."

"If you want my badge number you can get it from my fucking report." Masterson huffed.

Victoria narrowed her eyes on him, but it was clear the way her head tilted that Theo had started speaking to her again.

"No, that's not necessary, Uncle Theo... Of course, we'll wait for you to make the call. Thank you." She placed the receiver gently in the cradle before crossing her arms and giving Masterson a smug grin. "I appreciate your cooperation, Officer Bennet. I will ensure that my father and uncle are made away that you attempted to convince your partner to cease his inappropriate behavior toward my boyfriend."

"We'll see," Masterson shrugged, tossing his own smug grin Victoria's way.

The room fell into an awkward silence while we waited. I could hear more police outside of the office. There weren't a lot of patrons in the club at this time of day, but it was pretty clear we'd been raided. I just wasn't sure why it was happening at two p.m. on a weekday, or at all really. Az kept his business clear of the rest of our activities, they were fully legitimate. His name was on them all legal like and everything. The only thing that was criminal about the place was the five of us.

"*Mastersons, Bennet.*" A stern voice crackled over their radios, breaking the silence. "*Stand the fuck down and pull your god damned team from Temptat!on. **Now**!*"

"Oooh, somebody's in trouble. Nee-ner nee-ner nee-ner!" I grinned as I sang my taunt.

Bennet blanched and Masterson pressed me against the wall one more good time before stepping away. I turned just in time to see the promise of revenge light in Masterson's eyes. I had a feeling I'd be visiting him at some point to make sure he didn't act on it.

I moved across the room and grabbed Victoria by the arm and started to pull her toward the door. When we stepped out into the hall she pulled back and stopped me, leaning back into the door frame.

"Oh, and Officer Masterson. When this is all over and the dust settles, I hear they're always hiring at Walmart." Her voice was dripping saccharine sarcasm, and she gave him a little finger wave to accompany the mean smile.

"Are you trying to get fucked right here in the hallway in front of all these cops?" I chuckled.

"Not the time, Leighton." she replied, rolling her eyes.

"I think you mean *boyfriend.*"

"Why do I feel like I'm going to regret that?" she muttered as I pulled her toward the main club. "Hey, wait. Shouldn't we be heading out the back door?"

"I mean, we need to prep you for that sort of thing first, and like you said... not the time." I laughed before shaking my head. "No, wait. I was going to answer that for real, but it has to wait until we're somewhere with a little less heat. Just trust me, okay. I'll tell you as soon as we're in the clear."

"O...kay." Victoria replied, obviously confused.

Instead of trying to help her understand, I continued moving toward the main club. The guys were going to want any information I could gather about the raid, even if that just meant telling them I didn't find anything. Leading Victoria to the bar, I motioned for the bartender to fix her a drink.

"Stay here, ears open, okay?" I whispered.

"I-"

"Thanks, beautiful." I cut her off, kissing her on the cheek before moving toward the cluster of police officers near the emergency exit on the opposite side of the dance floor. I did my best to stick to the shadows, what few there were as I closed in on them.

"-supposed to plant the shit. So far, we've got nada and now the chief is crawling up all our asses." a cop that clearly went a little heavy on the donuts complained to the trio around him.

I paused, not wanting to draw attention to myself, and waited to see if they'd say more. If someone was planting shit in the club, we needed to know who to put a bullet in or else Az would have a fucking stroke.

"Our take from the Jackals isn't high enough to deal with the captain crawling up our asses like this, man. Without the plant we're gonna have I.A. up our asses too. We're gonna have to bust down a few of their street guys and make it real clear we need a bigger cut."

I fought the urge to snort. With as loose as these guys' lips were, I almost couldn't blame the Jackals for not holding up their end of the bargain they'd clearly struck. Creeping my way back toward the bar, I picked up my pace as soon as I was halfway across the dance floor.

"Ready honeybun?" I grinned at Victoria.

"Immediately, no." she replied, rising from her seat at the bar.

"Aww, what's wrong snookums."

"What the hell is with these pet names all the sudden?" she frowned, following me to the front exit.

"You said I'm your boyfriend, sugarplum." I shrugged. "I figured that meant we needed more pet names."

"For the love of God, Leighton. No." She groaned.

I chuckled and led her to my bike, handing her my helmet before climbing on. "I hate to make you wait for an explanation any longer, sweetie pie, but this place is crawling with pigs, and I need to fill the guys in before Az catches wind of it."

She grumbled something that sounded suspiciously like an insult as she jerked my helmet over her head and climbed on the bike with me. I decided not to worry about the speed limits since she'd already called in her uncle, and he'd managed to fuck up Masterson's whole day, instead burning rubber as I tore out of the parking lot and sped toward the house.

I nearly slid the bike into place as we pulled up at the manor, pausing long enough to let Victoria get off the back safely before I leapt off and made fast tracks toward the door. I threw it open, looking around as I made my way inside with Victoria walking double time behind me to keep up.

"We got a fucking problem, boys!" I yelled loud enough that my voice would carry through the house.

"GOD DAMN IT!" Joey's voice yelled back at me, and I blinked, realizing that he'd been basically right in front of me, sitting at the dining table, as I walked in. Somehow, I'd missed him there as I barreled through the front door.

"Fuck," I yelped, jumping a little. "You *are* a damned

ghost."

"You two are lucky you're cute," Victoria muttered behind me. "Since there's only one brain cell between you."

"Hey-" Joey grumbled.

"I resemble that remark!" I said at the same time. "But I'll let you get away with it since I'm your boyfriend."

"What the fuck is all the yelling?" Rich's voice cut through our banter as the rest of the boys made their way into the room.

"The cops raided–" I started, when banging on our front door drew all our attention. Everyone tensed up; Craig crossed the room and grabbed Victoria's arm.

"Come on, Bunny. Best make you scarce since we don't know what's going on." He said, pulling her upstairs behind him as quickly as he could.

We all waited until they were well out of sight before anyone moved. The banging became more insistent and louder. It was obvious whoever was on the other side of the door would beat it down if we didn't answer.

"How the fuck do people keep making it to our front door," Rich grumbled as he strolled past me to open it.

"Where the fuck is my daughter?" Hugo Bristol's face was red and mottled, his one good eye looked like it was about to pop out of his head, and I could have sworn I saw spittle fly from his angry little mouth as he raged at Rich.

"Mr. Bristol, how lovely of you to stop by." Rich replied dryly.

"You!" Daddy-O's eye narrowed as it landed on Az and he shoved past Rich. "I don't know what the fuck your little crew of idiots has gotten mixed up in, but this was *not* what we agreed on. You're supposed to be protecting my daughter. Instead, our home is blown to bits, you vanish with her for a month, and now I hear from my business partner that she was caught up in some sort of raid on your pathetic club. This is not proving your proclaimed innocence in the least bit, Casadei. You and the rest of your fucking criminals are fired. Bring me my fucking daughter, now!"

Az narrowed his eyes on Hugo, opening his mouth to say something. Rich, who had shut the door and moved into the room, stepped in front of Az and stared Daddy-O down with a look that said he'd clearly run out of patience.

"I think that's about enough of the theatrics, Hugo." He drawled, raising an eyebrow. "You don't get to come in here insulting us for doing exactly what we agreed to do. The *only* reason that Victoria is alive is because of us." Rich stepped toward Daddy-O slowly, causing the smaller man to take a step back. "We've pushed ourselves to the fucking limit to keep her alive, even taken bullets to make sure she's safe."

"Bullets you wouldn't have taken if you'd taken this job even remotely seriously." Daddy-O bellowed, squaring his shoulders and reclaiming the step he'd given up when Rich moved toward him.

Rich took another step closer, his body tense, and everything about him radiated a clear warning. "Hugo, with all due disrespect. Maybe if you stopped looking at your daughter like a business asset, she wouldn't be in this fucking situation. No one here sees her as a job *but you.* And as far as I care, we don't work for you anymore. We're going to make sure she gets through to the other side of this thing, whether you are backing us *or not.*"

"Damn straight!" I cheered. "Now, I'm just a little rusty on the law, but I'm pretty sure your job won't save you from being trespassed off the property. I'd suggest you get the fuck out of our house before we make that call."

"This isn't over," Hugo screeched as he backed toward the door. "As soon as I find a way to speak to my daughter, this little kidnapping scheme of yours will be over."

"Yeah, yeah. Get gone. Don't let the door hit ya in the ass on the way out." I mocked, pulling open the front door in time for him to stomp through it like a petulant child.

CHAPTER THIRTY TWO

Joey

Leighton immediately turned his attention to Rich once he'd shut the door on Hugo. "I knew it! We're still in a fight, but I fucking *knew it*!"

I smirked as Leighton threw his warm accusation on Rich. He'd given me the rundown about my idiot brother while we were out getting our house in order. When I asked him what happened, he looked ready to burst at the seams for an excuse to spill all the details. I laughed so hard I was in tears when he told me that Az had hit Rich and Leighton had offered to be his 'murder nanny.'

"Maybe you're gonna have a harder time walking away than you realized, big bro. Despite whatever you think is 'best.'" I said, a little more smugly than I'd intended. But as much as he was fighting himself, her, and the rest of us about what was evident, it seemed like he was losing ground whether he liked it or not.

"Just because I'm not willing to show all our cards to someone who may very well be our enemy doesn't mean I'm letting a *temporary* piece of ass get to me." Rich snarled.

The energy in the room shifted in an instant. Leighton and Az moved like they were both ready to fight him, but they didn't get the chance. I saw red when I started to move, going over the dining table instead of around it. My fist connected with his face as I came down from vaulting the furniture, causing him to stumble back. The room went quiet.

"I have had *e-fucking-nough* of this shit from you, Richard!" I growled. "You have been bullheaded and obstinate this entire time when she's proven herself over and over again. She saved Az's fucking life, she sat by *your* fucking bedside when we weren't even sure you were gonna make it through the night, she's the *only* reason we were able to get a car without resorting to violence to come home and we all know it. She's solved problems in my warehouse, quickly and efficiently–"

"She got us out of the shit at the club today, too." Leighton offered before falling back into silence.

"I am *so* over whatever the fuck is going on with you, and I will not stand here and listen to you insult the woman that I love anymore. You've gone from being stubborn to being disrespectful, and if it were anyone else, I'd already have dropped you for disrespecting what's mine."

Leighton cleared his throat, "Ours." he whispered with a fake cough, followed by the sound of a sharp slap indicating Az had smacked him in the back of the head.

"*Ours*," I relented. "You need to get your head out of your ass. At this point, you're as bad as Hugo with how you're insulting her."

Rich straightened up to his full height. "All of you have lost your fucking minds. You're putting that *woman*," he said the word as if it were a curse, "before our business. Before our *fucking family.* And not a single one of you chuckleheads can see why that's a goddamn problem!"

His fist lashed out too fast for me to react, and my nose crunched under the punch as if to punctuate his assertion that Victoria was a problem. I stumbled back against the dining table, holding my nose momentarily to check that it hadn't broken before narrowing my eyes on my brother again. I snarled as I launched off the table, charging my brother and getting low enough to have my shoulder collide with his waist in a takedown. He grunted harshly as his feet came out from under him, and we landed on the floor.

"You fucking moron! We haven't put anyone *before* our family! She *is* part of this family! Whether you like it or not, she's been claimed and she's fucking proven herself. You need to figure it. The fuck. Out!" I landed three quick blows to Rich's face to drive my words home before he recovered himself.

Rich wrapped his arms around my waist, trapping my arms at my sides and squeezing tight enough it was briefly challenging to take a full breath. He bounded back to his feet, reclaiming the few steps we'd lost when I tackled him to the ground.

"What is it going to take for you four to screw your heads back on straight?! Is one of us going to have to fucking *die* keeping her alive before you realize this whole thing is a fucking *MISTAKE*!?" He roared, slamming me into the dining table. The wood buckled and split in half under the impact of my body.

"Fucking hell, they're going to actually kill each other." I barely registered Az speaking as I scrambled to my feet, intent on launching myself at Rich again. "L!"

An impact from my right knocked me off balance, and then I was rolling across the floor with Leighton tangled around me.

"Sorry, bro." He grimaced as we came to an abrupt halt, slamming into the wall next to his bedroom door. I snarled at him, struggling to get away from his hold. "Don't make me hurt you, dude. You have to stop, or I'm gonna have to."

"Let me the fuck go, he deserves this." I barked, still trying to break free of Leighton.

My eyes were locked on Rich across the room. Az held him from behind in an almost bear hug. I was so focused on my brother struggling to break the hold Az had on him that I didn't notice Leighton's arm cocking back until I felt the sting of his palm against my cheek.

"No! Bad hetero-life partner. BAD!" He laughed as if this were all a game when I turned a wide-eyed gaze at him.

"What the fuck, Leighton! Did you really just bitch slap me?!" I snapped, pushing him away from me.

"Well, I had to do *something*." He rolled his eyes

dramatically. "You were going to make me hurt you if I didn't."

I laid my head back against the floor and stared up at the ceiling. "You know he deserved it, though. We've shot people for less than his disrespect."

"Yeah," Leighton shrugged. "But for starters, I told you *I* was in a fight with him over this, and for second, he's not healed all the way to take his proper licks over it, and..." He paused as if trying to figure out what number he was up to. "The man is clearly tearing himself apart because he just can't accept he's in love with *la petit démone* too. He can't even come up with new lines to throw around when he's having his temper tantrums about 'she's not suited to this' blah blah blah." he dropped his voice dramatically in an attempt to imitate Rich. "If he really meant that shit, he'd have a lot more lines than the ones he already used up on me and Az back at the cabin."

"That's... surprisingly insightful, L." I smirked. "Now, can you get the fuck off of me?"

"I say insightful shit all the time, I don't know why you guys always act surprised by it." He chuckled, unwrapping his arms and legs from around my body and climbing to his feet before offering me a hand.

I grasped his hand as he pulled me up and looked over as Az tentatively let Rich go. I narrowed my eyes on my brother but made no moves toward him.

"Next time you feel like you want to insult our girl, maybe think twice about it and keep your fucking mouth shut." I snapped.

"Hey now!" Leighton chirped, causing me to look at him. His hands were on his hips, and he had a look on his face that was scarily similar to the one my mother wore when Rich and I were in trouble as children. "That's not how this is supposed to go. You're supposed to kiss and make up or whatever brothers do so we can get back to the shit that went down at the club that got so rudely interrupted before I could fill everyone in."

"How 'bout no to most of that, and we just move on." I

said, rolling my eyes at Leighton.

"Joseph Innocenti, do not make me call your mother." L continued. "Because I will. Dawn *adores* me."

"I am not apologizing. And if you call her, make sure you tell her why I hit him. Dad would come down here with a belt. Now, can we *please* just move on? I've said what I had to say." I said sternly as I moved past Leighton and back into the kitchen, casting one more look at my brother. "And I meant every word."

"Whatever, I tried." Leighton shrugged. "But I'm still calling Dawn, I suddenly have a craving for her lasagna, and we've missed our weekly chats for the last... like month. She's gonna be so pissed when I tell her about this bullshit marriage arrangement my parents think is gonna happen."

"Tell her I said hi when you get her on the line," Az said, sidling up to the counter. "Leighton, you left your popcorn sitting."

"When the fuck did you make popcorn?" I asked.

"About the time you decided a fistfight required busting out the superhero moves and jumped off the table like fucking Batman or something," Leighton said, looking at me like I was crazy for even asking. "But anyway, we should talk about the raid."

"Share. Now, what happened at the club?" I said, hopping up on the island counter since we obviously wouldn't be sitting at the dining room table to discuss business for now.

Leighton filled us in on the raid and what he'd overheard from the cops on the take while shoveling fistfuls of popcorn into his mouth. At one point, I resisted the urge to slap the back of his head and tell him to stop talking with his mouth full out of concern the little psycho would derail into something unrelated if I did.

"We knew there were a few cops on the Jackals' payroll, but if they're interfering in *our* shit instead of just covering up for the Jackals, we need to have a meeting with our captains. They won't stop at hitting our legitimate businesses; they will make problems for all our dealings." Rich said when Leighton finished telling us everything.

As angry as I was with him, I had to admit even to myself that he was right. Hell, even *we* had cops on the take, but they weren't paid to interfere with the Jackals; they were paid to keep our guys out of jail. It was just the way these things worked.

"Have your guys meet us at the safe house on Brooks since we can't use the one on Senna anymore, thanks to our mole telling the Jackals about it. Fucking cockroaches. These assholes don't know that we know, so we need to leverage that and get the upper hand before they figure it out." Rich ordered as we started to make our calls.

CHAPTER THIRTY THREE

Victoria

Craig just stood silently beside me as I hid just out of sight at the top of the stairs listening to the guys deal with my father. I took a single step forward, intending to speak with my father myself when Craig gently grabbed my elbow and pulled me back with a soft shake of his head.

"No one here sees her as a job *but you*. And as far as I care, we don't work for you anymore." Rich's voice echoed up the stairwell.

I gasped, and for some stupid reason, tears welled in my eyes.

"What's wrong, Bunny?" Craig asked, causing the tears to spill over my lashes.

"I don't know why I'm crying." I sniffled, turning to wrap my arms around him. "It's so stupid. Rich made it clear he wants nothing to do with me, but now he's standing up for me to my *dad*."

Craig wrapped his arms around me, petting my hair and softly shushing me. "It's alright, Bunny. We already knew Rich was a confused idiot, and it's understandable it'd be upsetting for you sometimes."

A couple of minutes later, the front door slammed, making me jump slightly. I teetered on the edge of the stairs, thankful Craig had me pulled into a hug. The last thing I'd need was to fall backward down them and have all the effort to get me this far ruined because of an unfortunate fall.

The sound of a fight drew both my and Craig's attention, and I started to turn as we heard Joey and Rich shouting at each other. His hold around me tightened.

"You don't want to be in the middle of that, Bunny. Let them sort it out. It's... been a long time coming." Craig said carefully.

So, I stood at the top of the stairs listening. More tears fell when Joey told Rich that he loved me, and with every thrown barb and revelation, it only got worse from there. A deafening wooden crack filled the house.

"Jesus, they've killed each other," I said, pulling out of Craig's arms and rushing down the stairs. He caught up with me just as we reached the point on the stairs that brought the room into view, grabbing hold of my wrist.

My eyes grew wide as I watched Az grab Rich in a bear hug and Leighton launch himself at Joey to intercept him mid-air. I covered my mouth to stop the sob that tried to escape me as I watched the aftermath of what had clearly been a brawl. The dining table was collapsed, broken down the center, and Leighton was wrapped around Joey to hold him still, and Az looked like he was barely holding on to Rich's broad frame.

And it felt as though as fast as the brawl had started, it was ending. Leighton tried in vain to get the boys to make up, but they seemed content to just... move on despite the black eyes that were forming on the brothers' faces. Jarring didn't seem like a strong enough word to describe the shift as they moved into the kitchen and went back to talking about business.

Rich gave his orders and stormed from the kitchen, barely giving Craig and me a glance as he moved past us. The slam of his door echoed down to us a couple of seconds later.

"What the fuck happened?" I said quietly, unsure if anyone but Craig would even hear me.

Leighton's head snapped up from his phone and his eyes narrowed as they took in my red-rimmed eyes, and, probably, puffy face.

"What did you do to her?" he asked Craig, shock and concern evident in his tone.

"I didn't do anything, at least as far as I know." Craig answered, letting go of my wrist that he'd been holding and putting his hand on my lower back so we could finish descending the stairs and enter the room. "There was shouting, and she started crying."

"Is that popcorn?" I asked, catching sight of the bowl beside Leighton. "Oh, you know what would be amazing with that. A chocolate bar and some of that super amazing pizza from the place by my apartment." As the words left my mouth, it dawned on me what my problem was. "Shit."

"Are you pregnant for real this time, baby momma?" Leighton asked with a wide grin on his face.

"Uh, no. The exact opposite actually." I paused, not thinking as I squeezed my boobs to check, causing all four of the guys to let out a strangled choking sound. "Yep, they're sore. I'm about to start my period."

"I have something for this!" Leighton all but shouted before taking off for his bedroom. He reappeared a few minutes later with a stack of tampon boxes so high he had to tilt his head to the side to see where he was walking.

"Again, Leighton... I don't think I'll *ever* go through that much. I appreciate the foresight, but it's not necessary to buy the whole aisle." I sighed with a little smile. He meant well, at least.

"I didn't buy the *whole* aisle. I just know from having a sister that women tend to have a preference of brand and I didn't know yours." He frowned, moving to where the dining room table had been as if he would drop his haul. "Oh, right." He stepped around the destroyed furniture to deposit the boxes on the counter instead.

"You could have asked... But I suppose I can donate what I won't be using to the center." I considered as I stared at the pile of boxes.

"I sort of figured you would, that's why I just bought a bunch of different brands instead of texting Az to ask your preference." Leighton shrugged. The sentiment made my heart squeeze a little, and I couldn't help it when I started to tear up again.

"That's... really sweet, L," I said with a soft sniffle.

"Please don't cry again just because, ya know, I'm a psychopath, not an idiot." Leighton shrugged again.

"You're not a psychopath, Leighton. You can be really sweet when you're not being an ass." I sniffled again, wiping away my tears harshly. I hated the crying, but I couldn't stop it.

Leighton and Az were slowly backing away from the kitchen as I stood there trying to get a handle on myself. Which only made me feel worse. It wasn't like I *wanted* to cry over a pile of tampon boxes.

Leighton stepped behind Joey, where he'd hopped off the counter and come across the room when we entered and pushed him toward me by the shoulders.

"*Fix it!*" Leighton said in a loud stage whisper, causing Joey to roll his eyes.

"L, that's not how–" Joey started.

"Do your wholesome magic stuff, lover boy. Make her feel better." Leighton said, staying behind Joey and looking at me from around him.

"I can hear you, asshole." I snapped at Leighton, moving to where the bowl of popcorn sat abandoned and picking at it. I wasn't crying anymore; my mood had swung into irritation.

"We need a snack-rifice." Az said with a smirk, watching Leighton panic as he stood behind Joey.

"I can go–" Craig started.

"On it!" Leighton shouted, speeding from the kitchen toward the front door, and grabbing his keys. We could hear his bike start before the front door shut behind him.

".... I'm not that bad, am I?" I grumbled. Each of the three men left found something different in the room to look at, and no one answered the question. "Really?" I snapped.

"Not at all, Sweetheart. It's just... an adjustment." Joey offered.

"Though, to be fair, I don't think I've ever seen Leighton

move that fast." Az mused, snickering as he stared toward the entrance.

A sharp cramp in my abdomen caused me to grimace and I stalked to the counter and snatched a box of tampons off it. "Whatever," I muttered to myself, before practically stomping my way to the bathroom.

The rest of the evening was spent with the guys shooting me wary glances while plying me with snacks, hot water bottles, and foot rubs. Leighton had the foresight to bring back a bottle of Midol with his two bags full of candy that was working wonders for me. Rich still hadn't reemerged by the time I climbed into Joey's bed and passed out for the night.

I woke around lunchtime and was dying for some nacho cheese covered tater tots. After a quick shower, I made my way downstairs and started rifling through the cabinets. By the time I'd picked through all of them and come up empty, I was in tears again.

"Uh, shit." I heard Leighton whisper behind me.

My head snapped toward him just in time to see him backing away slowly and nearly colliding with Az.

"Wha-" Az started before noticing me. "Shit. What's the matter, Love?" His voice was gentle as he stepped around Leighton and moved toward me.

"I just wanted some tater tots with nacho cheese. Why is there no nacho cheese?" My voice sounded whiny even to me.

Az raised his hand and scratched the back of his neck in discomfort. "Craig usually does the shopping since he's the one that cooks." He glanced over his shoulder toward Leighton. "Go grab Craig for me, yeah?"

"Yep, you got it." Leighton replied, his relief at being dismissed from the room clear on his face.

"Why don't you go sit on the couch while I have a look, Love. Maybe I can find what you're after. If not, we can pick it up at the store on our way home from our meeting with our captains, okay?"

Without waiting for a response from me, Az started searching through the same cabinets I'd already checked. He was pulling everything from the second cabinet when Craig appeared on the steps, half his face still covered in shaving cream.

"Az Casadei, what the hell are you doing to my kitchen?" Craig demanded.

"Victoria wanted some nacho cheese." Az replied, glancing over to find me crying in earnest. "Why the fuck do we not have nacho cheese?!"

"Because I make it from scratch on the rare occasion you idiots ask for nachos," Craig replied.

"Of course you fucking do." Az grumbled, his voice lowering to the point it was clear he was speaking to himself. "PMSing, crying woman in the house, but you just *gotta* be all fancy like we didn't grow up on the processed shit. Fucking hell."

"I don't want homemade; I want the canned stuff." I wailed. "It's sooo good."

Craig looked at me with wide eyes like I'd just insulted him in the worst way.

"If the woman wants canned nacho cheese, that's what she's getting. You can just look the other way, Chef." Az said firmly. I could kiss him for defending my craving needs.

"Well, fine. We can get some of... *that* on our way back, but we don't have any currently. So..." Craig trailed off. I cried harder. This was dumb, I knew it was dumb. But the cravings were riding my ass, and I couldn't help it. If I were in my apartment, then I'd have my cheese, and none of this would be happening right now.

"Maybe... Can we afford to stop and get some on the way instead?" Az checked his watch.

"Dude, I'm not even done *shaving*!" Craig groaned. "We'd have to leave now."

"What about the tater tots?" I said between sobs and hiccups. "It's not the same without the tater tots."

"What the fuck is going on? Why is no one ready?" Rich's deep bass cut through the room in irritation. I turned to face him and had to look away. He was dressed in a sharp black suit with a pressed white dress shirt and deep crimson tie. "And can someone tell me why Ella is just standing outside staring at our front door?" He paused a moment and swept his eyes over the room. "And why is the Princess having a fucking meltdown?"

"Because of nacho cheese and tater tots. That's why no one is ready. And probably because she can hear that this is a bad time to knock." Az rattled off the answers to the questions as he moved toward the door.

"Wh– Nacho cheese and... How the fuck is this more important than the meeting with our captains. I would think we have more *pressing* matters." Rich said harshly.

"Because fuck you, Rich. That's why." I snapped. He could look good in a suit all day; didn't stop the fact he was an *absolute* dick.

Craig cut a glare at Rich and made a gesture at me, trying to control my hiccups and sobs. I caught sight of Leighton stepping up behind Rich and tapping him on the shoulder.

"I know Dawn taught you and Joey all about women's bodies and their monthly visitor, so how are you worse at this than me?"

"We don't have time for this. We're already going to be late." Rich clipped before moving toward the front door and jerking it open. "Ella, come in."

A short brunette with a deep tan and brown eyes strolled into the house, her eyes flitting around as if she was searching out a threat. Even in her black cargo pants and baggy black t-shirt, she was stunning. She definitely looked better than I did at the moment, and it had jealousy threatening to rear its ugly head in spite of the moth tattoo displayed prominently on her forearm.

"Ella, this is Victoria. Princess, this is Ella. She's your

bodyguard for the day. Do *not* leave this house."

"Yes sir," Ella's voice had a musical lilt to it that made me want to punch her in the throat, even though I knew I had no reason to feel that way toward the woman.

"I didn't know you guys hired fucking Disney Princesses for your crew." I huffed under my breath as I crossed my arms over my chest.

Rich cut his eyes to me with a glare. "*She* knows how to follow commands. Any princess that knows how to listen better than you do is worth having in the crew." He snapped.

Uncrossing my arms, I flipped Rich off with both hands, stuck out my tongue and pulled a childish, mocking face. Ella burst out laughing at my actions before her eyes moved to Rich and she stiffened.

"You can laugh, Ella. My girl is fucking hilarious." Leighton cackled.

"*Ours!*" Craig, Az and Joey corrected in unison.

Ella looked at me and grinned. "Damn, anyone with the balls to take on these five in *any* capacity is someone I want to be friends with."

"She's the job, Ella. Nothing more." Rich said with a scowl, before turning his attention to the other guys. "Why are you all still standing here, not ready to go?"

Ella shrugged almost to herself and strolled around Rich toward me, extending a hand. "We already know each other's names, but it's still nice to meet you, Victoria. I promise you will be safe with me. Az told me you've been stuck with just them for a while and thought you could use some time with another woman that gets it."

"Gets which part? The having my life turned upside down, or the multiple boyfriends?" I deadpanned.

Ella laughed again. "I only have the one guy, so probably neither. But it can't be all it's cracked up to be, being stuck with nobody but those five for as long as you have been. Yeah, they're my bosses, but they're still dudes."

Whatever hormone driven jealousy had been brewing

when she walked into the house vanished. "Hey, I like her. Can I keep her as a bodyguard?" I called out after the guys as they were retreating from the room to finish getting ready to leave.

Rich's cell phone rang and cut through the conversation. "Yeah?" Rich drawled, heading for the front door and stepping outside.

Ella and I fell into the casual get to know each other conversation until Rich stepped back into the house just as the other guys reemerged dressed in smart suits except for Leighton who was in his normal clothing with knives and guns strapped to him.

"We have a problem." Rich ground out as he slammed the door behind him, casting his gaze toward Ella as if deciding whether or not she should be present for whatever he was about to say.

"If you don't trust the soldier I chose to protect Victoria then you don't trust my judgment, Rich." Az spoke, noticing the indecision on Rich's face. "Just spit it out."

Ella practically preened under Az's praise, and I stuffed down the bit of jealousy threatening to resurface.

"The safehouse on Brooks is gone. We're down a captain and two others are injured. Somehow the fucking Jackals knew about the meeting, it's sheer fucking luck we weren't there when the bomb went off."

"Mother nature, one." Leighton snickered, winking at me.

"Absolutely not. We are not crediting the Princess having a meltdown." Rich grumbled. "We need to change into something more suited for clean up and get boots on the ground now."

"You do that." Leighton said, strolling toward me. "I'm not necessary for this part of the job, so I'm gonna hang here. Call me if there's someone for me to kill."

CHAPTER THIRTY FOUR

Victoria

"You're with us, Ella." Leighton grinned as the other guys moved to change again, and Ella stepped toward the front door. "Come on, Snickerdoodle, I'm gonna take you to do something nice for a change."

"Snickerdoodle? Seriously?" I huffed. "Absolutely not. And don't you think you should, I don't know, maybe cut back on the armory you're wearing?"

Ella's gaze flitted between the two of us, the way her face scrunched up betraying her desire to laugh.

"Nah, better safe than sorry. Come on. I got the perfect idea to make you feel better." Leighton grinned.

I rolled my eyes, and Ella covered a slight snicker with a cough. "Fine, but I need to change first."

Leighton's hands fluttered as if to say, 'hurry up,' and I made my way back upstairs to change into something more presentable than Joey's sweats and t-shirt. We hadn't been back long enough for me to buy a new wardrobe, but I did have some nice jeans and a blouse that would work for anything Leighton thought was a 'nice' outing. Throwing my clothes on, I made my way across the hall to the bathroom, quickly brushed my teeth, and pulled my hair into a ponytail. By the time I made it back downstairs, Leighton was leaning on the wall by the front door, twirling a knife in his hand, and Ella was nowhere to be seen.

I moved toward him, and his eyes jumped to me, causing a smile to spread across his face. It was so sweet that I felt horrible for the way I'd been behaving. Hormones or not, I'd been a jerk.

"Hey, thank you for whatever we're about to do. I'm sorry I've been acting like such a bitch. It's not really an excuse, but I'm pretty sure the implant is making my moodiness worse. The Doc said it might. It still doesn't make it–"

"None of that!" He said, sliding the knife he'd been playing back into its sheath on his thigh and grabbing my hand. "Just because I'm not the best at knowing what to do about it, doesn't mean I'm blaming you for it. We know it's not your fault. Now, let's go get you pampered!"

His words were so sweet, in his way, that I couldn't help it when my eyes burned with unshed tears again. His eyes got wide, and he took a small step back.

"Oh no, please don't start crying again. I don't... There's no one to fix it and no one for me to hurt to make you feel better! Come on, please?!" He said in a panic. The shift from sincerity to panic was so stark I couldn't stop the laugh that bubbled up out of me.

"Don't worry, I'm not going to rain all over your parade. Now, are you gonna tell me where we're going?"

"Definitely not." He grinned and pulled me outside. Ella waved from the front seat of the blacked-out SUV, but I didn't get a chance to respond before Leighton pulled me behind him and practically shoved me in the open sliding door of the back and climbed in beside me. "You know where we're going." He told his driver as he shut the door, and we pulled away.

A little while later, we pulled up outside of an upscale spa in Northside. A Touch of Nature Day Spa was such a popular spot, that it was usually reservation only.

"Love the idea, but... is it even safe to be here? Also, this place is reservation *only* usually. How do you expect us to just pull up and get a spot?" I said incredulously.

"Well, we usually don't have our gang wars in this part of the city," Leighton deadpanned. "And we own this spa, so we can roll up and get right in anytime we want."

"N-No, you fucking don't. There's no way you guys own A Touch of Nature. I've known Brenda for years. Me and Tiff have been coming here since college."

"If you don't believe me, call Az. His name is on all the paperwork and everything." Leighton said, raising an eyebrow and rolling his eyes. "Why the fuck would I lie about owning a *spa* of all things?"

"What... even is life?" I mumbled, catching Ella's chuckle from the front seat as she climbed out of the SUV. "Wait. Does that mean Brenda is a gangster? There's *no* way."

Leighton looked at me like he was explaining something to a child. "What? Of course not, but she's a fantastic manager. We can't staff our legitimate businesses with gangsters, or we would be very *bad* at our jobs. Az does have an actual payroll." He rolled his eyes at me again as he swung open the door and pulled me out of the SUV.

Without another word, he led me inside, Ella following directly behind us, and strolled to the counter. The petite redhead behind the counter smiled at him politely.

"G-Good afternoon, sir. How can we help you today?" she asked, struggling to ignore the weapons strapped to his body and remain professional.

"Give these two whatever services they want." He replied, pulling a wallet out of his pants pocket.

"Oh, unfortunately, we don't take walk-ins. I can make an appointment for your... companions if you'd like." the woman replied.

"No, they'll be taken care of *today*." Leighton demanded, pulling a black card from his wallet and sliding it across the counter.

"I sincerely apologize, sir, but we are fully booked out today. I am more than happy to book an appointment, as I've said."

"Ugh," Leighton groaned. "Where's Brenda? Just get Brenda out here. BRENDA!" he bellowed.

"Sir, if you insist on making a scene, I will have to call

the police and have them escort you from the property." The redhead clipped.

"BRENDA!" He yelled again, ignoring the woman.

The receptionist opened her mouth to speak again but didn't get the chance as Brenda strolled through the office door behind the counter. The woman was in her mid-forties, in a smart pantsuit, with her hair pulled up in a bun.

"Leighton, how lovely to see you!" The older woman smiled as she put her hand on the receptionist's shoulder. "Dear, you should have called, and I would have let Rebecca here know to watch for you."

"Yeah, it was sort of a last-minute surprise for my girlfriend. She's had a rough day, and I wanted to treat her and her new best friend." Leighton offered the woman a smile that didn't quite touch his eyes.

"Oh!" The woman's eyes slid over to me and lit up with recognition. "Victoria Bristol! It's been how long since I've seen you in here? The better part of a year, at least. Well, I certainly hope that you're keeping this young man on the straight and narrow. He needs to find someone to settle him down." She came around the counter, and we hugged briefly. She turned back to the receptionist. "Rebecca, start calling this afternoon's appointments to reschedule them, and if there's anyone in the back, please let them know that, unfortunately, their appointment needs to be rescheduled since we'll be closing for the day. Give them a complimentary appointment if needed. Once that's done, see me in my office. Since Tina didn't give you this portion of the training before going on maternity leave, I'll do it."

The receptionist looked baffled, blinking several times at Brenda before standing and moving out of the lobby to clear out any guests that were already here.

"She's new." Brenda sighed. "Tina is on maternity leave and delivered early. I wasn't aware she didn't get a chance to go over how we do things when you boys show up."

"So... those times that mine and Tiff's appointments

were rescheduled... were because the five of you needed a spa day?" I looked at Leighton. This day was getting more and more unbelievable.

"Perks of the job, sugartits." He grinned.

"Immediately, no." I rolled my eyes.

Leighton just shrugged before Ella cleared her throat to speak.

"I appreciate the... bonus, sir." Ella spoke softly. Her body language betrayed her uncertainty over being included in my impromptu spa day.

"It's not a bonus, Ella." Leighton frowned. "Az chose you to be our girl's new bestie, and this is just part of that. Consider it a promotion from bodyguard to best friend. Do you know how to walk in heels? I'm pretty sure that's something you're going to need to do at some point."

"Leighton," I sighed. "You guys can't just force someone to be my friend."

"Yeah, yeah." He replied, waving his hand in front of him. "You girls get whatever services you want. But make sure they include a pedicure on that list. I'll be waiting outside, keeping an eye out for any trouble, while you two become best friends. Maybe after I can take you two shopping."

Brenda snickered as Leighton moved toward the front doors. "If you ladies would follow me, I'll get you set up in a room and grab you some drinks."

Ella gestured for me to go first and fell into step behind me as I followed Brenda down the hall to one of the larger massage suites. I settled into one of the lounge chairs and picked up the tablet on the side table to begin selecting my services.

"You're not actually obligated to be my friend." I told Ella once Brenda left the room to grab our refreshments. "I'm pretty sure Leighton just doesn't know how that works. But you should definitely take advantage of him paying for the spa treatments. Consider it *my* apology for them trying to force you to become my friend."

Ella's face split into a genuine grin, and she moved to take the other open lounge chair, picking up the second tablet. "Thanks. The guys pay well and take care of us even at the bottom of the totem pole, but being at the bottom keeps me too busy to do something like this for myself."

I snagged her tablet and pulled up the menu to start selecting every service she could possibly want. "You're definitely going to want to take advantage of this then." I laughed as her eyes widened at the growing list I was putting together. Brenda came back with two champagne flutes and a big grin on her face. "Brenda, is there a 'select all' button on this list somewhere, or do I have to just keep doing them individually?"

Brenda set our drinks down on the table, tossing her head back with a full belly laugh. "There's not, sadly. But I like how you think, young lady."

Ella shifted uncomfortably in her lounge chair as she looked at my ever-growing list. "Uhm... Can we *not* do the micro....ablation and triphasic... combination facial? I don't even know what that is, and it sounds kinda painful."

I laughed. "Fine, we can skip that part. But pick whatever you want. Make sure it's the *good* shit. None of this basic services crap as a cop-out."

"Oh, don't forget, Leighton specifically requested pedicures. So, we've already got that ready to go while you decide what else you'd like." Brenda said, still smiling in amusement. "You ladies have fun. Give me a shout if you need anything."

Brenda stepped out of the room as the pedicurists entered. They introduced themselves and made idle chatter as they set up and started their work. It was almost amusing to watch Ella sit stiffly as they removed her shoes and socks. I didn't miss the raised eyebrow of the pedicurist as she set Ella's combat boots aside. They started with foot massages, and it wasn't until the woman working on Ella hit what must have been a sore place in her arch that the soldier's demeanor shifted. She let out a loud groan and visibly relaxed.

"Fuuuck, that's good."

"Told ya," I smirked.

Ella chuckled, and soon we were chatting like old friends. She told me about her life as a soldier for the guys, and I complained about managing four boyfriends and one raging asshole. Ella was surprisingly easy to talk to and before long it felt like we were old friends without all the craziness of the guys' world throwing us together. She was someone I could see becoming good friends with once the dust settled.

Hours later, we emerged from the spa, fully pampered and relaxed. I smiled softly at Leighton as I pushed through the glass double doors and stepped into the late afternoon sun. He was studying something on his phone and didn't see us exiting the building as a large body collided with my side, and a thick arm wrapped around my waist.

"Hey!" I shouted, just as I was jerked away from the entrance of the spa.

Leighton's eyes snapped up from his phone at the same time a gun cocked behind me.

"Let her go, or I'll blow your fucking brains all over the pavement." Ella snarled.

The man ignored her, letting out a whistle that had the sidewalk suddenly flooding with people. I lost sight of Leighton for a moment as the crowd overwhelmed us, and the stranger attempted to drag me further from the spa. The training Az put me through at the cabin kicked in, and I let my body go limp. The man grunted and stumbled, trying to hold on to my sudden dead weight. Taking advantage of him being off balance, I slammed my head back toward his, and was rewarded with the sickening crunch of his nose, and his arm releasing my waist as his hand flew to his face.

Gunshots sounded out in the crowd, and I finally caught sight of Leighton slashing his way through the mob. Ella was crowded against the building, firing her pistol in rapid succession, each shot hitting its mark as bodies dropped on the sidewalk.

"Come on, *ma petit.*" Leighton shouted as he reached me. "We've gotta go."

I allowed him to drag me back to the SUV and shove me inside.

"What about Ella?" I asked as Leighton clambered in behind me. My eyes flicked over his shoulder in time to see the woman fighting hand to hand with a man at least three times her size. "Leighton! We can't leave her he-"

Another shot rang out, and blood sprayed from Ella's face as her body slammed backward before falling to the ground. A horrified scream tore from my throat as Leighton slammed the door of the SUV and screamed at the driver to go.

He pulled me into his chest as the driver pulled away with the sound of screeching tires. Weaving his fingers in my hair, he shushed me until my screaming turned into sobs. I was so unbelievably tired of the people in my life dropping dead, being constantly in danger, or turning out to be enemies. It felt like something inside me was fracturing, and I didn't know how much more it would take before it broke entirely.

CHAPTER THIRTY FIVE

Leighton

The mood around the new dining table was heavy. The bombing at our safe house that had taken out one of our captains and injured two others was a clear declaration of war from the Jackals. The attempt to snatch Victoria outside the spa that resulted in Ella's death was something else entirely.

"You're sure they weren't Jackals?" Rich asked.

"Positive. None of them had the tattoo and our cleanup crew recognized a couple of them from one of the smaller drug dealer's crew. It's pretty clear this was part of that fucked up post Craig found." I replied.

"Where are we on our fucking leak?" Rich growled. "It's clear our mole has made the entire underground of Sacona aware we're back. We'll never get ahead of this shit if we don't plug the leak."

"Understatement of the fucking *year*, Rich," Az said dryly. "We've had three attacks on our territory, and we've barely been back a week. Four if you count being flushed out of the cabin."

"My guys are getting pretty antsy about all of it too." Joey added. "Had another one not show for work today, not that I blame them. We've been sitting with our dicks in our hands and not retaliating for anything."

"Except the vet, which you still owe me new rope for." Craig spoke.

"It's on fucking back order, get your panties out of a twist. Also, *not* the point here." Joey snarked.

"We have bigger fucking problems than some

goddamned rope!" Rich barked, slapping his palms hard against the table.

The doorbell rang at that moment, causing Rich to scowl and mutter about people managing to get to our front door unchecked. Shaking my head at him, I rose from my seat and strolled over to open the front door. Phil was standing on the other side, James, one of my trio of psychos I'd use for the big stuff, beaten and bound at his feet. Morgan, one of the prostitutes I used to frequent before she settled down with a Jackal, stood just behind Phil.

"Phil! My man!" I smiled, clapping him on the shoulder. "Good to see you, but what the fuck happened to James?"

The scrape of chairs on the floor was followed by the other four moving to stand at my back.

"Boss," Phil said, tipping his head in respect before bending down to hoist James over his shoulder. "I think we should talk."

"Yes, we should." Az snarled, surprising me. I expected Rich to be the one going Az-hole on poor Phil. "I'd like to know why you've shown up with a Jackal whore and one of Leighton's pocket crazies beat half to death."

"Hey now, you be nice to Morgan," I said in defense of the short, curvy woman. "It's not her fault the love of her life is a cockroach. No offense."

Morgan snorted. "Good to see you too, Leighton. Though, I gotta say, adding new scars after each visit hasn't been missed."

I stepped back, almost colliding with the others, before turning to shoo them all away from the door. Phil stepped into the house, moved toward the dining room, and dropped James on the floor. Morgan glanced around nervously before following him. Closing the front door, I gave the other guys my best 'behave yourselves' look and moved to face Phil.

"You never answered my question, man," I said, crossing my arms over my chest. "What happened to James?"

"I did," Phil shrugged.

"Normally, I wouldn't be happy with one of my guys turning up like this. But if he lost the fight, then maybe he's not fit for his spot. Good on you man," I put my arm up for a high five, and Az slapped me in the back of the head before grabbing it and putting it back down.

"Care to tell us *why* you happened to James?" Craig spoke up.

"He's the fucking mole." Phil answered. "It wasn't until he conveniently disappeared around the time you five showed back up in Sacona that I realized something wasn't right with the bastard."

"Yes, that is... Convenient." Rich drawled.

I whirled on Rich and pointed at him. "I *told* you, Phil was loyal. Now shut up and let him talk, fucker."

Phil blinked several times, looking at Rich before confusion gave way to realization. "Not gonna lie... I'm a little offended that notion would even be on the table," he sighed, "but I suppose I can see how it looked after what happened with the cabin."

"If I may," Morgan piped up. "Phil is telling the truth. James has been working with my ol' man for a hot minute now."

Az turned to glare at her, narrowing his eyes. "Why on earth would we believe you? You may not be a Jackal yourself, but you have every reason to cover for them."

"With how much Leighton paid me for my... time, before I met Carl, I'd have squealed regardless. But as it stands, my man wants out. He's not happy with the way things are going and I figured the information I have was just the right amount of leverage to buy him some protection from the horsemen."

"*If* you're telling the truth about your man wanting out, then we *might* be willing to cut a deal. Depending on how good the information you've got is." Rich said.

"Fantastic," Morgan smiled, swinging the purse that hung on her arm to her front and unzipping it. "I'm sure this will be plenty good enough."

She pulled out a small recorder and her cell phone, unlocking her phone, and opening her photo gallery before holding both out for one of us to take. Craig snagged the recorder at the same time I grabbed her phone.

"Got any nudes on here, Morgan?" I asked, waggling my brows at her as I started swiping through images of James and a man, I didn't recognize with a visible red spider lily tattoo on his forearm.

"You're lucky Victoria isn't down here to hear that." Joey snarked. "Doubt she'd appreciate that remark."

"What? I'm just trying to make sure I'm not gonna accidentally see something I shouldn't." I huffed.

"I followed Phil to their location." James' voice cut through the room, a slight staticky sound to it as Craig pressed play on the recorder. *"I covered my tracks, so he has no idea he was followed, but if you move fast, we can set him up to take the fall for it."*

I nearly burst out laughing at the expression on Phil's face. If we weren't his bosses, I had no doubt he'd have been telling us, 'I told you so.'

"How much for the information this time, James?" another male voice spoke.

"Seeing as making Phil the fall guy here is gonna make things tighter in the organization, I'm gonna need at least a hundred grand."

"Well," Rich said slowly, taking a few steps toward James. "That's all I need to hear." He drew his gun and shot the unconscious man between the eyes.

"What'd ya do that for?!" I whined. "I wanted to interrogate him!"

"That's gonna be hell to get out of this wood flooring," Morgan murmured.

"He sang like a canary when I was working him over, already, Boss." Phil spoke. "He's the one that took Jace out, leaked the safehouse locations, the warehouses, all of it.

Fucking psycho got greedy and thought he could stay on the payroll *and* be on the take for the Jackals."

"So," Morgan interjected. "About that deal. Do I have your word that my man has your protection?"

"I'd say this solves a lot of our problems, Rich," Craig said.

"Fine. You get your man to our territory and we'll get word out he's to be taken to ground. When the dust settles, get that tattoo of his removed and get the fuck out of town." Rich said with a sigh.

"God, Leighton liked to slice me up and somehow, *he's* the nice one." Morgan rolled her eyes. "But fine, we accept that deal."

"Actually, *Joey's* the nice one. But yeah, Rich is an asshole." I said with a grin, before turning to face Rich. "Phil deserves a raise by the way. I think it should come from your grumpy ass."

"We'll deal with that once we've sorted out just how much of our operations *your* man managed to leak," Rich replied. "Call the cleaners and somebody get this fucking body out of my house."

"Not it!" I sing-songed. "Somebody should check on Victoria after everything that's happened. Come on Az, I'm not doing this by myself in case she decides to throw something. I'd much rather it hit you."

CHAPTER THIRTY SIX

Victoria

I lay in Joey's bed, curled around the hot water bottle pressed to my abdomen. My cramps had been off the charts bad after lunch, and I'd opted to try taking a nap to sleep through the worst of them. It hadn't worked. I'd been lying in bed, counting down the minutes until I could take something for pain relief for the last hour.

The sound of the door opening was followed by two sets of soft footsteps and Az's voice. "How are you feeling, Love." he murmured.

"Like my uterus is trying to rip free of my body." I snarked.

"Oh, I think I know what might fix that." Leighton's voice called out from the foot of the bed. "I've been doing some research." He sounded so proud of himself.

"Yeah, and what's that?" I asked, rolling onto my back so I could see them both in the dark room.

"Sex," Leighton replied, clambering onto the bed to lay beside me.

"Not really the time, L." Az spoke, settling in on the edge of the mattress.

"Yeah, not the time. I'm bleeding like a stuck pig." I said, scrunching my nose.

Leighton barked out a laugh and threw an arm over my waist. "We're not put off by a little blood, *ma petit.* In fact, you should know by now that I *enjoy* it."

"How about a massage," Az interjected, his voice soft. "My dad... He'd rub my mom's shoulders and feet when she was having a... hard day."

"That... that actually sounds perfect." I said, sitting up.

Az chuckled, the corner of his mouth quirking up. "Thought you might like that idea. Come on, Love. I've got just the thing in my room."

He stood and held out his hand. I slid Leighton's arm off my waist, scooted to the edge of the bed, and took his hand as I stood up. He pulled me to him gently, throwing an arm around my shoulders.

"I'll take care of you, Love," Az said softly as he walked us toward the door.

"I fucking *bet* you got just the thing in your room, pervert." Leighton said, hopping out of the bed and following behind us. "I'm fucking coming too!" He paused, "maybe literally if things go well..."

"Who's the pervert?" Az sighed as we stepped into the hall.

"Never denied it." Leighton laughed. "I wear that title with pride," he said smugly.

Az opened the door to his room, standing aside so I could walk in first. I took in his room and felt a warm squeeze in my chest. It was so... *Az* and yet very different from what I'd expected. There was an expensive-looking China cabinet against one wall that looked filled with childhood things. A baseball glove, a stuffed clown, and a handful of ceramic Precious Moments figurines. A table set to one side was absolutely covered in Dungeons and Dragons things. Books stacked in piles, binders, and a 3D battle map dominated a good portion of it, with various minis and scatters of dice strewn across the surface.

I strolled along the wall, noticing a tastefully done gallery wall, completely covered with pictures from his life. I could see the guys from different points in their lives, and looking at the younger versions of them made me smile. There were a few older pictures centered on the wall, the color fading slightly around the edges. It was obvious that these were his parents when I spotted a toddling blonde boy who must have been him in one of them. I drew up to a stop as I came to the end of the wall, my eyes going wide. There was a picture of me that had obviously been taken during our time at the cabin. I stood on the dock, looking out over the lake with the warm sunset hues behind me. I had a slight smile on my face. I couldn't remember him ever taking a picture of me while we were there.

"When did you even take this?" I asked.

"Just one evening shortly after we'd gotten there. You... looked too beautiful not to keep that moment." Az said warmly.

"That is so sweet it makes me want to punch you in the mouth and remind you that you're a fucking gangster." Leighton chortled.

"We're not fighting in my room. I'm not gonna have you breaking something." Az said without any malice and rolled his eyes.

"Ugh, fine." Leighton groaned, moving to the side of Az's room that I hadn't looked over yet as my eyes trailed him. "Which one of these drawers do you keep the shit in, man? Why do you even *have* drawers when you got the rest of this shit hung up like some sort of fuck trophy to brag about?"

"I don't say shit about how you keep your toys, L. Don't judge *me* because I keep mine organized and rather enjoy my collection." Az snarked.

Leighton shrugged. "You don't exactly visit my room either. But back to the point, where's the good shit?" His eyes landed on something that caused his lips to tilt into a smirk. "Well, what have we got here? Az, you naughty boy, when did you install a parking space?"

Az huffed a laugh as he moved to that side of the room to help Leighton find whatever he was looking for. "When we moved in."

My eyes widened as I moved my gaze from the guys to take in the room itself. That side of his room was *very* different from the one I was currently standing on. It was like someone had drawn a line between the different sides of his personality. His bed was massive, dominating the space. The headboard was metal and elaborate. Several places looked like attachment points along the sides of the headboard and running across it.

The walls on either side had an *array* of toys along them. Floggers of varying thicknesses and lengths were hanging in a row, and long, thin canes of different materials and colors were mounted next to them. Restraints, leashes, straps, and a host of things I didn't recognize were positioned not just for ease of access but also for show. The other side of his bed had a large cabinet, with drawers ranging in size, that Leighton was standing in front of and Az was currently looking through. My eyes followed Leighton's gaze to the floor to a thick metal plate fastened with a large O-ring bolted to the floor.

"What... in the... torture chamber... fuck is all this?" I whispered to myself.

"Az's brand of kink." Leighton deadpanned, his eyes still watching Az pick through the drawers. "Honestly, it's almost genius, and I'm mad I didn't think of it first."

"And that brand is... what exactly?" I asked, my brows shooting up to my hairline. Az looked over his shoulder at me, a smirk on his face.

"Control." He said simply, but his voice had pitched low in a way that made my heartbeat pick up despite my earlier mood. Leighton's eyes cut to me, and a slow grin spread across his face.

"I think *someone* likes the way that sounded." He chuckled.

My face flushed, causing Az's gaze to darken and Leighton's grin to grow wider. Az turned with a bottle of oil in his hand and stalked toward me, stopping just out of reach.

"Is that so?" he asked in a husky tone. "Does someone enjoy playing the good little whore, at our complete and utter mercy?"

A strangled sound left my lips, and my face burned as I flushed harder.

"I already know you do, Love." Az murmured, leaning toward me until his lips nearly brushed mine as he spoke. "Leighton likes to brag. I know all about how you were such a perfect little slut for him and Joey."

I whimpered, taking a step back but unable to go very far as my back hit the wall of his room. Az's grin was almost vicious as he crowded my space.

"Joey was right. You do have the *prettiest* little whimpers." Leighton said his voice husky.

I opened my mouth as if I was going to say something, but my mind was totally blank on what it was, so I closed it again. Az raised an eyebrow, glancing down at my lips.

"What was that, Love? I couldn't quite hear you." he said smugly. "If you *want* something, you have to *ask* for it. You know the rules."

I gave him a contemptuous look, my lip curling slightly. He was always so smug, and it was equally thrilling and infuriating.

"Please give me an attitude, Love. You have *no* idea how much I would enjoy *correcting it.*" he said dangerously.

My mouth opened again, but he put two fingers in it before I could say anything.

"Close." He demanded, and I instinctively closed my lips around his fingers. "Good. Now, before you get yourself in trouble, let's keep that mouth of yours occupied."

"Az. *Share.*" Leighton bit out from over his shoulder, causing Az to chuckle.

He gave me a once over before pulling his fingers out of my mouth and grabbing me by the hair, his grip harsh as he pulled me off the wall and walked me over to the other side of the room.

"Strip," Az said, pushing me forward. It was not a request. His demands hit me like a jolt of electricity to my spine, and I made quick work of my clothing. "Good girl. Now, get on your knees. Leighton, stand in front of her."

"Just so we're clear," Leighton said as he moved to stand

in front of me, palming his dick through his jeans. "I'm not doing this because you told me to. I'm doing it for me."

Az didn't acknowledge his comment, his eyes still glued to me. "Undo his pants and take him out." I looked at him for a moment. He raised an eyebrow at me. "I *promise* you don't want me to repeat myself. Be a good toy for us and do as you're told."

"You heard the man, *ma petit,* I'd suggest you listen," Leighton said, a dark look in his eyes to accompany his smirk. My hands flew to his jeans, undoing the button and zipper before pulling them down enough to free his already hard cock.

"Now suck. Like the good little whore you are." Az demanded.

I licked my lips before taking Leighton into my mouth and sucking him in until he hit the back of my throat. He let out a strangled moan. His hands gripped my hair, and he moved in my mouth. His hold tightened, a low rumbling growl in his chest escaping, and he started to pick up speed as I swallowed him.

"Fuuuuck..." Leighton groaned out; I looked up at him from beneath my lashes. He had his head tipped back slightly as he enjoyed himself.

"That's enough." Az said, his voice sounding like he was facing away from us.

"What the fuck, man?" Leighton snapped as I tried to pull away from him, but his hand was still wound in my hair.

"Trust me," Az said, sounding closer behind me. "Let her go."

Whatever Leighton saw caused a wicked smirk to cross his face as he let me go and slid out of my mouth. I shifted away from him but made no move to get up.

"Very good. Already not moving until you're told." Az said. "You're a *natural* at this. Get up on the bed."

I scrambled onto the bed and turned to face them as they stood at the end. Az's shirt was off, and his belt undone. He held a long strap with thick leather cuffs hanging off one end. They were both looking at me intensely, and it made me shudder. Leighton wore a sadistic grin, and Az's smirk was nothing short of fiendish.

They moved toward me on the bed. Az stood as he reached me in the center, but when I went to look at what he was doing, Leighton grabbed me by the hair and pulled me in for a savage kiss that stole the air from my lungs. His tongue forced its way past my lips, exploring my mouth with his. Claiming it. He didn't pull away until the bed shifted again with Az's movement.

"Look at me." Az's voice was harsh with want. I turned to look at him where he knelt in front of me. When he spoke next, his voice was softer than before. "I know you've gone over safe words, Love. I expect you to use them if you need them. And if there's any part of you that *doesn't* want to do this, tell us."

My heart fluttered at how lust and sincerity mingled in his eyes at that moment.

"I want this," I whispered, unable to summon any actual volume to my voice. And with that, the air of dominance surrounded Az again, that vicious look falling back over his face.

"Wrists together then. Hold them above your head." He directed, and I did as he asked. I looked up when I felt the first cuff slide around my wrist. My eyes widened. I'm not sure how I missed the attachment point that protruded from the ceiling above his bed. The strap he'd been holding was secured tightly at the top, and he was fastening my arms to the cuffs that dangled down to just above my head.   He secured my other wrist and pulled on the strap to adjust the height, pulling my arms above my head and me up into a position that kept me on my knees. He and Leighton shared a look before climbing back off the bed and taking me in.

"You look beautiful like this, Love," Az said, his voice thick as he removed the rest of his clothes. Leighton followed suit.

Leighton gripped my thighs and pulled them apart before his hand slipped between them. There was a tug, and I flushed with embarrassment, turning my gaze slightly to the side and down as I realized he'd removed my tampon.

"None of that. If you're blushing in *my* room, it's because of something we're doing to you." Az said impatiently.

"Front or back, bro?" Leighton asked.

"She's been such an obedient bitch for us, as a reward, she can choose," Az offered.

My eyes flitted between them, unsure what to do. None of the men I'd been with in the past had been cool with period sex or made me feel so sexy if they had. Part of me was worried the guys would suddenly come to their senses and be grossed out.

Az gripped my face, turning me to look at him. "I told you, none of that, so stop it."

Leighton slapped my ass *hard*, causing me to cry out. "Self-doubt isn't allowed during playtime, *ma petit*. But if you're so worried about the fact you're bleeding," he took my face from Az's hands and turned it toward him, bringing his close enough for our noses to touch and allow me to see the feral gleam in his eye. "I *fucking love* blood play."

He released me roughly and I managed to speak, though my voice came out slightly strangled. "I can't deny you what you love."

Leighton barked out a laugh and climbed onto the bed, taking his place in front of me. "Looks like you're back, dude." He said to Az over my shoulder.

"Don't say it like it's a bad thing, our pretty toy has a *fantastic* ass." Az said, smirking.

"Just meant you're gonna miss all the cute little faces she makes when we make her cum. I plan to keep her eyes on me." Leighton shrugged, lining himself up with my entrance.

I gasped as Leighton filled me to the hilt in one smooth motion. He pulled out slowly, letting me feel each piercing in his thick cock before he slammed back in. I pulled against my restraints, desperate for something to cling to, as I cried out. I felt the bed shift again as Az positioned himself behind me. He didn't move for several beats, letting Leighton have his way with me for a moment before I felt his fingers, slicked with oil, move to my puckered hole. My entire body tensed, and Az drew his fingers away.

"Yellow." His voice came out more gently than it had been. Leighton immediately stopped moving and slid out of me.

"What's up?" he asked, peering around me at Az.

"Love, are you okay?" Az said, touching my chin with his clean hand to turn me slightly. "You're tense."

"I'm okay," I rushed out. "I just..."

"Just what, *ma petit*." Leighton asked. "You can tell us; this is a *safe* space."

I briefly worried my bottom lip before deciding to spit it out. "The last time I did *that* with someone, it hurt. Like *really* hurt."

I felt Az stiffen at my back, and then he breathed. "Love, did they not prepare you properly?"

"Uh... there was... spit." My voice was barely audible.

"So, no," Az said, his voice somehow soothing. "We don't *have* to do this if you aren't comfortable with it, but if we do continue, you will be prepared properly. It won't hurt."

"We should have a conversation at some point about your exes so I can get my murder list in order, *ma petit*. But Az is right. It doesn't have to hurt." Leighton added.

"Okay," I nodded, "I want to try."

Az smiled, a look of pride on his face. "Our brave girl." He said, kissing me on the forehead before turning me back to my original position.

Leighton's face came back into view as I was repositioned, and his eyes were still full of need. "Green?" He asked.

"Green," I confirmed with a nod. He pulled me into a shattering kiss, his hands teasing along my body until they reached my hips. He gripped me, his familiar rough touch immediately making my core ache all over again. Az's hand snaked around my side, grabbing my breast and playing with my nipple, rolling and pulling on the sensitive bud. I whimpered softly into Leighton's mouth as Az teased me. Leighton growled low in response, swiftly seating himself inside me again. The sudden full sensation had me pulling away from his mouth with a gasp and a shudder.

"Love how responsive you are." He groaned as he started to move. Az made a sound of agreement from behind me, his lips trailing across my shoulders as his hand slid down my torso. His fingers ghosted across my lower stomach while Leighton found his rhythm. My head fell back onto Az's shoulder as his fingers finally found their place, drawing slow circles around my clit.

I rolled my hips to match Leighton's thrusts, his piercings making the sensation mind-blowing. The wanton sounds fell freely from my lips as the guys worked in tandem to elicit the responses they wanted. My eyes fluttered closed as I was quickly lost in the pleasure they wrought out on me.

Az used his other hand to begin slowly caressing me from behind, teasing around my back entrance, using more lube than he'd had even the first time. He didn't stop his ministrations on my clit with one hand while he got me used to the touching with the other. He was gentle and patient as he moved with me. When he finally did begin to push a finger inside me, I stiffened slightly.

"Relax, Love. I've got you." Az whispered in my ear as Leighton rolled his hips into me, causing my mind to blank again.

He redoubled his ministrations as Leighton drove me forward before trying again, and this time, when he resumed his preparation, a moan fell from my lips at the sensation. It was unusual but not unpleasant as the pressure mingled with the full feeling of Leighton inside me. He held me close to him as we moved, eventually adding another finger as Leighton pushed me higher toward my climax.

"Get her to the edge, L. But don't push her over." Az bit out, his voice heavy and low with lust.

"Planned on it." Leighton groaned, his grip on my hips tightening. I could feel his nails scraping into the skin.

"Tell us when you're getting there. I want to *hear* you say it, understood?" Az ordered, adding another finger.

"Yes sir," I said, not so much words as moans.

"Good fucking girl." Az rewarded.

I mewled and moaned in his hands as Leighton pushed me closer with every stroke, the ribbed feeling from his piercings making my eyes roll back. I arched my back and rolled my hips as I approached the edge.

"Az..." I groaned out.

"Yes?" He answered; I could hear the smirk in his voice.

"I'm... almost..." The words were strangled as they came out of my throat. I could almost feel the desire to push me further before I heard him chuckle.

"Good girl," he hummed against my ear. I immediately felt the emptiness as he slipped his fingers out of me. Leighton slowed down slightly, enough to let Az line himself up with me, pressing into my backside slowly. "Just breathe, Love. And bear down a little."

I let out a soft whimper and nodded, following his instructions. There was a tiny bit of discomfort as he worked his way into my ass, which quickly gave way to pleasure. The moan that ripped from my throat surprised me with its intensity.

"Mikey, I think she likes it." Leighton chuckled as he began slowly thrusting into me again.

Az and Leighton alternated slow, shallow thrusts as I adjusted to being so full of *both* of them. As my moans and whimpers grew louder and my body began to writhe between them, demanding more, they picked up their pace. They worked in unison, one pressing in as the other pulled back.

"That's it, Love. Sing for us. We want to hear all the

sounds you make." Az bit out.

"Oh... God... I'm gonna–" My words were cut off by a deep moan that vibrated through my entire body as I clamped down hard around both of them.

"Fuck," they both groaned.

"She's milking my fucking cock like she needs it to live." Leighton moaned.

My body tensed, a second orgasm ripping me apart before the first had fully ended. I screamed, the sound echoing in my ears until my voice felt hoarse and raspy. I went limp, the restraints and my men the only thing keeping me upright as their movements became erratic. Their grunts and moans surrounded us as they chased their own pleasure, their thrusts losing rhythm further. Leighton's nails bit into my hip, roaring as he finished. Az followed right behind him, biting down on my shoulder.

They stayed inside of me until they went soft before Az slipped out of my ass and undid my restraints. I let him ease me down to the mattress, feeling it shift as Leighton climbed from the bed. My eyes closed, and I felt myself drifting off, only opening them briefly when I felt myself being cleaned with a warm washcloth. I was lulled to sleep by the hushed whispers as they finished their ministrations and climbed into the bed to cocoon me between their bodies.

CHAPTER THIRTY SEVEN

Craig

The next several days were spent working with Phil to determine which of our business locations and safe houses had been compromised. Looking at the map with markers on every place James had sold out to the Jackals, I was surprised we were still operating at all. Everyone in the house was on edge, realizing that we would have to give up a lot of territory to pull our operations in and move them to more secure locations.

While the other guys worked to move their men and products quietly, I holed up in my room, filtering through all the information my programs had scraped. I was determined to hunt down ArachnoWraith and end the bastard for putting the bounty on Victoria's head. I'd also been letting some plans for her piece of shit ex, Benson, simmer in the back of my mind while I worked. Unfortunately, it seemed the fucker had vanished into thin air. With our return becoming known on the streets, he'd disappeared from the public eye, and I couldn't find any trace of where he'd gone.

Footsteps pounding on the floor outside my room, coming to a halt before my door, followed by someone banging on it.

"We got *another* fucking problem!" Leighton's voice was slightly muffled by the door.

Groaning, I stood from my desk, walked over, and pulled the door open. "What now?"

"One of Joey's warehouses just got blown to fucking smithereens. Half his men were taken out in the explosion, not to mention the fucking product."

"How? I thought we had most everything moved?" I asked.

"It was the last spot that needed to be packed up and moved." Leighton said. "Most of our manpower went to moving our main ops first."

"How many did we lose?"

"Count is still coming in, but at least twenty. Maybe another couple hundred grand in product."

"Fuck," I breathed. "Where's Joey now?"

"He barely stayed for the call, as soon as he heard his place had been hit, he took off out the door. Rich and Az are following after him. I stayed long enough to fill you in and let you know I've called in Phil to sit with Victoria."

A ding sounded from my computer that caught my attention. Leighton jerked his head in that direction before turning away. I shut my door again and returned to my desk, slumping in my chair. A black window popped up over my other programs, and a cold sneer crossed my face when I saw it.

*Looks like you boys are having a hard time. Losing that much territory, manpower, **and** cash flow. I can see the forum headlines now: "The end of the Horsemen. Gentlemen gangsters put down."*

If there was ever a time I wanted so badly to reach through a screen and choke someone to death, it was now. The last thing I needed was to deal with this smug motherfucker's taunting.

But I must say, it's been more entertaining than my favorite shows. Nothing like a bowl of popcorn and watching an empire burn over a live camera feed after a hard day. Tell me, VoidPhase, what's it like to watch it all go up in flames?

I had to remind myself that punching my screen would only be a 'me' problem.

Arachno, it's about time you crawled out of whatever hole you're hiding in. I'm glad you've been enjoying the show so far, though it's regrettable you won't get to see how it ends. It's always a tragedy when someone with skill passes away, so it's a shame that you had to pick the wrong side.

My system pinged from another monitor, another window popping up with the words 'searching location' flashing slowly as my protocols did their jobs.

You're awfully cocky for someone standing on the edge of losing everything, Void. You're never going to find me, and when you're gone, my webs will run this space.

'Location Found' popped up on my other monitor, and a slow grin spread across my face as I took down the address.

*I'll see you **real** soon, spider. I'm going to enjoy pulling your legs off.*

I sent that last message and closed the window, throwing up some additional protocols to lock that motherfucker out. Pulling up my phone, I had to bark a laugh at just *how* close ArachnoWraith had been to me this whole time. It was funny, in a mostly infuriating way. They lived close enough to me that I'd probably even seen them, and it made me want to punch a wall. I holstered the gun on my desk, ensuring I had a silencer on it first, and pulled on the hoodie I had draped over my chair. Yanking open my door, I slammed it on my way out and moved to the stairs.

I took them two at a time to get down to the main area. I almost skidded to a stop as I noticed Victoria leaning casually against the counter, sipping from a teacup and chatting with Phil, who looked much more unusual, holding the dainty cup in his tattooed hands.

"–that going between the two of you? Did you make it official yet? She sounds like she'd be good for you." Victoria asked Phil, a little smile on her face. Phil scrubbed his hand across the back of his neck.

"Well, that's the problem. I can't, as much as I'd like to. If I ask her out, then it officially becomes a conflict of interest, and I gotta find a new therapist." Phil sighed.

"Well, maybe when the dust settles, we can look into something–"

"Hey, Boss." Phil cut her off, turning toward me. "Heading out?"

"Yeah." I clipped. There was a little squeeze in my chest at Victoria seeming to fit seamlessly into our lives, but now wasn't the time to acknowledge it.

"Good luck with all that. Don't worry, I'll keep eyes on your ol' lady like she was my own." Phil said, giving me a two-finger salute.

Victoria laughed and shook her head when she looked at me. "No. I promise you he won't."

Phil blinked slowly before his eyes widened with realization. "That's not how I meant that!"

"You're fine, Phil. I know what you meant." I huffed impatiently as I moved to the door and put my shoes on. I opened it to head out.

"Be safe!" Victoria's voice called out as the door closed behind me. I paused outside the door, considering going back for a goodbye kiss... but couldn't waste the time. I didn't want to risk losing the spider because they packed up and scurried away.

I climbed onto Leighton's bike, glad he didn't give enough of a fuck to hardly ever take the keys out of the ignition when it was parked at the house. I resisted the urge to speed away from the house and toward my location. The less attention I drew, the better.

The place was only a fifteen-minute drive going the speed limit, and the closer I got, the more amped up I got. We needed a fucking win right now. Squashing the bug might not fix all our problems, but we'd all sleep better knowing it was done. They were obviously very interested in our dealings, so there was no telling what kind of treasure trove we'd find in their system when I got my hands on it.

I pulled up to a small brick house with bright blue shutters, double-checking that the numbers on the mailbox and next to the door matched the one my computer had pulled. I raised an eyebrow as I eased into the driveway behind a silver Kia Soul and climbed off the bike. A well-tended flower garden along the sidewalk led to the door, with brightly colored garden gnomes placed throughout. The overall picture the place painted was vastly different from what I'd imagined for the spider's lair.

Shaking my head slightly, I approached the porch and knocked loudly on the door. The sound of someone shuffling inside was shortly followed by the door opening to reveal a smiling short, curvy, black-and-purple-haired woman. Her bright green eyes, tattoos, and piercings were shockingly familiar as I took in the sight of my favorite barista from the coffee shop I frequented.

"What the *fuck*, Shania." I managed to get out.

Her smile fell as she took me in. "Well, fuck."

"Not even gonna *pretend* to be the wrong person?" I scoffed.

Shania shrugged. "Eh, why bother? You wouldn't believe me; maybe you'd force your way in the house. We'd struggle, you'd probably toss my tiny ass like a shot put, I'd end up hurt, and we'd still finish in the same place. I'm not walking out of this situation, so why die tired?"

I was a little taken aback by her forthrightness. "Fair enough." I said, drawing my gun. "Now I'm gonna have to find a new person to make my coffee. God damn it."

She held a hand up, gesturing for me to stop. "Wait, just one favor for old times' sake. Make it quick and painless."

I raised the gun and shot her between the eyes. "Hope that was quick enough for you."

I looked around to make sure no one saw or heard anything before stepping over her body and pulling it into the house so I could shut the door. I pulled out my phone and dialed Leighton.

"Where the fuck are you man?" Leighton said when he answered.

"Taking care of a little bug problem." I clipped. "You got any street guys you can spare?"

"Did... you forget we have a bit of a situation going on here, dude?" He paused for a second. "It's Craig."

"Where the fuck is he?" Az barked in the background.

"He's apparently busy. And he wants some street guys." Leighton answered.

"Did you tell him that we're a little fucking *busy* here?" I heard Joey snap.

"Duh. What do you take me for? and *don't* say a criminal. That bit is over; we did it already." Leighton responded.

"Leighton!" I snapped. "I just need a couple of guys. Tell them to wear gloves. I need them to trash a house while I do some digging. I don't care who you can spare. I'll text you the address."

"Yeah, fine. I'll send someone as soon as we can." Leighton replied, hanging up on me.

I scowled down at Shania's body. Finding out the woman I'd been leaving massive tips for because she made my coffee just the way I liked ate away a little of the satisfaction I'd found discovering Arachno's location. Huffing to myself, I turned to look around the small living room and spotted the narrow hallway.

There were three doors along the hall; one went to a small bathroom, the other to what had obviously been her bedroom, and the furthest down the hall held her workstation. Leaning my head side-to-side to crack my neck, I stepped into the room and made myself comfortable as I booted up her system. I let out a derisive snort at the lack of password on her computer; it was clear she never expected to be found, let alone have *anyone* get into her office, and went to work.

Not long into my digging, I understood her laissez-faire attitude toward security. There was next to nothing saved on the system. It was evident that she conducted most of her business offline. That was more apparent when I stumbled on an email from the one man all five of us wanted to string up and burn alive.

A contact said that you could help me. I've been made aware that the men holding my fiancé have decided to target me, and I need to go underground while I gather my resources. I'm too well known in the public eye to use my personal contacts to disappear while I put my team together. Someone of your skills is what I require. I am happy to pay whatever your price to get the job done.
B. Prescott

"Fucking idiot," I muttered to myself.

I spent a bit longer trying to find any response or information to lead me to Benson, but there was nothing. If Shania had taken the job to help the weasel disappear, she'd done it offline. I decided to pack up her computer and take it back to the house. Some of my personal systems could potentially pull something off the hard drive that I wouldn't find on my own.

I unhooked her system and looked around the room for something to pack it up *in*. I'd have to give the setup to the guys Leighton sent because putting it on the bike to take back was impossible. I didn't trust them to move it around properly. Maybe I'd warn them that if it showed up damaged, I'd personally step on their throats for it. That would ensure it was handled with care.

There wasn't much in the room that was of use to help me pack the system up, and the more I looked, the more irritated I got. I found a small storage bin that looked big enough to haul everything underneath some stuff in the closet. I tossed some useless knick-knack over my shoulder, and when it hit the wall with a hollow thud, it caught my attention.

Turning around, I found a crack in the drywall that was only a few inches across and stopped suddenly. *What could the little spider have been hiding there?* I mused as I pulled chunks of the broken wall out to reveal a hollow space, and sitting inside it was another hard drive.

"No wonder she wasn't worried about that one." I scoffed. I picked it up and put it in my hoodie pocket. Still wouldn't hurt to take the other one; never know what could be on it. And if nothing else, I could salvage it for additions to my setup. I yanked the bin out of the closet and dumped the contents onto the floor. Then, I boxed up the tower and any auxiliary equipment that looked worth taking.

I carried it out into the hall, set it by the door, and stood inside, waiting for our people to show up. Fortunately, I didn't have to wait long before I spotted a pair in dark clothes heading up the walkway. I opened the door and let them in.

"Trash it. Take whatever looks valuable if you want, I don't give a fuck. Oh, and *this*," I indicated the storage bin with the hardware, "if it doesn't get back to our place *intact* I will hold each of you personally responsible. Understood?" I clipped.

"Yes, Sir." One of them said.

"Anything else?" The other asked.

"You can take things, leave nothing behind, so wear some fucking gloves," I pointed at the storage bin again, "and remember. *Intact,* or it's your asses."

They nodded as I let myself out and shut the door behind me, looking around as I moved back to the bike. I climbed on and headed for home.

I slammed the door a few minutes later as I walked in, kicking my shoes off, and stomped through the main room toward the stairs. Phil looked up from whatever he and

Victoria were doing.

"What's got you slamming doors, Boss?" he asked curiously.

"I had to *shoot* my fucking barista! I'll be in my fucking room!" I snapped loudly, stomping up the stairs two at a time.

CHAPTER THIRTY EIGHT

Victoria

Phil and I exchanged glances as Craig stormed through the house. It was almost shocking to see him in this state. He was always so level-headed that, for a moment, it felt like a different person had just walked in.

"I'm sorry Phil, I–" I started as I moved away from the counter.

"Go on, girl, what are you still talking to me for?" He said with a wave of his hand. I liked Phil. He was gruff and rough around the edges but a good guy.

I turned toward the stairs and rushed after Craig, starting up them right about the time I heard the door slam from the hall. Something must have gotten under his skin hard, and I couldn't help but worry about what happened. I knew there was trouble at the warehouse, but how had he needed to shoot a *barista,* of all things?

I stood outside his door for a moment, listening. I could hear the shuffling inside and his computer chair moving across the floor. I cracked the door open slowly.

"Craig?" I said slowly.

"What have I told you about sneaking up on a man while he's working, Bunny?" Craig snapped. His shoulders stiffened sharply, and he sighed. "I'm sorry. It might be best... to not be around me right now."

I slid into the room and shut the door behind me. "And that's exactly why I need to be with you right now." I said, moving through the room softly.

Craig's room was an interesting mix of him, kept to

organized little stations. His workspace dominated almost one entire side of his room. Different pieces of equipment almost wholly covered the long L-shaped desk. Six monitors formed a giant rectangle of screens, each covered with information that probably only made sense to Craig. Another corner of his room had a different kind of desk, with a few different types of jars and liquids set about it. A magnifying glass and light were positioned above a cotton pad, and several stacks of small white boxes sat beside it. Above that desk were artfully arranged frames, each with a different butterfly or moth pinned to it and labeled. They were beautiful and looked meticulously done.

A plush reading chair was next to a large shelf *stuffed* with books of all kinds. What couldn't fit on the shelf was stacked above it and on the floor in front of it. Next to that was his bed. It was as large as Az's, but it was a thick, uncovered canopy frame. It was some kind of brushed metal that was treated with a matte black finish. The square canopy frame had bars that ran in a grid across the top. There were similar attachment points all over it, and there were so *many* it was covered in them. They even seemed to go down the sides of the frame all the way to the feet of the bed. Behind the head of the bed, there was a large mirror. He had pegs lining the wall by his bed and rows and rows of rope stored in neat coils. I smirked as I took it in; he'd even sorted them by texture and color. He had a series of shelves below them with different containers that looked to have hardware inside them.

The man himself was sitting in his computer chair in front of his workstation. He pulled some kind of black rectangle from his hoodie pocket and worked on hooking it into one of the pieces of equipment on his desk.

"Craig?" I said as I moved further into the room. He sighed heavily and turned around sharply to face me.

"Bunny, I'm *working*. I'm not... in a good mood right now. I'm not the best person for you to be around right now." Craig said, his voice sounded measured as he looked at me. I could see the lingering glare in his eyes and the set of his jaw. He was angry, and it wasn't something I was used to from him.

"I just want... to check on you. This isn't like you, and I'm worried." I said carefully. Craig let out a bitter laugh.

"You are persistent aren't you, Bunny?" He said, standing. "You'd be surprised how much this *is* like me. It's just not a side that you get to see."

"I've been around you guys every day for months. I've never seen you yelling and slamming doors." My tone incredulously. "You're always so... steady."

Craig smirked virulently before shaking his head. "No, I'm not. That's who I'm *trying* to be. I have a temper, Bunny. Always have. I keep it on a tight leash because..." He trailed off, and I felt my heart squeeze painfully.

"Oh, Craig, honey. You're nothing like that. Being angry doesn't make you like that." I started to approach him as if to pull him into a hug. He stepped back.

"Bunny, I know you don't want to believe it, but there are times when calm and steady is the *last* thing you'll get from me. I have to... decompress. I have to work through it first. I don't want you to take the brunt of it." He sighed heavily, a sad expression on his face.

I moved toward him until I was standing almost chest-to-chest. I looked up into his face, my brows furrowed in concern, but I wouldn't back away from him like this.

"Craig Dougherty, you listen to me. You're human, and you have emotions like a human. Anger is one of those and having it doesn't make you a monster. Expressing it doesn't make you an abuser. *You* are not like that. The fact that you care enough to keep yourself in check when you're feeling your worst is proof enough of that." I put my hands on my hips and poked him in the chest. His gaze flitted between my face and the finger poking him in the chest.

His brows drew together like he didn't understand the words coming from my mouth. I wanted to laugh and shake him at the same time.

"Tell me how one of the two most emotionally intelligent men I've ever met won't give himself permission to be angry, when it's one of the most natural human emotions. It's just as natural as happiness, sadness, jealous, lust... all of them." I said, crossing my arms over my chest. "If the situation was reversed, you'd be standing here telling me that it's natural to be angry when the world around you burns. And you'd ask me what I needed to help me get through it. Give yourself the same fucking grace and tell me what I can do to help you get through it."

He looked at me for a long time, his gaze searching my face before something on his face cracked, and he smiled. It wasn't a bitter smile this time, and it wasn't sad. It was *my* Craig smiling back at me.

"Have I told you lately how lucky we are to have you even willing to tolerate us?" He chuckled, pulling me into a hug. I smiled softly against his chest before lifting up and putting my arms around his neck.

"I know you're still angry, but it's okay. What can I do?" I searched his gaze, trying to communicate that he was stuck with me without saying anything. He slid his hands down my back to rest on my hips, and an eyebrow raised as his smile turned into a smirk.

"I can think of something."

"Is that right?" I said, my breath hitching at how he looked at me. My body was still a bit sore, but the way heat pooled in my lower abdomen and I had to squeeze my thighs together said it didn't mind the idea.

"I want to make sure you're alright with what I have in mind, and if there's anything you want to change, you can let me know." He said, turning me toward the bed. "I don't know if any of the other guys have gone over scene negotiation, but it's to make sure we're both on the same page."

"Okay..." I said breathily, blinking several times to pull myself back to earth so I could focus on what he was saying.

"I'd like to tie you up. I... Rope helps. Something to focus on, something to pull me in and work out my shit in my head. I want to put you in a chest harness, something simple. Perhaps... work out from there if you're okay with a little improvisation on that part. Whatever it is, I will stay on the simple side since I haven't been able to tie you up before. If you decide that it's not for you, then just tell me, and we can get you out of them, okay?"

I nodded, imagining him tying me up, and decided that, in theory, I have absolutely no qualms with it based on how my heartbeat picked up speed.

"I'd prefer to use a natural fiber for how I feel, but we'll stick with something smooth so you–"

"Use what you want to use," I said quickly. "I want to give you what you need."

Craig smiled softly, cupping my face and leaning his forehead against mine. "I know you do, and I love you for that. But no, Bunny. Not yet, we'll experiment with it, but we won't start there. Your body will be in my hands, and I want to keep you comfortable. Besides..." He trailed off, leaning back to give my whole body a once over. "If I'm honest, I think you'd look better wrapped in silk."

I sucked in a breath at how his voice dripped with desire when he said that he wanted me in silk. I could only nod. He started to move us toward the bed, his hands on my hips as we moved.

"While I'm tying you up, I need you to pay attention to how your body feels. If you feel pinching, tingling, numbing, or burning, I need you to tell me immediately. What are your safe words?" Craig asked, his heavy-lidded eyes still sharp as they looked me over.

"Yellow for a break, red for stopping entirely." I spoke. It was becoming something automatic, which was probably the point.

"Good girl." He smiled. "Afterward, I'll check you over with standard rope aftercare, and we can lay together because I know you enjoy that afterward. We'll figure out exactly what you need for aftercare in different types of play, but if you feel like you want something in that moment, just tell me, okay?"

I nodded as my back hit one of the posts of his bed.

"Good," Craig growled, crashing his lips to mine for a kiss that I hadn't been expecting from him. It was aggressive in a way I'd not seen him before. His teeth nipped at my bottom lip, and he began to strip me of my clothes, only pulling away when he absolutely had to. His hands roamed across my body, teasing, massaging, and squeezing me as he explored me. I didn't stand a chance and melted at how he seemed to revel in me.

Finally, he pulled away, his chest heaving. "Get on the bed for me, Bunny. Sit comfortably in the middle." He said as he moved away toward his many rope coils on the wall. He looked back at me a couple of times as I scrambled into the center of the bed, his head tilted to the side slightly. He selected three colors of rope, pulling a few coils off the wall of each.

He laid them all out within reach of me on the bed and made sure there was a pair of sheers on his nightstand within easy reach as well. He stripped off his shirt before he climbed onto the bed with me. I raised my eyebrow as I realized he was still wearing pants. He laughed softly.

"You want me naked, Bunny?" He asked.

"Only seems fair." I said with a little smirk.

"Say please." He replied with an answering smug grin.

"Take off your pants, Craig. Please." I said, stretching the word out slowly as I said it.

"Mmm, now I rather like the sound of that. How can I say no when you ask so nicely." He said, making quick work of removing those as well. He climbed up on the bed with me, kneeling in front of me. He weaved his fingers in my hair and leaned down for a kiss, trailing his other hand down my neck and between my breasts.

He directed me to face the mirror, sat back, uncoiled the rope he needed, and set to work. I watched his face as he began wrapping my body in intricate lines and coils; he was exact in his positioning and careful in his tension. It was pulled across me, tight enough to feel it pressing into my skin but not so much as to be painful. He seemed to lose himself in the work, and I was content to sit and watch him. The silence was only broken by the occasional check-in with me about a knot or a coil in a sensitive area. The three colors created thick bands of designs around my chest, and as he worked, he added more additions, asking if he could move down onto my stomach. He adjusted me as he needed, moving slowly in circles around me. I watched the designs take shape in the mirror with wide eyes as I started to see them come together. Somehow, he'd managed to weave a heart in the center of my chest. The portions to hold its shape formed a weave over my breasts, around my shoulders, and continued in diamond patterns onto my stomach.

"Craig... that's beautiful." I breathed out as he reached the end of the last coils of rope and tied it off. He looked at me in the mirror, a little smile on his face, before he kissed the side of my head, leaning down until his lips brushed my ear.

"Only because you're wearing it, Bunny." He whispered. I blushed a deep red and looked away from the mirror. "Oh no. We'll not be doing that."

He traced two fingers along my cheek and moved my head until I faced the mirror again.

"Look at yourself," he said, his tone firm. I looked at myself in the mirror, my torso wrapped in his gorgeous design. He gripped my sides and sat me up on my knees, moving them a little wide so he could position himself flush with my back. I looked up at him, just above me in the mirror. "No, Bunny." He swatted me on the ass just hard enough to make me gasp. "Look at *yourself*. And don't move your eyes until I tell you. I'll swat you every time you do; it'll get harder each time. Understand?"

"Yes," I said softly.

He brushed my hair to the side, smirking at the bite mark from Az that still lingered. He kissed it before kissing a trail up to my neck, using his lips and tongue on the sensitive skin to send a fire straight through my veins to my core. His fingers teased the exposed skin between the ropes and moved across my torso before trailing down my stomach to my hips. He teased my thighs and core without giving me the pressure I was quickly starting to crave.

"I want you to see yourself as I do." He said quietly, kissing the back of my neck as his fingers ghosted across my inner thighs. "Do you know what I see when I look in that mirror?"

"What?" I asked, my voice breathy as I leaned back against his chest.

"I see..." He trailed off as his fingers finally found their way to the part of me that ached for his touch. He moved them in slow circles around my clit, his eyes on my face in the mirror. I looked back, catching his gaze. He swatted my ass a little harder with the other hand. "Eyes on *you*, Bunny. What I see is a woman who's so powerful that she's got five gangsters wrapped around her fingers."

I opened my mouth to say something, but he pushed his fingers against my clit roughly, and my words broke into a moan in my throat. I kept my eyes on myself and watched my lips part as I gasped.

"*Hush*," he said with a smirk. "The woman in that mirror is the most beautiful woman I've ever seen." His fingers moved faster; he shifted forward slightly so he could move them from my clit to my core, pushing them inside me slowly, using his thumb to continue where his fingers had left off. A low groan escaped my chest as he pushed them inside me.

"I see someone with enough compassion and kindness to make up for the lack of it in those around her." He pushed his fingers deeper inside me. I moaned as he crooked them, pumping his fingers faster. I could feel the coil of tension start in my spine. Something about him making me watch myself enjoying him was incredibly erotic.

"I see a woman I didn't know I needed in my life..." He

groaned as I arched my back, rolling my hips into his fingers as he moved them into me faster. I fought to keep my eyes on myself as my jaw was a little slack, my eyes fluttered, my face was flushed, and I was visibly panting. "But now that she's in it, I couldn't imagine it without her."

"Fuuuck... Craig..." I barely got the words out. The coil of tension in my body was about to snap.

"I see... a woman I want more than almost anything I've *ever* wanted." He said, his voice hoarse with need. "That's it, Bunny. Let go."

I dropped my head back on his shoulder as a loud moan ripped through me. My mind shattered as I came on his fingers, and my eyes rolled back in my head. He wrapped his free hand around my chest to hold me close as my body arched away from him. He didn't stop, didn't even slow down as the waves of pleasure washed over me. It wasn't until I was trembling in his arms that he slowed down and slipped his fingers from me.

"Stay here." He said, climbed off the bed, pulled open a drawer on the nightstand, and pulled out a condom packet. He ripped it open and slid it on quickly, returning to me on the bed. I'd fallen forward, resting myself on my hands and knees as I panted for breath. He took a position behind me, sliding his hands up my hips and lower back, over the ties on his rope, and to my hair.

"You have no fucking idea how good you look..." He said softly, almost reverently. "If we have our way, that'll change, though." He said as he entered me. I moaned, lowering my upper body to the mattress. He pushed his cock inside me slowly, every inch making my eyes flutter as I clenched around him.

Once he was fully seated inside me, he pulled out just as slowly. It was fucking *agonizing* how slow he moved. Still, it felt so fucking good I was useless to do anything but moan into the covers. When I started to get frustrated and needed *more*, he finally picked up speed. The sound that tore out of his throat was primal as he went from slowly savoring our session to grabbing my hips and slamming into me. It was like some kind of rubber band had snapped inside him.

"Craig!" I cried out. He pistoned into me with force, grabbing the ties of the rope and pulling me up from the mattress to hold me back against his chest as he thrust up into me. His name fell from my lips like a prayer as he wrapped his arms around me and rushed me toward the edge again. I was a moaning, mewling mess as he hit that sweet spot inside me that pushed me into delirium.

"Give me another one, Bunny. Just one more. I know you can." He grunted, pulling me down onto his cock as he thrust upward. His encouragement seemed all my body needed before I came undone at the seams around him. I came screaming his name, my head dropping back on his shoulder as he kept up his relentless pace. Wave after wave crashed into me until his thrusts stuttered erratically, and he followed me over the edge with a loud, guttural cry.

He held me against his chest as we panted for breath, resting his head on my shoulder and mine on his. We slowly returned to earth as our heart rate and breathing were under control. He kissed my shoulder as we began to shift, and he slid out of me.

"Let's get you out of these, and I'll look you over." He said slowly, his words still punctuated by deep breaths.

"That's going to take–" I started, and he huffed a quick laugh. I felt three sharp tugs, and the rope that had been hugging my torso fell into a pile on the blankets in front of us.

"Quick-release ties come in awfully handy in moments like these."

He laid me down and gathered up the rope to deposit on his nightstand before disposing of his condom. When he climbed back into bed with me, his hands tracing across where the rope had been, it was an odd sensation because I could almost still feel it on my skin.

"I think rope marks might be my favorite thing I've ever seen you wear."

CHAPTER THIRTY NINE

Az

We got two days of quiet before everything went to hell. Craig had found a number of leads on smaller crews that were targeting Victoria, thanks to that fucking messaging board. Leighton had even managed to snag a couple of them off the streets and put them down. We *thought* things were starting to turn in our favor right up until the six o'clock news came on the TV.

"Is- Is that my apartment complex?" Victoria's eyes were wide as she took in the inferno playing out behind the reporter. "That's my floor."

Craig caught my eye from near the stairs and jerked his head for me to follow him. Joey had already moved to Victoria's side and was comforting her as she watched her home burn to the ground on live television, so I silently turned and followed Craig upstairs to his room.

"You should see this. I was already on my way down to show someone when it came on the news." Craig said, tapping away on his keyboard and pulling up grainy security footage.

"What am I looking at here, Craig?" I asked, squinting, to try and understand the black-and-white video.

"This is her apartment complex, maybe fifteen minutes ago." he said, pointing at the screen before moving his finger to a figure exiting the building. "And that's Theodore Abrams."

"You sure?" I asked, knowing he wouldn't have said it if he wasn't. "We knew *Uncle* Theo was involved in some shit but seems a bit odd he'd dirty his hands so... directly."

"I'm sure. Just keep watching."

Craig swapped between the footage of multiple cameras, tracking Theo as he pulled away from Victoria's apartment complex before switching back to the one focused on her building. The man had barely been gone five minutes when a silent explosion rocked the building, flames bursting out of the windows on Victoria's floor.

"That's her apartment," Craig said, pointing at the windows.

"Why the fuck is he blowing up her apartment," I asked, my brows drawing down in confusion. "It's not like she was anywhere near the place. What purpose does it serve?"

"Seriously?" Craig frowned. "Have you not *met* Victoria? Something like this would absolutely draw her out in the open if it weren't for us, that is. I mean, for fuck's sake, she knows the front desk man on a first-name basis. She'd run down there to try and *personally* put the fire out with a bucket."

"Az! You're gonna wanna see this!" Joey's voice from downstairs had me turning back toward the door right about the same time my phone started going off. I pulled it out of the inside pocket of my blazer as I descended the steps.

"This is Az," I said as I stepped back down onto the main floor and looked up at Joey, who was motioning at the T.V. For a second, I didn't understand what I was looking at… again.

"Boss… it's about the art gallery." One of my captains said as I simultaneously realized what was showing on the news now.

"Son of a *bitch*!" I yelled as I watched the police tape off my newly acquired gallery. The glass was smashed outward, and it was a fucking inferno. "I had a piece on *LOAN* in that motherfucker. This is going to cost a fucking *fortune*!"

"Didn't you say that it was called The Flaming June? The irony…" Leighton laughed.

"Fuck you." I snapped as my phone started beeping that I had a call coming in. "I'll call you back, Mark. This is probably about the gallery." I answered the call and watched the other line disconnect when Mark hung up. "This is Az."

"Mr. Casadei, this is Detective Zhou." The man's voice came over the line. "I was calling about your–"

"The gallery I'm watching burn on the fucking news, I'm guessing?" I snapped. "Shouldn't I have found out about this from you *before* the reports on the news were able to tell me about it?"

"Mr. Casadei, this seems like a bad case of timing. There was a news crew headed back to the station, they were apparently the ones that called in the fire. Seems they decided to grab their cameras at about the same time. Our apologies that you're having to find out this way, I assure you our captain is already on the phone with their producer. Is this a good time? I just have a few questions I'd like to ask."

I scoffed, rolling my eyes as I shifted the phone to my other ear. "I'm not sure what would give you the impression that watching *millions* of dollars in investment burn on my fucking television would be a *good time*, detective. But ask your questions."

"I appreciate the gravity of the situation, Mr. Casadei. But unfortunately, this is just standard procedure. Do you have any enemies, or can you think of anyone who may want to do this? Former business partner, jilted ex-employee... scorned lover? Anyone that might stick out in your mind?"

The question was almost hilarious, given the situation. "No." I deadpanned without further explanation. It's not like I could tell him we were currently in a gang war with another Mafia family, and they seemed set on tearing down the city to draw us out. I'm sure that would go over *real* well with the good Detective Zhou.

The detective moved on to his next question, and I responded on autopilot. My focus was primarily on the scene behind the reporter, trying to pick out anyone in the growing crowd that looked suspicious. It wasn't until the screen switched back to the reporters in the newsroom that I noticed the sound of Joey and Leighton's phones both ringing. The looks on both their faces, as they listened to whoever was on the other end of their respective calls told me something was horribly wrong.

"Detective," I said, cutting off whatever the man had been saying to me. "I must apologize, but I need to make a few more phone calls to insurance and the artists who've had their work destroyed by the fire. I'll call and make an appointment to speak with you more in-depth tomorrow."

"Yeah, uh. That's fine. Let me just-"

"I have the number to the precinct." I cut him off again. "I'll be in touch."

I didn't bother waiting for him to say anything else before disconnecting the call. In the few seconds it had taken me to get the detective off the line, Rich and Craig had both come downstairs wearing matching expressions of worry.

"What's wrong?" I asked, noting the rolled-up map in Rich's hand and the way Victoria seemed to be unable to decide who she needed to comfort first.

"The entire goddamned criminal underbelly of Sacona has organized against us. That's what's fucking wrong." Rich snarled, moving to the dining table and unfurling the map.

"Every silent alarm I have set went off almost at exactly the same time." Craig added, stepping up beside Rich and producing a black sharpie.

I watched as he quickly began marking off different places on the map where we conducted business. Several of them were the new locations we'd secured after sussing out the ones James had handed over to the Jackals.

"Fuck!" Leighton shouted. "Fucking, fuck!

Joey was still on the phone, firing off directives to whoever he was speaking with. Victoria moved to look over Craig's shoulder as he continued marking off places on the map, and I couldn't help but notice that our territory was rapidly shrinking.

"Street guys have been pinned down here, here, and here." Leighton spoke, moving to jab his finger on the map to indicate the skirmishes. "An entire crew damned near was wiped out here."

"My warehouses on Tenth, Union, and Lotus are gone."
Joey piped in as he ended his call.

"What does this mean?" Victoria asked, her eyes
widening with a hint of fear.

"It means we have to fucking move." Rich snipped.

"What? Why? I thought you guys said this was the safest
place in Sacona for us." Victoria asked, her voice trembling
slightly.

"Not when they're taking out most of our men, Bunny."
Craig said softly, making the final mark on the map.

As he stepped back, I took in the picture his marks made.
We were being hit from all sides, and the circle was tightening
in around us. There was no way so many attacks at once were
the Jackals alone. Rich was right; the entire underbelly of the
city was targeting us. The only thing that I couldn't figure out
was who was pulling the strings. The small-time dealers and
thugs were usually too busy squabbling over their scraps of
territory to put their differences aside long enough to team up.

"Fucking hell." Rich bellowed, looking at his phone. "We
need a safe house, *now!*"

"What?! What happened?!" Victoria shrieked in a panic.

Rich turned his hard glare on her and spoke. "There's
a shootout less than five minutes away between some of our
associates and soldiers and what sounds like a fucking band of
mercenaries."

"Mercs? Are you sure?" Leighton asked.

"Pretty damn," Rich replied, holding up a blurry image of
a man that looked somewhat familiar.

"Holy shit, is that Damien?" Leighton blanched.

"This is bad, this is so bad." Victoria blabbered. "If
Leighton is scared, this is bad."

Joey grabbed her by the shoulders and turned her to face
him. "We worked with Damien way back when we were first
making a name for ourselves. The man is a war criminal. He
crosses boundaries that even Leighton would never."

"WHY ARE WE JUST STANDING HERE THEN?!" She shrieked.

"I agree with Princess for once. That is the appropriate response." Rich drawled. "Get your shit and let's go."

"Yes, go. Get *all* the guns. Please." Victoria whimpered. "These pants have decent-sized pockets, I can carry ammo or a knife or something if you need me to."

Under any other circumstances, I'd have found her words adorable. It was the panic underlining her words that had me hopping into gear. I barely caught Leighton handing her one of his favorite switchblades as I raced toward the stairs.

In a matter of minutes, we were all loaded into the armored SUV with our go-bags, each of us packing a gun. Victoria sat in the back, squished between Craig and Joey, holding the switchblade Leighton had given her tightly in her fist.

"Love, you need to put that away before you accidentally stab one of us," I said calmly as I slammed the passenger door.

"I'm not going to *accidentally* stab anyone," she snapped. "Leighton showed me how to use it. If anyone gets stabbed with it, it will be on purpose."

"We don't have time for you to squabble about this shit. Put it away, Princess, or I'll have Joey take it from you." Rich barked as he turned the key in the ignition.

"Fine, *dad*." She huffed, folding it closed just as Rich tore out of the driveway.

We rode in tense silence as Rich sped through the neighborhood, all of us watching for someone following us. We'd been so focused on who might be behind us that we didn't see the danger straight ahead. Rich slammed on the brakes with a soft curse and swerved to the left, taking a side street to avoid the blockade in front of us, only to find it blocked by vehicles.

"Fuck!" He shouted, throwing the SUV into reverse.

"Uh, Rich!" Leighton called out from the third row.

"Blocked this way too."

Not hesitating, Rich whipped the wheel so we were facing back the way we came. In the time it had taken us to take one side street and back out, we'd been boxed in.

"Shit." I hissed. "Looks like we're gonna have to do this here."

Three guns cocked behind me, and I knew Leighton, Craig, and Joey had all readied their weapons. I risked a glance behind me and nearly burst into laughter. Victoria's face was twisted into a feral snarl, and her blade was back in her hand. She looked ready to gut the first person she could, even though we weren't going to let *anyone* get close enough to give her that chance.

"That's precious, Love," I said as Rich slammed on the brakes and threw the SUV into park. "But stay in the fucking car."

CHAPTER FORTY

Victoria

Rich, Az, Joey, and Craig exited the SUV, leaving the doors open for cover before I could argue. Leighton slithered over the seat, flopping beside me, and gently kissed me on the cheek.

"Do what Az said, *ma petit.* Stay put while we deal with this." He said before slipping out of the vehicle to stand beside Joey.

I gripped the back of the front seats, watching as people poured out of the cars blocking the road before us. The guys were already outnumbered by at least three to one. I was terrified about how high that number might actually go if I looked around.

"What are you doing running with mercs, Candy?" Craig called out, his tone strangely friendly. "The Jackals can't do their own dirty work these days?"

"We don't have to do this, Craig. Hand over the Bristol girl and we'll let you walk away for old time's sake." A female voice called back.

"Not a fucking snowball's chance in hell," Az replied.

Against my better judgment, I took that moment to risk turning in my seat to look around. My stomach clenched as I realized there was no way we were walking out of this intact. Even with the doors for cover, there were dozens of armed men and women on each side of the SUV and at least twenty more to the rear.

"I didn't want it to come to this," the woman called out, pushing to the front of the group of armed men in black body armor to the front of the SUV. Her long brown hair was braided down the sides of her head, and tattoos covered every inch of visible skin. "I hoped what we shared in the past would be enough for you to have *some* sense of respect and hand the girl over. Hell, maybe we could have even picked up where we left off once the dust settled."

"We ended for a reason, Candy," Craig replied.

"A girl can dream," Candy shrugged, motioning to one of the men in the black body armor beside her. "Damien, if you would. Try to keep them alive so we can decide who to take in."

She melted back into the people surrounding her just as the mercenary grinned viciously.

"Leighton, good to see you, buddy," Damien called out as he stepped forward. "I've learned some new techniques during a trip to Kazakhstan."

"We're not buddies, Damien," Leighton called back. "And that's plenty close where you are."

Damien laughed and took another step forward. Rich responded with a warning shot that echoed loudly in the SUV and caused my ears to ring.

"Ah, come on now, bud. You're outnumbered and outgunned. There's only one way this ends." Damien called out. "Do you think it's the best idea to waste what few shots you have on *warnings*?"

"Fucking hell, Rich." Leighton hissed. "Just take the bastard out."

My eyes widened as Joey raised his gun and took aim over the top of the door. The muffled thud of a body hitting the pavement told me he'd hit his mark.

"Rich, if you're gonna pull the trigger around people like *these*, you *kill someone* with the shot." Joey snapped.

Several shots popped off from behind us, the bullets dinging loudly against the armored SUV.

"Yeah, well, I was trying to avoid exactly this." Rich retorted as more of the crowd began to fire on us.

"Good chance *this* was happening either way. At least now we don't have to deal with the sicko." Az clipped.

"Good riddance to him!" Leighton called, firing off shots toward our attackers. "Pretty sure he *literally* ate a baby once."

"Can we focus, Leighton! I don't think now is the best time for your exaggerations." Craig snarked. "We're in the middle of a fucking fire fight, at the center of a god damned kill box."

"Eh, seems like they're mostly shit shots." Leighton replied as bullets continued to bounce off the SUV. "With as many of them as there are, *one* of us should have taken a hit by now."

Seconds later, Leighton gave a pained grunt, and his free hand was pressed to his shoulder. I clapped my hands over my mouth to suppress the scream that wanted to break free as blood pooled under his hand and spread through the fabric of his shirt.

"You were saying?!" Az yelled, firing back.

"Lucky shot!" Leighton groaned.

"Bunny, in my bag." Craig barked into the vehicle. "There are some medical supplies; grab them. Leighton, let her wrap that wound before you lose enough blood that arm is useless."

Leighton slid into the SUV beside me, gritting his teeth in pain as I tore through the bags stacked in the third row. The first one I found had mainly weapons, and I held a hand grenade up in shock.

"Oh, perfect." Leighton chuckled, snatching it out of my hand and slipping from the vehicle before I could say anything. "Got something to thin the herd, boys, cover your fucking ears."

"*Another* god damned grenade?!" Rich yelled. "How is it you have one *every time*?"

"Well, obviously. It pays to be prepared." Leighton answered.

I saw the small object sail through the air toward the crowd at our rear seconds later. On instinct, I covered my ears. Leighton slid back into the SUV beside me, his fingers plugging his ears, just as the grenade exploded. The sheer amount of damage the small device had done was so overwhelming it left me too stunned to scream. I blinked my eyes rapidly, my brain trying to make sense of the sudden carnage.

"*Ma petit*, my shoulder," Leighton said, pulling me back to the task. "Quickly, if you don't mind. I think I just pissed the rest of them off blowing up their friends."

I tore through the rest of the duffle bags like my life depended on it, clothing, and various odds and ends flying around the inside of the car as I tossed them aside.

"Yes!" I cheered to myself as I finally got my hands on a package of gauze and a roll of medical tape.

"Uh, L… If you got another grenade, that would be handy right about now." Joey called out as I worked to bandage Leighton's shoulder. "We're running out of ammo here and these folks seem real keen on drawing blood."

I watched as Leighton peered through the windshield before whipping his head from side to side to take in our left and right as I finished wrapping his shoulder the best I could.

"Shit. Hold on!" He yelled, climbing over the center row into the back. "Where is it, where is it?"

He ferreted through the chaos I'd left behind and let out a whoop before he resurfaced with something in his hand. Without a word, he threw himself back over the center row and thrust his hand out the door toward Joey.

"Here!"

Joey looked at whatever Leighton had handed him, pulled something from it, and threw it as hard as he could toward the group to our left. Pink smoke filled the side street before it even hit the ground.

"What the fuck! Leighton, that was *not* helpful!" Joey yelled.

"Shit, sorry!" Leighton replied as he threw himself back in the third row. "Their visibility is down at least. That has to count for something."

"The one time we could really use you blowing something up and you're not ready?" Rich scoffed as he fired once more into the crowd, his gun clicking with the second trigger pull. "I'm out, what do we have to work with, Leighton? We're kind of counting on your crazy ass to get us out of this mess right now."

"I'm working on it!" Leighton snarled. "Just let me fucking think for a second!"

"I'm out too! Tell me you got something back there, man!" Az yelled.

I watched as Leighton's face lit up; his hand raised in triumph as he held an expensive-looking bottle of scotch. "I do! Thank you for being a bougie bitch that packs booze in his go-bag, Az!"

"If we live, you owe me a new bottle!" Az shouted.

"If we live, I'll buy you the fucking distillery that makes it, you snob!" Leighton responded, handing the bottle to me. "Open this for me, lover-muffin."

I did as he asked, watching as he grabbed one of Az's expensive shirts and tore it into strips. Leighton snatched the bottle back and began stuffing them into the bottleneck, tipping it slightly to encourage the alcohol to soak them through. Winking at me, he clambered back out of the SUV and stuck his hand down Joey's pocket.

"What the fuck man," Joey shouted.

"Oh, shut up, I just want your zippo you fucking firebug." Leighton shot back as he pulled the zippo in question free. I scrunched my face in confusion. I hadn't known Joey even *had* one, let alone that it was common enough knowledge among the guys for Leighton to immediately stick his hands down the man's pants for it.

"Hurry *up*, Leighton! I'm out too!" Craig yelled.

"Which side do you want me to aim for? Make it count, cuz this is it, boys." Leighton replied.

"Well, usually you take off the head, and these fucking snakes die; aim for the front." Az barked out.

Leighton raced to the front of the SUV, and I watched in horror as he left himself fully exposed. He didn't stop like I thought he would; instead, he cleared half the distance between us and the forward group of attackers. I heard the pop of shots firing off as Joey worked to provide him with strategic cover fire. My heart was thudding in my throat, threatening to burst completely free of my chest, when Leighton finally stopped moving, lit the strips of cloth on fire, and cocked his arm back. He threw the bottle with so much force that his body bent slightly forward and stumbled a few steps. Time seemed to slow as I watched the scotch bottle sail through the air.

"Good news, this side seems to be out of ammo!" Craig called out from my right, causing me to tear my eyes away from the scene through the windshield. "At least that means we stand a fucking chance, even if it means we're about to get rushed for some hand-to-hand.

As he finished speaking, he climbed into the SUV beside me and slammed the door, locking it. Az did the same in the front passenger seat before both moved to climb out of the vehicle on the left side.

"I didn't get as many as I wanted with that makeshift Molotov cocktail." Leighton's voice rang out nearby.

My body sagged with relief hearing him so close. My relief was short-lived as the guys all shared a look before Rich slammed the front door closed.

"Whatever happens, Sweetheart, don't get out of this fucking car," Joey said, dipping his head inside. "Get in the front seat, lock these two doors, and if shit goes south, run these motherfuckers down. Do you understand?"

My eyes burned as he gave me those instructions. It sounded... very much like a set of final instructions, and I didn't want to hear it. I tried to blink back the tears, but that only caused them to fall.

"Don't say it like that. You're getting back in this car when it's over." I snapped.

"Sweetheart–"

"No! You're getting back in this car when it's over. *Promise!*" I felt my voice get shrill as it raised. The sounds of gunfire were the backdrop of my panic despite them mostly coming to an end. Joey looked at me sadly.

"Lock the doors." He said before dipping back out and slamming them closed.

"Joey!" I screamed. He didn't promise me anything, and there was a voice in the back of my mind that told me it was a promise he couldn't guarantee he would be able to keep even if he had. I scrambled to the driver's seat and locked the doors, staring out the windows wide-eyed.

Fear, anger, and a feeling of uselessness had me in a chokehold as the boys–*my* boys–stood back-to-back to face the fucking mob of people that had surrounded us. It seemed like everyone was just sizing each other up. I could see Joey and Leighton fist-bump each other, and the urge to slap them both upside the head made me cry even harder.

Leighton slid a blade free from somewhere I couldn't see before reaching his hand out and making a 'come here' motion toward the group in front of them. I couldn't make out anything he said as he did, but the muffled sound of his voice was enough to tell me he was clearly goading them. Not wanting to watch as our attackers broke the temporary stalemate, rushing toward my men, I frantically began searching the SUV for a phone. It was a miracle the police hadn't already arrived, but if I could *just* find a phone, I could call for help. We'd deal with the legal consequences later.

The SUV rocked as someone slammed into the side, and my eyes widened in horror as I took in Az pinned against the vehicle. Adrenaline poured into my system, and I reached for the handle, intending to launch myself from it, if necessary, before the man landing brutal blows to Az's face was ripped away. I saw Leighton, covered in blood, take his place.

"Do *NOT* open that fucking door, Victoria!" Az shouted at me without turning around before he pushed off the SUV.

His tone was harsh enough to make me jerk my hand back from the door handle. I watched for a moment, my body trembling violently from the adrenaline coursing through my veins, before returning to my search for a phone. Coming up empty in the front, I climbed to the third row, hoping like hell I'd find a phone tucked into an unsearched pocket of one of the guys' duffle bags.

I looked out the window at some motion that caught my attention and watched as Rich palmed one of our attacker's faces and slammed his head into the concrete hard enough that it had to have killed him. A thought that was confirmed when he didn't move at all, his lifeless eyes rolled back. Rich moved on to pick up another man who had Joey pinned to the ground. He wrenched the man's head to the side sharply and dropped his body when Leighton ran up to him with a wide grin on his face. Rich's responding look said all I needed to know about the fact that Leighton had said something entirely out of pocket. I laughed, the sound coming out panicked even to my ears.

Taking a quick survey, it looked like my guys had nearly the playing field. I felt like I could breathe a little easier knowing that. Even though they were clearly tiring, the fact they'd eliminated so many people with ease gave me hope. My hands clasped together as I watched them work as a unit. If I hadn't been watching so closely, I would have missed the woman who slipped from the rear of the SUV, the dying sunlight glinting off of something in her hand. In three quick steps, she was behind Rich, and I couldn't stop myself when I saw the knife plunge into his lower back.

Launching myself over the center row in a move that would make Leighton proud, I clicked the door unlocked and ripped it open. A guttural scream tore from my lips as I pulled the switchblade he'd given me from my pocket and flipped it open, launching myself at the woman's back. All five of the guys turned toward the sound of my screaming slowly, as if time had only moved for me at that moment. I collided hard with the woman's back, causing her to slam on the ground, her chin bouncing off the pavement. I didn't think. I didn't hesitate. I plunged my knife into the back of her neck with a strength and ferocity that was usually only seen in mothers lifting cars off their children.

Time started moving again, and the sound roared in my ears, the sound overwhelming. I put my hands over them to shut it out and looked up, seeking out my guys. Rich moved as if to take a step toward me and stopped, all five turning slowly. Behind them stood Candy and six armed men holding guns at my guys at point-blank range.

"Wonderful performance." Candy smiled as she clapped. "But futile."

She jerked her head, and one of the armed men moved to step around the guys. Rich stepped in front of me as the man approached and growled low in his chest.

"Get up, Babygirl. Get up and start running. If we get out of this scrape, we'll find you." He said, not looking at me. I stared at his back as I stood slowly but couldn't move my feet. His light gray t-shirt was slowly turning red as the wound bled freely, starting to drip from the fabric.

Rich advanced on the man that was approaching us. He moved faster than a man who'd been stabbed should be able to, coming up in front of Candy's goon and knocking his gun to the side before he was able to get a shot off. He landed a hard punch to the man's face, which sent him reeling back a few steps. The man recovered quickly, rolling his neck.

Candy sighed loudly. "If you're gonna do this, Declan, make it fucking snappy. Some of us have places to be."

Our assailant nodded and grinned at Rich. Rich swung for him again, but the other man moved quickly and grasped his fist between his arm and torso. He twisted himself around and landed a harsh kick to Rich's gut. Rich grunted but grabbed the man by the ankle before he could pull his leg back. He growled with the strain as he picked the lackey up off the ground and lifted him to his eye level before slamming him into the concrete. The other man screamed, the sickening cracking sound of bones breaking accompanying the thud of his body into the ground. Rich leaned down and grabbed the gun from our assailant's holster, pointed it at his head, and pulled the trigger.

The sound of the gunshot made me jump, and I came fully back to the moment, realizing that I was supposed to be running. I turned and started to move, running nearly face-first into a smiling Candy.

"Well, hi there, sweetheart." She said brightly before grabbing me by the hair and pulling me close. She turned me around, and I heard a gun cocking right by my ear. "I don't think we've ever officially met."

"Don't fucking call me Sweetheart." I snapped, struggling against her hold.

"Aww, don't be like that, gorgeous." She crooned, walking me forward until we were a solid six feet away from the guys. "If you boys don't mind. I'd hate to put a bullet through this pretty lady's head. Go on and get on your knees for me, now, so I don't have to do that."

Rich turned to face us, his eyes widening as he took in the situation.

"Shoot her, Rich!" I yelled.

"Ah ah, I wouldn't do that if I were you, big guy," Candy said, clucking her tongue in her mouth. "She's a nice payday, but not one I'm willing to risk getting shot over, so go ahead and put it down. Let's all be civil here."

Rich sneered at Candy for a moment before his eyes swept over me. I watched in horror as his face fell, and he tossed the gun away from himself, put his hands up, and fell to his knees.

"That's a good boy." Candy crooned.

I watched as my other four guys were shoved forward roughly and dropped to their knees beside Rich. The five remaining thugs with Candy moved into position behind them the second they were on the ground and placed the barrel of their guns to the backs of my guys' heads. Candy released her hold on me and paced in front of my men.

"Now, see. I have orders to bring the girl and *one* of you

in alive. The rest are supposed to be in body bags." she said, tapping her chin as she paced, "But who to pick. They all look so good in a row like this, it would be impossible to choose."

"Shoot me and take the rest in alive," Rich offered, his eyes finding mine. "I'm so fucking sorry, Babygirl."

"No can do, big man." Candy shrugged. "But I have the most delightful idea. How about each of you make a speech to the pretty lady here, and then *she* picks." Candy clapped her free hand against the one holding the gun. "It's like a high-stakes version of the Bachelorette. Since you're so keen to speak, why don't you go first, Rich."

"Don't you pick me, Babygirl. I... I don't deserve it for how I hurt you. Pick someone who was honest with how they loved you. If I could have, I would have spent the rest of my life making it up to you. I'm so fucking sorry for being too stubborn. Too stupid to just... I love you, Victoria. And if I could go back, I'd have told you *so* much sooner... I was so caught up in my own bullshit, I couldn't see the forest for the trees. I wish more than anything I could take it all back. That we could start over at the beginning and I could do it right. I need you to know that. I might have been a better man with you, if we'd had the chance. If *I'd* given us the chance. But I'm serious, don't you pick me, Baby."

Silent tears started rolling down my face as I looked him in the eye, and the words poured out of him. My heart squeezed in my chest, and a sob escaped my lips. I looked at Candy, shaking my head.

"I *can't* do this. I can't choose between them. I love each of them. I can't do it. I won't." I said, my voice broke as I cried.

Candy frowned at me momentarily before turning her attention back to Rich. In one smooth motion, the man behind him stepped away, and Candy raised her gun, pulling the trigger. I screamed as Rich's lifeless body fell backward under the impact of the gunshot, blood pooling from the bullet wound between his eyes. My legs buckled, and I fell to my knees.

"Last chance. Choose, or I'll do it for you."

BOOKS IN THIS SERIES

The Horsemen Series

A Is For Arson

L Is For Larceny

C Is For Corruption (Pre-Order Available!)

J Is For Justified (Coming 2025!)

ABOUT THE AUTHOR

C. M. Bowen

 C.M. Bowen lives in the southern United States with her husband and son. When she isn't immersed in a writing project, she enjoys crafting, reading, and playing tabletop role-playing games. A proud member of the 2SLGBTQIA+ community, C.M. embraces opportunities to advocate for inclusivity while bringing her unique voice to the romance genre.

C.M. has been writing since adolescence, drawing inspiration from her early love of fantasy and later transitioning into paranormal romance. After attending university, she chose to pursue writing professionally, finding her place as both a fiction editor and author. C.M. specializes in romance, focusing on emotional depth and spice, always eager to explore new sub-genres and push creative boundaries.

BOOKS BY THIS AUTHOR

The Devil Inside

The Prince's Game

The Prince's Kiss

ABOUT THE AUTHOR

Zoe Dunn

Zoe Dunn is an American author who has been passionate about writing since childhood. With a foundation rooted in her love of horror and suspense, Zoe brings a Gothic-inspired edge to her romance novels, blending atmospheric storytelling with compelling character arcs.

Known for her skillful misdirection and unexpected twists, Zoe takes readers on journeys where love blossoms amid shadow and uncertainty. Her work showcases her ability to balance darkness and romance, creating narratives that keep readers eagerly turning the page. Zoe strives to craft intricate, immersive tales where passion, tension, and resilience take center stage, making her stories both unforgettable and deeply engaging.

BOOKS BY THIS AUTHOR

Meddling Memaws

The Wolf's Bite